# Nevermore

## A novel of Edgar Allan Poe
## and Allan Pinkerton

### BRENT MONAHAN

# CHAPTER ONE
*Saturday, October 27, 1849*

*When Allan Pinkerton awoke, he found himself securely bound to a chair. It was a damp and low-ceilinged interior, with rough-hewn beams exposed above. The floor was hard-packed dirt. There was not one window. He figured he was in the cellar of the townhouse where he had lost consciousness. An oil lamp identical to the one he had seen in the front room upstairs emitted a feeble, yellow light from its place on the floor. Moreover, the space seemed the same dimensions as the old townhouse had been.*

*The cellar smelled musty and dank. Under the steps, beyond a pathetic excuse for a bed, sat a closed trunk, topped by a carpetbag and a handyman's tool carrier.*

*The back of the detective's head, his shoulder blades, elbows and buttocks ached. He realized he had been dragged unconscious down those wooden steps. As he struggled vainly from side to side against his bonds, he realized that both peripheries of his vision consisted of wall. He looked up. Less than three feet above his head was a curving ceiling formed of hard-packed dirt and stone. He saw that he and the chair were inside a small alcove that had been dug out of the far end of the cellar. He registered the sand, the powdered limestone, and the trough for mixing cement directly in front of him. Beyond these lay several piles of bricks. Enough to wall him completely in the alcove, just as Fortunato had been sealed up for eternity, in Poe's* Cask of Amontillado. *Images flashed through his mind, in a sequence that showed him precisely how he had gotten from the streets of Chicago to this vertical grave.*

# CHAPTER TWO
*Tuesday, October 9, 1849*

Allan Pinkerton climbed onto the train thinking about confidence men. In neat, small script, he had filled thirty-four pages of the notebook he kept in his jacket pocket. It contained every fact, every anecdote related by victims and fellow lawmen, every personal experience he could remember. And yet he knew there was so much more to be learned. It never ceased to amaze and outrage him that men and women who were clever enough to devise and execute such complex crimes were too lazy to work half as hard at earning honest livings.

Within moments of boarding the awesome contraption, however, even the preoccupied lawman could not ignore his surroundings. When he had arrived in the United States in 1842, railroads were a novelty. The longest line of track ran about a hundred miles, and the cars were converted stagecoaches or storage sheds. Now, only seven years later, the engines were twice the size and the passenger and freight cars were custom built. The road he had paid to travel on, the Galena and Chicago Union, was less than two years old and the only railroad running into Chicago. The tang of multi-layered varnish could still be smelled on the wood. The plush, burgundy upholstery of the seats had yet to show wear. As he waited his turn while the other passengers stowed their luggage, he counted the seating. The car could accommodate thirty-two, and there were three passenger coaches on the train, coupled directly behind the closed car that had held dry goods on its outbound run and now shipped barrels of molasses east.

Three men stood in the coach's narrow aisle, one just in front of the lawman and the other two about eight feet beyond him. Pinkerton noted that only one among the three carried a suitcase. Immediately, this unusual fact focused his attention.

The man wearing the black, beaver-skin top hat had a sizable leather valise. As he shrugged out of his topcoat, freeing his right arm from its sleeve, the man next to him deftly ran his right-hand forefinger over the outside of his fellow traveler's just-exposed jacket.

Pinkerton reached under his coat and to the rear of his belt, where he always kept a pair of handcuffs, never taking his eyes from the "mark" being "fanned" for the bulging proof of his pocketbook. A moment later, a redheaded man appeared at the opposite entrance of the car holding a folded outer coat over his raised arm. Pinkerton saw the "fanner" nod his head almost imperceptibly to his right, indicating the position of the pocketbook. The mark set his coat on the seat he had claimed and then bent to lift the valise. The redhead took a hitch in his step, in order to time the "pick" perfectly. The man directly in front of Pinkerton was doing nothing to take the empty seat beside him, alerting the detective that he was part of the crime.

The one who had felt the pocket squeezed forward and jostled the man in the top hat just as the redhead walking from the other direction pressed up against him. Almost quicker than Pinkerton's eye could follow, the pocketbook was "reefed" and "tapped," and the "booster" moved on. Even as he apologized for squeezing by, he deftly slipped the wallet to the third man, who stood in front of Pinkerton.

The detective had never seen the technique performed, but he had read about it. While the pickings had to be divided among three men, it was virtually guaranteed to succeed. If the man wearing the hat suspected he had been robbed he could scream out his suspicion, and both the man who had passed him and the one who pressed against him from the back could be held and examined. The missing pocketbook would not be found. The immediate area and perhaps the entire car would be searched, to no avail. The two accused men could play either as understanding or outraged, with sometimes one taking one role and one the other. But the wallet would not be found on either of them. It would now reside in a pocket of the third man, who had since retreated to the rear car.

Leaving his carpetbag on the seat he had claimed, Pinkerton followed the third man through the door, across the narrow connecting platform, and into the last car. He waited until the thief, a small character with an old knife wound across both cheeks and the bridge of his nose, took a seat. Pinkerton quickly snapped one wristlock of his handcuffs around the man's left arm. The thief turned at the tug and the sound of the snapping metal, but as he attempted to pull his arm free Pinkerton closed the other wristlock around the seat's armrest.

"What the deuce! Bloody 'ell," the man exclaimed, in a London East End accent.

"What are you doing, sir?" a woman who had watched the action demanded.

Pinkerton produced a copper badge from his pocket. "I'm making an arrest, madam," he said coolly. "I am the detective for the Chicago Police."

"The what?"

The cuffed man thrust his free right hand into his coat pocket.

Pinkerton curled his fingers into a ball, cocked his arm, and delivered a hard right to the thief's temple, stunning him. Two women yelped in protest. Undeterred, Pinkerton dug into the man's pocket and produced a small flintlock pistol. He held it aloft for the other occupants of the car to see.

In a loud voice, he repeated himself. "I am the detective for the Chicago Police. This man is a pickpocket." To prove his point, he patted the stupefied man's inner pockets until he found the thick billfold and a thin one. He displayed both, waved the thick one above his head, brushing the protruding bills against the curving ceiling, then dropped the thin one on the thief's lap. "No one is to touch this man!"

Allan Pinkerton could make his low baritone petrifying when he wanted. He expected that his words would be obeyed. A conductor was climbing aboard as he exited the last car and came into the open air.

"Do not allow the train to move, sir!" he ordered. "There has been a robbery." Again, he did not wait to see if his command would be followed, did not even pause to read the reaction of the conductor. He rushed into the middle passenger car and up to the seated redheaded man who had boosted the billfold. He turned the captured flintlock around, grabbed it by the muzzle, swung the weapon in a short, swift arc and struck the man sharply between the eyes. The thief screamed out in surprise and pain. Blood spurted from both the split in the man's skin and from inside his broken nose.

Without pausing, Pinkerton strode up to the fanner. The man had cockily taken the seat next to his victim. When he saw his partner attacked, he had twisted out of his seat and begun reaching behind him. Pinkerton closed the short distance in two steps, swung his boot up, and delivered its sturdy tip into the man's groin.

The air whooshed from the booster's lungs; the knife dropped from his hand; he crumpled to his knees. Both hands thrust forward automatically to protect his private parts from further assault. Pinkerton drew back his leg, bent his knee, and unleashed an equally wicked blow to the man's face, knocking him backward onto the wooden aisle planking. Screams and exclamations of dismay filled the confining space.

Satisfied that the fanner was unconscious, Pinkerton turned around to face the man with the broken nose. In spite of being half blinded by blood and pain, he was digging into his coat. Pinkerton raised the flintlock and pointed it at the man's face. The thief wisely raised his hands.

Pinkerton cleared his throat and willed his heart to stop pummeling his chest. He drew in a deep, calming breath. "Ladies and gentlemen, I am a policeman. These two men and an accomplice in the next coach stole the pocketbook from the gentleman with the tanned leather valise. The one with the newspaper shoved under the straps."

"Me?" an astonished voice asked behind him.

"Check your pocket, sir."

"Blast if you aren't right."

Pinkerton reached into his coat and produced the billfold. The passenger noise changed from fear to anger.

"Who among you gentlemen is not afraid to use a gun on a criminal who will not keep his arms in the air?"

"I'm not!" an elderly fellow with a clean-shaven face exclaimed. He fairly jumped out of his seat to accept the flintlock from Pinkerton's hand. The detective reached under his jacket and produced his own weapon, a gleaming revolver.

A moment later, the conductor appeared at the rear of the car, along with the stationmaster. The latter man held an old muzzleloader. It took Pinkerton a minute to calm the passengers and explain precisely what had happened. Within another two minutes, all three thieves were escorted off the train. Two more male citizens of Elgin stood ready on the station platform with drawn pistols. Allan Pinkerton was not surprised. Even with Chicago and its thirty thousand citizens only forty miles away, the countryside of Illinois was largely wilderness, with ruthless men roaming boldly, looking for the weak and the unarmed to prey upon. Every second man in rural Illinois who traveled beyond his own land carried a weapon.

Pinkerton took a moment to replace the cuffs on his belt and then climbed back onto the train. He was greeted by applause and several pats on the back. The most enthusiastic among the group was the man who had been robbed.

"Please, sir. Do me the very great favor of sitting beside me," he invited.

Pinkerton accepted and brought his carpetbag across the aisle. While he stowed it, he studied the man whose wallet he had saved. The hair on his crown was beginning to thin, but he appeared to be about thirty, the same age as Pinkerton. The cut of his clothing indicated both taste and money; a faint smell of bay rum cologne wafted from his person. Pinkerton looked at the man's hands and saw that they were seldom if ever used for manual labor.

"You say you're a policeman?" the man said.

"Correct. Allan Pinkerton is my name. The one and only detective employed by the city of Chicago."

The man dipped his head with respect. "It's interesting there's even one, considering the city has allocated almost nothing for regular policemen. How many are there in all now?"

"Myself and ten regulars," Pinkerton disclosed. The car

jerked forward, indicating that the wood for the boiler and the water to make the steam had been replenished. The acrid smell of steam mixed with wood cinders penetrated into the coach. The two-hour ride to Chicago had begun.

"Not enough by a tenth," the man proclaimed. "And I should know. I'm a lawyer in Chicago. Edward Rucker." He held out his hand, accepted Pinkerton's, and gave it a hearty shake. "And how long since you left Scotland?"

Ever since he had arrived in the United States, barely surviving a shipwreck in Nova Scotia, Pinkerton had worked at limiting the sound of his Scottish burr. But neither was he so ashamed of his background that he took great pains to hide it. He told his traveling companion that he had been in the United States for seven years. He was not shy about relating his dramatic history and his grand plans.

As the miles rolled past, Pinkerton revealed that he had been born in Glasgow, Scotland in August of 1819. In his teens he had become a barrel cooper. Membership in the cooper's union had led him to Chartism, which was the first working class labor movement. His party enthusiastically campaigned for the right for all men over the age of twenty-one to vote, for secret balloting, and for more egalitarian election proceedings for Parliament. The liberal movement had been quashed.

Needing to flee Scotland to escape imprisonment, the young man had decided to immigrate to the nation that had won by blood and courage its independence from harsh British rule. Pinkerton had followed the trail of cooper work to Lill's Brewery in just-incorporated Chicago, but the almost unlimited opportunities had led him to conclude he could do better working on his own. He moved west of Chicago, to a hamlet named Dundee. His superior barrels, offered at a fair price, quickly sold faster than he could produce them.

Being as thrifty as any Scotsman, Pinkerton reasoned that he could eliminate his middleman if he found and felled the poles for fashioning barrel hoops. No one claimed ownership of one particular island in the middle of the Fox River, so he rowed out to it to cut lumber. Soon after he banked his boat and began to explore, the ashes of a recent campfire and other signs of habitation proved that people had been living and working there. He reasoned that the isolated island might be the hideout of the gang who had been counterfeiting and passing bad coins in the region.

Pinkerton led the only elected lawman within ten miles back to the island, where they camped out and soon surprised two members of the gang. Their leader, however, escaped. Using less than genteel techniques, Pinkerton wrung the ringleader's identity from his confederates. He then ran the third man to ground, bringing him to jail in handcuffs that Pinkerton himself had fashioned. His reputation for scrupulous honesty and hatred of criminals, teamed with his dogged pursuit and capture of the counterfeiting chief, soon got him nominated for and then elected to the position of deputy sheriff for all of Kane County. Not long afterward, the city fathers of burgeoning Chicago had learned of his record and recruited him for their newly organized police force. He did not, however, plan to work for others in his new profession any longer than he had as a barrel-maker. He confided to the lawyer seated next to him that he was learning as much about the schemes and operations of criminals as he could, and that this would turn him into a highly marketable private commodity.

"Marketable to whom?" Rucker asked.

"To railroads, for one," Pinkerton replied, gesturing to their surroundings. "To protect their clients from robbers of both the passengers in the coaches and the goods in the freight cars." He had reflected on the usefulness of a detective so often that he needed only utter the list he had long since memorized. "Hotels, for another. Banks from robbers and counterfeiters for a third. And then there's the needs of private citizens. Guarding the gifts at society weddings, tracking down daughters who elope, checking the pedigrees of fortune hunters, proving philandering spouses, catching white slavers."

"And runaway blacks?"

"No, sir!" Pinkerton exclaimed. "I would not sell my soul for that dirty job. I am a passionate abolitionist. My coopering shed served on half a dozen occasions to hide runaway slaves. I am proud to have provided a small link in the Underground Railway." His deep-set, button-shiny brown eyes flashed with pride, challenging his companion to debate him.

"Good for you, sir!" Rucker exclaimed. "I speak out against the infernal practice of slavery at every given opportunity, but I cannot say I would have the courage you have."

"It is a well-divided issue in Kane County," Pinkerton divulged.

"You need not tell me."

"So much so that when I ran for a local office, I came in dead last in a field of nine. Even my own minister, who often quotes the Bible about slaves, accused me of being a drunkard."

"Well, I'm sure it was a lie." Without waiting for confirmation of his opinion, Rucker confessed, "This is fascinating. I never thought of criminal detecting as a viable line of work. The only detective I ever read about was the one invented by Edgar Allan Poe."

"He's an English author, isn't he?" Pinkerton said.

"No, indeed! He's American through and through," Rucker replied, with surprise in his voice. "You've never heard of 'The Murders in the Rue Morgue,' or 'The Masque of the Red Death'?"

"Can't say as I have," Pinkerton said breezily, although he was feeling for the first time since beginning his conversation with the lawyer a bit defensive. As a man of business and strictly business, Pinkerton never found occasion to read fiction. He considered the escape an unprofitable waste of time.

Rucker blinked. "Then surely some of his poems: 'The Raven,' Eldorado,' 'Eleanore'?"

"Sorry, no." To break the little interrogation, Pinkerton refocused past the lawyer's shoulder and out the window on the passing landscape. He marveled at the train's speed and calculated that they must be traveling at no less than thirty miles per hour.

Rucker excused himself, stood, and reached to the overhead rack. He extracted the newspaper from under the straps of his valise. "I'd have thought you would have heard of Poe because no one had named your profession before he wrote about it. He created this French detective. A name like Auguste Maupin. I forget it precisely. But the character is a deducing machine." He sat again and unfolded the newspaper. "Strange coincidence that I should meet you only three days after Poe's death. You may read about him here."

Pinkerton accepted the newspaper. He was frankly amazed that a fiction writer's demise would occupy an entire column on the front page. But when he came to the third paragraph, he learned that the circumstances of Poe's death were not only unusual but also sinister sounding. He slowly stroked his carefully trimmed mustache and beard as he finished reading and then settled in on reflection, an unconscious habit he had developed in recent years.

"Interesting indeed," Pinkerton said as he handed back the newspaper. He realized that Rucker must have been staring intently at him as he read.

"You've revealed yourself as a most ambitious man," Rucker said. "Clever and courageous as well. Moreover, you proved yourself to me back in Elgin. I'm extremely ambitious myself."

"It would seem that your ambition has already paid off, given the thickness of your billfold," Pinkerton bluntly observed.

Rucker smiled. "True enough. I have made a great deal of money. When I was still a law clerk, I devised a simple yet thorough means of keeping track of every recorded instrument and legal proceeding pertaining to real estate titles in Chicago. My service saved attorneys much time and money, so they all depended on me. When I went into business for myself, I had plenty of customers. Right now, I'm investing every spare cent in land and convincing others to channel their capital through me for the same purpose. That's why I was out in Elgin the past two days. At the rate Chicago is growing, I can't lose. But I see in your dreams an equally intelligent means to gain wealth. Crime never ends. Your services will always be in demand. What do you say to you and me entering into a partnership, Mr. Pinkerton? You detect; I underwrite you until your receivables outweigh your debts. Then, for a set period of time, I collect a percentage of your profits. When it seems prudent for you to expand operations, you may bank on me again."

Pinkerton could not believe what he was hearing. He had estimated that he would need to work as an employee of the city of Chicago for at least five years, until he could save enough to launch his own private detective agency. If the streets of America were not in fact paved with gold, at least the legend about it being the land of opportunity was proving itself on ever-greater scales.

"I would very much like to continue our discussions," Pinkerton said.

"No time like the present," Rucker declared. He shook the newspaper and pointed to the article on Poe. "Between us, we possess the expertise and the capital. However, we need to launch this unknown service like a Chinese rocket. A great deal of publicity is called for. The most effective way to do that is for you to solve a very high profile crime. A national crime. Like the bizarre death of the man who invented the detective."

# CHAPTER THREE
*Monday, October 15, 1849*

In the few years since Allan Pinkerton had moved to Chicago, more direct transportation routes, overland turnpikes and railroads, had evolved. Although they were quicker than river and canal travel, the trip to Baltimore was still a long, frustrating, and arduous one. Pinkerton had taken only a single day to arrange leave from the police force, to collect money from Edward Rucker, and to put his own affairs in order. Then he was off, racing against time. He knew that every passing day made the solution of Poe's murder, if murder it was, that much more difficult.

Friends and acquaintances had volunteered their latest intelligence on the quickest and least wearing route to Baltimore, but they had neither been completely up to date nor wholly accurate. He had spent four very long days and two nights riding in horse-drawn coaches and on horse-drawn and engine-powered trains, wending from Chicago down through Indiana, across Ohio and thence to Pittsburg. The traverse of western Pennsylvania had been especially difficult, and he had awakened this morning in a town tucked among mountains named Harper's Ferry. From the evidence of construction all around him, he could see that it had just begun to grow as a rail hub.

Pinkerton's immediate objective was the station and tracks of the Baltimore and Ohio Railroad. He paused to put himself against a wood-framed building so that a passing carriage would not throw the street's mud onto his shoes and trousers. He drew into his lungs cool fall air, damp from the previous night's rainstorm. He set down his valise and carpetbag, hoisted his watch from its pocket, and compared it with the large clock dangling from chains above the building entrance. The difference between the chronographs was half an hour, and he doubted that either was faulty in its running. He sighed, wondering when time would become more standardized from region to region.

He moved on to the station and purchased a one-way ticket for Baltimore. He carefully counted his remaining money. He had twenty-eight dollars and fifty-seven cents on his person. Rucker had advanced him one hundred and twenty-five dollars, one hundred of which he had had wired to the Mechanic's Bank in Baltimore. He had also brought along twenty-five dollars from his own savings. By the size of his advance, he figured Rucker had allowed him twelve days to conduct and complete his investigation of Edgar Allan Poe's death, and then he would need to turn around and spend another five or six days traveling back to Chicago. His own money would give him breathing room and perhaps even a day or two to sightsee. He had been informed just that morning that he was below the Mason-Dixon Line, putting him for the first time in the South of his adoptive nation. He had been told that once he got to the states below Pennsylvania, he would find them to be fundamentally other countries, and he was eager to see for himself.

Pinkerton entered the last passenger coach and found a seat directly across from a refined-looking couple who appeared to be in their late fifties. He had discovered in his travels that his elders always had something valuable to share from a lifetime of experience. He learned that they were Hosea and Minerva Throckmorton.

The gentleman was a professor of literary studies at Richmond College, specializing in Middle English literature. He was on sabbatical and was returning from having lectured on

William Shakespeare at Cincinnati College, Capital College in Bexley, and American Western University in Athens, Ohio. From having already observed the careful cadence of the professor's language, his self-important bearing, his age, his prosperous and soft look, his bifocals, and the briefcase he kept tucked under his elbow, Pinkerton was not surprised.

When Professor Throckmorton inquired as to Pinkerton's profession, he eagerly replied. Before either husband or wife could think of another question, he asked, "Have either of you ever been victimized by a criminal?"

"My sister, Becky, was once," volunteered Mrs. Throckmorton, the sing-song lilt of the South in her soprano voice. "She was then married to a terrible scalawag, may his soul never rest in perdition. A liar and a drunkard. Drink is the work of the devil indeed. We abstain."

"We do have a glass of red wine each evening, Mother," Hosea corrected gently.

"Because the doctor said it was good for the constitution of persons our age!" Minerva shot back. "You can't count that or the thimblefuls of cordial we accept from hosts, Father."

"No," Father agreed.

Minerva uttered a little, annoyed harrumph. "Something about a man who claimed to have found money but only the top and bottom bills were real. The middle bills were all poor counterfeits."

"You lost five dollars to a counterfeit once," Professor Throckmorton reminded his wife.

"That's absolutely correct!" she chirped. "It was from the Bank of Maryland in Baltimore, with an issue date of 1836. But the teller at our bank informed me that the Bank of Maryland had failed in 1834. That's why I favor coin over script. So much safer."

The detective declined to estimate aloud how many times statistically Mrs. Throckmorton must have accepted and passed faked coins. Instead, he said, "Baltimore is my final destination. I'm investigating the death of a man named Edgar Allan Poe."

"Poe! Of course," said Hosea Throckmorton. "He spent his youth in Richmond, you know. And then he returned during this past summer. But Mrs. Throckmorton and I only moved to the city two years ago, and we were gone visiting friends and lecturing when he returned. Pity to have missed him. I count Edgar Allan Poe as one of America's best all-time writers, as do many of my profession."

Pinkerton wondered who the others were. He had heard mention of Washington Irving, James Fenimore Cooper, Longfellow and Hawthorne (whatever their first names were), but he had never read one of them.

"A shame to lose such a talent so young in life," Throckmorton went on. "Only forty. At the height of his career. Think how much more he might have produced."

"An even greater shame if he was murdered," Allan said, watching for the couple's reaction.

"Indeed. Murder it might have been." Professor Throckmorton reached under his elbow and moved his briefcase to his lap. "I'm sure you are aware of the remarkable aspects of his death, or else you would not be traveling all the way from Chicago." He opened the case and extracted three newspapers. "When I travel, I'm in the habit of collecting as many local journals as I can for the class our department conducts on writing editorials and reporting. Every one of these has something on Mr. Poe. He was supposed to have been on his way to New York, yet he lingered in Baltimore. He had several relatives and numerous friends there, but they didn't see him."

"Strange," said Pinkerton.

"Very strange indeed," Hosea amplified, shaking his large head back and forth. "To be found just outside a tavern that he had not been drinking at. And to linger on in hospital for days, ranting but never being able to say what had happened to him." He held up the newspapers. "Read these if you wish, Mr. Pinkerton, and keep anything that might be helpful to your investigation."

Pinkerton accepted the newspapers with no intention of doing more than to glance politely at them. He had been reading the few facts and many speculations of the writer's end in papers that he procured every time he switched to a new conveyance. He had read nothing that would shorten his need to visit all the major sites and interview the players mentioned in order to gain firsthand knowledge. He folded open a four-sheeted weekly gazette and saw with surprise that on Saturday, October 13th, six days after Poe had died, information on him was yet given front-page space.

"Are you well acquainted with the man's writings?" Throckmorton inquired.

"I am not even remotely acquainted," Pinkerton admitted.

The professor pressed his forefinger against the gazette. "Then this is as good a place to start as any. I'm sure they print 'The Raven' not only because it is one of his most famous poems but also because it captures so well the themes and style of his work."

Pinkerton nodded politely. The educator stared at him with expectation. He felt like a student beginning an assignment.

"I should have asked if you read, sir," Throckmorton said.

"Indeed. I read well," Pinkerton hastened to say. "It's just that my interests run to the happenings of the day. Or the Constitution of the United States and the Ten Commandments. Useful items." He smiled in apology. "I suppose that's disheartening for a professor of literature to hear."

Throckmorton nodded. "A bit. But this particular fiction might prove quite practical to you. In order to solve what occurred during Poe's last days, you might need to know the workings of his mind."

Recognizing the wisdom in the man's words, Allan set to reading the poem.

Once upon a midnight dreary, while I pondered weak and
    weary,
Over many a quaint and curious volume of forgotten
    lore–
While I nodded, nearly napping, suddenly there came a
    tapping,
As of someone gently rapping, rapping at my chamber
    door.
"'Tis some visitor," I muttered, "tapping at my chamber
    door–
Only this and nothing more."

Ah, distinctly I remember it was in the bleak December;
And each separate dying ember wrought its ghost upon
    the floor.

Eagerly I wished the morrow – vainly I had sought to
  Borrow
From my book surcease of sorrow – sorrow for the lost
  Lenore–
For the rare and radiant maiden whom the angels name
  Lenore–
Nameless here for evermore.

And the silken, sad, uncertain rustling of each purple
  curtain
Thrilled me – filled me with fantastic terrors never felt
  before;
So that now, to still the beating of my heart, I stood
  repeating
"'Tis some visitor entreating entrance at my chamber
  door–
Some late visitor entreating entrance at my chamber
  door–
This it is and nothing more."

Presently my soul grew stronger; hesitating then no
  longer,
"Sir," said I, "or Madam, truly your forgiveness I implore;
But the fact is I was napping, and so gently you came
  rapping,
And so faintly you came tapping, tapping at my chamber
  door,
That I scarce was sure I heard you" – here I opened wide
  the door,
Darkness there and nothing more.

\* \* \*

Deep into that darkness peering, long I stood there
wondering, fearing,
Doubting, dreaming dreams no mortal every dared to
dream before;
But the silence was unbroken, and the stillness gave no
token,
And the only word there spoken was the whispered word,
"Lenore?"
Merely this and nothing more.

Back into the chamber turning, all my soul within me
burning.
Soon again I heard a tapping somewhat louder than
before.
"Surely," said I, "surely that is something at my window
lattice;
Let me see, then, what thereat is, and this mystery
explore–
Let my heart be still a moment and this mystery explore;
'Tis the wind and nothing more!"

Open here I flung the shutter, when, with many a flirt
and flutter,
In there stepped a stately Raven of the saintly days of
yore;
Not the least obeisance made he; not a minute stopped or
stayed he;
But with mien of lord or lady, perched above my chamber
door–

Perched, and sat, and nothing more.

Then this ebony bird beguiling my sad fancy into smiling,
By the grave and stern decorum of the countenance it
    wore,
"Though thy crest be shorn and shaven, thou," I said, "art
    sure no craven,
Ghastly grim and ancient Raven wandering from the
    Nightly shore–
Tell me what thy lordly name is on the Night's Plutonian
    shore!"
Quoth the Raven "Nevermore."

Pinkerton read on, where the raven immediately perched on a statue displayed above the narrator's chamber door. The beast was minutely examined, asked if it be a prophet of life after death, a bird, or a thing of evil, only to have it repeat for nine more verses the one, enigmatic word.

At the last verse, Allan's eyes ceased scanning and concentrated once more on every word.

And the Raven, never flitting, still is sitting, still is sitting
On the pallid bust of Pallas just above my chamber door;
And his eyes have all the seeming of a demon's that is
    dreaming,
And the lamp-light o'er him streaming throws his shadow
    on the floor;
And my soul from out that shadow that lies floating on
    the floor
Shall be lifted – nevermore!

* * *

Pinkerton looked up at the professor. The man's eyes were wide, his bushy eyebrows elevated in expectation.

"And what is your assessment?" he asked

"He has a wonderful control of words," Pinkerton granted. "Especially the words that rhyme inside."

"Yes, internal rhyming. He is a master at that. His repetitions, his meters and cadences are music without notes. I love the 'pallid bust of Pallas.' Such inspired alliteration to express the inability even of godlike wisdom to fend off death. But what about the mood?"

Glad to have been asked a question he could answer, Allan said, "Sad. Depressing and dark. I assume that Lenore is his lost love."

"She figures in several of his poems. I don't know how many," Throckmorton revealed. "I have not studied him carefully. Do you understand the bird's symbolism?"

"The raven is black, like mourning clothing. I think it's a symbol of death."

"True. In Germanic tradition, ravens were connected to death because they fed on the flesh of the dead. A raven's cawing was a harbinger of death. But it's more than that. Celtic superstition holds that it represents the death of one thing to bring in the birth of another. In the case of this poem, it assures the narrator that his love will return nevermore, but this knowledge must be imparted for him to move on with his life. You will find that Poe is what they call a Gothic author. He revels in the dark, as you say. Also dreams, decay, destruction. He seems obsessed with lost loves, illness, and death."

"Perhaps he had a premonition of his own early death,"

Pinkerton hazarded.

"Do you believe in premonitions?" Throckmorton asked.

Allan said, "I've had a couple, so I can't discount them in others."

"So, literature can, after all, be both interesting and useful wouldn't you say, Mr. Pinkerton?

"We shall see." Pinkerton passed the newspapers back to the professor.

"I should be very much interested in hearing what you uncover, sir."

Pinkerton glanced out the window, at the receding countryside. "With any luck on my part, you will read about it in your home newspaper."

# CHAPTER FOUR

*Monday, October 15, 1849*

When Pinkerton arrived in Baltimore, his first objective was to visit the depot's telegraph office and send word of his arrival to the lawyer Edward Rucker, asking him to inform the detective's home and his police supervisor as well. He then left the terminal station at a brisk pace, grateful to exercise cramped muscles. He studied the enormous engine yard to his left as he trudged along.

The yard was still busy as the sun slipped behind the western verge of the city. Pinkerton observed the pulsing reds and oranges of great hearths burning beyond soot-stained, two-story-high windows. He listened to the ring of sledgehammers pounding enormous metal castings, heard the hiss and chug of steam, smelled not only soot but also grease as creatures of limited strength but mighty brain matter built and repaired gigantic metal beasts that were transforming the nation.

His long-term goal was to effect no less dramatic an improvement in confounding the nation's criminal element, and he counted on solving Edgar Allan Poe's death to propel his dream at the pace of a locomotive.

He reached a main thoroughfare called Pratt Street. A hotel sat opposite the train complex, but it and the clientele loitering around its front porch looked too seamy to endure for a protracted stay. He elected to move on to a more gentrified part of town. He had been told by the conductor that the center of the city lay about one-and-a-half miles to the east, and he wanted to be where the gas or oil lamps burned brightly in the dark, in spite of his being well armed. A solitary man burdened with two bulging bags was too tempting a target in the dark.

As he plodded closer to the Inner Harbor, the keen-eyed detective noted the difference between this outlying district of

Baltimore and those districts beyond the heart of Chicago. These residences and businesses had been in place before the first building had arisen on the southwest shore of Lake Michigan. They were structures of the Colonial, Georgian, and Federal periods, with the integrity, style and proportion reflective of professional architects. They were mostly made of brick, not like the ramshackle wooden structures that sprang up like toadstools on every spare acre of Chicago prairie. These streets were paved. The one he walked on had cobblestones and a brick sidewalk. He figured Chicago would look considerably better someday, but it would no doubt take cleansing calamities such as one he had read about the year before, when a Baltimore cotton factory burned down and took several blocks of surrounding dwellings with it.

After he had walked about three-quarters of a mile, Pinkerton regretted having been too thrifty, waving off the coach that had come out to the station specifically to meet the travelers and shuttle them to city homes, hotels, inns, and wharfs. His arms ached from the weight of his luggage. The first half mile had felt good to his stiff legs, but now he suffered the collective weariness of the long journey. He looked with increasing anxiety for a place to stay. None of the vehicles heading down Pratt Street toward the center of the city was a public conveyance. He crossed the Greene Street intersection and, after passing the eastside corner building, he caught sight of a large card in the window of a two-story brick townhouse. It read "Lodging and Board for Genteel Persons." The house looked tidy. Lace curtains hung behind the window glass.

Allan sighed with relief. He set his bags on the sidewalk, mounted the two granite steps, and used the curving brass knocker to rap on the green-painted door.

The woman who answered captured Allan Pinkerton's immediate and total attention. She was, in his judgment, about twenty-five years old. She stood almost as tall as he, which was five foot six. Her hair was thick and flame red, shot through with highlights of gold, set in ringlet curls up front and a high bun behind. A field of freckles dusted the porcelain skin of her face and neck, from her hairline to her upper bosom. Her face was a most pleasing oval that framed large blue eyes, a small and slightly upturned nose, and generous lips. The dress she wore was meant for house and day wear, made of a heavy cotton, full-sleeved with lace protruding from the wrists, with a plunging, triangular open panel from below her collarbones to her waist, covered with more lace. The length of the dress hid her shoes and feet from his view.

"Do I pass muster?" the woman asked, cocking her head to the side and placing her delicate hands akimbo on her hips.

"I'm sorry. What did you say?" Allan rallied.

The woman looked down to the two pieces of luggage. "Are you looking for lodging, sir?"

"Yes. Yes, precisely," he replied with enthusiasm.

"I'm afraid I do not lodge men."

Pinkerton glanced at the sign in the window. "But…"

"By 'genteel,' I mean lady folk," she expanded. "Occasionally, I admit a gentleman if he is accompanied by his wife."

"I'm a gentleman," Allan asserted. "I have a family."

"But not with you."

"No."

"Do you mean a family such as your mother and father?" she challenged.

"No, madam; my own family. A wife and children." He realized just how tired his arms, legs and feet were and decided to make a final effort. "One more moment of your time, if you please." He reached into his jacket pocket, pulled out a small leather case, and produced from it a calling card. He handed it to the defensive keeper of the door.

The big, blue eyes swept back and forth twice. "Mr. Allan Pinkerton. Chief Detective/City of Chicago." She regarded the supplicant again. "My, but you are a long way from home."

"And in desperate need of a place to rest my weary bones." He affixed his warmest smile.

"Well…it can only be for two nights. I have in the other bedroom Mr. and Mrs. Brand. They will be vacating on Wednesday morning this. I cannot allow a man without his wife to reside under my roof with no one else here."

"I understand perfectly," Pinkerton responded.

"I am Mrs. Brannigan," the landlady said, in a voice suddenly more soft and feminine. "It's a dollar-and-a-half a day, with a roll and coffee provided for breakfast and a full supper. Luncheon is on your own."

"Splendid," Pinkerton said. He dug into one of his trouser pockets and produced a two-dollar piece. "In advance. I'll get my belongings."

"Please, come right up the stairs to the third floor. I shall bring a plate to your room, since the rest of us have finished dining. The wash basin and towels are already set out."

And so it was that Allan learned no more of the intriguing young woman or of her other guests that evening.

# CHAPTER FIVE

*Tuesday, October 16, 1849*

Mrs. Brannigan had already built up the parlor hearth fire and set out coffee and rolls, as promised, when Pinkerton descended the narrow and winding stairs. He wondered how early she must have arisen, since the world beyond her windows was still shrouded in grey mist. She jostled a chubby baby on her arm. He was not surprised to see it, since its crying in the room below during the night had awakened him for a time.

"Good morning, Mr. Pinkerton," she greeted, offering a generous smile as well. "This is my daughter, Siobhan."

Allan noted that the child was about six months old. He did not wonder that it was pink-skinned and of a healthy weight; Mrs. Brannigan's breasts were full and round within her dress. His wife's breasts, by comparison, had been next to non-existent when he married her and could be completely contained in his two cupped hands when she had nursed. Mrs. Brannigan, moreover, seemed to have recovered her figure completely, as her waist was amazingly nipped in. Mrs. Pinkerton had grown thicker and continued to thicken as she neared thirty.

"And what brings the Chief Detective of Chicago to Baltimore?" she asked.

Pinkerton declined to divulge that he was the only detective on his city's force and that he had added the 'Chief' when he had his calling cards printed, in the logical expectation that burgeoning Chicago would surely have more detectives within a year or two. Otherwise, he had told himself, at least one hundred cards would have been wasted.

"I am here in the matter of the curious death of Mr. Edgar Allan Poe."

Mrs. Brannigan transferred her daughter to the other arm.

Her face drew long, and her eyes darkened. With no enthusiasm, she said, "I met him once."

Allan patted his jacket pocket, to be sure his notebook and pencil were at the ready. "Truly? May I inquire as to the circumstances?"

"It was in the winter of 1844…January, I think…that he returned to Baltimore on a lecture tour. He delivered a speech on the state of American poetry at Oddfellows Hall, in the Egyptian Saloon. It was extremely informative, except that he criticized the work of many of the persons he mentioned. He was especially unkind toward one man. An anthologist. I believe his name is Dr. Greenwald. I'd never heard of him, but the way Mr. Poe spoke you would have thought he was influential enough to infect the entire country with his compendium on American poets and their poems." Something wooden creaked on the floor above. The mistress of the house glanced upward.

"Am I keeping you from your duties, Mrs. Brannigan?" Pinkerton inquired.

"No, not at all. The Brands have left for the day."

Allan's head reared back slightly. "Already?"

"Yes. He's a farmer. Arrived from Germany. They're purchasing farmland west of the city. Please, make yourself comfortable. If you'll have coffee, I shall sit with you." She chucked her cooing daughter under the chinstrap of her puddinhead cap.

"I shall indeed," Allan happily agreed. He put himself in the chair closest to the hearth. The night had been cold, and there had been no fire in his attic room. "So, you found Mr. Poe to be an unpleasant man," he prompted.

"I found him to be very intelligent and extremely well educated, but overly proud of both. He possessed a mellifluous baritone."

"About five years ago, you say. Speak to me about the rest of his physical being."

Mrs. Brannigan poured herself a cup of coffee one-handed and lowered herself gracefully onto a wooden, turtleback chair. "I should say he was five-foot-eight and perhaps one-hundred-forty pounds. He had a great wealth of dark hair surrounding his very large forehead. His eyes communicated his intelligence. He rocked a bit when he talked, but he did not gesture as frequently as most men when they argue. He let his words rather than his hands and arms make his points. He carried himself altogether quite erect, like a military man. Or perhaps a peacock."

"His bearing and his attack on other poets took you aback," Pinkerton concluded, after swallowing a piece of roll.

The young matron cleared her throat. "Not nearly so much as when we approached him afterward. You see I, my mother, and my closest friend, Mrs. Winnifred Tucket, are all members of the Maryland Society for the Abolition of Slavery."

"I am a practicing abolitionist!" Allan was pleased to report.

"Are you?" She beamed, nodded her head, and seemed to regard her guest with a new appreciation. "Well, since you are a brother in arms, you must call me Molly!"

"And I am Allan."

"Allan it is. I don't mind telling you that you are in a city where we are seriously outnumbered. We three thought that, as Mr. Poe was clearly an enlightened man, had traveled to Europe, had spent so many of his years in Philadelphia and

New York, and was a long-time citizen of Baltimore, that his words against the infamous practice would carry great weight and influence."

Molly's passionate speech brought her forward in her chair, and Allan found himself drawn toward her. "But you were disappointed."

"To say the least. He not only declined to speak out, but rather defended the institution. He was very certain that slavery in our country was much more preferable to…how did he put it…'a miserable, short life in some grass hut in the jungles of Africa.' When we reminded him of the thousands who had died on the slave ships, he pointed out that those practices had been outlawed and were gone. He belittled our pleas that our black brethren were purposely kept ignorant and even treated like cattle, breeding children only to have them torn from their mothers and sold away. To his mind, the race was inferior and benefitted greatly from the care and protection of white owners. He even had the temerity to state that societies such as ours tend to encourage Negroes to resent both their masters and the labor they do. If he had spoken the same words during his lecture instead of after it, I would have demanded my twenty-five cents be returned!"

Pinkerton took out his notebook and pencil. Through a gentle grin, he said, "So, his death is solved already. He was killed by the Maryland Society for the Abolition of Slavery."

Siobhan began to cry. Molly Brannigan rose from her seat. "And yet they made you chief detective. Poor Chicago." Pinkerton checked her aspect and reassured himself that she was merely returning his teasing.

Molly gave Pinkerton a half-dismissive/half-preoccupied

nod. "Pardon me," she said, "while I attend to my hungry child."

"I shall be starting off immediately," Allan replied, finding the notebook page he sought. "Can you direct me to City Hall and also to the Washington College Hospital?"

"Washington University Hospital," Molly corrected. "It's on the east side of the city, almost at its limits. A tall, white building...perhaps five stories high, with a cupola on top. I believe it's at the corner of Broadway and Fairmount. Go out of my front door, turn to your left, and start walking. After about ten blocks, ask someone to point you toward City Hall. Supper in my house is served at six promptly. Good hunting, Chief Detective."

"I desire to speak with Dr. John J. Moran," Pinkerton said to the orderly at the hospital's front desk.

"And who might you be?" the man asked.

Pinkerton lifted his right hand, shook open two pieces of stationery, and laid them upon the desk. Though pressed to leave Chicago, he had not failed to secure a memorandum on letterhead from the city's sheriff, offering '...the aid of the most competent policeman on our force in the investigation of the affair of the death of Mr. Edgar Allan Poe.' The chief magistrate overseeing the Watch Force of Baltimore, William Foster, had been sufficiently impressed with the piece of paper and further impressed that his city's business was evidently being done at the expense of Chicago that he had penned and embossed his own directive that '...the reader of this document should, with all dispatch and diligence, assist Mr. Allan Pinkerton in the discharge of his investigation compassing the passing of Edgar Allan Poe.' This second piece of paper had required the expenditure of three morning hours to secure, but he expected it to pay off in short order. He had also been allowed to consult *The Directory of Baltimore Town and Fells Point*, a printed booklet that contained the names and addresses of more than thirty thousand residence owners. From this he proceeded to copy information on people who had appeared in various newspaper accountings concerning Poe's last days. They were Dr. John J. Moran (who lived next door to the hospital), Dr. Joseph Evans Snodgrass, Neilson Poe, Joseph Walker, Mr. John P. Kennedy, and several residents with the last name of Clemm.

"The chief physician is usually on the third floor at this hour," the orderly disclosed. He pointed. "Take those stairs."

Dr. John J. Moran had an aquiline nose and close-cropped hair, was thoroughly clean-shaven, and possessed a supercilious demeanor. Beside him stood a man in his early twenties, dressed in a suit. The younger man held in his left hand a long tube of light-colored wood with what looked like a trumpet player's mouthpiece on one end. Pinkerton recognized it to be a stethoscope. All this he absorbed before he spoke his first word.

"Dr. Moran, I am Allan Pinkerton, from Chicago. I would very much like to ask you several questions about Edgar Poe."

The physician blinked in wonderment. "Goodness me! I thought the man from New York had traveled far! Are reporters now arriving from the Indian territory?"

Pinkerton handed Moran his calling card and allowed the doctor to alter his surmise. "But I've reported everything I know already," Moran said with exasperation.

Pinkerton produced the letter from the justice building and waited again.

Moran sighed and addressed his companion. "Attend to Mr.

Muller and then find me." The young man nodded and walked off. Moran pivoted again to face Pinkerton. "This is a teaching hospital," he shared, glancing back for a moment at the intern. "Come to my office. Ten minutes is all I can spare."

Allan followed, thinking how he would have preferred spending no time in the building. He was ill at ease with the cries of the sick and dying and the peculiar smells he was convinced might be vapors of contagion. But Edgar Poe's last five days had been spent in the place, and so the visit was critical to the investigation.

While the doctor lowered himself into his chair, Pinkerton studied the walls. No diplomas were displayed. "To save time, why don't you tell me what you've read, and I'll confirm or deny each fact," Moran invited.

This was not Pinkerton's desired method of gathering information. He knew that if a person was quoted from his earlier testimony, he would be loath to contradict himself. Alternately, if he was compelled to repeat himself, more information might emerge, or he might prove from changed details that he had earlier fabricated facts. However, since the man was a professional and habituated to respect, the detective determined a more subtle, indirect course of action to gain what he sought. He produced his notebook and consulted it.

Pinkerton pretended to read. "Mr. Poe was carried to this hospital on Wednesday, the 3rd of October. He was brought by in a wagon by the police."

Dr. Moran shook his head vigorously. "No, he was found lying upon a bench in front of a large mercantile house on Light Street wharf. A policeman hailed a hack and directed the hack man to convey him here."

"That was about ten o'clock in the morning," read Pinkerton

"Correct."

"And he was placed in a ward."

Moran exhaled with exasperation. "Edgar Allan Poe placed in a ward? Do these reporters from other cities simply confect their articles? No indeed! He was immediately placed in a private room at my direction. I am the chief resident physician of this hospital, and he was given my personal and unflagging attention."

Pinkerton plunged on. "No one could tell you what Mr. Poe had been doing in the hours previous to his discovery."

"No. He was found unconscious and alone."

"The articles I read said that he seemed to be in an alcohol- or drug-induced stupor."

"It certainly appeared that way," agreed Moran, "but when I examined him, he had no smell of liquor on his person. Moreover, there were no tremors. His skin was pallid, with slight nausea at the stomach and a strong disposition to sleep."

Pinkerton moved the notebook closer to his nose. "A sleep so profound that he barely spoke."

"Stop reading and take notes if you wish to know the truth," the doctor ordered. "He was carefully undressed and critically examined by me as soon as he arrived. He complained of stomach pains. He was also thirsty. I suggested he might be inclined to take a little toddy, because the hair of the dog that bites them often produces a cure in serious drinkers. He was most vehement in his refusal and wished for water. From this I ruled out rabies, because that fatal disease produces a dread of water. Moreover, I found no puncture marks upon his legs or arms.

"Directly after my interview, he was sponged with lukewarm water, sinapisms applied to his feet, thighs and abdomen, and cold compresses applied to his head. I had the room darkened, and I directed that a nurse, Mrs. Lukauskis, be placed in a chair guarding the threshold of his room. Half an hour after I left him, he threw off his covers, opened his eyes, sat up, and asked where he was. The nurse fetched me right away. I drew a chair close to the bed and took the poor man's hand in my own. I asked him how he felt. 'Miserable,' said he. I asked what bothered him most, and he said that it was his head. He thanked me for my solicitation. I said that he was with people who knew his fame and respected him. He answered, 'If you respect me, then do me the great favor of blowing out my brains with a pistol.' I attempted to calm him, but he swept out his hand and moaned, 'I feel that I could sink through this bed into the depths of the infernal abyss, forsaken by God and man, outcast from society, unloved, bereft. Why is there no ransom for this deathless spirit?'"

Pinkerton concealed his incredulity. "What did you deduce was wrong with him?"

"I am convinced it was a deterioration of his brain, due to encephalitis or a brain lesion. And yet the regions of his brain controlling his thought and speech were not affected, as he later spoke of his family, his dead wife and poor mother-in-law. But, after some hours, his pulse increased to one-hundred-twenty beats per minute and grew feeble. He later expressed to me his everlasting regret–"

Not interested in hearing more patently fabricated soliloquies, Pinkerton said, "Excuse me, Doctor. Several reports state that his cousin, Mr. Neilson Poe, eventually arrived here."

"Yes. I sent for him. Sent for him and made inquiries concerning a Mr. Reynolds whom Mr. Poe kept calling for. By the time the cousin arrived, however, it was clear that the Grim Reaper had taken up vigil in the room."

"So, he said nothing to his cousin?"

"No."

"Nor to this Mr. Reynolds?"

"No, no. When next the patient's eyes opened, I adjured him earnestly to look to his Savior. He answered that he was surrounded by demons. In the last hours, I again entreated him to pray to Jesus, and he cried out that there was no buoy, no lifeboat to save him and that he could no longer reach the shore. A few minutes later, a muscular twitching and jerking set in, and, after one great tremor, he expired."

"During all of this rhetoric," said Pinkerton, "did you think to ask him how he came to be found lying on a bench out in the weather?"

Moran's head reared back as if he had been slapped. "Yes, of course. But he could not recall."

"I see. And the hour of his death?"

The physician hesitated. "What do you have down?"

"I have conflicting reports," Allan lied.

Without hesitation, Moran said, "About midnight. Midnight, the 7th of October." The doctor seemed content to stop there, but since the man sitting across from him continued to hold his gaze without blinking, he added, "After death, he was washed and laid out, in a suit of black cloth. He was placed in state under our rotunda. Hundreds of friends and admirers came to pay their last respects. Perhaps a dozen ladies were granted a lock of his hair, which was astonishingly thick and of the most jet-black hue. He lay there for an entire day. On the morning of...let's see...it must have been the 9th, he was interred in the Westminster burying-ground. I could not be there, but I was told by one who had attended that the collective grief was profound, and many eyes were sore from tears." Having completed his reconstruction, Moran threw up his hands, palms out, to show that he was finished.

"You said his hair was very thick."

"Thick and curly. No, not curly; wavy."

"Might such thick hair have hidden a blow to his crown or the back of his head?"

Dr. Moran blinked. "No. I told you that I examined him minutely. And he certainly would have told me if he was attacked."

"Did he have a wallet or a money clip on his person when he arrived at the hospital?"

"I...I don't know. I don't believe so, because all his care was done for free. Yes, I'm sure that he had nothing on him."

"Isn't that strange?" Pinkerton said, more into his notebook than to the doctor.

"Perhaps he was robbed by the hack driver."

"You completed no autopsy?"

"No. His condition was one of deterioration, and I had observed him long enough to be certain the cause lay within his brain. Moreover, it would have been a crime to have mutilated his noble head. He had a generous forehead, indicating a highly developed mind. It looked the same as that of the genius Napoleon. I have a death mask cast of the great emperor in my study."

"And this black suit he was buried in...was it the same suit in which he arrived?"

In answer, Moran pulled out his watch fob and consulted it. "I've given you considerably more time than I promised. I can only speak with authority from the hour he arrived in my hospital." He moved toward his open door. "I trust you can find your way out, sir."

"I can," Pinkerton assured.

After the doctor hastened away, Allan made a few notes in his book – far fewer than he would have hoped. His ploy of feeding incorrect information had induced the man to speak, but the words were almost certainly not accurate. The many newspaper reports had indeed stated that Poe was brought to the hospital in a hack. They variously gave the time of death on October 7th as 3:00 or 5:00 in the morning, but not one reported the hour as midnight. They also all claimed that he had been carried from Ryan's 4th Ward Polls or Gunner's Hall, the former being located inside the latter. Pinkerton determined to judge further how accurate or inaccurate Dr. Moran's testimony was based on whether or not "a large mercantile house on Light Street wharf" lay adjacent to Gunner's Hall.

That Moran was puffing himself up by lying about the conversations he had with Poe was obvious. If Poe had been half as lucid as Moran described, he would have given specifics of what had happened to him prior to his discovery in the gutter. The numerous newspaper reports agreed that Edgar's cousin, Neilson Poe, had been sent for and visited the dying man. However, none of the dozen papers Pinkerton had dissected had mentioned a 'Mr. Reynolds.' The very physician who might have shed noonday illumination on the case tragically shrouded it in confusion. If he got anywhere with the rest of his investigation, Pinkerton determined that he would return to the hospital with an official of the Baltimore police and force Dr. Moran to sift the wheat of truth from the chaff of his many embellishments and inaccuracies.

Allan turned down a flight of steps and found himself confronted by a nurse ascending. He recognized that her face had an eastern European bone structure, quite possibly Lithuanian. Rather than press himself against the wall, he moved in her way.

"Are you Mrs. Lukauskis?" he asked her.

The nurse took a moment to study the man blocking her way. "Yes, I am."

"Excellent!" Allan enthused. "You are precisely the person I was told to find."

"Me?"

"Yes." He fished one of his calling cards out of his pocket and handed it to the woman. While her lips helped her sound out the words, he unfolded his letter from the Baltimore Watch Force magistrate. "I am trying to get to the bottom of what happened to poor Mr. Poe."

Mrs. Lukauskis drew in a sympathetic breath and nodded with vigor.

"You sat guard at his door?"

"I did. Myself and Lucy, another nurse. We had shifts."

"Was Dr. Moran there most of the time?"

An incredulous look came onto the nurse's face. "No. Of course not. Dr. Moran has constant demands on his time. He appeared shortly after Mr. Poe arrived, and he looked in two or three times a day."

"Did he and Mr. Poe conduct any long conversations?"

A defensive demeanor pinched the corners of the nurse's eyelids.

"Not that I heard. But I wasn't there every hour, you understand."

"Of course, there was Lucy as well."

"And Dr. Moran would excuse me for short spells so I could catch a cup of coffee or visit the necessary."

Pinkerton pulled out his notebook and pencil. "Understood. And yet you were with the poor fellow for many hours. It's most important that I learn all the particulars of his arrival. He had no trunk, hand bag, or wallet?"

"No, sir."

"Did he carry a knife or wear a watch or other jewelry?"

"None of it. But he did have a cane."

"A cane. What happened to that?"

"His cousin took it away." She rolled her eyes. "I don't mind telling you, we had the devil's own time wrestling that cane away from him. He had a…"

"A what?"

"I was going to say a death grip on it, but that sounds so terrible, given the circumstances."

"Perhaps he felt he needed to protect himself," Pinkerton thought aloud.

Mrs. Lukauskis nodded. "Perhaps."

"And his clothes…he wore a suit of black cloth?"

The woman's blue eyes went wide. "No, not at all! He was dressed in the most shabby of clothes. They were cheap gabardine. Stained and faded. And ripped at several of the seams. The right arm was ripped up beyond the elbow. He wore what they call a bombazine coat."

"Wait a moment!" Pinkerton said, feeling positive for the first time in his investigation as he absorbed the news and scribbled notes. "What about his shoes?"

"Boots they were. Very poor quality. Worn out. Run down at the heels. Hadn't been blacked for ages, in my estimation."

"How curious," Pinkerton murmured.

"Not half so curious as the fact that the clothing did not fit."

Pinkerton looked up with amazement from his note taking. The nurse had clearly decided to confide in him, perhaps was eager to speak. "Didn't fit, you say. Too large, or too small?"

"Too small." She lifted her right forefinger. "And a hat came with him. It was old, too, and made of straw. A woven palm leaf thing you could hardly call a hat."

"Why is that?"

"Because it was bashed in at the back and had half its brim missing. Also, there was no ribbon around it."

"Bashed in," Pinkerton echoed. "Mrs. Lukauskis, this is most important: Might the hat have been bashed in the back because Mr. Poe had been struck hard on his head?"

"No." The nurse shook her head several times. "There were no bumps or splits in the skin. I stroked his head a number of times when I was applying cold compresses. His hair was so lovely. And he seemed to enjoy the attention, even though he couldn't say so."

"He was unconscious."

"Feverish. In and out, in and out." The woman's bright eyes lit up suddenly. "Come to think of it, his pantaloons didn't match his coat at all. They were lighter in color. Like new iron. And a different weave. What is more, he came in wearing neither a vest nor a neck cloth. No bow tie either. Also, the bosom of his shirt was crumpled and badly soiled."

Pinkerton found himself marveling at the stout nurse's powers of observation, thinking that she would make an excellent detective in her own right.

"Are these clothes still about?" he hoped.

"Oh, no. They were not fit for rags. I'm sure they were burned."

With one door closed, Pinkerton sought to open another with the help of the observant nurse.

"At any time in your presence, did Mr. Poe utter complete sentences?"

Mrs. Lukauskis paused to frame her words. "Well, yes. Sometimes, he would mutter or even shout a sentence. Here and there. He muttered a great deal about demons. But he would not answer me or Lucy or any of the doctors in clear sentences."

"Did he try to respond?"

"I think so. But he made little sense. He would say, 'Oh, my poor Virginia' or 'Oh, my poor mother.' Frequently, he said, 'I must...' But he never finished his thought. His last clear words were 'Lord, help my soul.' I pray the Lord has."

"Is Lucy about today?" Pinkerton asked.

"No. She's on when I'm off, and vice versa. But we traded news on Mr. Poe at every change of shift. Even though it was second-hand, I heard everything that she heard."

"And she got no words from Mr. Poe about how he came to his state or why he was dressed in rags?"

"No. Regrettably."

"Did he tell the doctor he felt miserable when he first came in?"

"I think he did."

"And he asked that someone help end his misery by blowing out his brains?"

"Not while I was in attendance. But he said something once to the effect of, 'My brain is exploding.'" Mrs. Lukauskis folded her arms across her generous bosom. "For all the world he seemed to be in either an alcohol or an opium fit when he arrived. I smelled no alcohol on his breath, but if he had laid out in the air all night, he might have lost the smell. And certainly opium would not have an odor. Now, I had heard of Mr. Poe by reputation. In this town he was infamous for being an inebriate. That's why we moved him up to the tower, to be away from the other patients. The ones with delirium tremens usually make a great deal of noise. But then Dr. Moran came in and examined him and pronounced that it was a fever or perhaps an advanced lesion of the brain, and as the days wore on and Mr. Poe deteriorated instead of improved, we all were inclined to agree. He was lucid enough on the first evening to ask for his cousin, Mr...what is it...Neilson Poe? And then, a day later, he started calling another name. The best we could make out was 'Reynolds.' It sounded like Reynolds. And once it seemed like he said 'Black Reynolds.' This led me to think it might be a Negro he meant."

"Perhaps 'Fetch back Reynolds'?" Pinkerton suggested.

"I'd be leading you wrong if I took a guess."

"Quite smart of you to say, Mrs. Lukauskis. When did his cousin visit?"

"On Thursday and again on Saturday. But conversation was impossible."

"And no appearance of any Reynolds?"

"No. We asked the cousin who that might be, and he had no

idea."

"No person named Reynolds ever visited," Pinkerton said one last time, silently cursing the physician.

"No, sir."

Allan put away his notebook and pencil. He beamed at the middle-aged nurse. "You have proven yourself a treasure, Mrs. Lukauskis."

"Have I?"

He dug into his pocket. "Indeed. Such powers of observation must be rewarded."

"Oh, no, sir."

"I insist!" He took the woman's hand, coaxed open her fingers, and pressed a dollar into her palm.

Mrs. Lukauskis shrugged. "Well, thank you very much indeed." She peered up the stairs and behind her before adding, "I can use it."

"They don't pay much, eh?"

"They can't afford to. I'm seeking other employment, to take you into my confidence. Our reputation is not the best. The doctors here kill as many in their operations as other doctors do cutting in the patients' homes. We have more empty beds than full ones. That's how I could afford to spend so much time with poor Mr. Poe."

As well as definite skills in detection, Allan Pinkerton had an excellent sense of direction. As soon as he quit the hospital grounds, he began walking briskly toward the Inner Harbor. He figured the business district would be more likely than the eastern edge of the city to offer a public transit line or else a hackney for hire, but fifteen minutes later he was still on foot.

As he marched along, he admired the houses and shops. The town seemed to have been laid out in a roughly rectilinear fashion early in its history, so that he did not feel as if he had stumbled into a brick version of a garden maze. At last he came upon a café. He ordered ale, a plate of cold cuts and cheese, and a side dish of pickled vegetables. The beer schooner was very generous in proportions, fashioned of pewter with the sort of glass bottom that had inspired the phrase, "Here's looking at you!"

As soon as he finished eating and paying, Pinkerton consulted his watch and hurried from the café. The day was quickly wearing on, and in his mind's eye he envisioned sands rushing through the neck of an hourglass. The man who had waited on him in the eatery had directed where Allan might most successfully find conveyance. He hailed an unoccupied hack, read out the address of Neilson Poe, and climbed aboard. As they bounced and rattled toward Baltimore's elegant Mount Vernon section, Pinkerton became aware of a very tall, circular monument with a figure on top, looking down from the city's western heights and surrounded by stately town homes. The driver explained that it was twenty years old, constructed of white marble, and had been erected in honor of George Washington. Allan suspected that Chicago would be established and rich enough in short order to create its own marble spectacles.

Soon, the hack arrived at Neilson Poe's home. As Allan despaired of finding another cab in the residential area, he asked the hack man to wait. He silently applauded his foresight when a Negro servant informed him that Mr. Poe was at his place of business and that it was located within a few blocks of the harbor. They moved off again, and Pinkerton shook his head with impatience as he registered how far the autumn sun had descended from its zenith.

Not too long afterward, the detective found himself seated in a well-appointed office, directly across from Neilson Poe. He was a calm and soft-spoken gentleman whom Pinkerton judged to be around forty years of age. Everything about him and his surroundings indicated 'comfort' to Pinkerton. The man was most inviting and pleased to learn that the search for the solution to Cousin Edgar's mysterious death had not been buried with the man.

"I was afraid you were yet another pesky reporter," Neilson shared.

"They can be tiresome," Allan commiserated.

"Tiresome and rude. No respect at all for our privacy or emotions."

"I have heard that you were not able to converse with your cousin," Pinkerton steered.

"That is unfortunately true. He seemed to recognize me on my first visit, and he smiled once. But he was unable to answer my questions. This was in spite of the fact that he uttered several coherent words together every now and then. I think once he recited a line from one of his poems. 'Lost Lenore,' he said at one point."

"You were given his walking stick?"

Neilson's expression pinched. "It is not his cane. I remember his distinctly. Before this last visit to Baltimore, he was in Richmond. Here is the one given to me and said to have been found with him." He reached behind for a fancy cane with a brass top. He gripped it in both hands and turned a ring at the neck of the handle. From the wood, he withdrew a short sword.

"So, he was armed."

"Indeed. He may have purchased it in Richmond, but I am quite surprised that he was willing to part with the other. It was as a friend to him, an accomplice in affectation as it were, since he did not limp or require support. I have written to two parties in Richmond, making inquiry as to the cane and whatever they may know of his intentions in Baltimore when he met with whatever misfortune overcame him. He grew up in Richmond, you know."

"I had read something of it," Pinkerton replied. "But I would welcome knowing more."

"His mother and father both were accomplished actors. His father was a drunkard and abandoned his family when Edgar was very young. His mother, Elizabeth, followed performance prospects South to sustain them. There were three children: William Henry – called Henry, older than Edgar – and Rosalie, younger." Neilson's eyes grew sad. "Elizabeth died, however, when Edgar was just turning three. It was not a quick death, I understand, and he, being very precocious, was well aware of her passing all the way. I believe he never had a completely happy day after that."

"How did he get on once she had passed?" Pinkerton asked.

"The family was split up. He went to a friend of the mother's. Allan is the family name. Edgar added it to his own out of gratitude. But it was ever a tumultuous relationship between him and the father."

"Was he adopted?"

"No. Never. I understand the mother adored and spoiled

him, but the father was very demanding and more like the wrathful god of the Old Testament than the forgiving one of the New. Edgar was happier when he was invited to visit the home of another Richmond family, the Roysters. I have sent letters to both houses with inquiries."

Allan murmured the name and marked it down in his notebook. "I understand Edgar did not stay with you on this last visit," he prompted.

"True enough. While I respected him greatly for his talents, I did not deem him a proper guest."

"Because of his drinking?" Pinkerton asked. According to several of the newspapers, Edgar Poe had the same curse as his father.

"No, not that," Neilson said, tilting back his chair slightly, making it creak. "He could keep himself sober as a judge when he wanted to. No, I mean that he was a decidedly obstreperous individual. You had to weigh every phrase you uttered in his presence, because he would challenge it and not stop arguing until he was convinced he had proven you wrong. I think this was because he felt defensive around people of even moderate financial success. The only superior station he could show was that of the mind. He was almost perpetually poor."

Allan inhaled the smell of freshly tanned leather. The couch to his right looked new. In fact, most of the items in the office gleamed or shone with no patina of age. He remembered reading that Edgar Poe was carrying a large sum of money when he had disappeared. He wondered if Cousin Neilson's business was doing well enough to merit new furniture purchases or if he had come into money another way.

"Did he seek to borrow from you?" Pinkerton asked.

"Oh, occasionally. But he was constantly lamenting his state in front of my children and making the world to be a terrible and unfair place. To listen to him, there was nothing he could do about it. This was simply not true. He was more than smart enough to open a shop or work at a bank. But those labors he deemed beneath him."

"Can't editors make a decent living?" Pinkerton asked.

"I am sure some can. But even if he could not find such a position, other writers should have served as examples. I know that Emerson spent his early adulthood teaching at several schools. Nathaniel Hawthorne, who is easily as successful as Edgar in writing, earned his steady income by working in a customs house. I understood that Edgar knew an acquaintance of President Tyler's son and tried to use the relationship to secure a sinecure in the Philadelphia customs house. But he failed to appear for the interview. Most likely he was drunk. But my final reason for not welcoming Eddie was that he did not tolerate children well. He was of the opinion that children should be seen and not heard. My wife and I revel in their youth and antics and did not want Eddie dampening their ardor."

Pinkerton did not comment on Neilson's last words. His attitude toward the young aligned more with the writer cousin than with the businessman.

Neilson added, "And, then again, if you let him overnight within your walls, there was no telling how long he would overstay his welcome. He often had not a cent on him."

"That I have read," Allan said. "Several newspapers also reported that your cousin called on a Dr. Nathan Covington Brooks on either the 28th or the 29th, but that this gentleman was, unfortunately, out of town."

"I read the same," Neilson said. "Moreover, I took the trouble to check this out. I was able to speak with both a servant and Mrs. Brooks. They told me that Eddie had paid a surprise visit. He seemed to the servant confused. The man could not tell whether Eddie's state was due to illness or intoxication."

"One of these reporters learned from persons in Richmond that your cousin was on his way to New York, via Philadelphia. The purpose was to launch a literary journal."

"So I understand…but I learned this from second-hand sources, just as you have," revealed Neilson.

"So, where might he have stayed in your city?"

"Not so very long ago, maybe last year, he used Bradshaw's Hotel, on Pratt Street, opposite the train depot. But I checked there, and they had no record of him lodging within a week of his rescue from the street."

Pinkerton suspected that his host spoke of the seamy hotel he had refused to consider the previous evening. At such places, any form of mischief was possible. Cut-rate often betided cutpurse or even cut-throat.

"I have checked at half a dozen inns and hotels personally and put out the word with friends who have promised to help me track down his recent history," said Neilson. "I am thinking that he surely had a trunk or valise with him. When found, it might provide clues to his purpose here and who he met."

Pinkerton consulted his notebook. "Indeed. Are you acquainted with a local friend or acquaintance of your cousin by the name of Reynolds?"

"Ah, the mysterious Reynolds. They asked me about him at the hospital. I never heard Eddie mention the name. Why do you ask?"

"Both the doctor and one of the nurses who attended him said that he seemed to be repeating that name over and over toward the end."

"Strange. Perhaps he was on his way to meet with a Mr. Reynolds. Which means the person might not even be in this city."

"You are correct," agreed Pinkerton.

Even as they spoke, the sun declined another degree and now shone into the westward-facing office window. Its rays struck the polished brass head of the cane and reflected onto Pinkerton's face. He thought how the cane had been present for all the hours preceding Poe's discovery in the street, and yet it could tell nothing of its travels. Nevertheless, he wondered if it might indirectly provide information.

"May I?" the detective said, leaning toward the halves of the cane.

"By all means."

Allan searched the blade of the sword for signs of blood or threads of cloth. Finding nothing, he picked up the wooden end and examined it for nicks or bits of telltale earth. It was, in every way, as clean as if it had been purchased at a store that morning.

"Perhaps there was no foul play at all," Neilson posited while Pinkerton examined the cane. "My cousin was never a well man. He complained frequently of headaches. I personally believe he was a lifelong victim of that humour called melancholia. He was obsessed with the fear that he was going insane. He spoke of all the bizarre thoughts he had whilst he dreamed. But then he would credit his creativity, the ideas for his stories, on the selfsame dreams. I am sure he felt as ambivalently frustrated as Hamlet. He believed his moods were what caused him to drink and not the other way round. Likewise, the taking of opium and laudanum. Some argue that these have medical benefits, but I only hear bad things associated with them. The drink and drugs fed the mood, which fed the vices. A vicious cycle which, inevitably, killed him."

As he spoke, Neilson reached into a small, silver-plated box on his desk and took out a lucifer – a friction-ignited match. From a larger box, he extracted a pinch of tobacco in a neat tube of paper. Allan's nose had told him the man partook of tobacco, and yet he had noted neither a spittoon nor the telltale sign of brown stains upon the oriental rug that betrayed usage. He had only recently seen the appearance of machine-rolled cigarettes. He knew that the publisher of the New England Almanack and Farmers Friend had declared tobacco a pesticide and a poison to man, but he also knew that smoking would not be stopped. He personally disliked the smell, but he was not about to complain. Nor would he point out the irony of his host deploring drink and drug use even as he filled his lungs with the first intake of habit-inducing smoke.

"I'm here because I'm not certain what killed him. He had virtually nothing but that cane left on his person when he was found," Pinkerton reminded the cousin.

"He owned virtually nothing most of his life," his interviewee countered. "I personally think that he was overcome with illness and lay all but helpless in a hidden place. An opportunist saw his state and robbed him of his watch and billfold."

"And his clothes as well?" Pinkerton asked.

This news produced a remarkable alteration in Neilson Poe's placid face. It suddenly went rigid. His eyelids drew wide apart.

"His clothes?"

"Indeed. You saw him laid out under the hospital rotunda?"

"I did."

"Those clothes were donated." Pinkerton turned the pages of his rapidly filling notebook and read aloud the detailed description of the rags that had been provided by Mrs. Lukauskis.

"I'll be dashed! Well, it still might be robbery of an unconscious man," Neilson supposed, tapping the ash of his smoke into a tray and then taking another puff.

Pinkerton tucked away the look of genuine surprise on Neilson Poe's face concerning news of the clothing. The look supported the man's innocence in his cousin's death. "Robbery where? Certainly not on the street. I cannot imagine the most bold of rapscallions daring to take the time to exchange clothing with an unconscious man."

"Even in a back alley?" asked Neilson Poe.

"What robber would trouble himself to dress his victim in his old belongings? Would he not just drop them there in a heap and nip off?"

"Surely you are right," the businessman agreed.

"Someone said to me, 'Since he had no money on him, it was most probably a simple robbery. How can you solve such a random crime of opportunity in a giant city like Baltimore?' But the switching of the clothing and the long period of time between your cousin's arrival here and his discovery prove that this was more than random."

"I see what you mean," Poe said.

The mention of an alley reminded Pinkerton of an important question he needed answered. "Does Gunner's Hall sit next to

Light Street wharf?"

The businessman laughed. "No. They're a mile apart. Why?"

"Dr. John Moran is not a reliable fellow."

"He and his hospital have less than sterling reputations, I'm afraid," Neilson Poe said. "There have been several graves in the cemetery closest to the hospital that have been reopened within hours of burial and the bodies stolen. One theory is that the hospital is strapped for money and needs dissection corpses for teaching the young doctors."

Pinkerton rolled his eyes as he tore a page from the back of his notebook and began writing. "I want nothing to do with that crime. Mr. Poe, you have been most helpful, and I thank you kindly. I expect to travel to Richmond in a day or two. If you learn that the cane came from there, would you please send it to me so that I may convey it thence? Here is the address of the place where I'm presently staying. I expect to change addresses soon, but I will be sure to inform you."

Neilson stubbed out the remainder of his cigarette in the ashtray and rose to accept the slip of paper. His eyes stole to a clock fixed to the inner wall of his well-appointed office. "My manservant should be waiting downstairs with my carriage. May I transport you somewhere on my way home?"

Pinkerton also consulted the clock. He had approximately ninety minutes until Mrs. Brannigan laid supper "at six promptly."

"Gunner's Hall is on the east side and away from the harbor?"

"That's correct."

The detective did not wish to abuse Poe's offer. "What about Westminster Cemetery?"

Neilson lifted his coat from a tree just inside his door. "You desire to see my cousin's grave?"

"I do."

"It's at West Fayette and Greene."

Pinkerton stood and fetched his derby hat from the corner of Poe's desk. "That's closer to your home. How far would you judge Fayette to be from West Pratt?"

"A brisk walk."

"Then Westminster Cemetery it is."


Westminster Church was actually two impressive structures, both designed and built in the classic English Presbyterian style. The tall windows of the church proper narrowed to lancet arches. Stunted buttresses hinted at Gothic ancestry. Its very high central tower overlooked the gentrified neighborhood. The cemetery, which lay to the right of the church front doors, was small in comparison.

Pinkerton entered the burial ground with his hat removed. He searched out a fresh grave in the front and then the middle of the yard but found only markers, trees, and grass. At the very back rose a mound of earth strewn with white chrysanthemums.

"Edgar Poe is under there," a raspy voice declared.

Allan looked to his left. A man was seated on a small stone bench. The seat had recently been dragged a distance of about fifty feet, as evidenced by the wide marks made in the gravel walkway. Whoever had moved the bench had not bothered to rake the path back into an aesthetic pattern. Allan wondered if it had been the man sitting on it. He wore a rather elegant black suit. Stretched between his hands was a newspaper. His brass-rimmed spectacles had earpieces. Small ears, around which the wires were bent, were set close to his head. Allan was able to observe this because the man's hair, as black as his clothing, had been slicked back with a shiny pomade. He looked up at Pinkerton and blinked several times.

"Did you know him?" Allan asked, able to think of nothing better to say.

"I knew him well. And I knew him long." The man folded the newspaper and set it to his side. Allan noted that an apple also sat on the bench. "But I've never seen you, so I'm guessing that you did not know him well."

"That's true. My name is Allan Pinkerton."

The man stood, and as he did he winced slightly and favored his left side. Pinkerton noted that the mourner was about five-foot five, an inch shorter than his own stature. The detective judged him to be in his mid- to late forties. He was of a thin, diminutive build, in contrast with the detective, who had developed a sturdy, muscular physique from years of wrestling wood and iron into barrels. The man extended his right hand.

"Aaron Pelglade. I came all the way from New York for this." His neck turned to the left, so that Pinkerton assumed he was indicating the grave. Then, confusingly, his head swiveled to his right. "So, Pinkerton is a Scottish name?"

"It is. And Pelglade?"

"English. It means through the glade. I trust you won't hold my ancestry against me. We're both Americans, aren't we?"

"Indeed," Pinkerton agreed. The man had shifted the focus of his gaze through his thick lenses to the bridge of the detective's nose and kept it there. This, combined with his rapid blinking, held Allan's attention.

"I'm a whiskey drummer," Pelglade announced. "Whiskey.

From the Irish, meaning 'water of life.' That's how I both came to know Mr. Poe and kept running into him."

"He frequented drinking establishments that you supply?" Pinkerton followed.

"Correct. I travel the middle coast, from New York to Richmond, representing three distilleries that make three different types of whiskey: bourbon, rye, and Mr. Poe's favorite: Tennessee straight."

"Aged in charred oak barrels two years or more," Allan said.

"Just so! Do you favor Tennessee straight?"

"I used to be a barrelmaker," Pinkerton shared.

Pelglade maintained his fixed, batting focus. "And what, may I inquire, is your profession now?"

Allan was damned if he would lose the staring contest. He lowered his gaze to the stranger's philtrum, the creased indentation between nose and upper lip. "I am a detective."

Pelglade exclaimed with a loud but pleased noise. "Now isn't that interesting? Are you here to pay homage to the popularizer of your profession then?"

"It would be fitting," Allan granted.

"Then you have found him," said Pelglade. He turned with a jerky motion, uttered a tiny sound of pain, and plopped himself down on the bench. As his posterior descended, his right hand dug into his pantaloon pocket and emerged with a jackknife. He flipped it open. With his left hand he retrieved the apple.

"He and I became tight immediately. It was our mutual obsessions with dying and death, reanimation, premature burial...in short, the gruesome and macabre. Have half with me," the salesman offered, cutting the apple.

"No, thank you."

"You know what they say about apples and doctors," Pelglade said, finishing his cutting. "If Eddie had eaten more apples perhaps he wouldn't be here."

Pinkerton thought the remark was quite flippant, given the circumstances, but he merely said, "Thank you, no. I shall be dining soon."

"Suit yourself." Pelglade wiped the blade of the knife on the edge of the newspaper, folded it into the handle, and stuck the knife back into his pocket. Then he inspected both parts of his apple and tossed the smaller section onto the ground very close to the freshly dug grave. He bit into the remaining half and, before he finished chewing, said of the discarded part, "It's white now, but soon it will be a disgusting brown. And then, if the weather is damp, base creatures will devour it. If the weather is dry, it will shrivel into a fourth its size." He took another bite, chewed for several seconds, looked directly at Pinkerton, and asked, "And now that you have paid homage, are you going home?"

"Not directly," Allan said. "I also intend to learn more than what is reported in the newspapers about the circumstances of your friend's death."

The staring eyes behind the spectacles turned away, glancing again left and right, as if he expected momentary company. "From what I've read, the circumstances were rather curious."

Pinkerton mentally added Mr. Pelglade's name to his list of sources. He was about to ask if he might arrange an interview, when the whiskey salesman lifted his hand and waggled his forefinger.

Pelglade stood and flung the remainder of the apple over the iron fence beyond Poe's grave. "Perhaps I might be of help in your investigation."

"You might indeed. May I interview you tomorrow?"

"What's wrong with tonight?"

"I dislike venturing out in a strange city at night," Pinkerton said truthfully.

"Perhaps we lodge not too distant from each other," Pelglade pursued. "I am at Maryland House, on the south side of Lexington Market." He pointed. "Just over there."

"I am on West Pratt at Greene Street."

Pelglade took several steps toward the entrance to the cemetery, as if reconsidering his offer. He paused within the mottled shadows of an ornamental tree, then turned with a graceful pirouette. "There's a saloon just three streets to the east of where you're staying. O'Grady's. It's not one I supply, but it would be convenient."

"At eight?" Pinkerton suggested.

Pelglade's head elevated. The sun caught the lens of his spectacles so that the detective could no longer see his eyes. But his smile was exceedingly broad.

"Excellent! Eight it is!" He spun around again and walked briskly toward the street.

"You've forgotten your newspaper," Pinkerton called out.

"You may have it," the reply came from over the salesman's shoulder. "There's no news worth reading anyway."

Pinkerton picked it up. He needed the advertisements seeking boarders if he stayed in Baltimore beyond Wednesday.

# CHAPTER SIX

*Tuesday, October 16, 1849*

Allan returned to Mrs. Brannigan's house just in time to wash his hands and face and change his shirt. A mirror, which could be pivoted, was attached to his dresser, and he canted it to place his image dead center in the glass. He caught himself stroking his beard and mustache, both of which had not had a trim since the previous Friday. He took scissors from his travel bag and began neatening the thickly massed hairs. From his prolonged, critical study of his face, he decided that he looked permanently grim. He noted that his all-but-invisible upper lip was not entirely concealed by his mustache. He considered his brow ridge too heavy and his eyebrows too low. Although his shiny, brown eyes communicated intelligence, he judged that they were set too deeply to be attractive. He turned from his reflection and thought about writing a letter to his wife. Her faithfulness balanced out her silent martyr demeanor. And she was a good mother. Among the women he had known, the two things counted for much. He knew he should be more grateful. Then he thought about tales of letters taking a month to wend their way to Chicago from the East Coast. He would likely be back home before a letter arrived. He sighed and went down to supper.

Molly Brannigan's ear was not attuned to German accents. The Brands turned out to be the Brandts. The husband was twenty-two and his bride eighteen. Upon their marriage, they had been doubly dowered and were determined to take the opportunity in the United States to quadruple the farmland they could afford to buy in Saxony. Frieda Brandt was shy and barely spoke English. Wilhelm was outgoing and eager to practice his adopted language. From German neighbors in Illinois, Allan had picked up *Plattdeutsch* words and phrases, so that he was able to support Wilhelm's bubbling monologues. The couple had that day bought eighty acres of bottomland to the west, and prosperity seemed to them unavoidable.

Molly divided her time efficiently among her baby, her guests, and feeding herself. Allan reflected that her soft poke bonnet and her apron enhanced her femininity. He also noted that she did not seem so much to walk as to glide from kitchen to parlor. Several times, as he supplied "Willie" with English words, he caught her watching him with an approving smile. The German couple was visibly impressed by the profession of detective, and first the husband declared and then the wife echoed that it was a noble career. When Allan was asked about the progress he had made that day, however, he became uncharacteristically shy, declaring that he had just begun his investigation. Following the meal, he volunteered to help his landlady clear the dishes. She shooed him off.

"Then I'll be stepping out for a time," Allan told her.

Molly's head tilted back slightly. "To drink?"

"To a saloon, but not to drink," he assured her. He told her about his chance meeting with Aaron Pelglade in Westminster cemetery, that the man was a whiskey drummer, and that he could not afford to walk away from a person who claimed intimate acquaintance with Edgar A. Poe.

Mrs. Brannigan dipped her head. "Very well. My door locks at ten o'clock sharp, and I will not take kindly to being roused after that time."

"I will be at a place called O'Grady's," he said. "If you want, you may have Mr. Brandt come and drag me back here at half past nine."

"You're a grown man," she replied, "and I trust your pocket watch works." She stepped back into the parlor and resumed talking with the young German couple.

Chuckling at her spunk, Allan went out the front door.

When Pinkerton arrived at O'Grady's Tavern, Aaron Pelglade was already seated with a half-finished glass of whiskey in front of him. Perched on his table was a rectangular case, finished in black leather and with metal guards riveted to each corner. It appeared to be new, with not one nick on it. It was large and had a polished wooden handle attached to its top. Pelglade half rose from his chair when Allan approached. As he had in the cemetery, his face pinched a bit and he favored his left flank.

"Did you hurt yourself recently?" Allan asked.

"Just a little unaccustomed labor," Pelglade replied. "I'm drinking bourbon. What will you have, Mr. Pinkerton?"

"Hot tea," Allan replied, taking one of the other chairs.

The whiskey salesman guffawed. "Do you want to get us thrown out on our tails?"

Pinkerton imagined with longing the welcome taste of whiskey on his tongue, the heat going down his throat, the sense of well being radiating from his stomach. He longed for just one shot. But he rejoined, "Surely not everyone who steps into this saloon orders liquor."

Pelglade looked around, blinking away as he did. "Surely all the men do, and I see no women."

Pinkerton put up his hand to halt the conversation. He rose and walked to the bar. He returned carrying a mug.

"Beer?" Pelglade asked, as he glanced mechanically left and

right.

"Yes. Birch beer." Pinkerton smiled wanly. "I flashed my badge at him. I'm sure he also saw my revolver. I told him I was on duty. He gave me no trouble."

"Well, if you wish something stronger when we're ready to leave…" The salesman flipped back a latch and spread the hinged halves of the case. Inside, six flasks of whiskey were secured by leather straps. "Kentucky bourbon, Tennessee straight, and Pike's Hill rye from right here in Maryland. I can get you a very good volume price to take home to…where is it you hail from?"

Pinkerton gave a brief description of his deeds and his rise to "chief detective" of Chicago. He did not, however, share with the stranger the plan he and Edward Rucker had cooked up, using the famous dead writer to make Pinkerton's name a national household word. When he had divulged enough to merit Pelglade's confidence, he said, "Where did you and Mr. Poe first meet?"

"Eddie," Pelglade corrected. "Eddie to his close friends and relatives. And I'm Aaron."

"I'm Allan."

As he repeated his glancing habit, Aaron Pelglade asked, "Allen with an 'e' or Allan with an 'a'?"

"The latter."

Aaron exclaimed loudly again. "No wonder you're investigating on Eddie's behalf. The selfsame name spellings prove this must have been fated!"

"Perhaps," said Allan, at the same time thinking that ninety-nine percent of what people thought was fate was either pure chance or a decision for which they were not willing to take the blame.

The drummer lifted his shiny, black shoes onto the seat of the free chair and crossed one ankle over the other. "We go way back. I first met him when he was working in Richmond for Thomas White, the publisher of the *Southern Literary Messenger*. That was in late 1835, I believe."

Once he began, Pelglade was like a primed pump that continued to gush without prompting. According to him, Poe switched his main focus from poetry to prose soon after the two met. Within a few weeks of his hiring, however, sloppy and unfinished work due to drinking caused him to be fired. Poe returned to Baltimore, where the virtual gypsy had been living. There, he married his thirteen-year-old cousin, Virginia Clemm. Soon after that, White gave him a second chance, and he moved back to Richmond with his wife and mother-in-law.

He worked at the *Messenger* for about eighteen months. Pelglade's opinion was that, between Poe's literary contributions and his taste in selecting the works of others, the periodical increased subscriptions from 700 to more than 3,500. When White refused to up his ten dollar per week salary, he quit and moved to New York City.

Unable to find editorial employment for an entire year, Poe moved again, this time to Philadelphia. During the year 1838, he could only find freelance work, albeit with quality periodicals such as Franklin's *Saturday Evening Post, Godey's Lady's Book, Burton's Gentleman's Magazine,* and *Graham's Casket,* whose name was later changed to *Graham's Magazine.* During this particularly hard period, Pelglade calculated that he and Poe had written to each other some dozen times and met in bars perhaps half that number.

Poe finally convinced William Burton to give him editorial work for two hours each day in exchange for ten dollars per week.

"This is where he blossoms," Pelglade declared with emphasis, taking the first sip of his second whiskey. "He was still uneven, mind you. Do you know his works, Mr. Pinkerton?"

"Only 'The Raven,'" Allan answered.

"Oh, you must immerse yourself. I have with me...not here, of course, but in my hotel room... almost all his published efforts. Only some are in books. Many I've had to cut out of magazines. I'd be glad to lend them to you, one at a time."

Pinkerton had no intention of spending his hours reading fiction. Moreover, he did not expect to see Pelglade again. Nevertheless, he thanked the man.

The whiskey seller nodded and then shooed away a mosquito that had been pestering his head. "At any rate, he was wildly uneven. For example, 'The Devil in the Belfry' and 'The Man Who Was Used Up' are like something a schoolboy would write. Filled with execrable puns, overdrawn humor, and, above all, poor plots. Names like 'General John A. B. C. Smith,' a droning preacher called 'Reverend Doctor Drummummupp' and, at the opera, 'Misses Arabella' and 'Miranda Cognoscenti.' But the worst is the Dutch clock-making town: 'Vondervotteimittiss.' Get it? 'Wonder what time it is.' I tell you, they are no better than campfire yarns."

Pelglade's sour expression suddenly softened to one of fond reminiscence. He rolled his eyes upwards, as if peering into the distant past. "Ah, but then comes 'William Wilson.' That, and 'The Fall of the House of Usher.' Here are displayed true genius!"

"I suppose all writers have good and bad ideas," Pinkerton mused.

"But 'why' is the question!" the bespectacled man shot back, his wide eyes magnified by the lenses. Apparently, he meant his outburst to be rhetorical, because he plunged on with his history of Poe the writer. After a year, he recited, Poe jumped from *Burton's* to the position of assistant editor under George Graham, the owner of *Graham's Magazine*. According to Pelglade, his salary was $800 per year, with extra for literary pieces he produced.

"In 1841, he produces the masterpiece that is the prototype for your profession, Allan:" Pelglade said. "'The Murders in the Rue Morgue.' Do you know what a sensation it was? Within nine months, the circulation of *Graham's Magazine* quadrupled! Quadrupled!"

Picking up speed, the man who had vomited more than enough intimate information to convince Pinkerton that he was a genuine friend of Poe's chattered on. He described how the writer became furious that Burton would not reward his successful efforts with a salary raise. Poe's drinking and disregard for deadlines caused increased tension. Finally, Poe learned with shock that Burton was selling the magazine to return to acting but had never given his assistant editor the opportunity to buy it."

"Would you say Mr. Burton acted unjustly?" Pinkerton inquired.

Pelglade seemed irked into silence by the constant buzzing of the indefatigable mosquito. The blinking eyes behind the thick spectacles followed its unceasing, circling flight. Tired of its interference, Pinkerton clapped his hands and sent the insect falling lifeless to the tabletop. Pelglade inverted his whiskey glass over the corpse.

"Would you say Mr. Burton acted unjustly?" Pinkerton repeated.

"One must walk a mile in an Indian's moccasins, as they say," his companion replied, in an off-hand manner. "I don't know Mr. Burton and only heard Eddie's side of it. According to him, he maintained long periods of total abstinence. His argument was that others constantly used drink to create a spirit of conviviality. Around them, he felt as I made you do when you came in here. Unlike you, he succumbed to their pressures. To him drink was like a poison. Once he began, he could not stop until he fell over and was confined to extended bed rest."

"Then you must have been responsible for many of his falls," Allan boldly pointed out, nodding at the black display case. His eyes caught sight, at the same time, of Aaron's fingernails. There were traces of embedded dirt under the ragged tips.

Pelglade withdrew his hands to his lap. "I know. Not in keeping with the rest of my appearance. It's that bit of unaccustomed labor I mentioned before. In retrospect, I should not have helped that gentleman replace the wheel on his carriage."

"Of course you should have," Allan verbally applauded, as he privately wondered how such an effete-looking specimen of manhood could possibly wrestle a wheel onto an axle or hold up a damaged carriage.

Aaron shrugged at the approval.

"But you were speaking of Mr. Poe's drinking problem," Allan prompted.

"Yes. I suppose I was responsible for three or four of Eddie's drinking jags. That is, until I truly believed what he was saying was not just an excuse for his excessiveness. In later years, I would happen upon him when he had already begun his binges, and then I did more good than bad."

"How so?"

"Well, because I knew no one could stop him. So I merely waited until he was too drunk to resist me, and then I brought him home. Actually, left him off at his door and ran away is the truth. I did not want to earn the unenviable reputation of being the man who created the downfall of America's greatest fiction writer."

"Greatest indeed? Surely not everyone thinks the way you do," said Pinkerton.

Pelglade bristled. "They should! I assure you that I am the most discerning of critics. I declare, with the authority of one who has devoured more than a hundred novels and anthologies of fiction, that he had no peer. Do you know how much reading time a man who travels up and down the coast, year after year, has in his evening hours?"

Allan knew the constant traveler at the other side of the table did not expect his question to be answered, so instead he said, "I am told that because he valued his talents at least as highly as you do he felt free to publicly criticize other writers."

Pelglade crooked his fingers at the bartender for a new glass of bourbon. "True. All but the adored Miss Browning. Why, he even found fault with Longfellow and Dickens!"

"Would you say this created actual enemies?"

"Most assuredly," said the whiskey salesman.

"I mean enemies who might want him dead."

"Ah. Now I see where you are driving! Writers are mostly

persons of reflection and not action. They truly believe the pen is deadlier than the sword, so they attempt to wound each other mortally with words. And yet I can think of one man who clearly would have enjoyed being Eddie's executioner. And wouldn't you know, my naive friend assigned this same man to be his literary executor."

"That is quite astonishing," Pinkerton said, feeling the visceral sensation that told him when he had been presented with an important clue to solving a case. "What is the man's name?"

"Dr. Rufus Wilmot Griswold. Have you read any of his poetry?"

"No, but I seem to recall his name." Suddenly, gears meshed in his mind, and he remembered Molly Brannigan's near-correct recollection of "Greenwald." Allan snapped his fingers and pointed. "He is also an…anthologist."

"Correct. Of American poetry and prose."

"Poe excoriated him right here in Baltimore a few years back. During his lecture on American poets."

"Not just in the salons and lecture halls," shared Pelglade, after he downed in a single gulp an inch of his third drink. "Even more damning, he mocked the man's efforts in print."

"Then why on earth would he name Griswold his literary executor?"

"Because Eddie hid his criticisms in print behind a pseudonym. And obviously because he naively believed word would not travel from distant lecture halls to Philadelphia. He knew that Griswold adored his work, and that as an editor he has the connections to see that Eddie's legacy continues to be printed."

"Dr. Griswold is an editor in Philadelphia?"

"He is the editor of *Graham's Magazine*." Pelglade smiled and raised his eyebrows as if awaiting certain reply.

"The same magazine where Poe was editor."

"Until he drank so much that his work suffered terribly and he was let go. This, however, was also after his genius and taste had grown subscriptions to 40,000!"

Pinkerton was deeply impressed. He had no idea that fiction writing was so popular. The readership of a magazine he had never heard of was larger than the population of Chicago. Clearly, a world of literary refinement existed parallel with the world he knew, and he had never known it.

"Oh," the salesman went on, "modesty forbids me to repeat the language Eddie used when he attacked Griswold and Graham in my presence. But do you know how desperate the man was for a dollar, Allan?"

"I do not."

"In spite of his hatred, he continued to submit manuscripts to Graham's. He had sunk to such depths that he could not afford pride. No fools they, they continued to publish him and increase their circulation. And why shouldn't they? Philadelphia was also my home then, and I will admit that whenever I was there I went to his favorite haunts and sought Eddie out. I should be ashamed to say this, but the unending tales of his personal horrors were simply too interesting not to hear."

"The Germans call that emotion *Schadenfreude*," said Pinkerton.

"Trust the Germans to have a word for something so negative. But I also sought him out in the matter of his stories. Those were his days of greatest productivity." The head swung left, then right.

"Rather ironic," Pinkerton judged. "Failure at editing but success at writing."

"Not at all! The fictional life of an artist may have nothing to do with his factual life. In truth, they may coexist as two completely separate persons!"

With each new glass of bourbon in him, Pelglade had become more aggressive in his assertions. Pinkerton understood how he and Poe became friends. Birds of the same feather, overly proud of their intellects, they pontificated black-and-white opinions and would not tolerate dissent. He could imagine how the two complemented each other, even as they complimented each other. And who else would an alcoholic prefer to cozy up to more than an enamored whiskey drummer?

"Surely the history behind an artist's life and especially his sufferings may be the wellsprings from which he draws some portion of his creations," Pinkerton asserted.

Pelglade regarded his listener in silence for a moment. Then he affixed a smile as hard and fake as a Greek mask. "You have a point, sir. Obviously, you were born in Scotland. Eddie spent time there in his youth. I am certain his images of desolate heaths and ruined castles derived from those days. His obsession with lost loves assuredly came from losing his mother and, not long after, the love of another older woman he viewed as a kindred spirit. His troubled dreams figure prominently. But those elements alone cannot account for the sudden upwelling of inspired ideas in 1843. 'The Pit and the Pendulum,' 'The Tell-Tale Heart.' That, inarguably, was his high-water mark."

Pelglade's eyelids narrowed, and his expression became solemn. "Then he slipped back into mediocrity. 'A Tale of the

Ragged Mountains.' Ridiculous. 'The Spectacles.' Banal. Until he wrote 'The Raven.'"

"A marvelously crafted poem," Pinkerton contributed, recruiting his scant knowledge. "Excellent symbolism, alliteration, and internal rhyme."

Pelglade reached across the table and tapped Pinkerton on the back of his hand. "So, you're more informed than you let on." Pinkerton noticed that he no longer blinked his eyes every few seconds; nor did he glance left and then right. The liquor had evidently dulled his nervous habits. Pelglade added, "He swore to me that he was only paid nine dollars for that deathless wonder."

"You say it as if you doubt it," Allan observed.

Pelglade's somber face changed to one of disgust. "If he sold that poem for nine dollars, then he was an imbecile. And Edgar Allan Poe was no imbecile."

"Perhaps he was desperate," Pinkerton theorized. "Alcoholics and opium eaters do desperate things when the craving is upon them."

"Yes," Pelglade softly replied, "the effects of corn, rye, and the poppy seed. 'A Tale of the Ragged Mountains' is in fact the dream of an opium addict who has previously died. Inspired by experience, but a ridiculous plot nonetheless."

Pinkerton took out his watch and glanced at it. Pelglade's digressions were getting longer and the detective's time shorter. "So Griswold lives in Philadelphia. Who in Baltimore would be dangerous to Mr. Poe?" he asked.

"I don't know," Aaron returned. "I only visit this city. I can tell you much more about Philadelphia and New York. Do you believe that just because Eddie was missing for several days and then found outside a tavern that foul play occurred?"

Allan then disclosed the information about the clothing Poe was found in, both too small and far shabbier than anything the proud writer had ever been seen in.

Pelglade nodded vigorously. "That is compelling. Then combine these with the bizarre business reported of him getting on a train drunk, without a ticket, and being sent back to Baltimore. I am no detective, but I certainly would have made specific inquiries around this town last week if I had lived here. First of all, as his friend I should have attended his viewing and funeral. But I have a work schedule and a living to earn."

The liquid in Pelglade's third glass of whiskey was down to half an inch. From an inside coat pocket he withdrew a tiny case, opened it, took out two pills, and popped them in his mouth.

"Foxglove," he supplied without being asked. "My heart tends to race when I become upset or overexert myself, and these do wonders. Bless the apothecary!"

"And it is to be taken with three glasses of whiskey?" Allan doubted.

Pelglade shooed away his concern and downed the last of the liquor. "I note that you follow the amber every time I lift the glass to my lips. Are you sure you won't have a parting shot? It's on me."

Allan declined with thanks. In spite of Pelglade's elegant clothing and his shiny display case, the man did not look in healthy condition. After three generous glasses of whiskey he showed no outward sign of having become drunk other than the disappearance of his facial motions, indicating that he was used to such consumption. Allan pictured the relentless routine of journeying up and down the coast selling whiskey, cycling perpetually back and forth like a rodent in a long cage, sitting for hours without exercise, his only breaks from the routine being drink, literature, and the occasional company of a friend. Now, the poor man with the nervous, off-putting tics and the scratchy-sounding voice had lost both literary friend and drinking companion.

"Are you married?" Allan inquired, rather sure of what the answer would be.

"No, Allan, I am saddened to report that joy has never been mine. I was not without relationships, mind you. My first love was my greatest. I believe she was truly my soul mate. However, she died of a fever when she was sixteen. My relationship with the second lady went so far as engagement, but she grew tired of my many days away from her on the road. The third pretended to love me. She spent my money. I foolishly endeavored to keep her by lavishing on her all my savings. She ruined me, and when I had no more coin she said, with the most carefree air, 'I dismiss you.' I understand that I am no Don Juan. I know I can be tiresome. I have been dismissed by women, by both sexes who think themselves better than whiskey salesmen, and worse of all by editors. So I thank you for your forbearance tonight, Mr. Pinkerton."

Because his recitation was stated in a calm, matter-of-fact tone, it was all the more pathetic. Allan did not consider himself an overly sentimental man, but his heart went out to the whiskey drummer. "Nothing of the sort," he insisted. "You are too hard on yourself. I judge you a fascinating–"

"Character?" Aaron interrupted.

Allan laughed. "Just so."

Pelglade broke into a beaming smile.

Allan observed, "If you have been dismissed by editors, that means you write as well."

"I do. I should rather say I did. Until I met Eddie, I made an earnest effort at it. But then I looked at greatness from close up and lost heart. I despaired in knowing my control of language, my inner ear could never be as finely attuned as his. Why should the world have interest in the merely good when we are blessed by the great, such as Shakespeare, Chaucer, Homer, Milton…and Poe?"

Pinkerton had no answer and merely shrugged. He pushed his chair back from the table. "I'm afraid I have a curfew where I'm staying."

"Really? I believe I can be of more help to you than merely what I have spoken tonight," said Pelglade, with an air of desperation. "I should like to assist in any way possible."

"I don't know what that might be," Allan said. He curled his fingers around the chair in order to shove it forward.

"Wait!" Pelglade exclaimed in his raspy voice. "What have you accomplished so far?"

The detective sat again and related his strategy of working methodically backward from the place of Poe's death and the people who last saw him. He disclosed that on the morrow he would hunt down the friend who Poe had asked for at Gunner's Hall and then visit the hall itself.

"If you still have not satisfied yourself at that point," Pelglade said, after listening carefully, "you should travel down to Richmond. I read in one newspaper that Eddie had raised money there to begin his own periodical. He had been making the attempt for years, but his fame was not yet sufficient. He was going to call it either The Penn or The Stylus. Perhaps someone followed him up to Baltimore, got him drunk or waited for it to happen naturally, robbed him, and dumped him at the tavern. I can recommend a capital place to stay while you're there: the Linden Row Inn on East Franklin Street."

Pinkerton stood again. "You said you are staying at the Maryland House?"

"That's right."

"I shall contact you if I have any question related to Mr. Poe."

Pelglade brightened. "I shall depend on it."


Allan arrived at Mrs. Brannigan's green front door at ten minutes before ten. He found that the Brandts had already retired, all the better to get an early start on their move to their new property. Molly Brannigan had doffed her bonnet and apron and looked tired but pleased to see her lodger.

"Will you sit in the parlor with me and allow the day's cares to slip away?" she asked.

"I would very much welcome it," Allan returned.

"I have tea brewing. It won't be but a moment." Molly disappeared into the kitchen.

Left alone, Allan surveyed the parlor carefully. Over the fireplace mantel hung a rather primitive oil painting of a Baltimore clipper ship plying deep ocean waves. He also spotted on the mantelpiece a clock under a glass dome, a scrimshaw carving of a unicorn and a thick piece of glass with a round top and a pyramid bottom. He recognized it from his transatlantic crossing as the type of glass incised into ship decks. They picked up sunlight, and the pyramid shape dispersed it around the deck below.

"It's called a deck prism," Molly said, as she entered the parlor carrying a loaded tea tray.

Allan set down the prism and hastened to relieve her. "Your husband is a sailor."

"He is captain of a clipper and a part owner of its cargo, which is tobacco."

"Ah, yes. The growing mania across Europe."

"And in our country," Molly returned, grimacing and shaking her head.

"You do not approve of it?"

Molly sat beside the stand that held the tray and began pouring tea into two delicate china cups. "No, I do not. It stinks; fire is always a danger; it stains carpets and makes clothing smell; and it causes its habitués to cough. Coal soot and wood ash clog our lungs enough without seeking more irritants. My husband insists that I disapprove of everything enjoyable, but that's only because I, unlike most persons, find the courage to disapprove publicly and demonstrate against the things I oppose."

"Such as alcohol and slavery."

"Correct. You take a bit of sugar with your tea."

Allan smiled at her attention, watched her ladle out the sugar with a dainty hand and a dainty spoon, and accepted the tea. "I thank you. What else would you change?"

"I would give women the right to vote, I would limit drinking to private dwelling places, and I would mandate education for every citizen. Thomas Jefferson wrote that the only way a democracy can survive is if its citizens can read and write."

Allan said, "You do know that you are extremely forward

thinking."

"I believe I am extremely right thinking," Molly countered.

"And I agree with your every tenet," Pinkerton hastened to say.

"Even women's suffrage?"

"Why should I tell you what you want to hear, considering you are tossing me out tomorrow morning?" he riposted.

Molly's mouth opened. She nodded several times. "Have you secured new lodging yet?"

"I have not had the opportunity," he replied.

She set down her teacup. "I have never had a male lodger alone in this house, and I daresay I may never again, but there is much about you, Mr. Pinkerton, that makes me trust you. Moreover, in the past week this neighborhood has had two break-ins, and I believe it would be far safer having a detective under my roof than for me and my daughter to sleep here alone."

"I am greatly flattered by your trust. However, if you feel this way, you must remember to call me Allan."

"And I shall be Molly from now on," the young woman asserted.

"For how much longer will you be without your husband?" Allan asked.

"He sailed for Hamburg Wednesday past. Then he drops the remainder of his cargo at Southampton."

"Perhaps I can be of further assistance by chopping up the tree trunk lengths I saw in your yard. Winter will be upon us before we know it."

"That's kind of you." Molly raised her teacup without averting her eyes from Allan's. "But we engage a man who lives in the next street. Mr. Burton. He looks after such things."

Something had been itching at Pinkerton's mind since Molly had entered the room. Suddenly, it surfaced, and his face lit up. "I must compliment you on possessing a most astonishing memory, Molly! I learned something about the writer Mr. Poe vilified at the lecture you attended. His name was Griswold, very close to Greenwald."

"Yes, that's it!" she replied.

Allan was pleased when she blushed at his praise. He went on at some length relating his two meetings with the strange Aaron Pelglade. Again, as he spoke, a memory scratched to escape its dark, cerebral dungeon. And then he had it.

"I forgot to mention that this fellow has black hair, slicked down and back with Macassar oil. It does his appearance no benefit, except to announce before he opens his display case that he is a salesman. Dr. Moran averred that Edgar Poe had jet-black hair. Does your prodigious memory recollect this to be true?"

"No," Molly replied. "I stood very close to him for some time and noted his hair. It was beautiful. Thick and wavy, and very neatly combed. But it was a dark brown and not black. Very few persons in my experience possess truly black hair."

"In mine as well. This further proves that Dr. Moran was at least not observant, if not that he lies with no sense of guilt. I should be glad not to have him attending to me."

Molly's daughter began to cry in the cradle that had been set just between the parlor and kitchen. "That's my cue to retire for the night," Molly said.

"I'll see the fire down and bank it."

"Thank you. Good evening, Allan."

"And to you...Molly."

She picked up her daughter and moved toward the stairs. When she had mounted the third step, she paused and looked at the detective with an enigmatic smile. "Try my husband's rocking chair; it's very comfortable."

Other than the fiddleback chair Allan sat on and the turtleback chair Molly seemed to prefer, the parlor had room for captain and mate dining chairs, a small sofa and a rocking chair. Allan stood and moved the quilt from the rocking chair onto a small lady's travel chest, painted a pale yellow and decorated with bright blue and yellow pansies. Under the quilt lay a long and not very thick book with a plain buff cover. It was volume one of Edgar A. Poe's *Tales of the Grotesque and Arabesque*, published by Lea & Blanchard of Philadelphia in 1840.

Allan turned the rocking chair so that the light from the fireplace spilled over his right arm. He studied the table of contents for several moments, opened to "The Fall of the House of Usher," and sat.

# CHAPTER SEVEN
*Wednesday, October 17, 1849*

According to the newspaper reports, a man named Joseph Walker had come across Edgar Poe lying on a bench outside Gunner's Hall. In a lucid moment, Poe had asked the man to get in touch with Dr. Joseph Evans Snodgrass, who was a friend and admirer of Poe's. Allan had found two J. Walkers in the city directory, along with one Jos. Walker. Reckoning the law of averages, he figured he would hit the right one on the second try. However, because he had so many persons he wanted to contact that day, he started at seven, before Molly Brannigan or her temporary tenants had arisen.

To his delight, Pinkerton found that the first home he visited belonged to the man who had discovered Poe. To his dismay, the man was out of town on business and would not return for two weeks. Pinkerton hailed a hack and directed the driver to the home of Dr. Snodgrass, which proved to be a most elegant townhouse surrounded by generous lawns and planted borders and containing a separate carriage house and a servants' wing. Heavy clouds were gathering overhead, threatening rain.

The door was answered by Dr. Snodgrass himself. His annoyed expression changed to one of ire when he heard the reason for Pinkerton's visit.

"What do you mean knocking on a gentleman's door when it is not even nine o'clock of the morning?" he demanded. Before Allan could reply, he added, "I have had more than my fill of curiosity seekers banging on my door about poor Mr. Poe."

Prepared to prove himself, Pinkerton resorted to his badge and his letter from the chief magistrate of the Baltimore Watch Force. The doctor's reaction was to crumple up the sheet of paper and let it drop to the ground. He attempted to shut his door.

Allan stepped forcefully into the doorjamb and held the door open. "I appreciate your irritation over this business, sir," he said, struggling to maintain his composure. "However, the other people who have bothered you did so out of morbid curiosity or to earn a living by reporting. I have traveled a great way to try to see that justice is done to 'poor Mr. Poe,' as you have put it."

Snodgrass's jaw relaxed a bit. Pinkerton could discern the doctor's tongue moving around behind his pursed lips. "What do you want to know?" he asked at last, not inviting the trespasser inside.

"Mr. Poe was found outside Gunner's Hall, lying on a bench."

"The place is more commonly known as Ryan's 4th Ward headquarters. According to Mr. Walker, who is the man who found him, he was alone and laid out semi-conscious on a bench. His moaning attracted Mr. Walker's attention. He was able to get from Mr. Poe the name of a friend. That name belonged to me."

"How long had you been friendly with Mr. Poe?"

"About fourteen years. Mr. Walker then smartly penned a note to me, giving Edgar's name and his woeful condition. He asked that I come to his immediate aid. I summoned Henry Herring, who is an uncle of Edgar's living close by, and together we hurried down to Ryan's Ward."

"You found him still on the bench?"

"No. He had been helped by a few men to a chair just inside the tavern door and then again abandoned. He appeared to be drunk."

"Did he smell of liquor?"

"Your name is Pinkerton?"

"Yes, sir." Allan bent and retrieved his abused letter.

Snodgrass did not appear apologetic for his act. "Mr. Pinkerton, the whole of that entryway smelled of alcohol. Alcohol, piss, and vomit. It is a drinking establishment of the lowest nature."

"I see. And you found Edgar wearing shabby clothing."

"We certainly did. This is the reason why I have not pushed you out my door. Only when he first began his writing career did I know him to be poorly dressed. He won a prize for writing in Baltimore that launched him. He was invited by the head judge, Mr. John Pendleton Kennedy, one of the true worthies of this city, to dine at his house. Edgar begged off because he was ashamed of his dress. Mr. Kennedy bought him a suit, shirt, collar, and tie because he was damned if something so piddling would serve to deny him the company of young genius. Since that time, no matter how low his state had sunk, Edgar dressed well. The clothes Henry and I found him wearing were a mockery to the man's pride."

"He had a cane with him."

"He did."

"What else?"

"A straw hat that even a mule would be embarrassed to wear."

"Did you check his clothing for a wallet or other belongings?"

"No, sir. He was in such terrible shape that we immediately stopped a hack man and paid him to drive Edgar to the nearest hospital, which is the Washington University Teaching Hospital on Broadway."

Recalling the testimony of Dr. Moran, Pinkerton asked, "Was it you or a policeman who summoned the hack?"

"It was I. I know at least one newspaper reported the other, but that is not the case."

The detective observed that Snodgrass had calmed considerably since trying to close the door, his voice had lowered in pitch and intensity. Allan was now ready to ask his most important questions.

"If I was Mr. Poe's good friend, I would have done my best to get out of him what had happened. I am sure you did this."

"Of course."

"And what did he say, even in partial phrases or mutterings?"

"He told us how awful he felt. He asked where he was. He offered no recollection of getting to the polling ward. When we asked, he could not remember if he had walked there by himself, had been carried, or walked supported by one or more others. In short, he revealed almost nothing."

"That is most unfortunate."

"Except that he did say the name 'Reynolds' three times," Snodgrass added. "However, it was without context."

"And without given name attached?"

"Correct."

"Do you know any friends or acquaintances of his, white or black, named Reynolds?"

"I do not."

"Perhaps it was a name that only sounded like Reynolds?"

"Perhaps. It was extremely difficult to understand him. He slurred his words. Sadly, saliva dripped from his mouth, and his nose was clogged and dripping. The air was cool, and so were his hands. His head, however, was fevered. He might have lay outside for some time."

"And this definitely took place on October 3rd?" said Allan.

"Which I believe explains precisely what happened to Edgar," Dr. Snodgrass declared with pat assurance.

"And that is...?"

Snodgrass folded his arms across his chest. "You are not from this city, Mr. Pinkerton, so you may not know that a major election was conducted on the day of Edgar's discovery. I am convinced he had been prepared for cooping."

"I do not know that term," Allan confessed.

"Then allow me to explain it to you. It is not enough for some unscrupulous politicians to bribe judges and to steal ballots to win elections. This city currently has, by best estimate, 162,000 people residing within its limits. It is, furthermore, one of America's greatest harbor cities, a magnet for both foreign immigrants and those leaving farms and other cities. Consequently, it is all but impossible to keep accurate records of where men live and who is eligible to vote. Men move away without notifying the government. It takes months for the record of deaths to be reconciled with the directory."

"Cooping is a form of election fraud," Allan understood. He carefully folded his letter and replaced it in his pocket.

"Fraud in the parading of men from ward to ward, giving them aliases, and stuffing the ballot boxes. It is my firm belief that certain persons spotted Edgar to free drink wherever he was staying. Ultimately, one must say that he was the cause of his own death, you see? They plied him the night before the election until he was all but unconscious, with the intent of driving him from ward to ward and using him as a warm body to vote for their candidates. They probably had no idea that too much drink had nearly killed Edgar in the past. They were astonished at how sick he became in relatively short order. Panicking, they dumped him outside the polling station."

"Who would be most likely to have done this?" Allan asked.

Snodgrass shrugged. "Pick from among five or six factions of rank hooligans. The boys at Ward's are as good a gang to question as anyone. I frankly don't know how you could pressure any of those rough characters into telling you the truth, Mr. Pinkerton, but I'd wager a week's earnings that one or more of them know exactly why Edgar was lying on that bench two weeks ago."

Behind Allan Pinkerton, the clouds let loose with a torrent of raindrops.

By the time Pinkerton arrived at 44 East Lombard Street, he was soaked to the skin. The cloudburst had let up a little, but it had already done the worst it could do to the detective. Pinkerton stood in front of the tavern in a dark mood. He stepped off the street and noticed a broad plank stretched across two low barrels and positioned partway into the alley. This, he thought, is what everyone has been calling a bench. Not even a real bench for the poor man to lie on! He pictured the writer lying prostrate, ignored. He walked into Gunner's Hall.

The tavern was of good size, with a grand room in the center that was open to the second-story roof. An open walkway with railings ran around two sides of the second level. A number of private rooms enclosed the back and sides of the first floor. The grand room held some dozen tables and about forty chairs. The bar was tucked into one corner. Pinkerton read an amateurishly painted sign over double doors in the back wall: Ryan's 4th Ward.

His practiced eye told Pinkerton that he was in a neighborhood hangout. Although the hour was not yet eleven in the morning, half a dozen denizens were ensconced at two tables, drinking and chatting as if time or gainful employment did not exist. He walked up to the bartender, who was semi-busy arranging mugs on a back counter.

"I need to talk with Reynolds," Allan said, omitting introduction or small talk.

The bald-headed bartender did not bother to turn. "Reynolds who?"

"The Reynolds who drinks here."

"Nobody I know."

Pinkerton plunked a two-dollar piece noisily on the bar. "How about now?"

The bartender turned and picked up the money. "Why do you need to talk with this Reynolds?"

"I want to buy some of his time."

"Wait here," the man said. He crossed to the double doors, opened one, and slipped through the doorway.

Pinkerton turned to face the room. Conversations stopped. Six sets of unfriendly eyes stared at him. He unbuttoned his sopping-wet coat.

The double door flew back with force, and a pug-ugly fellow who was at least five foot ten strode into the grand room. The burly figure looked forty and going to fat, but Allan imagined he had spent his youth in hard labor such as wrestling cargo back and forth between wharves and ships. The hair on his crown was thin, and that around his ears white, wild, and wiry.

He wore a flannel shirt whose sleeves he had rolled up to the elbows. His tan trousers were held up by braces, and his boots had thick heels with studs that clacked as he bestrode the wide wooden floor planking, heading directly toward Pinkerton.

"Are you Reynolds?" Allan called out boldly, before the man could draw near.

"I'm Monk," the man said, displaying his Irish heritage in only two syllables. "Who are you that you t'ink you have the right to ask for anyone here?"

Allan watched Monk's hands flexing and curling into fists. "I'm a detective. If you know the whereabouts of a man named Reynolds who was involved in the death of Edgar Allan Poe, you had best tell me or else become an accessory."

The men who had been sitting at the tables had been galvanized by Monk's appearance. In two groups they rose and drifted toward Pinkerton. Allan backed toward the bar, to prevent any from getting behind him.

"I know all the coppers in this town – you ain't one of them," Monk declared. His focus shifted to the man behind the bar. "Hold him, Passano."

Warned, Pinkerton spun around and punched Passano hard in the nose. He did not wait to see the damage he had caused but continued his circle, reaching under his coat and jacket to the shoulder holster that held his revolver. He had the weapon halfway out when three members of the table crowd reached him. One grabbed his arm and jerked it hard, causing Allan to lose his grip on his gun. It sailed into the air, hit the floor, and slid under a table.

Allan elbowed one of his assailants in the stomach and managed to punch another hard in the ear, but two clawed into his coat and then two more pressed him hard against the bar. Within moments, he was pinned and helpless.

Monk came forward and explored Pinkerton's clothing. He found the detective's billfold, badge, notebook, pencil, and two letters. He handed the letters over to the bartender.

"What do they say?"

From behind Pinkerton came the sounds of sniffling and then a blowing. The bartender said, "He's a detective all right. From Chicago."

"Chicago!" exclaimed Monk. "Jesus Christ! It ain't enough we got reporters from our own town accusing us of Poe's death?" He came up almost nose to nose with Pinkerton, his face turning red. "Well, you need to go back to Chicago right away, and here's something to encourage you."

Monk cocked his arm and delivered a swift jab at Allan's midsection. The air whooshed from Allan's lungs. Only his quick turn, which put his coat and jacket in the path of the punch, kept him from losing his breath entirely. As it was, the force partially doubled him over. Monk followed with a left hook into Allan's right cheek just below the corner of his eye. Allan felt the bite of the man's ring.

The grand room boomed from a sharp report. Every man jumped and turned toward the sound. Plaster and fur drifted down from a newly made hole in the ceiling. Aaron Pelglade stood by the table under which the revolver had disappeared. He held his display case in his left hand and the revolver in his right, pointing upward. Smoke curled out of its barrel. When he had everyone's attention, he swung it down and then left to right in a slow arc.

"Everyone back away from the detective," he said in his

raspy voice.

A widening space formed around Pinkerton.

"Don't anybody think of running, because I will shoot him in the back," Pelglade announced, in a surprisingly calm voice. "I'm a crazy son of a bitch, and I've killed before."

"Be careful with that, friend," someone in the crowd cautioned.

"I'll be as careful as you let me be…friend," Aaron returned. "Now you, the coward in the flannel shirt…walk over there." He gestured to the center of the room. Once the man had moved, he glanced momentarily at Pinkerton. "I'm sure you have something to say to him, Mr. Pinkerton."

Allan bent to the floor and reclaimed his derby hat, which had been stepped on several times. He dusted it off, re-blocked it, and set it on the bar. Then he removed his coat, his jacket, and his shoulder holster with unhurried speed.

"Listen, you two," Monk said. "We had nothing to do with Edgar Poe being outside this hall."

"First things first," said Pinkerton, unbuttoning his vest as he slowly moved toward the obvious leader of the crowd. He massaged his bruised cheek, felt the line of blood from the split skin caused by the ring, moved his hand to his eyes to survey the quantity of blood, and then said to Monk, "You choose: no holds barred or London Prize Ring rules."

"No punching below the waist, no gouging, no spitting, no biting," Monk said, smiling grimly. "When I get done with you, you can tell me why a Scotsman would follow London rules."

The pair circled each other for several seconds. Then Monk came forward with all the grace of a log rolling downhill, swinging hard with a roundhouse. Pinkerton ducked under it and delivered two quick jabs to the larger man's left shoulder. Angered but chastened, Monk settled in to a clockwise dance of leading with his left and following with his right. Again and again, Pinkerton blocks the blows and counterpunched, punishing Monk's left shoulder until gradually the man's guard lowered. Then three times, he caught the ward leader in the side of the head. The last one staggered Monk, who abandoned all rules of engagement, bull-rushed into Allan with a yell, and drove him toward the floor. Everyone in the tavern was shocked to see the Chicago man's foot come up under him as he fell, plant into Monk's belly, and launch him head over heels onto his back. Like a cat, Pinkerton was up and delivering strikes with the toe of his boot into Monk's side.

"Enough! Enough!" Monk yelled. "You win."

Pinkerton stepped back.

Monk held up his arm to one of his cronies for aid. Two men rushed forward and hoisted him upright. He swiped at a trickle of blood that dripped from under his ear.

"Mr. Poe was found outside this hall wearing the rags of a beggar," Allan stated, as he struggled to regain his breath.

"And we know exactly what that makes everyone think:" Monk returned. "Somebody wanted to use him for cooping that day. But whoever would do that would be an idiot. Edgar Poe was practically a citizen of Baltimore. He spent plenty of time here. His family is here. The ones who take in the ballots would recognize him no matter what he wore. Whoever dumped him on our doorstep did it to draw attention away from them and put it on us. We been asking around just like you, and we don't know who that was!"

"Poe did," Pinkerton said. "He spoke the name Reynolds

several times. Who is Reynolds?"

Monk's eyes moved from man to man. The detective could not tell if the look warned them not to speak or invited someone to come forward. Finally, the eyes of the ward boss settled on Pinkerton.

"Nobody here knows."

"Hey! Back off, unless you want another hole in your head!" Aaron Pelglade commanded. Two men from the crowd had been stealthily sidling in his direction.

Pinkerton went to the bar and reclaimed his belongings. He glared at the bartender, who had a bloody rag pressed against his nose. "You were less than useless. Where's my two-dollar piece?"

The bartender sullenly handed over the coin.

Allan moved toward the whiskey drummer. "Let's go. I won't get anything more here."

They quit Gunner's Hall Tavern by backing out. Once in the open, they sprinted down Lombard for two-dozen paces. After they crossed High Street they slowed, and Pelglade handed the revolver back to the detective.

"These…revolving pistols are becoming… popular," Aaron said, gulping air. "We live in amazing times. Bicycles, macadam roads, rubberized tires. Machine-made carpets, a tunnel under the Thames. They say you reap what you sew. Now we have machines for both."

"Yes, this is made by a man named Colt," Allan divulged. "He has an assembly line process, and all the parts are interchangeable. It is an astonishingly accurate and reliable weapon. Perfect for cowing mobs such as we faced in that hall."

"Slow down, please," Pelglade called from slightly behind

Pinkerton. "Your pace is too fast for my heart."

"Sorry." Allan slowed.

"No, I'm the one who is sorry. The damned thing is pummeling my ribs. I tell people it never recovered from being broken three times by women." Pelglade did not smile as he made his pronouncement. He set his wares case down in the street and reached into his pocket for his tin pill box.

"They didn't recognize you in the tavern," Allan observed, staring down at the new case. It sat in a shallow puddle of water. He reflected that it would not look new for much longer if the salesman treated it so poorly.

Pelglade popped two digitalis pills into his mouth. "You mean professionally? True enough. A few of the older ones should have. I certainly recognized them. But I believe their brains have probably gone soft. No, Gunner's Hall was very loyal for the past several years to my competition. However, I had gotten wind that there was a shift in control. That's what encouraged me to pay a visit. Sure enough, I had never seen that Monk fellow or the man behind the bar. I dare say I won't step in there again in the near future. You should be glad I decided to try for a sale."

"I am glad indeed," Allan allowed. "Thank you."

"Don't thank me. Thank Providence. If ever I was given proof that I am fated to help you in this investigation, it was in Gunner's Hall."

"Have you ever killed someone?" Allan asked, remembering Pelglade's threatening words.

Aaron burst into a raspy cackle. "No! Of course not. I was appalled at the size of the hole your revolver made in that ceiling."

"It makes a good-sized hole going into someone, and an even bigger one coming out," Pinkerton said.

Pelglade's eyes grew larger behind his spectacles. "Then you have killed."

"Unfortunately, yes. I would rather not speak of it."

"Not another word on the subject."

"I'm miserable in these wet clothes," Pinkerton said. "You must be cold as well."

"I am," Pelglade deemed.

Allan suggested, "Then why don't we go into a saloon which you do serve and sit before the fire for a spell? I will pay for the libations."

"Here is a more refined establishment," Aaron said, pointing to a coffee parlor. "I am not unaware of your abstinence from whiskey, and I love a good cup of coffee almost as much." He took Allan's elbow in a familiar grasp and guided him across the street's slick cobblestones. "Baltimore loves its coffee," he imparted. "Ever since the British navy blockaded the import of tea during the War of 1812. This place looks inviting."

The men mounted the steps and entered the establishment. A few other victims of the morning rain had drawn themselves close to the roaring fire, but Allan and Aaron were able to find a table close enough to benefit from some of the dry heat. They were served by a woman whose face proved she had survived smallpox.

"There is another reason why I am delighted to have happened upon you, Allan," Pelglade declared. He opened his black case and pulled out a newspaper. He laid it carefully on the table.

Allan saw that it was the *New York Tribune*. He read the date of October 9, 1849. Pelglade opened the paper with almost reverent care, turned it back, and displayed the second page.

"You wondered to me if Eddie had any true enemies? Here is one...in black and white."

The headline was 'Death of Edgar A. Poe.' Pinkerton was frankly amazed that the two center columns of the second page of one of the most important newspapers in the country had been entirely devoted to Poe. He began to read, stroking his beard unconsciously as he did.

### Edgar Allan Poe has died.

He died in Baltimore the day before yesterday.

This announcement will startle many, but few will be grieved by it. The poet was known, personally or by reputation, in all this country and he had readers in England and in several of the states of continental Europe, but he had few or no friends; and the regrets for his death will be suggested principally by the consideration that in him literary art has lost one of its most brilliant but erratic stars.

The family of Mr. Poe – we learn from Griswold's "Poets and Poetry of America," from which a considerable portion of the facts of this article are derived – was one of the oldest and most respectable in Baltimore.

The article then spoke in glowing terms of the contributions of members of the family during the Revolutionary War and especially of David Poe, a decorated major who was loving referred to as "General" and who was beloved of no less man than Lafayette. Pinkerton scowled, however, when he read the line:

> His father and mother – both of whom were
> in some way connected to the theater, and lived
> as precariously as their more gifted and more
> eminent son – died within a few weeks of each
> other.

Allan was about to remark to Aaron that although the article started with a pair of strangely negative statements, it went on to be neutrally informative and often quite positive. It praised Poe's handsome calligraphy, saying that "His conversation was almost supra-mortal in its eloquence. His voice was modulated with astonishing skill, and his large and variably expressive eyes looked repose or shot fiery tumult into theirs who listened." Having heard Pelglade's warning words, however, he determined to read to the end. As positive as the first column had been, so negative was the second.

> He was at all times a dreamer – dwelling in
> ideal realms – in heaven or hell – peopled with
> the creatures and the accidents of his brain.
> He walked the streets in madness or melancholy,
> with lips moving in indistinct curses, or with eyes
> upturned in passionate prayer (never for himself,
> for he felt, or professed to feel, that he was already
> damned), but for their happiness who at the
> moment were objects of his idolatry…He
> regarded society as composed altogether of

Villains. In him…were the worst emotions which mitigate against human happiness. There seemed to him no moral susceptibility, and, what was more remarkable in a proud nature, little or nothing of the true point of honor. He had a morbid wish for success. As a critic he was little better than a carping grammarian.

The piece ended by presenting Poe's recent poem, "Annabel Lee," which "…the writer was handed just before he left New York." As the hardened detective read the poem, he realized his eyes stung from pent-up tears.

The whiskey salesman noted that Pinkerton had all but finished the second column. "Is Rufus Griswold a man who wants to kill Eddie or not?"

"The signature, however, is LUDWIG," Allan noted, reaching into his pocket for his notebook and pencil.

"Of course it is!" Aaron fumed. "The man is a coward. Of course, he would argue that he is simply copying Eddie's method of criticizing in print behind the safety of a pseudonym." Aaron's forefinger tapped on the newspaper. "Who else but a shameless self promoter would stick in an advertisement for his own work? Have you ever seen such a thing in a supposed eulogy? Poets and Poetry of America indeed! That is the very work that Eddie deplored on his lecture tour. What cheek! What calumny! And to belittle Eddie's powers as a critic. The man was brilliant in that role. To reduce Poe to the role of 'carping grammarian' is to admit that he had been personally wounded by Poe's insights in print. The sniveling, sneaky bastard! Well, you can certainly prove that Ludwig and

Griswold are one and the same by determining precisely to whom Eddie gave this last poem in New York."

"You think this is serious enough for me to visit Griswold?" Pinkerton asked.

Pelglade straightened up to his full height. "I most certainly do!"

"I shall give it consideration," said Allan. "However, if I do not get any farther here in Baltimore soon, I believe my next action should be to visit Richmond."

"Absolutely! Just as I said. I will be wending my way down there on business ere long. Perhaps we can travel together."

"Perhaps," Allan allowed. He glanced at "Annabel Lee" in the newspaper and thought of Molly's book left on the rocking chair. Like raindrops softening hard soil, Poe's words had worked on Pinkerton's prejudice. "I got my hands on your friend's *Tales of the Grotesque and Arabesque* last night. I read 'The Fall of the House of Usher,' 'William Wilson,' 'The Devil in the Belfry,' and 'The Man Who Was Used Up.'"

"Good for you!" croaked Pelglade. "And was I not right? Are the first two not works of pure genius and the second two silly drivel?"

"I enjoyed them all," Allan found himself admitting. "However, I do rather agree with you. The ones about the devil and the remains of the soldier are forgettable. But the other two are difficult to dismiss. Mostly because they are such disturbing ideas, disturbingly described."

"Yes, but where else, in textbook or literature, is the descent into madness so well captured as in the Usher family tale?" Aaron argued. "How clever he was to have the house decaying at exactly the same pace as the family!"

"It drives relentlessly to the result of its theme," said Allan, hoping he would not be forced to say much more, since he had such a tiny font of knowledge about fiction to draw from.

"And is not 'William Wilson' a story we can all learn from? Do we not all have within us two men, one good and one evil?" Aaron drove on.

"Certainly Mr. Poe seemed to," Allan said. "I believe that he saw clearly what he was and, therefore, his inevitable fate."

"Being murdered, you mean?"

"Not murder, but certainly a steady dissolution and decay. An early death. Just as in the tale of the house of Usher."

"Yes," agreed Pelglade. "However, if one pursues your theory, Eddie would have been wrong about his persistent vision of one day being buried alive."

"Did he have such a vision?"

"Assuredly. He was obsessively fixated on the theme," said Poe's friend. "It appears again and again. Not just with the sister in 'The Fall of the House of Usher.' Oh, my god, the permutations." He wrote a story called 'The Premature Burial"; which I believe was based on his own experience. The teller is sure he has been buried alive, only to remember he has been partaking of opium – one of the other obsessive themes of Eddie's life – and then collapsed in a narrow hammock on a sailing sloop." He began that tale by relating several historical instances he had found of persons who were actually buried alive. One of them was, in fact, a woman here in Baltimore. Or what about 'The Tell-Tale Heart,' where the narrator has killed a beloved old man just because he has an evil eye, and then he buries the man beneath the floor boards? But the heart lives on! And then there is his masterpiece on this theme: 'The Cask of

Amontillado,' where one man buries another alive behind a wall." Pelglade's croaking voice softened and a smile suffused his face, strongly suggesting to Pinkerton that this was among his favorite of Poe's stories.

"Behind a wall? Why did he do that?" Allan asked.

"Revenge. Truly cold revenge for…how did Eddie put it? 'The thousand injuries of Fortunato I had borne as best I could.' Or 'Ligeia,' where the narrator's first love lives on somehow after death and takes the body of the second wife. But we now know that Eddie need not have worried personally after all."

"In that fear he was dead wrong," Pinkerton said.

Pelglade shot him a surprised look. And then he laughed. "Dead wrong, dead wrong. Indeed." He suddenly stood. "I must hurry to my next appointment. You know where I am staying."

"The Maryland House, on the south side of Lexington," Allan recited.

"Just so. Please let me know if and when you are going to Richmond. I realize that you have been working backward from Eddie's death, but I suspect that starting at the beginning of his final journey may be more valuable."

"You may be right," Allan allowed.

"And if I should somehow miss you from this point forward, it was a distinct pleasure." Aaron Pelglade held out his small hand for shaking. "Shall I give you my address in New York so that you can write me if you find that Eddie's death was indeed a crime?"

"I am certain if that is the case you will read about it in the *New York Tribune*," Pinkerton replied. "The editor clearly adored him."

"Yes, of course." Pelglade clicked his heels together in the continental fashion, glanced left and right, bowed with a jerky motion, picked up his muddy-bottomed whiskey case, and walked out of the coffee parlor.

Watching the man go, Pinkerton shook his head. He reflected that if Edgar Poe was merely as strange as Aaron Pelglade, then there was no wonder that critics found him peculiar and erratic.

Space directly in front of the fire became open. Allan moved closer and ordered a second coffee. While he waited, he thought about all he had learned of Poe in the past week. The writing in the newspapers shed conflicting lights. Even the few persons he interviewed in Baltimore had not been in complete agreement. But the detective was sure that the writer's words told the absolute truth, if one had the wisdom to peer beyond the fiction and realize the facts that had informed and helped create it. Poe's life had certainly been a dark and negative one. Being orphaned at three and having a family with a history of drunkenness could not have been positive influences.

The man whose house he had entered as a very young child had expected much of him but had not been willing to adopt him. Yet Poe had adopted his name, had craved that respect. People had died around him constantly, many of them young. But deaths at every age were, Allan reflected, a fact of life. Everyone bore losses. He had once heard a statement that genius and insanity were extremely close, and that only a gentle shove was sometimes necessary to nudge the hypersensitive person from the brilliant side to the utter darkness.

In Allan's personal experience, the simpleminded folk usually had more bad things happen to them than the clever, and yet precisely because they were simple they did not worry to mental exhaustion about it until it happened. He suspected that heightened awareness of the world, of its many dangerous possibilities, of the frailty of life and the ultimate payment exacted of every mortal must take its toll. And yet Benjamin Franklin, Thomas Jefferson, and many of the founding fathers had been brilliant and had not dwelt on the negative. Otherwise, they would not have had the courage to conduct a revolution. Allan was sure he needed to know much more about Poe to understand what made him unflaggingly morbid and so enamored of the grotesque.

But one thing Allan Pinkerton already deduced, in spite of the fact that he had virtually never read fiction: Edgar Allan Poe was a master writer. Whatever criticism one cared to level against his themes and obsessions, the man had an incredible imagination. He had an astonishing vocabulary and unerring ear for the juxtaposition of words. His combined skills created moods and images that could not be easily shaken off. He was the dark archangel of the worlds of delirium, dreams, and death.

Allan sensed the annoyed stare of the shop's proprietress. He felt the legs of his trousers and realized he must have been sitting by the fire longer than he had thought. With a guilty nod, he rose and placed his empty cup on the trolley near the front door. He left on the saucer a shiny twenty-five cent piece.

The home of John Pendleton Kennedy sat on North Calvert Street, just off Monument Square. It was a large house, and Mr. Pendleton, who practiced law, worked out of it. In spite of having arrived unannounced, Pinkerton was invited in after a half-hour wait with none of the annoyance or suspicion shown to him that morning by Dr. Snodgrass. He was particularly impressed by the library, where ceiling-to-floor shelves crammed with books ran all around the room except at the windows and doorways. Allan imagined that there were towns of 10,000 in America that did not have libraries as large.

"My ancestors were Scottish and Irish," Kennedy said amiably as Allan drank in the splendor of the room. "But I don't think we have any Pinkertons in our past."

"That's probably a good thing, sir," Allan replied. "We're a shady lot."

Kennedy laughed. He tilted his head to study the cut and bruise on Allan's cheek. "And apparently inclined either to fists or to falls."

"Not everyone is as gracious as you, sir, when it comes to being interviewed," Allan replied.

The lawyer looked to be in his fifties. He was a handsome man, with peaked eyebrows, piercing eyes, a long nose, and clean-shaven cheeks.

"Do you like fiction?" Kennedy asked.

"I have a rapidly-increasing interest," said Pinkerton.

"Perhaps you've read one of my novels? I wrote *Swallow Barn* and *Horse-Shoe Robinson*."

"I'm sorry, no. My reading leans heavily toward the practical side."

"I see. And yet you had enough interest in Edgar Allan Poe to travel all the way from Chicago."

"Yes, sir. Because what I read in the newspapers suggested he might have been murdered." John Kennedy did not look at all convinced of the explanation, so Allan added, "And since he made detectives famous with his stories, I thought someone of my profession should investigate on his behalf."

"Well, I'm glad you have the financial wherewithal to fund such a noble venture," remarked the lawyer. "Certainly his estate could not have paid you for this work."

"I understand. I also understand that you were kind to him both in promoting his career and in lending him money."

"I was. To possess even a small spark of the divine creative fire is a wonderful thing, but to nurture those in whom it flares is both an honor and a duty. Would you care for a spot of sherry?"

"No thank you, sir."

Kennedy gestured to a chair in front of his desk. Instead of sitting behind the desk, he took the one directly to its left. "And what makes you think Edgar was murdered?"

From constant consulting of his notes and verbal repetitions, Pinkerton replied without hesitation. "The unaccounted days between his arrival in Baltimore and his discovery. His missing trunk. The fact that he was dressed in ragged clothing not his size. And his attempt to speak about someone named Reynolds."

"Reynolds? There is a judge in the city by that name, but I seriously doubt that he and Edgar crossed paths. I shall ask him when I see him tomorrow."

"You were a friend to Mr. Poe for some fifteen years, I understand," Pinkerton said.

"I would like to think one of his best and most loyal friends."

"But not a minute of the time between when he arrived… which should have been the 28th of September…until his discovery outside Ryan's 4th Ward did he spend with you." Although Pinkerton could not think of a single reason why Kennedy should lie to him, he nevertheless kept his gaze fixed on the man's face, searching for even a hint of disingenuousness.

"Not one minute…unfortunately."

Pinkerton nodded. "And what do you think of the possibility that your friend was purposely made drunk so that he might be used for cooping?"

Kennedy smirked. "I think with all the unknown faces drifting into Baltimore, that Edgar Allan Poe's would have been the last one I would have chosen for cooping."

"Then what do you believe befell him?"

Kennedy shook his head for several moments, his eyes cast down, his lips narrowed. "I watched his personal descent into the maelstrom over a period of years. He drank himself to death, Mr. Pinkerton. Not all at once. Just a little at a time, year after year. Like toeing a statue toward the edge of a precipice. The first, the second, the twelfth push may not send it into the abyss, but eventually even the smallest nudge will do the trick. Edgar died from the effects of one too many debauches. He knew drink and drugs would be his end, and he fought with all his will. But men have varying degrees of natural resistance, and his was not strong. Organs shut down. The candle guttered and failed. And we are all the poorer."

"But he did have enemies," Pinkerton argued, weakly.

"Yes. Those men of lesser talents he insulted. Those men he constantly promised to pay back and never could. Small crimes. He did not steal or kill or bear false witness." Kennedy dipped his head with a defending lawyer's apology. "Ironically, he made his enemies not by lying but by telling the truth. He did commit adultery once or twice that I know of, but the husbands seemed pleased that such a genius would lust after their wives.

"Poe was nothing but a writer. And, as you the practical

reader would say, not even an Isaac Newton or an Adam Smith or an Immanuel Kant. A mere fiction writer. It was all he cared about. He once said to me that he knew from youth that it was to be his profession and that he pitied any man who did not have the talent to write fiction. In that, he shared the same kind of hubris as the immortal Wolfgang Amadeus Mozart. I read a letter that the one 'beloved of God' wrote to his sister, in which he proclaimed, 'I have contempt for anyone who cannot compose as a sow pisses.' We all should be happy to support such golden nightingales with a coin now and then.

And how can any other writer take insult from such unique souls? Those who can best appreciate these rare creatures should be the ones to applaud the loudest. Their talents are innate and not developed. They have no understanding of what we lesser mortals suffer to create, so if they insult us it is out of the most innocent ignorance. Many may have cursed Edgar out of jealousy, but to kill him over it?"

Pinkerton was dumbstruck by the lawyer's eloquent logic. When he left Chicago, he had had no notion that his investigation would immerse him in a world of erudition. He felt dangerously out of his depth during his interviews, at some points as if he were one who spoke English as an adopted language. He longed for those simple days when he had been tracking counterfeiters, kidnappers, and train thieves. He struggled to erect a smile as he stood.

"Well, thank you so much for your time, Mr. Kennedy." He reached into his pocket for his notebook and scribbled down Molly Brannigan's address. "If Judge Reynolds did cross paths with Mr. Poe or if you happen to hear anything suspicious, please send a note to this address. I would be most appreciative."

# CHAPTER EIGHT
*Wednesday, October 17, 1849*

The outhouse at the rear of Molly Brannigan's property was, in relative terms, a clean one. The wooden seat plank was highly varnished and had a hinged cover, both of which assisted in sanitation. High openings cut in the shapes of moons and stars provided light and ventilation. The floor was of brick. To one side of the wide seat lay a small pile of newspapers, under a shallow bucket containing corncobs.

After Allan finished buttoning up, he went to one of the rain barrels and used the scoop to pour over his hands. A clean, dry rag hung thoughtfully inside a little wooden enclosure. He stepped from slate to slate up the alleyway and around to the green front door. In one hand he held a large bouquet of yellow chrysanthemums. In the other he held a book wrapped in brown paper and string.

The Lexington Market stood roughly halfway between the homes of John Kennedy and Molly Brannigan. Allan had walked there specifically to purchase flowers, and then he spied the book stall. He was certain that a city the size of Baltimore supported several independent bookshops, but the discovery of two carts – one for used books and one for new – was delightful enough. He inquired of the owner if he had any volumes of Edgar A. Poe, only to have the man laugh at him and offer to buy anything of Poe's the detective might have to sell. Apparently, nothing whetted the public's appetite for artistic works like the recent death of the artist.

The cart of used books was filled, but the choices among those new were, at least to Pinkerton's desire, few. *Elements of Geometry*, Sir John Herschell's *Outlines of Astronomy* and *The Timbrel*, a collection of scared music were all too practical. He rejected two novels, *The Invisible Gentleman* and *The Dowager*, out of hand, since their authors were not important enough to have their names on the covers. His choices devolved to James Fenimore Cooper's *The Sea Lions*, Charles Dickens' *Dombey and Sons*, *The Works of Michel de Montaigne* and *The Poetical Works of Percy Bysshe Shelley*. Although he had not seen any book except Poe's *Tales of the Grotesque and Arabesque* in the Brannigan home, Allan assumed nonetheless that more than a few other volumes resided in the owners' bedroom or behind closed cabinet doors. Allan had fretted over his selection for a full minute, then thrust out his hand and grabbed the novel by Cooper.

Molly opened her front door. Allan anticipated her breaking into a broad smile at the sight of the enormous blooms. Instead one eyebrow raised, she glanced up and down the street, then she grabbed the collar of his coat and pulled him with force up the last step and into the house.

"If these flowers are for me, Mr. Pinkerton, you are very kind. However, I cannot have my neighbors thinking I am entertaining a gentleman caller whilst my husband is at sea."

"I'm sorry," he apologized. "I wasn't thinking clearly."

Molly closed the door and leaned against it. "I'm sure you were thinking with the most innocent of motivations. Many do not. It's ridiculous, but appearance is important. I know for a fact that the woman to the left of us is beaten soundly every other night."

The subtle scent of green apples came into Allan's nostrils. Mrs. Brannigan had daubed herself with cologne.

"And the man two doors down–" Molly stopped suddenly. "What happened to your face?"

Allan handed over the chrysanthemums and then removed his derby. "I met with some resistance in my quest for the truth."

As his landlady accepted the bouquet, he noted that she did not wear her usual cotton housedress. Instead, she had on a beguiling, cream-colored evening gown of moiré silk. Mrs. Brannigan's freckled porcelain skin was beautifully on display thanks to the gown's off-the-shoulder design. The upper flesh of her breasts thrust prominently out of the gown's center panel.

"Are you going out tonight?" Allan inquired.

Molly blushed. "No. I was just…trying it on to see if it still fit. This was the great fashion when I was married. The dress was part of my trousseau. But you are the worse for a rainy day, and I prattle while you stand there."

"I'm fine," Allan assured. "I returned too early. I'm imposing on your time."

"Nonsense. Siobhan is sleeping, and supper is all but prepared. Take off your suit, and I will press it later."

"Something else for you," Allan said. He laid the wrapped book down atop the woman's decorative traveling chest with the painted pansies. Before Molly could respond, he crossed to the narrow stairs.

"I've moved your belongings to the larger guest room," she called after him.

Allan paused on the second step. "But what if a couple should appear in the next hour?"

"I shall turn them away."

Molly's voice had become considerably more gentle. Allan turned her words over in his mind for a moment and then finished his climb.

Precisely at six, Allan descended. He was upset to see that Molly had pulled the gate leg table from the inner parlor wall and set it and the chairs up by herself. His gift of flowers sat in a Delftware vase at the far side of the table; his setting was placed to Molly's immediate left. The captain's chair remained close to the wall, nonetheless a reminder of the master of the house.

Supper consisted of cornbread, Mulligan stew, lemon tarts, and lemonade. Molly, who had changed back to a cotton day dress, drew Allan out on the events of the day and listened with spare comment to his tale of frustration. She seemed most interested in hearing the news about Rufus Griswold's harsh words on Poe in the New York Tribune, but she did not hold much stock in the possibility that the man would seek physical revenge as well. When she professed confusion as to why Allan had traveled so far when there was neither proof of murder nor any possible chance of remuneration, he confessed the plan hatched by Edward Rucker to launch the Pinkerton Detective Agency into national prominence. To his relief, she did not condemn either him or Rucker.

"Whatever happens, it will not affect Mr. Poe's condition," she said, adding immediately, "I must thank you for the wonderful gift of *The Sea Lions*."

"It is my thanks for your introduction to Mr. Poe's stories. I am not a reader of fiction."

"Neither is my husband. I have read five other of Mr. Cooper's novels, and I have found every one of interest. I wonder if, in his dotage, he has outgrown his obsession with manners, rank, place in society, and ambition."

"Do most novelists have obsessions?" Allan asked.

"Don't we all? They simply exercise their drives on paper." Molly dabbed her lips. "Have you not just confessed to me that, like so many Americans of our era, you are obsessed with ambition?"

"I suppose I did," Allan replied. As long as his hostess declared no revulsion, he did not feel any guilt.

"My husband is consumed with ambitions. Thank the Lord he has finally realized some of his. Two years ago, just a month before we married, he received his captain's papers. And early last year, for the first time he contracted for a percentage of the cargo he delivered."

"He is how old?" Allan inquired.

Molly stopped chewing, took the time to swallow, and fixed her eyes on Allan. "Forty."

While Pinkerton knew of many instances of women marrying men almost old enough to be their fathers, both widowers and prolonged bachelors, he found himself surprised that this was the case with Molly Brannigan.

"You expected to hear that Shamus would be a younger man," Molly observed.

"Well...frankly, yes."

"Why?"

Allan took a moment to order his thoughts. A person of Molly's intellect merited a thoughtful reply. "Because you strike me as a woman guided by spirit and emotion. I should have thought you would marry a man close to your age with whom you would be desperately in love."

Molly set down her fork. "I have so many emotional parts to me that the rest of my existence must be pragmatic. Do you think a young man would allow me to race off to meetings and demonstrations on women's suffrage, temperance, universal education and other utopian causes?"

"I had not thought of that," Allan confessed.

"I am a headstrong and independent creature," Molly asserted. "It is a good thing that the man I married is gone at least eight months of each year. Further, I will not apologize that I enjoy a roof over my head and enough to eat. According to Shamus, we will be able to move up closer to the monument within two more years. That will give me a higher standing in society, and from there I may possess the leverage to accomplish some of my difficult goals. I board strangers not because we need the money to live; I do it so that we may move from here all the sooner. I can afford to board only those persons who interest me. Such as yourself."

Allan did not blush easily, but he felt a certain heat begin to suffuse his head and neck. "What do you make of Edgar Allan Poe's obsessions?" he asked, to deflect the course of the conversation.

"He was more ambitious than you, I, and my husband combined. But I strongly suspect he was also lazy and self-indulgent and inclined to blame the world for his relative lack of success. I think he believed that inspired and skillful writing alone should guarantee wealth and adulation. He was troubled and deeply embittered."

"But he had a difficult early life, and that cannot be blamed on him," Allan argued.

"So have many of us," Molly proclaimed, in a tone that suggested her youth had not been all sweetness and light. "But the time comes when the adult must take the child within us, put it over his or her mental knee, and tell it to behave. I suspect when you have finished your investigation, you will find that Mr. Poe obliquely murdered himself."

Increasingly, Allan was feeling the same way, but he had come too far and was gambling too much to walk away without turning over every stone. He thought that, at the very least, he would need to put into print his thorough investigation to impress future clients, even if he was compelled to hire a ghostwriter. The phrase brought him right back to the subjects of death and Poe.

"I have one clue that may serve to prove you wrong about Poe killing himself," he said.

"And that is...?"

Allan pulled his chair a bit closer to Molly. "He had written a poem just before he left New York, bound for Richmond. Griswold got his hands on it and included it in his article. It is called 'Annabel Lee,' and in spite of the fact that yet again the love of the narrator's life has died, it is most positive. He states that they were very happy, that her soul is with his even now, and that nothing can ever sever them, even death itself."

Pinkerton's eyes unfocused in memory.

"I must say, it touched me more than any other poem I have read. I believe I can even recall the first verse:

It was many and many a year ago,
  In a kingdom by the sea,
That a maiden there lived whom
  you may know
By the name of ANNABEL LEE;
  And this maiden she lived with
  no other thought
Than to love and be loved by me.

Allan waited for Molly to comment. When she did not and simply stared at him, he reached for a tart out of nervousness.

"And from this you believe that Edgar Poe would not drink

himself to death."

"Yes," Allan said with conviction. "The other pieces of his I have read all breathe an air of doom and despair. This was nearly the opposite. He was traveling up and down the coast this time not to avoid creditors but in regard to his future. Aaron Pelglade, the salesman friend of Poe, shared with me that he was in the process of raising money to publish his own periodical. He must have believed his fortune was turning."

"Are detectives not supposed to deal with fact rather than conjecture?" Molly asked, through a doubtful look. "Might a detective and those who depend upon him not starve because of such leaps of logic?"

Allan looked down at the tart in his hand, still unsampled. He thought of the importance Molly Brannigan put on enough to eat, and from there he thought again of her husband.

"You have not asked me how old my wife is," Pinkerton noted.

"I have not asked you anything yielding more than that you have a wife and children," Mrs. Brannigan returned. "I do not mind at all talking about Shamus. I have the impression that you are not inclined to speak of Mrs. Pinkerton."

Allan rarely discussed his wife without prompting, but he now felt obliged to speak. "Her name is Joan. Her maiden name was Carfrae. She was a friend of my friend and a professional singer. I was a rebel and thought that any woman with the nerve and talent to earn a living on the stage had to be interesting. She saw me as a rebel as well, campaigning for utopian causes. I suppose you could say we were impressed with each other. My family did not approve of her; but I got her in the family way, so the only thing to do was to marry secretly. Then my revolutionary actions caught up with me: I belonged to a group called the Chartists."

"I am well acquainted with the Chartist movement," said Molly, again fixing him with a pensive stare. "A noble outcry for social and political justice, outlawed by the Crown."

"I was forced to flee Scotland. Joan had little choice but to follow. Our marriage nearly got her drowned when our ship foundered off Nova Scotia. She has endured several moves and my several changes of occupation without complaint. I know she resents me for getting her with child and keeping her from pursuing her art on the stage, but she is a silent martyr. Which drives the wedge further between us. We have two boys. William is the elder...no longer a child but not yet a man. The other is about three years older than your daughter."

"You never experienced desperate love?" Molly asked.

"Unfortunately, no. But perhaps it is best never to ascend to those heights," Allan philosophized, "since what goes up must inevitably come down. The 'happily ever after' variety of white-hot passion may only succeed in fairy tales, novels, and theatrical presentations."

The landlady rose from her chair and lifted her empty plates. "Oh, I think that variety might last with the occasional couple. But I suspect that generally the flint and steel romances are famous precisely because they did not have to endure. Take Romeo and Juliet or Héloise and Abelard. When both lovers die or one is castrated, nobody expects more." She paused and tilted her head to look at Allan's discolored and swollen face.

"That disturbs me," she said.

Allan started at the remark. "I'm sorry. I should move my place to the other side of–"

"No. I mean on your behalf." Molly walked into the kitchen.

"One minute."

Left for more than the promised minute, Allan mulled over Molly's words about passionate love. He thought about the ironically positive elements of losing a beloved, such as Edgar Allan Poe had done, while the romance was still in bloom: She could never disappoint him, never nag, never be sick, never cheat on him. She would never age. As the years wore on, her faults would be forgotten and only the beautiful and endearing remain. He reflected that a man could feel less alone living with a memory than with a woman in a loveless marriage.

Molly returned carrying a spoon heaped with white powder in one hand and a half-filled wash basin with a bunched-up towel in the other.

"This is crushed powder derived from the bark of the willow," she said, as she dipped the spoon into the cooled remains of his mulled cider. She stirred the spoon into the golden drink. "Have you used it before?"

"No," Allan replied.

"It does not remove the pain of swelling, but it lessens it. Finish your drink."

While Allan obeyed, Molly took her seat and put the towel up against Allan's cheek. She had obviously immersed it in water from one of the outside rain barrels, both because it was quite cold and he had heard the back door open and close. He attempted to take it from her.

"No. Let me do it. And in a few minutes we shall switch to heat. I have the kettle beside the kitchen hearth." Molly locked eyes with Allan. "Now, what were we talking about?"

"I believe the subject was castration," he said.

She laughed lightly. "No. It was passionate love. If you have never tasted it, that is a sorrow and a misfortune. For many men – blacksmiths, carpenters, boot makers, railroad engineers – the opportunities for meeting women beyond church and formal introductions are few and far between. But I should think that your line of work would place you alone with women many times in a year."

Molly's eyes, sparkling in the parlor firelight, were taking a leisurely tour of Allan's face. Even as his cheek cooled, the rest of him grew warm.

She continued. "If you are disappointed in marriage, believe me, so are many women. More so than men, I suspect, for the men are not ransomed off by their fathers or brothers."

"But you are talking about adultery," Allan said.

"I am talking about uniting the two topics we discussed: pursuing the needs of your heart and yet being pragmatic. I would strongly disapprove of a married man seducing an unmarried woman, because he is taking her time and affection and depriving her of security. However, a circumspect affaire de coeur with a married woman may make two comfortable but passionless marriages bearable. Might save them, in fact."

Molly dipped the towel in the basin and squeezed most of the water out. She again pressed it gently to Allan's cheek. "So, one of my liberal views at last shocks you."

Many replies came to Allan's mind. He settled on, "It gives me pause. Have you tasted passionate love?" he dared.

"Once. Before I was married. But after marriage? The answer is no." Molly drew in a long breath and then exhaled. Allan could feel her warmth.

"Tell me about Chicago," she said.

# CHAPTER NINE
*Thursday, October 18, 1849*

During the night, Allan awoke to what he thought was a creaking of the hallway floorboards. He had called out Molly's name softly, wanting to be certain that the house had not been invaded by the break-in artists she had said were preying upon the neighborhood. He heard a faint but definite movement of boards in reply but no voice. He rose, lit a candle from the embers that still glowed in his fireplace, went to his door and opened it, but found no one. He climbed the steps to the attic as noiselessly as he could and saw nothing among the sweeping shadows. Likewise, he descended to the parlor, accompanied by the ticking of the mantel clock, and found it unoccupied.

He returned to the double bed, but despite the comfort of the mattress and down comforter, he did not fall asleep for a long time. When he did, he dreamt of approaching a tall cliff by the ocean. It was a cloud-shrouded night, with a full moon peeking in and out. Beyond the edge of the cliff the ocean pounded against rocks. As he came nearer he saw the backlit figure of a woman in a gown. When moonbeams caught the dress, it shone as if it were made of silk. The woman's hair was full and wavy.

He walked toward her for what seemed like a full minute, barely gaining ground. A sudden gathering of clouds made the place stygian. When the clouds parted, he saw that the woman in the gown was motionless and not breathing. Again, the clouds closed in. This time, when they parted, he saw the familiar face as if it had been dead and desiccating for a month. Molly Brannigan and Edgar Allan Poe were denying him rest, haunting his days and nights.

Mrs. Brannigan was in the kitchen feeding her daughter when Pinkerton emerged to begin his day. Molly displayed no embarrassment for the words she had spoken the night before. However, to the roll and coffee that she had promised, this morning she also added bacon. She filled the breakfast conversation with a retelling of the first chapter of *The Sea Lions*. As he listened, focused on her expressive blue eyes, watched her sensuous lips moving, he knew that he had fallen into the desperate form of love they had touched upon the night before. He waited until the last moments before rising to deliver his unhappy news.

"I intend to leave tonight by train for Richmond," he told her.

"Well, that is not a good plan," she replied. Allan's wild imaginings had the woman following her words with an impassioned speech of why he should not leave her. Instead, she said, "The railroad is not complete between Washington and Richmond. You would do much better to travel by boat."

Allan smiled weakly. "Thank you. I do intend to return here as soon as my business there is concluded."

"By 'here,' do you mean this house?"

Again, Allan was jolted by the woman's words. "Am I not welcome?"

"Of course you are welcome. I simply do not want to have no room available when you return. How long do you think you will be gone?"

"Three nights."

"Very well." Molly smiled. "That's settled. But your bill to date is not."

Finally, as Mrs. Brannigan gave him a constrained look and held out her hand for payment, Allan felt that all the familiar words, her compliments, and even the advise she had given him on love outside marriage were only expressions of sisterly fondness. Even so, for these attentions he was grateful.

Pinkerton paid his bill and insisted on leaving another three dollars in way of reservation. He went upstairs to pack one suitcase with belongings. He would leave behind the other as a further promise of his return. When he came down again, Molly Brannigan was outside beating a rug.

Pinkerton's plan for the day was full, demanding that he stay on the move until dark. He first purchased a copy of the *Baltimore Sun* and read the notices of the ships arriving and departing, from Baltimore and from every port that Baltimorean ships visited. He learned that the only ship sailing that evening for Richmond was the *Joe McGinity*, a two-masted schooner that shuttled passengers and holds of heavy cargo back and forth between ports. He searched out the business shed and purchased passage on the boat.

Next, Allen found the nearest telegraph office and sent messages to his wife and to Edward Rucker. Five minutes later, he was inside the Mechanic's Bank, withdrawing money for his trip. He then went to the office of William Foster, the chief magistrate of the Baltimore Watch Force, and reported on his activities to date and those he intended for the day. Foster was not at all surprised by the news about the ruckus at Ryan's 4th Ward. He shared with Pinkerton that a reform association was in the process of organization to secure order and fairness at the city's polling places. The slipshod methods of verifying voters and the blatant acts of intimidation during the recent election had simply become too apparent for honest citizens to ignore. Until the tide of public outrage had reached a certain peak, however, the ward bosses carried political weight and would be given latitude by the judges. Pinkerton took Foster's words to be an oblique counsel; if the only way of finding out how Poe had come to the alley bench or learning Reynolds' identity was to wrest it from one of the wards, the cause of death might never be determined.

Toward eleven, Pinkerton entered the business of Neilson Poe. He learned via a secretary that a letter had arrived from Richmond and that the cane belonged to a Dr. John F. Carter of that city. Allan was given the brass-headed cane to return. As he exited the building, he noticed two young men loitering in the shadows of the three-story structure across the street. One wore a knit cap and plaid mackinaw-type coat, which set him apart from the sidewalk traffic. The other wore a thick, ecru-colored sweater.

William Foster had shown Pinkerton a map and indicated the locations of the other city ward halls. Clutching the cane, Allan started briskly toward the west side of town. As he turned a corner, he caught sight of the two men behind him. He noted for the first time that the one in the mackinaw coat held a stick. It was thicker than a cane and crooked, like a shillelagh. He set off at a slow jog, putting distance between himself and the followers. Then he resumed his normal pace. When he turned again, pretending to show interest in the displays behind a store window, he saw that the stalkers had not lost ground. Pinkerton continued on his way another two blocks, to be absolutely certain he was being followed. When he caught the colors of the plaid coat out of the corner of his eye, he went around a fence, entering the gate of a small park. Shrubs still holding their leaves lay just beyond the gate, and he crouched behind them and readied himself to spring on the young men.

The stalker in the sweater came alone to the gate. He stopped there and searched for his quarry, cursing under his breath.

"You there, in the bushes! What are you doing?" a female voice called out. An elderly woman walking a dog on a leash had paused on the park path and was peering hard at Pinkerton.

The stalker turned. Pinkerton stood and leapt over the bushes, the cane raised.

Forewarned, the young man thrust up his shillelagh and met Pinkerton's attack. They closed into one writhing mass, free hands clawing into coats, armed ones striking with shortened blows.

Having experience in several hand-to-hand fights, Allan smoothly slipped his right foot behind the left heel of his adversary. He let go of his grasp and shoved with all his might. The young ruffian fell hard to the pavement. Behind them, the women remonstrated loudly, calling out "Someone, anyone, help this poor young man!" Had he not been so preoccupied, Allan would have shouted at her.

Pinkerton cocked the brass-headed cane and prepared to deliver a strike on the stalker's head. Before he could, a blow landed on him, first catching the edge of his derby and sending it flying and then striking his shoulder. Knowing without looking that he was being attacked by the second tough, Allan pivoted and let his cane fly.

The standing tough jumped back, giving Pinkerton just enough time to twist the ring on the cane neck and withdraw the short sword. He offered the standing attacker, who held a blackjack, a confident grin.

From the end of the block came the shrill sound of a whistle.

"Get up, Bill!" the standing tough commanded, even as he backed away and lured Allan from the prone young man. The one in the plaid jacket rose to one knee, then stood, all the while swinging his shillelagh without effect.

"Reynolds sent us to say 'hello,'" the one in the sweater said in a mocking tone. A moment later, both were tearing down the street, heading east.

A man a little older than Allan came panting to his side. A Watch Force badge was pinned to his rough-spun shirt. Secured to his business hand by a long leather strap was a hardwood nightstick that had many nicks and scrapes.

"In broad daylight!" the man exclaimed.

From the park, the old lady continued to yell, causing her dog to howl in chorus. Her free hand gesticulated wildly at Pinkerton.

"Shut up, you stupid hag!" Allan yelled.

The constable's head reared back.

"I'm sorry," Allan apologized, not to the busybody--who continued to bark at him unabated – but to the watchman. "I have had several very frustrating days, and being accused of attacking my attackers is a bit much." He shoved the sword back into the cane. "I'm a policeman myself." He fished out his badge and held it up.

Ah," the man said, his face lighting with understanding. "You're the one from Chicago. Well, you must be getting somewhere," he decided. "Otherwise, you wouldn't have somebody's bully boys after you."

Allan thanked the officer, took directions to the closest polling ward, retrieved his hat, thumbed his nose at the muttering old woman, and went his way.

The reception at the ward hall was relatively more cordial than Pinkerton had met at Ryan's 4th, but the information given was just as useless. The man who spoke with him introduced himself as Jean Claude. He swore that, in comparison to the other wards, his was "the front gates of heaven." His opinion was that the rumors of cooping were greatly exaggerated. Too many men were willing to sell their souls for a pint of ale rather than to be dragooned. He also stated that he did not know what Edgar Allan Poe had looked like, which killed Boss Monk's theory that no one would have touched the author for that reason. Finally, Jean Claude alleged that he knew "every man, woman, and child in this ward," but he was not acquainted with anyone named Reynolds. Allan silently questioned the man's veracity on both counts. He decided at that moment to abandon his visits to the other wards.

Pinkerton was not surprised when he visited the Maryland House in the middle of the afternoon and did not find Aaron Pelglade. He estimated that the hotel was more swank than his own billfold could afford. Some of the lobby furniture looked like it had been imported from Europe; the floor planking was varnished; the windows were clean; several mirrors had been hung on the walls, both to offer the patrons a chance to assess their dress before leaving and to reflect sunlight through the lobby. The detective wondered just how much profit there was in selling whiskey.

Allan put himself down on a couch for a time and contented himself with watching the parade. Growing rapidly bored, he approached the clerk at the desk. As he did, he caught a whiff of a pleasant scent. He could not be sure if it was the same spring apple aroma he had inhaled the night before.

"Was a redheaded woman here not long ago?"

"Excuse me, sir?" the clerk said.

"A pretty, redheaded woman, about twenty-five years of age…was she here?"

"No, sir. I last attended to a patron and his wife. They were an older couple." The clerk had a clipped, English accent and a chirpy voice. "How may I help you?"

"Is it possible that the hotel keeps recent editions of the city newspapers?"

"Indeed we do, for all manner of uses. We do not keep them as the publisher would, but you are welcome to search through the piles. They are in that storage room past the potted plant."

In the large closet Allan found four stacks of newspapers. Issues of the *Baltimore Sun*, the *Baltimore Gazette*, the *North American*, and even the *Philadelphia Evening Bulletin* were mixed together. It took him some time to search out Baltimore editions with dates between September 29th and October 3rd, the day Edgar A. Poe first arrived in the city from Richmond and the morning he was found. He brought the papers back to the couch and began scanning, with the purpose of seeing if any strange events might have caught up Poe and resulted in his death.

The California gold rush was constant news, with one periodical reporting each day under the heading "From the Gold Region." Pinkerton read about the U. S. treaty with Nicaragua, about Canadians favoring annexation by the United States, about California organizing for statehood and the status of the Hawaiian kingdom. But, other than local news of the impending election, the city had been peaceful and its happenings largely uneventful. And then Pinkerton's eyes settled on the story of Margaret Jensen. She had gone missing. The noteworthy part of the story, however, was that she had disappeared after she died. The cause of her death was listed as "rupture of the appendix" and her age as fifteen. Notices of her demise had been placed in all the city papers, inviting friends and relatives to view her at her home before burial. The viewing was to have been on September 30th, but when the family descended from their bedrooms that morning, they found the coffin empty.

"What's so interesting?' the familiar, raspy voice asked from over Allan's shoulder.

Allan smiled at the whiskey salesman and handed him the newspaper. "You've heard the term 'busybody'?  Well, here is one."

Pelglade's eyes swept back and forth, down the column. "Talk about insult to injury. I wonder if the casket company will accept a return?"

Pinkerton figured the New York man's callous persiflage was in response to his own pun. He decided neither of their remarks was respectful and said, "Perhaps the poor mother or father will die of shock or sorrow, and they won't need to return it."

"It says here the family was not in the habit of locking their doors. Well, this should be sufficient lesson to them. Come up to my room, Allan! Why are you reading old news?" Aaron asked, handing the newspaper back to Pinkerton.

Allan gathered up the papers he had not yet read and tucked them under his arm. As the men climbed the stairs to the hotel's second floor, Pinkerton discussed his idea that Poe might have gotten innocently involved in some shady action.

"Then you really do need to visit Richmond," Pelglade said, "because it appears that you are grasping at straws here."

Allan noted that the drummer wore a more casual suit of wool and did not carry his display case. "Did you not work this afternoon?"

"No. No one wanted to listen to my pitch."

Reaching the second floor, Aaron sounded winded. "Baltimore has not been especially thirsty of late, it turns out. That's quite a handsome cane you're carrying."

"Your friend Eddie had it when he was found outside Gunner's Hall," Allan replied. "But it wasn't his."

"No, it wasn't. He had his own, which was elegant in its own right. He didn't need it because of age or affliction, naturally. It was an affectation. Now, that is more interesting than those newspapers." Aaron nodded at the several issues Allan had carried with him.

"And you have never seen it before?" Allan replied to make certain.

"Not I. Did you get it from the hospital?"

"No. It was passed to his cousin."

"Ah. Do you think it belongs to the Reynolds person you were asking about inside Gunner's Hall?"

"No. I now know for a fact that it belongs to a physician in Richmond named John Carter."

Aaron produced the room key and opened the door. "So, Eddie picked up the wrong cane before he left Richmond and did not notice? Would that not suggest he was drunk before he arrived in Baltimore?"

"I shall have to ask Dr. Carter."

"Then you are going!"

"I sail this very evening," Pinkerton said, following his host through the door.

Pelglade moved into the room, but Allan remained at the threshold, drinking in what he saw. Elegant as the hotel was, it evidently did not provide daily maid service. The bed covers were in disarray. A pair of stockings attached to their garters lay on the floor. The suit that Aaron had worn when Allan met him in the cemetery lay over the back of the room's one chair. A brown paper bag lay crumpled at the foot of the bed. Atop the room's desk, beside the oil reading lamp, sat several newspapers and an open and inverted book. The doors of the armoire lay open.

The salesman grabbed the black suit and took it to the armoire. He offered no apology for the mess. Instead, he asked, "What do you think happened to Miss Margaret Jensen of this fair city?"

Allan closed the door. "From what I hear, the most logical explanation is that her body was taken for medical use. The hospitals – especially the one Poe died in – seem desperate for dissection corpses."

Pelglade lifted his display case from the seat of the chair and set it on the small desk beside the bed. "I hope that is the explanation. More persons should donate their remains to further the knowledge of medical science rather than letting them rot in the ground." He opened the case. It needed restocking

"In that story you told me about," Allan said, "the one called 'Premature Burial,' you said that Poe related an actual live burial."

"Are you thinking Miss Jensen was not dead and stepped out of her own–"

Allan waved the idea away. "No, sorry. I've changed the subject a bit. What were the circumstances of the case in the story?"

A sly look swept over Aaron Pelglade's face. "I will tell you only on the condition that you have a nip with me."

"Just a finger width," Allan allowed. After seven days of abstinence, the thirst had come powerfully upon him. "I favor rye, if you please."

"Good choice, as this is from Pike's Hill, right here in Maryland." The whiskey drummer set the two glasses on the desk side by side, bent to one of two open wooden cases on the floor beside the desk, and withdrew a sealed flask.

"He said the woman was the wife of a lawyer who had been a member of Congress. According to Eddie's tale, she lay without moving for three days and even became rigid. They laid her in a family vault and did not have reason to open the vault for three years, when another member of the family died. When the husband unlocked the door and pulled it open, his wife's shrouded, skin-on-bones figure fell at his feet." He poured the whiskey out, an inch for Pinkerton and two inches for himself.

"A lawyer and member of Congress," Pinkerton mused aloud, accepting his glass. "Was he not making a playful nod at his friend John Kennedy?"

"Quite possibly," Aaron allowed. "He did not name the woman. But I would bet that the situation actually happened."

Allan sampled the rye. It was indeed well made. He let the liquor trickle slowly over his tongue and down his throat, anticipating the feeling of well-being that would follow. "Why would you think that?"

Aaron took his drink to the bed, threw one pillow atop the other, sat, and swung his legs up onto the pile of bedclothes. "Because Eddie never invented a story when he could borrow one." He relaxed back to a semi-recline and tipped the glass to his lips. "A convenient truth always works. One is sure the facts support the tale, since it actually happened. Eddie was a Hercules with language but a Procrustes when it came to making plots convincing."

Allan had heard of the supernaturally strong hero Hercules and assumed the other name belonged to a mythological character. Rather than admit his partial ignorance, he asked, "Are you saying that his stories are not all his?"

A small belly laugh sounded through the alcohol. "Half the vituperation in the literary world comes from one author accusing another of stealing his idea, or a line, or an image. As a critic, Eddie was always calling out other writers for borrowing from him or someone else. But in that he was a hypocrite."

Aaron took the chair from in front of the desk and brought it close to the room's window. Seeing how careless Aaron was with his belongings, he dared to place his ankles on top of the salesman's rather large travel trunk. "Hmm! I imagine that, since there are only so many words, phrases, and ideas floating around, that a writer might believe his creation is inspired and then find that it has already been used. Perhaps several times."

"Well, to hear Edgar Allan Poe speak of plagiarism, it was the greatest sin known to man. And yet, at the beginning of this very year the Boston *Flag of Our Union* published Eddie's little story called 'Hop-Frog.' The eponymous character is a jester, dwarf, and cripple in a king's court. He is constantly mocked and made drunk, but he bears it all with good humor until his friend, a semi-dwarf girl comes to his defense and is kicked and wounded by the king. Then the jester tricks the king and his brutish nobles into masquerading in costumes made with pitch and flax. He conspires to hoist them into the air where they are all set on fire, forming a human chandelier. Do you know the source of this ending?"

"No."

"Mad Charles VI of France once chained himself to his nobles during a masquerade revelry. They caught fire, and since they were attached, six nobles burned and four died." Aaron took another large gulp of rye.

"But how many average readers know this? I think that borrowing from history…especially little-known history… should be allowed," Pinkerton opined.

"If you were a man of letters, Allan, you would right now be shouting that Eddie obviously stole the characters and plot of 'Hop-Frog' from Victor Hugo. Some sixteen or seventeen years ago, that great Frenchman wrote a successful play called 'Le Roi S'amuse.' The king amuses himself – and does so at the expense of his jester, who plots revenge. Great writers may not be great idea men, compelling them to steal.

"The topper of all Eddie's borrowings is a singular non-fiction editing job: a textbook on seashells called *The Conchologist's First Book: or, A System of Testaceous Malacology.*" He snorted. "The subtitle sounds like the study of evil gonads! It was intended for school use, and he put his name to it. This was ten years ago. The only problem was that he knew not one thing about seashells. He stole the whole treatise from a limey by the name of Captain Thomas Brown. His book was called *The Conchologist's Text Book*. Not even a unique title!"

The subject of Pelglade's rant seemed strange to Pinkerton, given the degree to which the man had previously defended Poe. He sought to draw him out. "Are you saying your friend would have been nothing without stories he stole?"

"No, no, no! He was a great wordsmith. More than that, he was a great deviser of detail once he had a plot. And he was even more. I'll wager you don't know that he was a wizard at ciphers and all sorts of riddles."

"This is news to me," Allan admitted.

"He wrote a series on both cryptography and autography. He solved any and all cryptograms submitted by the public to *Alexander's Weekly Messenger*. This became the rage for a time. You must also read his story 'The Gold-Bug,' which is based around ciphers. He had a mind as complex and precise as a watch made by Patek Philippe. It served him particularly well for his detective stories, of course. He was a veritable demon at ratiocination." Pelglade drained his glass. He pointed to the newspapers that Pinkerton had set down. "But his greatest personal triumph, to my mind, was in solving a real murder simply by reading the newspaper reports."

"Surely you are exaggerating," said Pinkerton.

"Not in the slightest. In real life he surpassed the detective he invented. It was the murder of a girl in New York by a sailor she had been secretly seeing. By means of such seeming trifles as reports of a torn slip and a missing rudder, Eddie proved who had to be guilty. And then he stole the true story, moved it to Paris, and called it 'The Mystery of Marie Rogêt.'"

"So, what you are saying is that he was two-faced; he

deplored those writers who borrowed but borrowed himself, even as he took them to task," Allan reasoned.

"Me?" Aaron said, bouncing off the bed to refill his glass. "Who am I to criticize the immortal Edgar Allan Poe? I am a mere Poe taster." He began to laugh, at first lightly, then with more and more gusto, until he began to cough from the effort.

"Are you all right?" Allan solicited, rising from his chair.

"Right as rain in the desert," Pelglade gasped. "Nothing that a little of my own wares won't cure. Finish your drink, so I can pour you more!"

"No, not in the afternoon," Allan declined. "I must keep my legs. I need to get myself down to the wharves."

"Well, you have a fine cane to serve as a third leg," Aaron observed. "It will serve you especially well if you meet a sphinx."

Allan was about to mention how the cane had served him well already that day, defending him from the two thugs who had sought to harm him. But then Pelglade's latest obscure comment stopped him dead. He figured it must be another literary illusion. Then Allan's normal, taciturn nature prevented him from passing along the incident. He had never been in the habit of sharing his investigations with anyone outside the law before he met Aaron Pelglade, and he feared that the man might end up inadvertently blabbing specifics of Pinkerton's investigation to some guilty party who happened to sit next to him at a saloon.

"I'll keep it handy," Allan said.

"Unfortunately, I cannot travel with you tonight. I have two appointments here in the morning," Pelglade shared. "But I shall follow you to Richmond on the morrow. How long do you expect to be there?"

"One or two nights, depending on what I find," Pinkerton answered.

"And then back to Baltimore?"

Allan thought of Molly Brannigan. "Yes."

"But surely, in light of what I have told you about Rufus Griswold and shown you in black and white," Aaron said with force, pointing to a newspaper, "you will need to travel to Philadelphia as well."

"We shall see," was all Pinkerton was willing to return.

The whiskey drummer fairly dashed to the desk and pulled a literary journal from under the book and newspapers. He thrust it at Pinkerton.

"Here! Since we shall certainly cross paths at least once more, you must borrow this from me. It has Eddie's first detective story in it."

Poe stared at the journal. It was a copy of *Burton's Magazine*.

"1841," Allan read. "But this would be difficult to replace," he argued. "And fate might determine that we do not meet again."

Aaron patted the detective's hand and shifted to his display case. "From what Fate has arranged so far, I am convinced otherwise. I fully expect to find you at the Linden Row Inn on East Franklin Street. Are you sure you will not have another finger's width of rye? It seemed to do you much good. "

Pinkerton acknowledged to himself that he felt the relaxing effects of the little whiskey he had drunk, and he longed to accept the drummer's offer. But then he thought of Edgar Allan Poe's inability to stop drinking once he had begun and where that man now lay. Whether by fate or coincidence, the fact that he was investigating Poe was more than a little disturbing to the

Chicago man.

Although he had led a life of physical labor and hard reality and Edgar A. Poe had led the soft life of the thinker, every day he had discovered anew how fundamentally alike they were. They both had fallen prey to "demon alcohol" many times. Although he had not admitted it to Molly, his periods of drunken belligerence had as much to do with his loveless marriage as fleeing Scotland, Joan almost drowning on the Atlantic crossing, or his constantly changing location and jobs. He and Poe also agreed in believing that children should be seen and not heard. Allan loved his sons from their births, but he often fled the house when they cried or threw tantrums, and he found himself acting stern and demanding to counteract his wife's overindulgences.

He and Poe were careful about their dress, believing that it helped define a man. Both were fascinated by crime and the criminal mind. If Pelglade was correct, both he and Poe were wizards at what the little whiskey man with the enormous vocabulary called 'ratiocination.' Finally, Poe was said to be an adulterer. To this point, Allan had not sinned in the flesh. But, since shortly after laying eyes on Molly Brannigan, he had committed adultery in his mind. Allan determined to be a better man than Poe. He would resist the second drink. And as long as Molly did not throw herself upon him, he was sure he would never embarrass himself by touching her or confessing his absolute infatuation.

"I'll take that second drink in Richmond," Allan said, offering as well a conspiratorial wink that he hoped would make the rather pathetic man standing in front of him feel like he had gained a friend to replace the one he had lost.

"I shall drink to that," Aaron said, as he refilled his glass.

Walking to the Brannigan residence, Allan kept a vigilant eye for anyone who might be lying in wait for him. He thought about what the ruffian in the sweater and wielding the blackjack had called out. There seemed to him only two possibilities: either the real Reynolds had gotten wind of Pinkerton's investigation and was anxious to frighten him away, or else Monk had sent the pair from the 4th Ward to get even. In the latter case, the men from Gunner's Hall either knew who Reynolds was or had no idea and were merely taunting the detective. Frustrated as he was with his investigation, he would have risked another confrontation, even with both boys, if it meant he could beat the truth out of one of them.

The whiskey still had not worn off completely as Allan came up West Pratt toward Greene Street. When he was still several townhouses distant from the Brannigan residence, he saw the green door draw back. He expected to see no one else but Molly and was astonished to view a man exiting the house. Allan noted that he was fairly tall. He was also a bit underweight. He wore work clothes rather than a suit. His face was clean-shaven, and the brown hair of his crown was all but missing. As near as Pinkerton could tell, the man was close to forty but good looking.

Allan had come to an abrupt halt from his surprise. Recovering as quickly as he could, he made a casual about-face and retreated to the end of the block. He watched the man walk down to Greene Street and then disappear, heading west.

*So much for appearances' sake*, Allan thought bitterly. He wondered if Molly Brannigan may only have been flirting with him the previous evening to practice for an assignation this day. She, who had spoken so matter-of-factly about women disappointed in marriage being justified in taking lovers, had followed her own advice. What upset Allan so much was that she could be so honest in such thoughts but lie to him about her own dalliance. He knew that it was not his business, but he could not refrain from feeling personal about it. Which made him feel foolish.

Allan resolved to watch the Brannigan's front door while he perused the last of the newspapers. After scanning each page, which took about thirty seconds, he looked up and made sure no other movement occurred. At one point, he consulted his pocket watch. He saw that he should be heading toward the wharves even now, since the tide would reverse within the hour and the seaward breeze would come in soon after. And yet he waited and read, until the last page of the last paper revealed no event that might have caught Poe up. He had hoped to read of another unsolved crime like the death of the sailor's girlfriend, over which the writer might have gotten killed investigating.

Allan dropped the newspapers in a rubbish cart. He pushed his derby hat lower on his head, tucked Dr. Carter's cane under the pit of his left arm and strode toward the sea captain's home.

Molly Brannigan appeared at the door only a few seconds after Allan knocked. Dressed in a blouse and wrap-around skirt with a kerchief on her head, she seemed disheveled and winded. In fact, a strand of her hair had fallen onto her nose, and she blew it out of the line of her eye.

"Allan! I saw both your bags and wondered if you had changed your mind," she said, stepping back out of his way.

"No. I didn't want to drag the one I'm taking to Richmond

around with me all day."

"So, you are indeed going." She focused on the brass-topped cane but made no comment.

"Indeed. The ship sails quite soon." He jerked his head up and down twice. "I'll just fetch my valise and be on the way."

"Very good. Well, I'm quite busy cleaning, so I'll simply say 'Au revoir' and see you when you return. Allan. Your name means 'noble' or 'fair to the sight' in Celtic, don't you know?"

Allan was in no mood for her flirting flatteries. He nodded and took the stairs two at a time. For a few seconds, he heard his landlady humming the old folk tune *Barbara Allen*. And then there was suddenly silence. When he descended with his valise, less than a minute later, Molly was no longer in the house. He did not bother to learn where she had gone.

# CHAPTER TEN
*Friday, October 19, 1849*

The Virginia landscape was not as "Southern" as Allan Pinkerton had expected. Beyond the open window of the coach that carried him from Williamsburg, the old capital of the state, to Richmond, the new capital, the countryside did not look very different from that of southern Maryland or Pennsylvania. The only difference he could spot from the rolling coach were the stands of pines and stately, shiny-leafed magnolias. He noted that this was as far south as he had ever traveled, but he hoped his detective agency would eventually become national, requiring him to journey around the entire, magnificent country. *At the rate I'm foundering with this investigation, however,* he reflected glumly, *I will never again leave Chicago.*

Thinking of foundering, Allan was at least glad to be on dry land once more. He had been assured by the captain of the *Joe McGinity* that the largest segments of the voyage between Baltimore and Williamsburg were placid, inland waterways. To him, the waves looked just as wet and just as liable to drown him as those out in the Atlantic. Clouds had blown in at sunset and, with them, a seaward breeze that churned up the iron-grey water. The schooner was heavily laden, running low enough in the water that salt spray was felt everywhere but below deck. There were no accommodations on what was essentially a cargo vessel, so one had to sleep sitting up. However, even a hammock would not have guaranteed Pinkerton rest, since the other passengers were all engaged in card playing, tobacco smoking, drinking, tall-tale telling, and even the occasional singing of a sea shanty. Allan figured the revelry had subsided around three in the morning, so that he had caught three hours' close-eyed rest. He expected he would sleep well that evening.

The coach pulled into Richmond precisely at two o'clock in

the afternoon. He was pleased that the coachman was willing to stop at the Linden Row Inn. He was delighted to find that they had a room available. After he inspected the quarters and dropped off his valise, he inquired as to the location of the Allan family home. He was directed to walk five blocks, to Fifth and Main. There sat a house that Allan reckoned in his mind as a mansion. Apparently, it was well known to everyone in the city and had its own name: Moldavia. Fashioned of brick, it seemed to rise higher than its two stories. What made it look all the more impressive and imposing were the double-storied columned porches running the entire width of the right side, capped by a roof emulating that of Greek temples. It possessed a wide and ornate front doorway and tall, wide windows.

Allan walked the elm-shaded path, admiring the lush, well-cared-for lawns and English-style gardens as he went. He paused as he thought of Edgar Poe standing in this very place. *How much more difficult his adult life must have been,* he thought to himself, *after growing up in such privilege? If it had been me, I would have assumed such luxury would extend to my entire existence. And then to sink to abject poverty. No wonder he was bitter and morose.*

Allan climbed the steps, and knocked on the door. A Negro manservant in livery answered. Allan presented his calling card and waited, holding Dr. Carter's cane in both hands.

A good-looking young man dressed in modern fashion and who Allan judged to be seventeen or eighteen came to the door. He neither offered his hand nor a smile.

"I am William Galt Allan," he said. "What can I do for you, Mr. Pinkerton?"

"I have come to Richmond concerning the business of Edgar Allan Poe's death."

"Edgar Poe," the young man corrected. "We do not consider his taking of our name as legitimate."

"Would you allow me to ask a few questions?" Allan persisted.

"Who is it?" a female voice inquired from inside.

"A policeman asking about Edgar," William called out.

"Well, do show the gentleman some hospitality, William," the woman said, moving into the foyer. "Sir, please come in."

Allan expressed his thanks and ventured half a dozen steps into the house. He glanced to his right and left and saw that the ceilings had to be at least ten feet high. The large windows served to allow the afternoon sun to penetrate and throw warm, golden patterns upon the expensive furnishings. On one side was a large, octagonal dining room; on the other was a sitting room with a harp and a grand piano. The front rooms were shrewdly calculated to serve for impressive entertaining.

The woman sashayed forward, her dress swaying gently back and forth as she moved. The dress was of silk, with a plunging neckline and sleeves to the elbows decorated with fringes of lace. A large brooch depended from a black velvet ribbon around her neck. Her wealth of blond hair was worn up, held by several ivory tucking combs. Pinkerton noted that she was not a particularly handsome woman, but she could not have been older than forty. He suspected that she was a stepsister to Poe. William handed her Pinkerton's calling card.

"Chicago. My, my. I am Mrs. Allan," the woman said, holding out her hand. "Welcome to Moldavia."

Allan accepted the proffered hand, bent from the waist, and kissed it.

"I know that you are busy, William," she said, without

looking at the young man. "I can entertain Mr. Pinkerton."

William expelled a nasal sound of annoyance, turned, and stalked up the ornate stairs.

"The day is so delightful, and winter will so quickly be upon us," Mrs. Allan said, "that I try to take enjoyment outdoors now whenever I can. Will you partake of some sun tea with mint with me, sir?"

Allan allowed that he would be delighted. He walked beside the woman out the back door and into yet more gardens. The land declined steadily toward the James River, which could be spied here and there beyond copses of trees. A black female followed at a distance, waiting until her mistress crooked her hand. Then she hurried forward and accepted the order for tea and shortbread cookies.

Mrs. Allen gestured to a round, wrought-iron table and chairs under a vine-covered pergola. After they had seated themselves, she said, "You wish to know about Edgar's days here before he met his end in Baltimore?"

"Yes, ma'am, I do."

"Well, there are persons in Richmond who can tell you much better than I. I do know that he was here in July, August, and September. He left our fair city for a time to deliver a lecture in Norfolk. He lectured here as well, but no one in this family attended. He and we have been alienated since before John's death. They had become increasingly at odds in the last years, especially since John's first wife, Frances Keeling Valentine – of the illustrious Richmond Valentines – died."

At last, Pinkerton knew the woman's place at Moldavia. She was the replacement wife and much younger than Allan would have imagined. The sullen young man who had spoken to Allan at the door was then Edgar's step-foster brother.

"In fact, he tried to borrow money from John while the poor man was on his deathbed," the hostess went on.

"How long ago was that?"

"That was 1834. My husband, rest his soul, died on March the 27th. Edgar demanded to see him. He pushed past two servants. My husband refused to speak with him and even raised his cane to keep him at bay."

"I'm sorry they quarreled," Allan offered.

Mrs. Allan shrugged. "I heard from friends that the speech he delivered in Norfolk was quite impressive."

"Did they say he was sharp and positive?" Allan asked.

Mrs. Allan smiled. "If I may be so bold as to translate, you are asking if he was sober and not spewing his usual darkness and depression. They said he was in positive spirits and showed no sign of drunkenness."

The refreshments arrived, and Mrs. Allan played hostess with bravura charm.

"The people you need to interview are the Roysters," she said, as she poured. "He was usually on good terms with them. Of course, bless his soul, Edgar was not misspending their money. My husband lavished the equivalent of two fortunes on him because he saw the boy's great promise. Edgar should have been ever so much more grateful, coming from common theater folk. The father, a drunkard, passing that disease on to both his sons. His mother birthing an illegitimate daughter. Him an orphan with no relatives willing to take him. Edgar received private education his entire youth, do you know! When the family was in the British Isles, he went to grammar school both in Irvine, Scotland and the Stoke Newington section of London.

I know this for a fact because John related it many times. And then John enrolled him in the University of Virginia during its second year. How did Edgar repay him? He ran up $2,000 in debts, much of that to gambling. So that was one fortune down the fox hole in a matter of months." The woman raised her chin high, leveled a haughty look at Allan, smiled vaguely and said, "Is it any wonder that we are not kindly disposed to him at Moldavia? I, for one, do not care a whit how he came to his predictable end."

In order to explore Richmond further, Allan took a different route back to the inn. On the way he encountered a bookshop. Inquiring of the proprietor, he was shown the second volume of *Tales of the Grotesque and Arabesque*. The price was more than he wanted to pay and more than he thought it was worth, even given the recent death of the author. Against his thrifty nature, he dug into his pocket and produced the coins. Like the James Fenimore Cooper novel, it would be a gift for Molly, and the cost of presents held no weight. His wanderings took him to Seventh and Broad Streets, where he came upon Sadler's Restaurant. The place looked clean and inviting. Allan had not eaten a meal since morning, so he sat down. After placing his order, he opened the volume and read "The Unparalleled Adventure of One Hans Pfaall."

Pinkerton found the story from its very outset absurd and ridiculous. It detailed the trip to the moon by a man who invents a balloon that compresses the vacuum of space into breathable air. The protagonist had previously murdered several of his creditors, but the people of Rotterdam are so impressed by his trip that they decided he should be pardoned.

Nevertheless, Allan continued to read, finishing all but a few sentences when his food arrived. This plot, he decided, was less than "one hand's full" and one that Poe had not borrowed.

Dusk was descending as Pinkerton returned to the inn. He thought of Molly Brannigan's cozy townhouse, of her pleasant if liberal discussions, of her feminine attentions. He realized that, in stark contrast, he was now leading the life that Aaron Pelglade had described to him; he was alone in a strange city, in a room with no personality, with a book for his companion. He imagined the whiskey drummer on the road for perhaps a hundred nights a year, desperately seeking to attach himself to whomever would show him a little friendship and, the many times he failed, being compelled to the substitute solace of a book. Allan wondered how lonely he himself would feel in another two weeks. He suspected that he would be very glad to return to Chicago, his job, and his family, whether or not he had solved the secrets of Edgar Allan Poe's death.

At the hotel, although feeling a pressing need for sleep, Allan elected to read a second of the tales in the volume he had purchased. The hour was not yet nine. He knew that if he allowed himself to close his eyes, the next thing he knew he would be wide awake in the middle of the night, and his internal clock would be a kilter for days. He turned to 'Metzengerstein.' Frederick, the last of the title family of Hungarians, is historically obliged to continue a feud with the Berlifitzing nobles. When the latter family's patriarch is killed in a stable fire, the cruel, young Baron Frederick is suspected. From that flaming stable gallops an untamed stallion with a brand that seems to prove it was owned by the dead man. No one, however, will claim it. The wild and brooding Frederick believes he sees within a wall-hanging tapestry moving images of a Metzengerstein killing a Berlifitzing. Frederick becomes obsessed with riding the horse, and when his own home catches fire, the horse carries him into the conflagration and to his death. Witnesses see a huge cloud rise above the flaming castle, in the shape of a colossal horse. As if the tale were not dark and depressing enough, Allan found Poe's style overly complex and confusing, filled with bewildering images and phrases. In order to be able to present solid evidence of his opinion when he later expressed it in conversation, Allan copied down a typical passage in his notebook.

"From this date, a marked alteration took place in the outward demeanor of the dissolute young Baron Frederick Von Metzengerstein. Indeed, his behavior disappointed every expectation, and proved little in accordance with the views of many a manoeuvering mamma; while his habit and manner, still less than formerly, offered any thing congenial with those of the neighboring aristocracy. He was never to be seen beyond the limits of his own domain, and, in his wide and social world, was utterly companionless – unless, indeed, that unnatural, impetuous, and fiery-colored horse, which he henceforward continually bestrode, had any mysterious right to the title of his friend."

Pinkerton did not deem the tale good in any way, the failure of mood and style overshadowing content. When he checked the original date, he found that Poe had seen it first published in 1832. It seemed that Aaron Pelglade was right; Poe's early tales were not the stuff of genius.

Pinkerton set the book aside and looked for a time through the room window, watching the movement of walkers, riders, and carriages on the street. He thought to lie down, but Poe's story had so jangled him that he could not. He decided he was more annoyed by it than disturbed and tried a third tale from the book before sleeping. He chose a short one entitled 'Berenice.' This one, Allan read, had first been published in 1835. A man named Egaeus is affianced to his cousin Berenice. He seems to be highly distracted and inclined to daydreaming. His fiancé contracts a disease that consumes her, part by part. Only her beautiful teeth seem unaffected. One passage so struck Allan that he was compelled to read it three times.

"I saw them now even more unequivocally than I beheld them then. The teeth! They were here, and there, and everywhere, and visibly and palpably before me; long, narrow and excessively white, with the pale lips writhing about them, as in the very moment of their first terrible development. Then came the full fury of my monomania, and I struggled in vain against its strange and irresistible influence. In the multiplied objects of the external world I had no thoughts but for the teeth. For these I longed with a frenzied desire. All other matters and all different interests became absorbed in their single contemplation. They – they alone were present to the mental eye, and they, in their sole individuality, became the essence of my mental life. I held them in every light. I turned them in every attitude. I surveyed their characteristics. I dwelt upon their peculiarities. I pondered their conformation. I mused upon the alteration in their nature. I shuddered as I assigned to them, in imagination, a sensitive and sentient power, and, even when unassisted by the lips, a capability of moral expression."

On the one hand, Allan was awed by Poe's power of capturing the essence of obsession. The use of so many sentences to show just how deeply and in how many ways the teeth had taken over the narrator's thinking was brilliant. On the other hand, Allan did not know how anyone not at least partly insane could have conceived of the details of such all-consuming obsession.

Allan finally tore his eyes away from the disturbing passage. He read that Berenice dies, and still the narrator cannot forget the teeth. A servant tells him that her grave has been disturbed. This is enough to revive him from his reverie, where he sees he is covered in blood, and at his side are dentistry tools and a box with thirty-two white teeth.

Allan realized when he closed the book with force that his lips were drawn back from his own teeth. He knew that if he had dreamt such a story, he never would have shared it with anyone. Certainly, he would have pulled out several of his own teeth before he would have written the story down and then sought to have it put into print under his own name.

More and more, he was feeling less sympathy for the dead man. Not one character in any of the three tales was a sympathetic one; not one had a single redeeming feature. Even a man who had suffered losses, reversals, disappointments, and poverty should not have thought the worst of the entire human race.

Had his first taste of author Poe been the three stories in the aptly named *Tales of the Grotesque* and had he read them on the trip to Baltimore, Allan knew he would have turned directly around and given Edgar Allan Poe not another thought. But he had first heard the praise of Molly Brannigan and Aaron Pelglade, and he had read the brilliant 'The Raven' and the beautiful 'Annabel Lee,' and he knew that some events or people had demonstrably improved the man over the past fifteen years or so.

He reflected that this was a mystery as great as that of Poe's last days, and he wondered if the other interviews he would conduct in Richmond would shed some light. He knew with near certainty that he had to sit with the unkind Poe critic Rufus Griswold and get that literary man's point of view before he returned home. Allan Pinkerton realized that his goal now was to solve both the riddle of a death and of a life.

# CHAPTER ELEVEN

*Saturday, October 20, 1849*

The Royster family was well known in Richmond. Pinkerton had no trouble receiving direction to the ancestral home. When he visited and made himself known, however, he was politely told that the best person in the family for him to consult with was Mrs. Sarah Elmira Royster Shelton. He was given her address and assured that Mrs. Shelton would be pleased to speak about Edgar Allan Poe.

Mrs. Shelton was a good-looking woman with kind eyes and a ready but rather wistful smile. She had a long neck and long, thin arms, and she kept her hands folded primly on her lap. She appeared to Allan to be in her late thirties or perhaps early forties. His suspicion was soon borne out.

"I am indeed happy to speak of Eddie," Mrs. Shelton said, from her seat in front of her parlor window. Allan had been invited to sit directly across a spindly, well-crafted serving table. "He was ever dear to me, since the first time I met him. Has anyone told you what a magnificent swimmer he was?"

"No, ma'am," Pinkerton admitted.

"I was thinking of that just this morning. He could swim the James River as quickly as I could walk along its banks." Her eyes, focused down and to the side, were seeing well into the past, and although Allan was in no especial hurry, he sought to bring her to the point of his visit.

"Did Mr. Poe have any enemies in Richmond?" he asked.

Mrs. Shelton's expression changed to one of light embarrassment. "Oh, only the half of my family, I suppose. You see, Eddie and I fell in love when I was quite young. When he put his mind to it, he could be the most charming man on the face of the earth. And, of course, he had memorized hours of poetry, and he would recite sonnets to me with his melodious voice. Every now and then, he offered a verse he had composed especially in my honor. What young woman can resist such attention?"

"I understand," Allan said.

"You called upon the Allans yesterday," Sarah Shelton said with pat confidence.

In strolling the streets of Richmond and gazing down its long avenues, Allan had formed the opinion that it was a large city. "Evidently," he reflected, "the upper social tier is quite intertwined and intimate."

"I did," he confirmed.

Mrs. Shelton's face screwed up into a look of distaste. "Horrid, horrid people. The only good one was Frances Valentine, John's first wife, and she had not a drop of Allan blood in her. She died so young, so young. In 1824, if I am not mistaken. But I digress. She and John had no issue…although everyone in the city knew that John had fathered a bastard named Edwin Collier."

Allan held his tongue at the reference to illegitimacy. Within the space of a few days, he had learned that Edgar Poe had affairs with other men's wives, that Poe's mother had delivered a daughter who was not her husband's, and that Poe's foster father had at least one offspring out of wedlock. He reflected that he was either naive in regard to the general adult population's sexual behavior or else he had happened upon a particularly randy and amoral segment.

"So Eddie was the heir apparent to their fortune," Mrs. Shelton went on smoothly. "It was not John's fortune, to be technically correct. He managed to fail his businesses…more than once. Shoddy ones they were: tobacco, slaves, and headstones! He inherited his uncle, William Galt's, fortune. My family expected the very best from Eddie. He was so smart and well educated. He spoke three languages! They were certain he would receive at least annual support until he inherited a portion of the fortune. Not to forget that he was admitted to Mr. Jefferson's University of Virginia."

The woman's face turned patently sad. "And then, toward the end of the first semester, he was forced to withdraw. The boys going there had servants, lavish lodging, stabled horses. They were used to spending all manner of money on carousing and gambling. John had not even given Eddie enough money for books! So Eddie sought to gamble to earn his way, and he was defeated by astronomical pots even when he did hold good cards. So, he was reduced to shame, and my parents broke the engagement. He fled to New York."

"But why would your family be against him now?" Pinkerton asked.

"I'm coming to that. I was prevailed upon to marry Alexander Shelton. He was a good man, a good provider, and loved me. But he was no Edgar Poe. We come now to this past summer. Eddie and I had both lost our spouses. He had returned to Richmond rather triumphant. His poems and stories were celebrated here and abroad. He was lecturing to sold-out salons. And he had finally secured funding to start his own literary journal. We renewed our relationship, and he pressed me ardently for my hand. My family, however, argued that Eddie had experienced many peaks and valleys in his life, and that this good fortune was surely only temporary. They callously stated that his renewed interest in me was the security of my home and bank accounts."

"In spite of your family, were you determined to marry him?" Allan dared.

Sarah Shelton paused for a moment, and in that moment Pinkerton saw the doubt that told the truth.

"Yes, I would have," the well-off widow asserted of a dead man, one no longer capable of failures. She drew in a deep breath. Her eyebrows knit. "Do you actually suspect that a member of my family hired someone to murder Eddie just to prevent him from marrying me?"

"Do you think that is possible?" Pinkerton countered.

"No," his hostess decided. "Because every one of them continued to work on me after he left for New York in late September. If one knew Eddie was going to die, he wouldn't have continued to badger me relentlessly. And they all said that he would show his true colors long before we actually married…which could not have been until next summer, given our time-honored traditions in Richmond. Merciful me, murder would have been ridiculously premature! We had not even become engaged."

"What did they mean by his 'true colors'?"

"His propensity to drink to delirium," Mrs. Shelton said with candor.

"Did he drink during this past summer?"

"To my knowledge, he did not partake of a drop. He told me several months ago that…how did he put it…'Alcohol is poison to me. I have foresworn it for good.'"

"No one among your family left Richmond around the same time Mr. Poe departed for Baltimore?"

"Heavens, no! I am afraid you have come a great distance to bark up the wrong tree, Mr. Pinkerton. Now, won't you take some refreshment?"

Following a light lunch and a return to the Linden Row Inn to change his collar, Allan planned to pay a visit to Dr. John F. Carter and return the cane. As he entered the inn and put his foot on the first step leading up to his room, however, the hotel was pierced by a series of shrill screams. Pinkerton withdrew the revolver from his shoulder holster and bounded up the steps two at a time. He turned into the second-floor hallway and saw a Negro woman dressed in a maid's uniform standing in front of an opened room two doors down from his own. Her hands were clapped over her mouth, but they hardly impeded the screams that continued from her throat. At her feet lay a line of dropped towels and linens and a ring of keys.

Pinkerton continued to the open doorway. The maid stepped back, colliding with the wall behind her. Her legs failed her, and she slid slowly to the carpet. He saw that she was unharmed and turned his attention to the sight that had so unnerved her.

A fully dressed woman lay in the room, face up, feet toward the door. Blood covered the front of her dress and formed a pool in the carpet under her. He noted that her right hand was bloody as well.

Shoes pounded up the stairs. Pinkerton turned. The inn manager and another male member of the staff arrived.

"A woman guest appears to have been murdered," Pinkerton announced.

The men's strides faltered.

"I am a policeman," Pinkerton said, shoving the revolver back in its holster and fetching out his badge. "Allan Pinkerton. Your guest, Mr. Rounsville."

"Yes, Mr. Pinkerton," the manager recognized. "I greeted you this morning."

"Summon your sheriff," Pinkerton ordered in a cool voice. He was now in his element, self-assured of his capabilities, and relieved that this murder was not several weeks old.

The manager instructed the other man to block the stairs to curious onlookers and then find the sheriff. He glared down at the black woman. "Get up, Claudia! What happened?"

Through quavering gulps of air, the maid related that she had only opened the door and taken one step inside the room when she saw the body. She had touched nothing and backed out as quickly as she could.

"Why don't you go downstairs and rest, Miss," Allan suggested.

The maid rushed away.

"I know this woman," Allan marveled, studying the body.

"She is Mrs. Augusta Manley," Manager Rounsville said in a soft, respectful voice, as if speaking in a normal tone might make the corpse sit up.

"No. Her real name was Yvette Benoit. She was a confidence artiste, out of Montreal, Canada," Pinkerton countered. "She used to work with her husband, in Montreal, Quebec, Toronto and other Canadian cities. They used many tricks, but a favorite was for her to meet a wealthy man somewhere and take him to her apartment or hotel room. Then, when they were in flagrante delicto, the husband–"

"In what?" Rounsville asked.

"In the act of sex," Pinkerton said, hoping that his bluntness would save him from further interruption. He knelt close to the body and made sure her chest did not rise or fall or her eyes blink. He noted that the pupils were dilated in death. He studied the wounds. "The husband would burst through the door and threaten to kill the man unless he paid them an enormous sum. Generally, they selected married men with upstanding reputations in the city. I count one stab wound to the right hand, one in the throat, and five in the chest. Whoever did this wanted to be very sure she died quickly."

"Did you once work in Canada?" the manager inquired.

"No. She moved to Chicago to escape arrest. Her husband was not so lucky. He is serving several years in a Canadian prison. I became acquainted with her when two of our larger emporiums experienced a sudden rash of missing goods." Pinkerton did not bother to continue the story. The reason Yvette Benoit had not been caught before Pinkerton was called in to observe was that she dressed, spoke, and acted like one of Chicago's upper crust. Her habit had been to alternate visits to the two establishments. As it was early spring, she wore a coat lined with beaver and carried a beaver muff. She would ask to inspect an article, which she would handle with her right hand. At the same time, she would set the hand warmer down on the counter on top of the thing she wished to steal. The muff had a slit on its underside, and Yvette would wriggle her fingers through it and draw the item inside.

When Pinkerton caught her, he learned that she had grown greedy and careless because she had two children plus an opium tears habit to feed. A Chicago judge bargained with her to give up her children for adoption in exchange for being set free. The other stipulation was that she leave the state of Illinois permanently or serve consecutive terms for her next crime and the one for which she had been excused.

Pinkerton wondered if the court's decision would have been different if the very pretty – and well-proportioned – Yvette had not spent private time with the judge in his chambers before the lenient sentence was passed. Looking at the same woman lying dead on the hotel room floor, he thought that she had hardened in six months. Then he reversed his opinion, believing it was only wishful thinking on his part for a woman who was such an unrepentant sinner. Certainly, some of what he read on her face was due to the shock of being attacked and the pain of death. What was most astonishing to Pinkerton was not that she had migrated to old-wealth Richmond but that he had taken lodging two doors from her. He touched the corpse's forehead.

"She is still fairly warm. I would say, judging from the temperature of the air in the room, that she has not been dead an hour."

"It must have been a bold robber to come up here in daylight," Rounsville declared, surveying the scene.

The room had been ransacked. The contents of the desk drawer and armoire had been strewn haphazardly around. The woman's suitcases were opened and emptied. The mattress had been stripped and pushed onto the floor. The pillows were cut open and feathers scattered. One pillowcase had traces of blood along the slit. The thorough search proved to Pinkerton that this was not a simple crime.

"The murderer was not merely a bold robber," he declared, straightening up. "Does that back stairway provide a means to an entrance other than the one in the lobby?"

Rounsville interlaced his fingers, in an effort to keep them from trembling. "Yes, but we lock it from six in the evening until eight in the morning, specifically to prevent any person from entering the inn without passing the desk."

"So, the night but not the day. Are you afraid of touching her?" Pinkerton asked.

"I would rather not," said the manager.

"The dead are not to be feared, Mr. Rounsville," Allan said. "It's only the living who will do you harm. Please assist me. I need to see if she was stabbed from behind as well." The two men rolled Yvette Benoit halfway over. No rents in her dress appeared on the back.

Pinkerton stood and examined the door. He saw that, like his own room's door, it had a tiny, fisheye glass porthole installed so that the lodger could see out into the hallway.

"The latest thing," Rounsville declared. "We just put them into the doors last year. A lot of good it did this woman."

"Which is quite curious," said the detective. "Yvette was a professional. She trusted no one."

"Well, she must have known and trusted this person," the manager decided. He followed his pronouncement with a sudden, sharp intake of air. "Oh, my Lord!"

"What?"

"She has been staying at the Inn for the past three days, and each late afternoon Judge Early went upstairs without pausing in the lobby. I believe he wished not to be noticed. And, to think of it, I never saw him come back down. He must have left by the back way."

This did not sound like the correct solution to Pinkerton. In the first case, the judge had to have suspected he was seen, whether or not he paused. Second, even the worst political appointments to judgeships were seldom made to foolish men. In the third, Yvette would not be so stupid as to blackmail a judge.

"Is he a sitting judge?" he asked.

"Yes. And he's married!"

"Let us hold our suspicions until I've finished here," said Pinkerton. He swung the door closed and then back. He looked down, bent, and pressed his hand against a dark spot on the carpet.

"Blood I will not touch," Rounsville exclaimed.

"It's not blood." Pinkerton held up his fingers for inspection. "This is water. And there is a larger spot just outside the door."

Rounsville stepped out into the hall and looked down. "What could that mean?"

"It means I should find…" Pinkerton got on his knees and inspected the place where the room carpet ran against the wall molding. Several times he lifted things and placed them on the palm of his left hand. Then he stood and held out the hand to the manager. "Fresh petals and a bit of fern."

Rounsville squinted at the lavender, purple, and green pieces. "True enough. What do they mean?"

"That unless I'm mistaken, the person who came to your Mrs. Manley's door disguised himself as a delivery person by holding up a bouquet. A bouquet that he had just removed from water. You provide envelopes downstairs, do you not?" When Rounsville confirmed this, he asked, "And where is that flower shop I saw yesterday?"

A commotion at the bottom of the stairs indicated that several persons wanted to come up.

"The closest one, Milady's, is on East Grace Street and Fifth."

Pinkerton closed the door. "That's the place! You may allow people up to pass the room but not to enter it. Do not abandon your post, Mr. Rounsville! I will return as quickly as possible."

"The smaller petal is from a purple aster," the owner of Milady's said of the tiny clues that Pinkerton had shaken from the envelope. "The larger is coneflower."

The shop catered to a well-off clientele, selling soaps, toiletries, perfumes, potpourri, stationery, and floral bouquets. The owner was a woman of advanced age who, nonetheless, seemed quite sharp of mind and sound of body. She spoke with a measured cadence and the hint of an educated English accent. She also wore too much perfume.

"You are correct in thinking that the last piece belongs to the fern family," she added. "This is maidenhair."

"Did you sell a bouquet containing these plants today?" Pinkerton asked.

"I did. Two or three hours ago."

"And do you know the name of the person who purchased this bouquet?"

"I am not in the habit of giving out information on my patrons, sir," the woman replied coolly.

Pinkerton produced his badge and flashed it just long enough to be sure the woman was chastened.

The owner said, "He is not a frequenter of this shop, but I know his name nonetheless. We are both members of St. John's Church. He is Charles Tippett."

"Might you know if he is married?" Allan asked.

"He is indeed."

At first, the sheriff of Richmond was unwilling to believe that a prominent pillar of the city's society, a philanthropist, and one of the foremost traders of wheat and other grains could ever lower himself to murder. And then Allan Pinkerton laid out for him the modus operandi of Yvette Benoit when it came to rich men. She would present herself as both married and well off, so that her mark would be lulled into thinking his charm and not his money was what had attracted her to him.

She would also arrange to first encounter him in the least suspicious place, such as in a church, where she would say that he had been referred to her by reputation and might well serve her as an investment advisor. A luncheon meeting would lead to a tryst, and then another and another. The highly attractive bait would dangle herself, the hook would enter the flesh, and the prey would be played to exhaustion, until the angler was ready to reel him in. She would meet him in tears, with the terrible news that he had made her pregnant. From a moderately rich man, her going extortion rate was two thousand dollars "to help raise the child properly," since she was "far too religious to consider abortion." She would accept one thousand but no lower. If he balked, he would be threatened with a visit from her to his wife.

"Do you know Charles Tippett personally?" Pinkerton asked the sheriff.

"Only by reputation," came the reply.

"Then I suggest you do some asking around very quickly and, while you do, put a couple men in front of his office and his home. Find out--"

"I know what to ask," the Richmond policeman said.

"Excellent."

The sheriff looked around for a spittoon. Not finding one, he continued to chew. "If it turns out that Mr. Tippett is indeed the murderer, do you wish your name in the newspapers or kept out?"

"Put in, by all means," Pinkerton said. "I would, in fact, appreciate an interview. I can expect no other reward, can I?"

"You can expect two free nights in this inn," Rounsville chimed in.

"Let us not get ahead of ourselves," the sheriff said.

At seven fifteen that evening, a breathless reporter from the *Richmond Enquirer* visited Pinkerton. His name was Oscar Penn Fitzgerald, and he had an accent with more nasal twang than did other citizens of Richmond, suggesting to Allan that he had been raised farther to the south. He was quite earnest in his speech and mature of demeanor and later revealed himself to be only twenty years of age. He told Pinkerton that Charles Tippet was found to have had the chance to visit the inn, to have purchased a bouquet of asters, coneflowers, and fern fronds, and finally to have drawn eighteen hundred dollars from two of his bank accounts four days earlier, only to redeposit the funds this afternoon.

As Pinkerton had suggested to the sheriff, Yvette's latest conquest, Judge Eustus Early, was only too willing to sign a warrant allowing a search of the suspect's bank accounts and his home. At just before six o'clock, two officers of the law had knocked on Tippett's front door. The answer they received was the report of a pistol. Prominent businessman, devoted husband, loving father, paragon philanthropist, and church elder Charles Tippett had taken on three more roles – as his own efficient judge, jury, and executioner.

"And how is it that you find yourself in Richmond, Detective

Pinkerton?" Fitzgerald asked. When Allan revealed his motivation, the young reporter gasped. "Why, I am – that is I was – a close, personal friend of Mr. Poe! You see, I do not write only reportage. I work at fiction as well. Eddie was most kind and helpful to me."

Allan was delighted to learn the news.

"That is why," the young man went on, "I was part of the committee formed to raise the funds necessary for launching his long-delayed periodical, *The Stylus*."

Allan's delight redoubled. The main reason he had undertaken the time-consuming side trip to Richmond was precisely because he had read that Poe had supposedly raised a large sum of cash in Richmond. Allan knew that money caused the same law as that of physical masses: the larger the pot of money, the exponentially greater the attraction to criminals.

"And may I inquire how much money was raised in this campaign?" Allan asked.

"The figure I heard was $1,500," said Fitzgerald. "As Eddie told it, he had been trying to raise money for the magazine since 1840. And then this past May, like some 'deus ex machina,' a fellow named Edward Patterson sent him a letter. He was quite young and quite enamored of both Eddie's poetry and stories and of his work as a critic and literary theorist. He lives in a town in Illinois with the singular name of Oquawka – obviously an Indian name – and he inherited from his father a newspaper called *The Spectator*. Not knowing anything about Eddie's plans for *The Stylus*, Patterson proposed that Eddie become the editor of a quality subscription journal. Patterson promised to put up a good deal of the start-up money. Eddie told us he got from the man $100, and this was what he was using to travel from New

York to Richmond and thence back to New York via all the major cities."

"And this was above and beyond the $1,500," Pinkerton said.

"I believe so. Regarding the subscription funds, I did not serve as the treasurer. That person was Osgood Lee. However, I personally brought in five per cent of that," Fitzgerald said proudly. "Fifteen subscriptions."

Pinkerton's mind reeled. The amount was about what a successful lawyer or doctor would make in a year. "Was the money deposited in a local bank?"

"No, Osgood said it was turned over to Eddie in a lump sum, outlining for us the many associated costs of starting such a venture--and he knew them well, since he had worked for so many magazines. There was the rental and set-up of an office, the purchase of quality paper, the engagement of a reputable printer. But first of all, several months of contributions had to be purchased or contracted for. One of the main reasons Eddie was stopping at several cities on the way to New York was to meet with various writers and solicit their best work."

"Was he in good health when you last saw him?" asked the detective. "No fevers, sweating, trembling, fatigue?"

"None of those. No trouble walking, breathing, or speaking. Other than being thin, he seemed fine." Fitzgerald pointed to Pinkerton's notepad and pencil. "I see you work just as I do."

"It helps me to look at facts together. Turning pages later on lets me create associations." Pinkerton took out his folding knife and began to whittle a new point on his pencil.

"Since it doesn't appear to have been ill health, do you think the money figured in his end?" the reporter asked.

"He was found penniless."

"But not beaten."

"Penniless and in a fog from which he never emerged," Pinkerton said, choosing his words carefully.

"It was not an alcohol- or opium-induced fog," asserted the young man. "I know that his reputation was that of a drinker, and he often wrote with authority concerning opium, but he indulged when his life was miserable. You know, the mercy of oblivion. Of late, everything was going his way. He knew it, and he vowed that he would let nothing deter him from realizing his literary dreams."

"When the spirit is willing, the flesh may yet be weak," Allan responded.

Fitzgerald shook his head vigorously. "You didn't know him. I did."

As far as Pinkerton was concerned, the reporter's minute detailing of facts about the young benefactor from Illinois more than demonstrated his closeness to Edgar A. Poe. However, to tweak Fitzgerald for displaying his superior attitude, Pinkerton said, "Prove it to me."

Fitzgerald folded his arms across his chest and tilted his chair back against the wall. "I can do that easily. You must know the poem 'The Raven.'"

"It was my introduction to the man's genius," said Pinkerton.

"Then this is perfect proof. In an essay he wrote three years ago, entitled 'The Philosophy of Composition,' Eddie stated that he selected the word 'Nevermore' because of its rhythm: two short, hard syllables, followed by a lingering, long one. Not true. He confided in me that the word was put in his head by the son of a woman he was sleeping with in Sarasota, New York."

Pinkerton reflected that this was probably one of the wives that Aaron Pelglade had so casually mentioned.

"If I remember correctly, it was the name of a pet owl," Fitzgerald finished. "What, beyond your solution to the murder of Yvette Benoit, can you furnish to prove you are a veritable C. Auguste Dupin – the class of detective who can get to the bottom of Eddie's death?" he countered.

Pinkerton could not have hoped for a better invitation. He launched into the well-honed, dramatic account of his life. Duly impressed, the young reporter filled half a dozen pages of a notebook with jottings. During a pause in his recitation, publicity-hungry Pinkerton solicited the knowledge whether the *Richmond Enquirer* traded news with other papers. Unfortunately, the farthest this exchange went was to Norfolk and Washington. Allan made sure to ask that Fitzgerald stress that "the famous chief detective from Chicago" was in Richmond to make inquiries about the death of author Edgar A. Poe. It would mean spending another night in the city waiting for a possible informant, he knew, but such a person might just crack the case wide open.

When the reporter left, Allan was so elated that he knew he could not sleep until at least midnight. He rejected out of hand reading any more of volume two of *Tales of the Grotesque and Arabesque*. Then he remembered that he had the periodical, *Burton's Magazine*, that Aaron Pelglade had loaned him, with 'The Murders in the Rue Morgue.'

# CHAPTER TWELVE

*Sunday, October 21, 1849*

While it was not the two columns the *New York Tribune* had devoted to Edgar A. Poe on its second page, Oscar Fitzgerald's article on the Benoit-Tippett murder-suicide mentioned Allan Pinkerton's name five times on the front page of the *Richmond Enquirer*. Allan purchased six copies and took them back to his room, to pack for home and to reread at his leisure. He made a note to telegraph the news to his investment partner in the detective agency on the morrow.

Following an unhurried breakfast, Allan found the address of the residence of Dr. John F. Carter. He waited until church services would be over and strolled to Seventh and Broad. Dr. Carter was at home and invited him in with a spirited welcome. His wide, upward-curving lips, prominent cheeks, and rosy complexion complimented his positive attitude. He accepted his cane with gratitude and went to the stand that held other sticks and two of the relatively new invention, the umbrella.

"I've been using Edgar's," he said, "but it's good to have mine back." He shook his head slowly. "Not good, however, to hear that it was with him when he met with misfortune."

"Tell me about how the canes came to be switched," Allan said, as he was led into the doctor's study/office and invited to sit.

Carter said, "He paid a call here. He was imminently leaving for New York, with the twin objectives of raising more money for his publication and to fetch his mother-in-law, Mrs. Clemm. He wished to move her, along with their belongings, back to Richmond. The home of his youth was to be the home of his advancing years. A happy symmetry that sadly did not come to be."

"Did you happen to hear the sum of money that was raised

to that point?" Allan asked, to confirm the rather astonishing figure quoted by Oscar Fitzgerald.

"I had heard $1,500," said the physician.

Pinkerton noticed a framed photograph among three others decorating the wall behind the doctor's desk. He was fairly certain, based on a drawing he had seen in a newspaper during his trip to Baltimore, to whom the image belonged.

"That is Mr. Poe, is it not?" he asked, coming out of his seat to put himself closer.

"It is. He was quite pleased by it and had a number of copies made for friends. I was one he favored."

Pinkerton knew that the relatively new fad of sitting for photographic portraits was quite expensive. His wife, Joan, had pestered him to arrange to have one of the Pinkerton family taken, but he had resisted, thinking that by the next year more photographers would be in business and therefore the charge would be considerably less. Yet somehow, perpetually impoverished Poe had found the money. Allan supposed that the man's selfish nature and vanity had won out over his poverty. The image captured him straight on, no doubt sitting on a chair and looking up at the photographer. His dark, thick hair was parted on the left. His left eyebrow and eye sat lower than his right, both sides dominated by his overlarge forehead. As if in counterbalance, his moustache was longer on the right side than on the left. He had premature bags under his eyes. Beneath the moustache, his lower lip was quite small. He wore an extremely high neck cloth. Around it was a floridly wrapped silk tie in an oblique striped pattern. His opened black frock coat collar appeared to be made of velvet of the most stygian shade.

"Forgive my interruptions," said Pinkerton reseating himself. "About the canes?"

"Think nothing of it. Let's see. He left Richmond on a Thursday night." The physician bent forward and consulted a calendar on his desk. "That would have been September 27th. Yes. Mrs. Freeman was the patient. He stopped by, without letting me know beforehand, at about 8:30. My wife told me he waited almost an hour. I suppose the boat was leaving quite late. I was unfortunately out on a call to Mrs. Freeman. He said he could wait no longer, and she walked him to the door. He said to tell me that I could find him for a time across the street at Sadler's restaurant. I supposed they were so engrossed in discussion that he took the wrong cane. They do look alike."

Pinkerton was not half as positive as Carter. It was true that both canes were of the Malacca variety, mottled brown and fashioned of rattan. Both had brass heads. But Carter's was more ornate, with the rough shape of a lion's head, while Poe's was smooth. Furthermore, Carter's had a crosshatched brass ring between the grip and the stick, the secret to releasing the sword within.

"Do you think he visited you because he was concerned about his health and the damp voyage?"

"Possibly," Carter allowed. "He also left behind a copy of Thomas Moore's *Irish Rhapsodies*. It may have been that he was in good health and had stopped by specifically to lend me the Moore book. Or it might have been that he was not feeling well, and his state caused him both to confuse the canes and to forget the book. I understand from the owner of Sadler's that he met with some other acquaintances. Who these were the owner did not know, so that I unfortunately cannot name them for you. Mr.

Rattle – he's the owner – however reported that there was much merriment made. Quite some time after midnight they accompanied him down to Rockett's Landing and the Baltimore boat. Mr. Rattle said Edgar was sober and cheerful to the last. Edgar complimented him for the good fare and said he would soon patronize him again."

"Had you seen him earlier in his visit, to judge the state of his health?"

Carter moved his calendar out of his way and set his elbow on his study desk. "I did not conduct an actual physical examination upon Edgar, but I observed him to be about as fit as a man of forty should be. You are hinting around the common apprehension that he drank constantly and in great excess."

"I have been assured of that…" Allan said, "…and of the opposite."

"Well, I can relate a personal incident from about two days before he left. He was invited to a party given by the Talleys. He was in the very best of spirits. He said that he had written to a dear friend of his, a Dr. Griswold who lived in Philadelphia, asking him to serve as executor of his literary estate should some fatal accident or disease befall him. It seemed that just that afternoon he had received a reply from the doctor. He had it on his person, and he showed it around. I glanced at it. Griswold said that he was flattered by Edgar's request. I distinctly remember that Mr. Talley declared the news deserved a toast. Those who had filled glasses raised them, and Edgar was asked to join. He simply shook his head and said, "That, like Satan himself, is behind me."

Allan's mind swam with the strange news. He could not

fathom how Poe would put the fate of his reputation for all the generations to come in the hands of a man he had so insulted. As he carefully wrote down Carter's words, Allan asked, "Did Edgar own a shabby jacket and iron-colored pants, both a little small on him, intended perhaps for him to do physical labor in?"

Carter laughed. "Physical labor and Edgar Poe never shook hands. You must remember that he was raised in a well-to-do family who not only took pride in their dress but also in being up with fashion. They had servants for all the labor. When I saw him at the party, I noted that he had settled on a 'look.'" He pointed to the photograph on the wall. "It was exactly the same as in that photograph." As he spoke, his expression grew increasingly somber. "I read that he was found in shabby clothing, and I took it only one possible way."

"And what was that?" Allan was eager to know.

"That someone who disliked him intensely expended the time and effort to dress him like that purely out of malice. They knew how much his physical appearance meant to him, and they were determined to mock him by having him end his days dressed in beggar's rags. As opposed to how he left us in Richmond, Eddie must have become a physical wreck in quick order to have allowed it."

Pinkerton did not bother to take down the doctor's thoughts, because they were precisely his. The period between Poe's departure from Richmond on the 27th, dressed in his habitual finery, and his discovery outside Gunner's Hall on the very early morning of October 3rd was not even seven full days. It was not as if the man had fallen on prolonged hard times, had worn out his black suit and been compelled to purchase second-hand rags. Pinkerton was convinced that there was a premeditated meanness, perhaps even a controlled rage behind the act.

"I wonder, then, why whoever dressed him in those rags did not take the cane from him as well," said Carter.

The detective remembered the observation of Mrs. Lukauskis: Poe had maintained a death grip on the cane, even inside the hospital. He also remembered that the gabardine coat's sleeve was torn "beyond the elbow." Ripping open the sleeve might have been the only way to pull the coat on if Poe would not let go of the cane.

"I am sorry to relate that I have no idea. Well, it has been a distinct pleasure meeting you, Doctor," Pinkerton said, rising. "Let me not take up any more of your Sunday."

The remainder of the day went slowly for Allan. No one banged on his door in search of his autograph or to offer congratulations. He received no notes from eager informants. Toward dusk, he took a stroll into a district of Richmond he had not explored. When returned to his room, he found himself bored and lonely. He thought of Aaron Pelglade and his solitary, peripatetic life. He found himself staring at the book and the periodical lying one atop the other on the nightstand next to the bed. He knew he had no interest in reading any more of Poe's earlier efforts in *Tales of the Grotesque and Arabesque*. He elected instead to reread 'The Murders in the Rue Morgue.' The story fascinated him.

It was the first piece of fiction he had ever read twice. What captured his attention most was Poe's innate understanding of the detection process. The crime scene was minutely observed.

Clues were laid out in precise, unambiguous detail. When normal explanations proved impossible, the next most possible scenario was searched for. The witnesses were interrogated just as he would have done, weighing the conflicting observations based on each person's unique set of limitations and biases. He was especially impressed by how Poe had C. Auguste Dupin place an advertisement in the newspaper based on what he suspected had occurred, tricking the owner of the murderous ourang-outang into coming to his door.

The pragmatic detective could now see a sound argument for fiction. It not only entertained but it could also thrust the reader into worlds that, if carefully and accurately created, would allow them to experience many lives. At least as interestingly, it could expose the mind, the spirit, and the very soul of the author, perhaps even more than if one had been the author's boon friend.

*I had always thought of myself as a complicated person,* Allan thought to himself as he finished the story for the second time and set the magazine down. *But Edgar Poe makes me look simple.* He deeply regretted that he could no longer get to know the man personally, but he was more determined than ever to piece together drives and motivations filling Poe's last days and how, quite possibly, the sum experiences of the writer's life took him to an alley beside a tavern.

# CHAPTER THIRTEEN
*Monday, October 22, 1849*

By eleven o'clock in the morning, Allan was convinced that no one in Richmond was rushing to him to offer a solution to the mystery of Edgar Allan Poe's death. He had already inquired about the next boat sailing to Baltimore. He learned that it was the *Pocahontas*, a packet small enough to navigate the James River all the way up to Richmond and meant primarily to transport passengers and mail. It sailed shortly before midnight. When Pinkerton badgered the dock manager, the man checked his back logs and determined that the *Pocahontas* was indeed the vessel that had sailed after midnight on September 27th.

Allan paid the Linden Row Inn desk clerk to forward a telegram to his silent partner, Edward Rucker, succinctly announcing his triumph in solving a local murder. He had begun to pack his belongings in his valise when an unexpected knock sounded at his door. He checked the image on the other side of the safety porthole and saw a face he recognized. For a moment, he could not place who the face belonged to. And then he had it. He threw back the door.

"Professor Throckmorton!" Allan exclaimed. "What a pleasant surprise!"

The male half of the couple who had shared the train ride from Harper's Ferry to Baltimore with Pinkerton stood just outside the door, holding a book in his left hand. He offered his right.

"I'm flattered you remember me," said the teacher. "I never in a million years thought I'd see you again, but then I saw your name in the *Richmond Enquirer* yesterday, credited with solving the murder right here at the Linden Row. I simply had to come over and look you up."

"I'm honored that you did," Pinkerton said, truthfully. At

least the next hour he would not have to spend alone.

"I finished teaching a class not long ago, and my only other class of the day is at ten minutes to three. I thought we might seek refreshment."

Refreshment turned out to be fermented.

Professor Throckmorton led Pinkerton to a chic café with all the assuredness and enthusiasm of a hound on the scent of a fox. The café, created in the Parisian style, had several tables with chairs set out on the brick pavement. The October sun was warm and inviting, but Hosea insisted on sitting inside. He shrugged out of his frock coat as he moved.

"I'll have a hot buttered rum," the Professor told the owner as he lowered his girth onto the chair.

With some twelve hours until sailing and no need to stay completely alert, Allan gave in to temptation. "Spiced rum," he said. When the owner left to fill the order, he said to his companion, "Pardon me for my professional inquisitiveness, but I am certain I remember that Mrs. Throckmorton said you were both teetotalers."

Hosea shooed the notion away. "She sneaks a nip when she's out. I know she does. She just doesn't want us to be like her sister and the sister's ex-husband."

"The one who frequented the racetrack?"

"The same. When Becky drinks, she has a tongue like a Muslim scimitar. When Noah drank, it made him loose with his fists. An unfortunate combination. So I don't fight it at home. I confine my drinking to occasions such as this."

Pinkerton marveled at how many players involved with his Poe investigation had secrets. Dr. Moran lied about his conversations with the dying man in order to puff himself up.

The brute with either the first or last name of Monk, being a politician and therefore among the least respected of citizens, had drawers filled with secrets, even if the mysterious Reynolds was not one of them. Molly Brannigan had her lover. Yvette Benoit and Charles Tippett had died from their shared secret, aided by the libidinous Judge Early. And now Professor and Mrs. Throckmorton were exposed as less than truthful as well. Allan reflected that in such a world he would never be out of business.

"Have you read beyond 'The Raven' since we last met?" asked the teacher.

Both because he had concentrated so hard on the investigation and needed some rest from discussing it and because he had developed such an interest in Poe the writer, Allan welcomed a scholarly chat. "I have, sir. And there is a question that you, as an authority on literature, may be able to answer. I know this to be a bad thing among writers of fact, but how great a sin is it for a fiction writer to borrow from other writers?"

Throckmorton thought for a moment. "Do you mean to borrow phrases, images, and symbolism, or to borrow someone else's plots and characters?"

"The latter."

The professor took a good sip of his drink and wiped the froth from his upper lip. "We are talking about plagiarism."

"Exactly."

"You might think that lifting only a few words and inserting them would be the lesser crime, but actually it is the greater. To my way to thinking, fascinating and convincing characters are so unique that one cannot borrow and change them without fatal loss. If they are slavishly copied, critics and readers alike will call the thief out, and his career will be ruined. Regarding plot, I may not be the one to ask."

"Why is that?"

"Because I am biased. You may recall that I am an authority on William Shakespeare. It is indisputable that he borrowed from Ben Jonson, Francis Bacon, Milton, and Marlowe. And he was copied in turn. He certainly borrowed liberally from North's translation of Plutarch. It has not been verified whether or not he read Greek or Latin, but he somehow learned the plots of Seneca and Horace. If you want a specific plagiarism of the Bard, look up Masuccio's *Il Novellino* of 1476. There you will find the salient plot points for his *Romeo and Juliet*. But..." Throckmorton lifted his forefinger and waggled it around dramatically, "...he *always* improved what he stole. He turned straw into gold, made pedestrian materials immortal. Who other than a dusty old academic such as I knows of Masuccio's *Romeo and Juliet*? The other authors may have created bodies, but they were like the dry bones in Ezekiel; they were all but buried and needed a god to breathe the soul into them. Shakespeare borrows because he finds the plots the right-sized vessel, as it were, to hold the immortal characters that show us so much of what we are."

Having read on Allan's face that he was impressed by the speech, Hosea paused to take a long sip of his hot buttered rum. "I have heard the charge leveled against Mr. Poe that he borrowed from others, even as he railed against the practice. Is that why you ask?"

"It is."

"Well, this issue pales in comparison with the problem of

copyright laws being ignored. Hiring a lawyer is never less than expensive. Compared to what you would receive from the periodicals and newspapers who flagrantly reprint your work, it isn't worth the pursuit. And the worst lawbreakers are the Europeans. The French, Germans, and English. They reprint entire books without rewarding the authors."

Pinkerton thought of Aaron Pelglade's mention of Poe stealing the conch shell textbook, but he said nothing. Instead, he asked, "If someone stole your ideas, even if they improved on them, would you ever entertain the thought of doing physical violence to that person?"

"Heavens, no!"

The name of Rufus Griswold flashed into Pinkerton's mind. "What about devising a means to thoroughly embarrass him?"

Professor Throckmorton's eyes twinkled. "Now that I might entertain...if I was sure I could get away with it without retribution or punishment of the law." He drained his mug and pointed to Allan's near-finished drink. "What say we have another?"

Ten minutes after Allan Pinkerton arrived at the wharf where the *Pocahontas* was tied up, Aaron Pelglade appeared. He walked slowly and with a rolling gait, his suitcase in one hand and his display case in the other.

"And there he is!" Pelglade called out, his raspy voice even more shrill and high than normal. "I did not have the time to search you out, but I hoped that I might find you ready to return to Baltimore."

"You finished your business here?" Allan replied.

"Just twenty minutes ago. After one very busy and profitable day. I did, however, grab a moment to read about your latest exploits on the front page of the Sunday *Richmond Enquirer*." Pelglade set down his burdens, reached up to his hat, and doffed it with smiling deference.

"That was a most strange and fortuitous event," allowed the detective.

"Sometimes these things are preordained," declared the whiskey drummer.

"Just as my never solving the riddle of your friend's death may be."

"What a pity to contemplate," Pelglade commiserated.

Pinkerton nodded to the boat. "A fortuitous event is that we both happen to be taking the selfsame vessel to Baltimore that Poe took on his last trip." Pinkerton's half-lowered eyes moved slowly left and right, registering the busy and rough-looking crew, an unspoken communication to Pelglade.

"Ah," understood the man who had saved Allan from the Gunner's Hall ruffians. "And the crew would most likely be the same only four weeks later."

Pinkerton patted the revolver under his coat and jacket. "But let us not concern ourselves with that until we are within swimming distance of Baltimore's shores. Shall we board?"

The night was nearly as warm as the day had been. The breeze was gentle. There were six other passengers. The safety of numbers heartened the Chicago man. He and Pelglade elected to stay on deck even when the crew cast off and the packet moved from the bouncing ripples near the shore to the smooth flow of the central river channel.

Not satisfied to view the passing scenery in silence, Pelglade fired off a fusillade of questions as to what the detective had learned that might have a bearing on the case. He seemed most interested in hearing about the money raised to finance Poe's long-desired periodical.

Aaron paused from wiping his spectacles with his pocket handkerchief. "They said one thousand five hundred dollars, did they? That would certainly be more than enough reason for anyone who knew about it to do harm to Eddie. One or more are lying about the figure."

"Why do you say that?"

"Because Eddie tried to start the same magazine at least twice before, and he never raised as much as two hundred dollars."

"But he was never so famous as this past summer," Pinkerton argued. "You said so yourself. The man's reputation was like an avalanche descending a mountain."

Pelglade shook his head almost violently. "No!" he snapped, and then with less force, "No. Think about it. That is three hundred subscriptions in Richmond alone."

"It is the place where he grew up and still has many friends," Pinkerton said, playing devil's advocate.

"It is not Philadelphia, New York, Boston or even Baltimore. There are not three hundred literati in the entire city. Trust me; something is wrong. Now that the money has disappeared, friends are inflating themselves like Aesop's toad, bragging how much they loved him. Bragging how willing they were to put their money behind him. Easy enough when he's dead and can't refute their claims."

"You make me want to turn around," Allan said, looking back at the lights of the city receding behind the trees that lined the riverbank.

"For what purpose? If you could get to the bottom, I assure you that all you would find would be several thoroughly embarrassed people. Amateur liars." Aaron saw that his companion had retrained his gaze on him. He shrugged. "Unlike me."

"I think I know whiskey, and yours is good," Pinkerton said.

"I'm not talking about selling my whiskey," Aaron replied. "It is the best. I'm talking about my efforts at fiction. First, all fiction writers aspire to be the most professional liars…liars who must either have or develop multiple personalities. That is not beyond me. But mainly I was a convincing liar to myself, because I was certain I was a master with the pen. And then I met Eddie. He disabused me…a few times by lecture but mostly by example." He sighed. "Let's go below and get a drink. "

Since consuming his two spiced rums earlier in the day, the thirst was fully upon Allan. He wanted to look as abstemious as an alderman when he returned to Molly Brannigan's house, but that would be some eighteen hours away. Moreover, if he could not cajole or distract his shipboard companion from his self-pitying mood, he was damned if he would listen to the moaning and groaning sober. Finally, he reasoned that a couple stiff drinks would calm his terror of the sea.

"Below it is," Allan said, gesturing for Aaron to lead the way.

The packet bar was a disgrace, the contents of the displayed bottles suspiciously light in color, and the prices maritime robbery, so the pair stole forward and away from the other passengers. Aaron opened his case and handed Allan his own flask of Maryland whiskey, while he broke the seal on one of bourbon.

"I have read 'The Murders in the Rue Morgue,'" Allan

announced, before Aaron could begin the second verse of his personal lament. "Twice, in fact."

Aaron removed his lips from the mouth of his bottle long enough to proclaim, "Excellent! And what did you think?"

"Many things, all positive." Allan related his wonder and awe at Poe's understanding of the methods and the psychology of detective work. Then, without pause, he said, "I was also struck by how much of his own self your Eddie threw into this story. You know, the beginning words about–"

Pelglade had closed his eyes. Without opening them, he suddenly interrupted, in an overloud voice, "'...I there became acquainted with a Monsieur C. Auguste Dupin. This young gentleman was of an excellent, indeed of an illustrious family, but, by a variety of untoward events, had been reduced to such poverty that the energy of his character succumbed beneath it, and he ceased to bestir himself in the world, or to care for the retrieval of this fortune.'"

"Formidable!" Allan said with respect. "You truly have immersed yourself in your friend's work."

Pelglade merely nodded.

"That is precisely the passage I was thinking of." Pinkerton stretched out along the bench that only he occupied. "What do you think of the idea that Edgar Poe feared he was becoming insane by the time he turned to solving murders and therefore felt the need to prove his continued hold on sanity by developing the most ingeniously complex stories?"

"I fervently hope that this scow holds as little water as that theory," his companion said in a dismissing tone. "Eddie prided himself on his cleverness right from the start. Long before I knew him. Are you aware that when his foster father disowned him, he joined the army?"

This was a side of Poe that Pinkerton had never heard, and he acknowledged both his ignorance and his fascination.

"I can only imagine Eddie under fire," Aaron said with contempt. "At any rate, he went under the name of Edgar A. Perry. He told people the A. stood for Admiral. Even before that, he went by the name Henri Le Rennet. Allow me to spell the last word." He did. "The little game is that the extra 'n' and 't' don't matter a whit in French pronunciation. Like the word for 'waters' – eaux – is pronounced 'o.' René means 'rebirth' in French, as in 'renaissance.' 'Henry the Reborn.' The first name in honor of his dead brother, Henry."

"He was saying he considered himself reborn after leaving Richmond," Allan echoed.

"But only so the cognoscenti could understand. Those 'in the know' were the only ones Eddie cared about. Too clever by half and far beyond the common man or woman, the mass of readers who determine whether you're merely in print or successful. So, you give your highest marks to the 'Rue Morgue' story."

"The situation was highly unlikely…" Allan began.

"But that is precisely what made the solution so spectacular!" Aaron argued in a rhapsodic tone.

Rather than fall into a debate, Allan said, "Tell me more about how he misused his wit and playfulness."

"Very well. Anything to pass the time," Poe's friend obliged in a suddenly glum tone. "It wasn't enough to show how clever he was. He had to make fools of everyone."

"I have noticed how there are few good people in his stories," Allan observed. "They are usually insane, morbid, stupid, vengeful, jealous, foolish in the extreme or other equally distasteful types."

"Except for his heroines," Pelglade pointed out.

"And they're always on the point of death or dead already." Pinkerton sat up for a second. "And if the protagonists are good or clever, they're modeled after him. I feel it is quite sad how he felt the constant need to build himself up by tearing others down."

Pelglade belched. "Yes, even the universally venerable, such as Henry Wadsworth Longfellow. You want to hear the ultimate irony? Eddie accused him of plagiarism. When Longfellow failed to rise to the bait, Eddie planted letters of protest under false names supposedly addressed to the magazines he edited, worded so that he could effectively knock his own weak protests down." Aaron took a swig from his flask, laughed as he was swallowing, and choked for several moments.

Allan shifted his attention from the overhead beam he was studying and glanced across the narrow aisle. "Are you all right?"

"I spilled some bourbon, dammit." And then he laughed heartily again.

"What?" asked Pinkerton.

"I should have called him Puck. You know: 'What fools these mortals be.' Edgar A. Puck. Now it's too late."

Allan had no idea as to what his highly literate friend referred, so he occupied his mouth by tipping more whiskey into it.

Pelglade said, "Yes, a mischievous gremlin. He was always thinking of ways to gull the public. I suppose his first hoax was 'The Narrative of Arthur Gordon Pym.' It was modeled on

Morrell's 'Narrative of Four Voyages to the South Seas and the Pacific.' But it was exponentially more bloody and macabre and set at the frozen South Pole. Related as gospel, but not a word of it true."

"Just the same as that 'Adventure of Hans Pfaall'!" Allan supplied.

"'The Unparalleled Adventure of One Hans Pfaall'," Aaron corrected gently. "So you've read that, have you? Well, you are certainly going back to before his inspired work. You know, he wrote another hoax dealing with a balloon. It was printed in the New York Sun not so long after I befriended him. He reported as truth the successful crossing of the Atlantic Ocean by a manned balloon, to an island near Charleston, South Carolina. He knew the public was primed to believe because of a genuine attempt shortly before to cross the English Channel in a balloon. A great many newspapers were sold, but those who were convinced have never forgiven Eddie." Aaron yawned and continued, "But the biggest hoax of all was publishing that conch book under his own name. Fortunately for him, few even knew it existed. He told me his total pay was thirty copies, most of which he never unloaded. So, for once the joke was on him!"

*He offended so many and with such glee*, Allan marveled. So strange. *To crave adulation and fame to the point of obsession and yet make it so difficult for people to like him.* Allan recalled how two men in Glasgow had murdered each other in broad daylight fighting over a gold coin lying in the street, a coin that was actually a brass button. If this was possible, then any one among hundreds who might have felt slighted or belittled by a callous remark or even Poe's malice in print could have caught him at a weak moment – just as Hosea Throckmorton in the café or

Aaron Pelglade and his case of whiskey had with Allan this very day – gotten the writer who vowed alcohol was poison to him roaring drunk, stolen his money, switched his clothes, and dumped him in the gutter. *Who could solve such a crime?* Allan lamented.

A lull set in. Toward the stern of the packet, a pair of men were arguing loudly. The other passengers were quiet. Allan concentrated on the increased bounce and roll of the boat. He figured that they had reached tidewater and found himself stroking his beard only to realize that his jaw could not feel the attention. He looked at the flask of whiskey clasped tightly in his other hand. He had emptied half the bottle, and in the process his face had become rather numb.

"Do you mind if I catch forty winks?" he asked his companion. "I'm feeling quite drowsy."

The only reply was the slow rhythm of light snoring.

# CHAPTER FOURTEEN
*Tuesday, October 23, 1849*

The packet *Pocahontas* left the heavy chop of Baltimore's Outer Harbor waters and tacked toward the city, with Fort McHenry looming on the left. The bulk of the day had run its course, and the nose of the craft swung toward the lowering sun.

More than an hour earlier, Allan Pinkerton had worked out with Aaron Pelglade just how they would interrogate the five-man crew of the packet. Allan would move methodically from stem to stern, ending with the captain. While he buttonholed each man, Pelglade would watch his back. Allan did not swim well, and he did not want a purposely unsecured block swinging into him and knocking him into the grey-green waves.

The first man Allan approached was a bit smaller than he and built on the wiry side. He had swarthy skin and a ponytail and sported several tattoos of marine themes. He was coiling rope as Allan came to his side.

"Were you serving on the *Pocahontas* four weeks back?" he asked.

"Why do you ask?" the man returned without looking at Pinkerton.

"Because one of the passengers was a man named Edgar Poe." Pinkerton went on to describe Poe in detail, including his black suit, wavy, dark hair, oversized bow tie, and brass-headed cane.

"Yeah, I remember him," the sailor answered. "A real dandy."

Pinkerton dared to hope. "I am a friend of Mr. Poe's. It is worth money for me to learn about his trip on this packet."

The man stopped coiling rope. He glanced momentarily at Pinkerton. "How much money?"

"What is your name, sir?"

"Hewitt. Jack Hewitt."

"A bit of simple information is worth five dollars."

"Six," Jack bargained.

"Very well."

"Let's see three dollars right now," the sailor said.

Allan scanned the boat, to learn if others among the crew had stopped work to observe them. Everyone else seemed to be going about their business. He reached into his pocket and pulled out three coins. He let the sailor see the glint of their surfaces in the red sunlight, then closed his fist.

"Did anyone come onto the boat with Mr. Poe?" Allan asked.

"I know that. Give me the money first." Hewitt stuck out his hand. When he held the coins, he said, "No. He was by himself."

"Was he sober?"

"He was. But he talked as much as a drunk man. He acted like he was a member of royalty or something, holding court. He even spouted poetry."

Pinkerton then knew the sailor had indeed been in Edgar Allan Poe's presence. "So, he got off this boat hale and hearty?"

"He did."

"Was he met by anyone on the dock?"

The sailor glanced behind Pinkerton, down the length of the packet. "Not on the dock. Out by the street. The fellow was standing in the shadows, like he didn't want to be seen. But I seen him."

"You got a good look?"

"Good enough to describe him."

"Go ahead."

A crafty smile curled up the corner of Hewitt's mouth. "I can't talk here. I'm thinking what I know is worth a total of eight dollars."

Fighting to conceal his elation, Pinkerton nodded slowly. "Five more and that's it. Where can we talk?"

The captain barked an annoyed-sounding command in Hewitt's direction, and the man saluted in a casual manner and moved to adjust the headsail.

"There's a place called the Tavern on the Wharf not five hundred feet from where we berth, " he said over his shoulder.

"I saw it."

"That's where I stay in Baltimore. I'll be out back of the place about an hour after we tie up. Now let me work."

Pinkerton strolled to the whiskey salesman's side, laboring not to grin like a lottery winner. "I struck gold on the first try."

"Good for you," Pelglade said. "What did he say?"

Allan repeated the conversation verbatim. "In less than two hours, I may have a description of the man who robbed your friend, dressed him in rags, and left him for dead. Of course, it may just as well be an innocent friend come to meet him who I did not interview."

"Sailors are not known for telling the truth," noted Pelglade. "What member of the police will believe you when you present a story second-hand from some denizen of the docks?"

"Come behind these crates," bade Pinkerton, moving aft. When he and Aaron stood among the battened, shoulder-high pallets of bundled mail, he reached into his left trouser pocket and withdrew a ring holding three keys. One was quite small. He took this between his thumb and third finger and put his hand under his coat and behind his back. Then he passed the key to the other hand and repeated the process. This time, his hand emerged with the ring of keys and a set of handcuffs.

"I keep the cuffs closed around two of my back belt loops," Allan confided in his companion. "Believe me, I will not merely take down the sailor's words. He will no doubt resist repeating them to the law, so I will cuff him and march him to the Watch box at the top of the wharf and see that his testimony is duly recorded. He'll either cooperate, or he won't see that five dollars."

"Don't plan on traveling on the *Pocahontas* again," Aaron advised archly. Immediately, he added, "My plans require me to leave for the Pike Hill Distillery early tomorrow. Too many tavern keepers forgot the taste of my wares and have depleted my sample rye."

Pinkerton wondered if he and Pelglade had not drunk as much as all the samplers combined, but he offered no comment.

Pelglade added, "Between my hectic schedule yesterday and that uncomfortable voyage, I'd like to get into a bed as soon as possible. But I wonder if I should linger and assist you first."

"I thank you, but your presence would no doubt spook Mr. Hewitt. I'm sure I can handle him," Allan said.

"I'm certain you can as well." Aaron tapped him forcefully on the lapel. "Be assured that I will seek you out when I return from my detour; you still have my copy of 'The Murders in the Rue Morgue!' Where will you be staying?"

Allan described the townhouse with the green door, close by the northeast corner of West Pratt and Greene. The packet had caught a good breeze and was heeling along at about six knots. The broad curve of Baltimore's cityscape expanded rapidly. The passengers, including Allan and Aaron, busied themselves collecting their belongings.

* * *

When the packet docked at Spear's Wharf, Allan took his time, becoming the last passenger to leave the boat. He was tired and impatient for the hour to pass until he could confront the sailor behind the Tavern on the Wharf, but his anticipation of hearing a strong lead imparted a new energy to his being. He found himself needing to give his legs exercise. With Edgar Poe's cane and his valise in his hands, he took a stroll toward the far end of the long wharf.

Thick hawsers secured a medium-sized clipper ship named the *Fleetwind* to the pier pilings. Allan studied the various types of people readying the ship for its departure on the reversing tide. He saw a sailor with a belaying pin standing guard over a collection of suitcases, trunks, and even an ornate but empty birdcage. Then his eyes fixed on one item. It was a small lady's travel chest, painted pale yellow, with bright blue and yellow pansies on its side.

Pinkerton walked up to the sailor guard. "Excuse me. Does that yellow chest belong to a woman, about twenty-five years of age, with red hair?"

The sailor grinned. "It should. But it was brought here by those two characters." He jerked his head up toward the ship's rail, where two men conversed with their back to the wharf, oblivious of the conversation down by the pile of luggage. Allan noted that both wore soft woolen clothing. The observation was not an idle one.

Pinkerton reached into his pocket and produced the last of his dollar coins. "How soon does this ship sail?"

"In about an hour."

Pinkerton pressed the coin into the sailor's palm. "It is very important that those two men do not leave here. If they should try, be sure they do not do so with that chest. It is stolen."

"I suppose I could see to that," the sailor allowed.

"I shall be back directly," Allan told him, even as he began walking away from the *Fleetwind*. Only when he was more than two hundred feet distant did he break into a trot, and then a run. His objective was the Watch box located between wharves near Pratt Street. He did not slow his pace until he spotted the pair of policemen standing in front of the box. He fished out his badge and dug into his inside pocket for the letter from Baltimore's chief magistrate. While he held the sources of identification up to the two surprised men, he said, "The section of the city around Greene Street has been experiencing a series of burglaries."

"That's right," one of the policemen said. "Those streets and several streets around the monument."

"I believe I know where you can find the two robbers. Come with me!"

The astonished officers gave no objection as Pinkerton reversed his direction. However, they refused to run. Four minutes later, all three men came to the gangplank of the *Fleetwind*.

The men had disappeared from the rail.

Pinkerton and one of the policemen stood guard at the foot of the gangplank while the second officer went onboard. Ten minutes later, he emerged with the two men, the captain of the vessel, and the ship's mate at arms by his side, the latter holding a pistol. The thieves were both loudly protesting their innocence as they descended to the wharf.

"Show us your luggage, if you please, Mr. Kelly," the officer standing next to the captain requested.

"Those two," Kelly said, pointing to a trunk and a large suitcase. Although he wore a businessman's suit and shoes, his face told a tale of a hard, dissolute life. His sullen partner was cut from the same pattern.

"What about the small, yellow chest?" the officer asked.

"Don't know who that belongs to."

"You filled out a tag and had me attach it," the sailor guard accused indignantly.

"Never did nothing of the kind."

Pinkerton had approached the three pieces, which stood touching each other. He bent close. "The handwriting on all three are identical. But you needn't bother with the lady's chest for the moment. Where is the key to open the trunk?"

"I lost it," second thief said with a cocky air.

"Bad luck," Pinkerton said, and to the captain of the Fleetwind, "And who do they say they are?"

"Devon Kelly and Hans Stroheim."

Pinkerton noted that at least their names conformed to their faces. "Let me help your problem." He produced his folding knife and wrestled the trunk lock open. It stood upended. When he spread the two halves, all that could be seen were several secured items of clothing. As soon as Pinkerton undid the leather straps and lifted the apparel out of the way, out tumbled two small jimmies and a pair of nippers. Next, a bundle of baize cloth fell onto the dock and unrolled, exposing a small gimlet and a couple of bureau picks, followed by several jointed keys, a thin glazing knife, a container of common matches, and a few yards of strong twine. Remaining jammed into the one side, taking up most of that space, was a folding ladder.

"Behold the tools of the housebreaker's trade," Pinkerton

declared. He shoved his foot into the bottom of one side of the trunk and kicked out a pair of very large shoes. He smiled at the two thieves. "Which one of you is in truth Sir Jimmy, Knight of the Night?"

Neither man replied.

"Your investigators found enormous shoe prints in at least one of the victims' back yards, no doubt," Pinkerton said to the two lawmen. One nodded. "You will find that one of these scoundrels wears shoes that will fit nicely inside of these. You must make your men look for a very large man with gigantic feet. If you will observe their clothing, everything is soft. Even the soft sound of starched shirts, collars, and the like can awaken light sleepers."

One of the policemen slapped his nightstick against the palm of his opposite hand in a semi-threatening manner. The mate at arms kept his pistol leveled on the housebreakers. The second policeman linked the two thieves together with his set of handcuffs, even as they protested that there were no complaining witnesses and the materials inside the trunk were used for their business of house repairs.

Pinkerton laughed at their brass. Those with enough nerve to enter the houses of others uninvited invariably had more than enough gall to protest their innocence, even in the face of a mountain of evidence against them. He pointed to the lady's chest.

"The reason I recognized that is it belongs to my sister, Mrs. Shamus Brannigan," Allan said  He delivered her street address. The objective of his lie was to take the chest away rather than have it vanish from a police storage area.

Another policeman said, "It's no doubt filled with the booty from all their robberies, so we can't let you have it yet. You can help us by carrying it to the city jail."

Allan gave an involuntary glance toward the Tavern on the Wharf. "I can't. I have to meet someone."

The policeman shook his head. "I'm sorry, but you lodged the complaint, so you–"

One of the robbers broke into a hoarse laugh and thumbed his nose at Pinkerton with his free hand.

"I lodged no complaint," Pinkerton protested. "I simply pointed you two to the robbers your force was unable to catch."

"It will take no more than an hour, sir," the second policeman said in a coaxing tone.

Pinkerton sighed. He knew that the hour would quickly become two. He would miss his meeting with Jack Hewitt, but he also had been told by the sailor that Hewitt lodged at the tavern. He also knew the Pocahontas would not sail until the next morning. He would simply hurry back as quickly as he could and hunt down the man.

"All right," Allan relented. "But let's be damned quick about it!"


"Jack Hewitt!" exclaimed the bartender. "Is that Duke's real name? He went out the back door about an hour ago."

Pinkerton glanced around the tavern saloon. *These lads make the ones in Gunner's Hall look like choirboys,* he thought. Among their number were ladies of the night, trying not to look bored. Allan's hand itched to wrap around his revolver.

"And he didn't come back?" Allan asked.

"No, sir." The bartender jerked his bald head toward a door nearly hidden in the deep shadows of the rear of the room.

Allan walked through the door and found himself standing among a welter of crates and buckets, cans and barrels, dispersed between piles of garbage that fed legions of rats and flies. The stench, even on a cool October night, was enough to make Pinkerton's stomach roil. The only reason why he could imagine the sailor would pick such a place to meet was because no one with eyes or a nose would elect to be there for any longer than it took to give fresh trash a good heave-ho. Less than a hundred feet away was the harbor's edge, below a wooden walkway. Allan moved to it and looked around. There was no sign of any human activity. The water splashing against the pilings was scummy and decorated with curving lines of oil. On his return reconnoiter, he spotted a white square of folded paper. It looked virginal in its cleanness and wildly out of place.

Pinkerton bent and retrieved the paper. It had been carefully folded, twice. He opened it and read.

*My continued gratitude for helping bring*
*Poe to me. If you wish to remain free and*
*unconnected to his death, you must help*
*me take care of another man. I will again*
*pay you $20. I am staying in the same place.*
                    *LUDWIG*

Allan walked through the door and went up to the bar again. He flashed his badge and leaned forward so that the barman could not miss seeing the butt of his revolver protruding from his jacket. "About Duke Hewitt…"

"Yeah?"

"Were you holding a note, probably inside an envelope, for

him?"

"Not me."

"Then who was?"

"I didn't say anybody was," he said, gazing around his bar. "Hey, have a listen! Did anybody pass a note to Duke Hewitt when he come in?"

"Duke, who?" one of the group called back. Everyone laughed. Pinkerton was not especially surprised when no one took responsibility.

Allan leaned in toward the man behind the bar. "Does he keep a room in this tavern?"

The bald man's eyes glanced down at the exposed revolver butt. "I don't want trouble here."

"There won't be unless I'm provoked. Does he keep a room here?" Pinkerton repeated.

The barman smirked. "Like by the month?"

"Exactly."

"Duke can barely afford by the night."

"But he paid for tonight."

"Yeah, he paid for tonight."

Pinkerton made sure to swing his head right and left. No one in the crowded establishment had moved, but he had everyone's attention. To the bartender he said, "I need someone to take me up to his room. Someone with a key."

"Isaiah!" the barman called out, looking at an unlit alcove.

As if by magic, an old Negro man dressed in black materialized out of the deep shadows of the alcove and moved without haste toward the bar. He half supported himself on a well-worn broom.

The bartender tossed a ring of keys at the tavern's custodian.

"Room Four! Knock. If Duke don't answer, open it up for this copper."

As they climbed the stairs, Pinkerton said to the black man, "Duke Hewitt is a regular?"

"If he be the man I think you mean, he been coming here the past six weeks or so."

"Did you see him leave in the last hour?"

"I seen him come in tonight, come up here, come down and have a drink fast like. Then I seen nothing," Isaiah furnished. He led Pinkerton to a poorly made door and knocked. No reply came from inside. He knocked again and waited.

"Open it!" Pinkerton ordered.

The custodian obliged and stepped back.

The room was small and dark and exuded the faint odors of sweat and semen. The bed had been made and not disturbed. Atop the cover lay a sailor's duffel bag. Its neck was drawn tight. Jack Hewitt had dumped his belongings and taken off.

Pinkerton yanked open the bag and shook the sailor's belongings out. He searched for an envelope or any other slip of paper, but all he found was clothing, toiletries, a handkerchief with old blood on it, and a Hohner harmonica.

Shaking his head, Pinkerton exited into the narrow hallway. "Thank you for your trouble. Lock it up," he told the custodian. Without pause, he rattled down the stairs, strode across the saloon, and hurried out onto the wharf. The *Pocahontas* floated quietly at its berth. Only a single lantern hung on a main mast hook provided light. The gangplank had been pulled in.

"Ahoy!" Allan called out. "Ahoy the *Pocahontas*!"

Several shouts later, the packet's captain appeared, looking unhappy at having to answer the call.

"What did you forget?" he called back.

Pinkerton uncupped his hands. "Nothing. I need to speak with you about Jack Hewitt. I am a detective."

"Yeah, I caught a little of you and the two cops rousting those gents earlier," the captain, a man named Massey, nodded. "What's Hewitt done?"

"Lower the gangplank," Allan ordered.

Moments later, both men stood on the dock. Without comment, Pinkerton handed the captain the note.

"I found that among Mr. Hewitt's belongings," Allan said, to simplify the story. "How well do you know the man?"

Massey handed back the note. "As well as I need to. He walked up to the boat about two months ago, claiming to have crewed out of New York and Providence. I asked him to tie me a bowline, a sheet bend, and two half hitches. He did so straightaway. How much more can I demand of a man who receives four dollars for each round trip between here and Richmond?"

"He was part of your crew for the last month?"

"That's right. That and longer. You're tracking him down because of that piece of paper?"

"Do you understand the implications?" Pinkerton countered.

"Yeah. That he helped kill Edgar Allan Poe. I don't believe it."

"Did he spend money like the proverbial drunken sailor exactly one month ago?"

"The twenty dollars your note mentions? I have no idea. I don't hang with the man. Why didn't you arrest him in Richmond or right after we landed?"

Pinkerton tucked the note in his pocket. "I told you. I only just found this in Hewitt's belongings."

"And now he's gone, but he left his belongings behind," the captain sought to understand.

Pinkerton's eyes swept the dark silhouette of the Pocahontas. "Exactly. Now, I am relying on your captain's integrity that he is not onboard your vessel."

"Search below if you want. I never invite trouble with the law," vowed Massey. "My fortune depends on my mail contract."

"Then you will do yourself and everyone else involved a great service by not warning him and by notifying the police when he returns. I intend to show them this note right now. His detention will be worth that twenty dollars to whomever turns him in."

The packet captain said nothing, but Pinkerton could see that, as in every other corner of the world where he had walked, money spoke loudly.

"I had him. I had him!" Pinkerton ranted as he marched along West Pratt Street, Edgar Allan Poe's cane tucked under one arm and his valise swinging in long arcs from the speed of his stride. "Six hours. That's all it took in Richmond!" he yelled into the street, not caring who heard or thought him insane. "Two hours tonight. Ten minutes in Elgin."

A murder, seven house robberies, and a train boosting were what Pinkerton meant. He had solved and resolved all three crimes in less than half a day's worth of hours. But the mystery of Edgar Allan Poe's end he had not opened up enough in nine days to shed a thin crack of revelatory light on.

He would receive no monetary reward even if he did. The

money Edward Rucker had laid out and which he had supplemented was disappearing as if he had a hole in his pocket. The solutions of the murder in Richmond and the serial robberies in Baltimore would surely help Rucker in promoting him as the nation's most successful expert. *So,* he thought, through the anger that felt as if it would lift off the top of his skull, *why don't I just quit and go back to Chicago right now?*

And then his feet faltered. He set his valise on the sidewalk and looked down West Pratt. He could almost see the townhouse with the green door from where he stood. Molly Brannigan was there. Molly Brannigan, to whom he could do nothing more than gaze upon and listen. "Well," he said to himself, "at least I've done something for her tonight." With that thought, his anger and frustration drained away. He drew in a long, slow breath, retrieved the valise, and continued his walk.

When the green door opened, Allan received a reception that he never would have expected.

"My God!" Molly exclaimed. "I am so glad you're back! Come in, come in!" She fairly pulled him up the two steps and into the house. The moment she had the door closed, she threw her arms around the flabbergasted detective. "While you were gone, I was robbed!" she said, still holding herself tight against his coat.

Allan looked into the piles of beautiful red hair directly in his line of vision. "I know. I retrieved your yellow traveling chest."

Finally, Molly let go. She took a step back and regarded her houseguest with astonished eyes.

Allan set down the valise. "And your husband's scrimshaw.

And, I suspect your silverware and several other items as well."

Molly's next reaction was to collapse onto her turtleback chair. "How can this be?"

While he took off his coat and derby and then pulled the captain's chair in front of her and sat, he related the entire episode. All the while, Molly kept her hands on her knees and occasionally shook her head.

"Well, I must get down to that jail house first thing in the morning," she said, "because my pearl earrings, my rings, and my charm bracelet were stolen as well. One of those monsters came into my bedroom while I slept and took them. I feel utterly violated."

Allan glanced at Molly's left hand and saw that her engagement and wedding rings were missing. "When was this?"

"Two nights ago. I trembled all day, and last night I slept with a knife under my pillow. And the police made matters worse. They told me I was partly to blame. They found the kitchen window unlocked and partway opened. I was sure–"

"Idiots," Allan said. "Unless victims happen to leave a door or window open, this pair come in through an upper window. Most houses leave the upper windows open a crack for air circulation until the real cold sets in. You do this in your guest bedroom."

"That's correct."

"They had a folding ladder with them when I caught them. One enters from above, works those rooms, descends, and leaves a downstairs window open when he leaves. They were clever sons of perdition. They alternated nights between the rich part of town and here, to keep the police confused. I'll wager they rented a place not far from this house. What interests me is learning how they picked you to rob. Let me describe them to you."

While he went over every detail of each man's face, Molly excused herself to make a pot of tea and invited Allan to follow her into the kitchen. Even before he had finished describing the one who called himself Stroheim, Molly started jerking her head up and down.

"The chimney sweep," she said, and a light seemed to turn on in her eyes. "How stupid of me. He came to my door offering his services to clean the tar from our chimneys. Very cheeky. Put himself right on my front doorstep, and when I answered he took a step forward. I naturally stepped back and then held my ground. He pointed to the fireplace and delivered his pitch, but he was busy at the same time assessing our wealth."

"He was indeed," Allan agreed. "As you can no doubt verify, you and your husband are better off than most living on this block. Was this before the robberies began in this area?"

Molly thought. "Yes."

"Then don't be hard on yourself," Allan said.

"But I am," she replied. "He was the cleanest chimney sweep I had ever seen. I should have taken a good look at his fingernails." She patted Allan on the shoulder and gave the same shoulder a squeeze, and he wondered fleetingly through her welcome distraction why dirty fingernails meant something to him. "Well, I shall be a better detective from now on," she said with conviction.

Allan longed to toss off a wry remark about how Molly's lover failed either to protect her or to get her precious property back. But he knew it was none of his business, in spite of her hand on his shoulder.

"Enough about my trials and tribulations. Tell me about your adventures in Richmond," Molly invited.

Allan fetched one of the copies of the *Richmond Enquirer* from his valise. While Molly read, and cooed, and asked a barrage of questions, Allan took over the pouring and brewing of the tea and the setting out of cups and saucers. He glanced at little Siobhan, who slept peacefully in the floor cradle opposite the hearth. The warm, well-lit kitchen, the common routine of the tea preparation, and the back and forth with the woman dispelled every feeling of loneliness he had had. She insisted on bringing the tea and the remains of a batch of scones she had baked that afternoon into the parlor, trailing praise for her guest as she did.

When they were both seated at the table, Allan switched the topic to his continued investigation of Edgar Poe's unhappy end. Visit by visit, he spoke of the persons he had interviewed in Richmond. He told her about the $1,500 supposedly raised and missing. He omitted the reunion with Aaron Pelglade, because Molly had already heard of the whiskey drummer, and he did not want to have to lie about the amount of drinking he had done.

"Something is definitely wrong about the $1,500," Molly reasoned. "If having his own periodical was indeed Poe's fondest dream and if he had worked at it for almost a decade, he would not be so careless as to carry such a sum on his person. He knew the reputation of the street crime in Baltimore and New York. One only has to read their daily newspapers to know that. Since Richmond was to be his home and the home of the magazine, unless he was naive beyond reason he would have deposited everything except traveling and relocation money and the money he needed to purchase excellent new literature from those he admired."

Both in Scotland and the United States, Allan had dealt with many men who belittled women, who assured each other that smaller heads meant smaller brains and who judged the opposite sex merely by the shine of their tresses, the narrowness of their waists, and the generosity of their hips. Allan was not such a fool. In the past few days, he had been impressed by the Washington University Hospital nurse, Mrs. Lukauskis, who had prodigious powers of observation. But among all women he had ever met, Molly impressed him most.

He realized that she possessed two talents that preoccupied him: clear reasoning and deduction. He granted that if she was relieved of her day-to-day wifely duties and focused her attention purely on detective work, she might rival him. Certainly, her ability to capture information and retain it, as proven by her near-recollection of Rufus Griswold's name from a lecture delivered years earlier, far exceeded his. Molly did not scribble constantly into notebooks, and yet she grasped and then retained all the facts he had delivered to her about his Poe investigation. He told himself that before he left Baltimore he would praise her for her gifts, but now was not the best time.

Having avoided the subject as long as he could, Allan dug into his pocket and pulled out the folded piece of paper. He told Molly of the circumstances of finding it and how Jack "Duke" Hewitt, the likely key to solving the case, was missing. Then he handed her the note. She turned it toward the fire to read it, and her brows knit. She looked up at Allan with a pained expression.

"This must mean you, Allan. You are apparently the only one

still pursuing the truth behind Mr. Poe's death."

"I think you are right," he replied. He tried to take the note from Molly's hands, but she instead gripped his hand with her own and squeezed. He added, "The man must fear that I am closing in on him…although I have none of the confidence that he does. Maybe Hewitt fled without his belongings because he saw me with the policemen on the wharf. In which case, this opportunity was wasted."

"Good luck for me meant bad luck for you," Molly commented.

"Truly, one does win some and lose some," Allan answered. "If my presence gives you the slightest fear for your safety or that of Siobhan you must tell me, and I will leave directly."

"You will not!" Molly declared. "Not after saving my treasures for me. What sort of ingrate do you think I am?"

"One has nothing to do with the other," Allan said, folding his other hand over hers, so that it was captured. "You owe me nothing. It is I who owe you for trusting me from the beginning."

For an instant, Molly's lips tightened and her neck muscles worked up and down. Embarrassed, Allan, popped up from his chair and bounded to his valise. He opened it and pulled out the copy of Tales of the Grotesque and Arabesque, Volume Two.

"I have found another present for you. The companion to the book I bought you several days ago. But I warn you: the tales, at least in my opinion, are not very good. I think they are too macabre and bloody for a lady."

Molly smiled. "Oh, are all ladies faint of heart? Don't forget: Like Mr. Poe, I am Irish. We adore the macabre and the maudlin. And as far as blood is concerned, what other warriors in the world go into warp spasms before battle?"

Allan deemed the reference far too esoteric for his understanding. He realized that if, as a private detective, he expected to move in higher circles, a wider reading knowledge would be clearly be demanded. He knew that he had meant to say something else about the discovered note, and he searched his mind and found the fact.

"I believe I know who this Ludwig is," he shared.

Molly's blue eyes brightened. "Who?"

"The very same Rufus Griswold that you heard Poe excoriate in his lecture. Although, it would seem strange enough that a man who works in Philadelphia would have been in Baltimore a month ago to do harm to Poe."

"Not if Poe had communicated his itinerary to the literary world," Molly opined. "After all, you have said that he was on a deliberate tour from here to Philadelphia and to New York, to engage writers and to raise more subscriptions for his new periodical."

"Then why did Griswold not wait until Poe had reached Philadelphia?" Allan challenged, delighted to employ Molly's sharp mind to aid his reasoning.

"Because if Poe died in Philadelphia, suspicion would surely have fallen on him."

"You have a point," Allan allowed. "And now he returns to Baltimore from Philadelphia because I am asking many questions? How would he learn about my presence?"

Molly's eyes grew enormous. "How? Goodness gracious, I am a stupid woman! And I promised myself that it would be the first thing I related to you when you returned."

"What?"

"I told my closest friend, Winnifred Tucket, all about you, and wouldn't you know she was able to produce a copy of the *New York Sun*, dated October 12th. Her cousin collects various papers, rolls them up, and sends them inside brown paper each week. The *Sun* had a small article about you coming to Baltimore to investigate Mr. Poe's death!"

"How could that be?" Allan wondered. "I had not even begun investigating." He reached into his pocket for his ever-ready notebook. He consulted the first page. "Yes, I was still in transit."

"You confided in me that you have a lawyer backing you. Since your journey is just as much to promote your extraordinary skills as to solve Mr. Poe's death, would it not be that he released the information?"

"That's the only explanation that makes sense. I will telegraph Rucker tomorrow, directly after we reclaim your property," Allan decided. "Indeed, the *Sun* would publish an article like that. After all, they allowed Poe to convince them to publish his great balloon hoax."

"I don't not know of that," Molly confessed, "but if at least one newspaper in New York carried the article, why should one or more in Philadelphia not? In which case, Rufus Griswold would have known not only what your purpose was but also when you were arriving."

Allan gave her an admiring look. "All right, then, if you're so very smart, why would Poe call him Reynolds?"

"Perhaps that's the back end of his pseudonym: Ludwig Reynolds. Your friend, What's-his-name Pelglade, might know."

Allan swallowed the last of what he intended to be a first cup of tea. He had not found time for supper, and he thought the tea and the plate of scones might get him through the night until breakfast.

"No. Aaron would have picked up on that in Gunner's Hall." He snapped his fingers. "But Hewitt could have gone by the name Reynolds! If I can't find this sailor in the next day or two, I will certainly travel up to Phil–"

Siobhan suddenly launched into a series of petulant cries.

"That's the cry of a wet bottom," Molly said. She looked reluctant to leave Allan alone in the parlor.

"Thanks to your kindnesses, I know my way around your home," he said. "Do not neglect your daughter on my account."

Molly nodded, rose, and disappeared into the kitchen. Allan poured a second cup of tea and downed all three scones, listening to the young mother singing a lullaby softly to her child.

# CHAPTER FIFTEEN

*Wednesday, October 24, 1849*

Allan snapped awake from the sound of his bedroom door hinges barely squeaking. In spite of the reassurances he had made to Molly Brannigan only hours before, he was so perplexed by his investigation of Poe's death that he had no idea if they were safe or not. Before lying down, he had hung his shoulder holster over the left-side bedpost. It was a single-motion matter for him to reach across with his right hand, draw out the revolver, swing back with his thumb on the hammer, and point it at the door.

"Allan?" The voice belonged to Molly.

Allan lowered the weapon. "What's the matter?"

In answer, the door swung fully open and Molly entered. He could just barely make out the solid shape of her within the gloom of the room. She came to the edge of the bed, and he waited for her to speak. Instead, she reached down with both hands for the hem of her nightgown. He saw the movement and heard the rustle of fabric. She let it slip to the floor, and he knew that she stood naked.

"Don't speak," Molly said. She sat on the mattress and reached for the covers.

As she did, Allan placed the revolver in its holster. When Molly relaxed backward, she met with the crook of his elbow. She turned her head and kissed his upper arm.

Allan's excitement was already evident by the time she pivoted fully against his flank and slid her fingertips up his thigh to where it joined his torso. He felt the weight and warmth of her breasts against his ribs.

Molly adjusted her position and moved up so that her lips found his. Because she had come to him, he allowed her to dictate. He felt the lightness of her kiss, the playful teasing of it.

And then, while her right hand moved lower and worked its magical ministrations, she began to kiss his face all over. She pursed her lips and drew his flesh slightly into her mouth. Then she found his mouth again and explored it with the tip of her tongue.

Allan was helpless to resist such determination and skill, even if he had wanted to. He gathered Molly into his arms and planted passionate kisses everywhere he could reach, while he ran his fingers through her thick hair, stroking, petting. The woman began to make purring noises. She insinuated herself under his strong frame, adjusting herself so that he was fully on top of her, with her legs winging out, inviting.

"Don't worry," she said in a whisper. "This is my safe time of the month." Immediately, she stretched her hands down the small of his back, reaching for his buttocks, to guide him into her and to dictate the motion that she favored.

Allan had long since abandoned thought. Guilt had no place. He moved from pure passion and need. He entered the magnificent female and took his pleasure, even as he strove to use every one of his senses to learn how most to please her.

They thrust and pitched and grunted and sweated to a mutual, mind-numbing climax. Then he collapsed upon her and shuddered involuntarily as she continued to stroke and kiss him. Even after his ragged breath had returned to normal he lay without moving, waiting for Molly for tell him what to do.

"Again," she whispered.

When Allan awoke for a second time, Molly had left the bedroom. The faint rays of dawn reflected into his window, above a world still in shadow. He knew that his very first thought, which was of the captain's wife, would lead to a successive chain that could not possibly allow more sleep.

Allan moved to the window and gave a casual glance outside. Immediately, his head jerked around, and he stared at the dark figure he saw in the Brannigan back yard. It was that of a good-sized man. The figure made no noise and was moving toward the back door. In his right hand was what looked like an ax.

Allan grabbed his nightshirt and yanked it on. Climbing directly across the bed, he snatched his holster on the move. Molly had closed the door. He threw it back and raced down the steps. When he reached the parlor, he heard the house's back door open. The parlor fire was little more than glowing embers, and the room lay in near-total darkness. Allan took two more steps forward and cocked the revolver.

"Stand where you are!" he commanded in his riveting baritone.

Something fell to the kitchen floor.

Upstairs, Siobhan began to wail.

"I'm pointing a gun directly at you!" Allan warned.

"I'm not moving," the male voice assured him through the portal.

Allan shuffled cautiously forward. The coals in the kitchen hearth gave more illumination. It was just enough for him to make out the image of the good-looking man who he had seen leaving through the Brannigan's front door the Thursday before.

"I'm Glenn Burton," the man said. He held his hands up, and they were trembling. "I help Mrs.–"

"What is happening?" Molly demanded, coming down the steps with her crying daughter over her shoulder.

"Good morning, Molly," Burton said, sheepishly.

With that greeting, Allan understood exactly who the man was and how foolish he had been in jumping to conclusions.

"Glenn," Molly said. Even in the gloom, Allan could see that she was flustered and struggling to maintain her calm. She kissed the child and joggled it lightly.

Hammer uncocked, Allan lowered the revolver. "You help Mrs. Brannigan with the heavy chores."

Mr. Burton merely nodded.

"I believed it would be comforting to have a detective lodging under my roof, given the robbery," Molly said to Burton. "Perhaps not always."

Burton stopped to pick up the short-handled ax he had dropped. "I'm afraid I put a gouge in your floor."

"Don't mind that," said Molly. "It will give Shamus something to do when he's home other than bothering me. He's dropped several things in here. Allan Pinkerton, this is Glenn Burton and vice versa. Detective, meet handyman."

While she spoke, the man Allan had supposed was Molly's lover set the ax on the kitchen counter, reached for a box of "lucifer" matches, and brought an oil lamp to glowing life.

"I forgot my whetstone to sharpen the ax," Burton explained to his neighbor. "I figured to borrow yours rather than go home."

"Of course," Molly allowed.

While they talked, Allan took a good look at Glenn Burton. He wondered if it was that he was obsessed with thoughts of Edgar Allan Poe or if the handyman actually looked like the writer. Allan judged him to be five foot ten, an inch taller than Poe had been. He also had the slightly down-turned eyes that gave Poe a lugubrious look in the photograph Allan had viewed in Dr. Carter's study. Allan had already seen that Burton was thin on the previous Thursday, as well as noting the fact that the man had a high forehead, aided by pronounced baldness on his crown.

"Hush, Siobhan!" Molly encouraged to her whimpering baby. "Why don't the three of us put some decent clothes on while you sharpen your ax, Mr. Burton? Then we should sit down to breakfast, and Detective Pinkerton will tell you how he solved the robberies plaguing our city."

Glenn Burton did the man's work around the house during Captain Shamus Brannigan's absences, and Mrs. Burton minded Siobhan whenever Molly needed to shop or to socialize. Without the baby, Molly and Allan were able to travel quickly, arriving by hack at the city court and jailhouse as the day employees arrived. Molly signed a document pressing charges against the two burglars and stated that she would testify as to the visit of the German in the guise of chimney-sweep and the taking of her property.

"You can claim your jewelry and silverware," the property clerk said, "but the lady's chest and the scrimshaw must remain as evidence."

Molly did not complain, although Allan could see that leaving the two items behind pained her. He watched with his own slight pain and discomfort as she fitted her wedding and engagement rings onto her finger. As she and Allan were leaving the office, two other sets of aggrieved victims arrived.

The clerk who had handed over the property called out, "Oh, might you be Detective Pinkerton?"

Allan pivoted. "I am."

"Magistrate Foster said that he wished to speak with you if you came in. He might have arrived by now." The clerk gave directions to the top floor.

The building had only been constructed two decades earlier, around the time John Quincy Adams was visiting Baltimore and giving it the name the Monument City. Nevertheless, the structure had suffered the city's exponential growth and had walls opened and doors moved. Molly and Allan climbed, meeting dead ends and reversing themselves.

Allan mused how the search for the chief magistrate's office was a good metaphor for his Poe investigation. At one point Molly led the way. As she turned up a flight of steps and gripped the banister, the charm bracelet that she had fastened around her wrist tinkled softly.

"It is quite a handsome piece," Allan admired.

"More importantly, it has considerable sentimental value," Molly said. She raised her wrist for inspection. "The windmill was purchased by Shamus when he was in Amsterdam. The shoe he brought me from Paris and the theater mask from London. They are promises from him that he will show me these places once our children are old enough to travel. The heart was Winnifred's gift when Siobhan was born."

They found William Foster's office without further trouble. The walls were decorated with several lithographs of patriotic scenes. From a vase sitting on a delicate display stand, blossoms of Joe Pye Weed, Goldenrod, and Sneezeweed burst in abundance like fireworks on the Fourth of July. Foster glanced up from his desk and sprang from behind it when he recognized Allan. Pinkerton introduced Molly and asked that special care be taken to protect her stolen belongings.

"Whatever you may desire from the city of Baltimore will be my pleasure to satisfy," said the chief magistrate. "Your presence investigating Mr. Poe's death has been gift enough, but to have solved the many burglaries in one fell swoop is more than anyone could expect."

"Nevertheless, I am at an impasse over this Poe business," Allan admitted. "Can you spare me ten minutes so that I can tell you what I have learned?"

"Please!" Foster beamed at the detective's companion. Allan knew that Molly's beguiling presence in the magistrate's office guaranteed an extra five minutes if he required it. When Molly interrupted softly to remind him of an important fact Allan had omitted, Foster's face showed that he, too, was capable of admiring her for her brains and well as her beauty.

In conclusion, Pinkerton handed over the note he had found behind the Tavern on the Wharf and allowed Foster to read it. Then he described Jack Hewitt in detail, which the official copied down.

"I will see that this is delivered to every man under my command."

"He is an itinerant," Allan said. "So my guess is that he would be in a gin palace, a cheap hotel, or haunting the harbor area, looking for a ship. By now, he should know that I found the note meant for him alone. If I were he, I would hie myself out of Baltimore as quickly as possible."

"Do you have any idea who this Ludwig is?" Foster asked.

"I do. And I will see to that myself."

Foster put up his hands in a pleading manner. "I'm sorry to say I'm happy to hear that. We are perpetually strained to perform the policing duties of our burgeoning city as it is."

Pinkerton asked, "And you have heard nothing from any sources about a person named Reynolds or more about the possibility that Mr. Poe was gotten intoxicated for the express purpose of cooping?"

Again, Foster made the same gesture. "Unlike Chicago, we have no detective. I have asked my men to make inquiries, but no one has yet come forth."

Pinkerton wrote the Brannigans' address down on the back of his calling card and handed it to the chief magistrate. "You can find me through this kind lady," he said. He saw that Foster's attention had become stuck on the "kind lady."

"Shall we be off, Mrs. B?" he asked.

"We shall," she agreed.

Both men watched her glide from the office.


Molly and Allan walked down North Charles Street toward Pratt and the Inner Harbor. Lexington Market, one of the largest shopping venues in the New World and with as many as 600 wagons converging on market days, catered primarily to commonplace needs. The great city of Baltimore, however, was big enough and rich enough to have its own specialty shopping districts.

As a harbor city, it supported dozens of ships' chandleries, naval stores, commodity brokers, and underwriters businesses along the wharves. North Charles Street was a hodgepodge of caterers to higher society: musical instruments, millinery, wigs, travel items, purveyors of porcelain, and the like. Even to the most hard-pressed of individuals, the temptation was to slow the pace and peek into each passing store. However, compared to other women moving along the sidewalk, Molly was positively tarrying. Allan suspected that being a mother had made the young matron into more of a homebody than she liked.

After she registered aloud the many desirous items in a shop that specialized in buttons, hooks, ribbons, and bows, Molly said to Allan, "You have had several opportunities to mention last night, but you have not taken them."

"I..." Pinkerton swallowed and tried again.

"It is complicated for you," Molly said, turning from him for a moment to look in a shop window.

"Very."

"Because you are married and I am married."

"Those are two of the reasons."

Molly said, "Can you tell me with absolute honesty that you have never had an affair before?"

"Never!" Pinkerton said with fervor. "My wife is the only woman I have ever lain with...until..."

"Mr. Brannigan is the only other man but one who I have known." Molly consulted the sky. "I want you to understand how special you are to me, Allan."

"I cannot begin to tell you how deeply I feel about you," he returned.

"Even so, I cannot say unequivocally that you three will be the only men I sleep with my entire life. Mr. Brannigan does not take his vows of "forsaking all others" as sacrosanct. I have found a blue garter that was not my own hidden in the lining of his sea trunk, along with a small packet of love letters to him, dated several months after our marriage. But this does not justify my behavior last night."

"What does?" Allan needed to know, considering the matter-of-fact tone of voice Molly was using.

"I know that marriage is ever so much more than physical passion. In fact, if that is all there is in a marriage, it is eventually doomed. The Germans are a pragmatic people. They have a famous saying: 'Love fades. Good cooking lasts.'"

"They also say a woman's place is 'church, kitchen and children,'" Allan responded.

"That saying is not nearly as wise," Molly judged. "Marriage should not be entered into lightly. However, at a certain age one must dive into the matrimonial sea or risk being a dry spinster all one's life. I do not believe in divorce. I do believe that the day after you marry you may turn a corner and meet the man of your fondest passions. In that case, the answer is to satisfy your passions, then return to your marriage and never look back."

"So, along with temperance, universal education and the vote for women, you believe in free love."

"Love is never free," Molly replied. "I will pay a price for last night, as will you. If you are wise, you will do your penance in private and manage the memory in silence. Do you regret that it happened?"

"I don't know," Allan said. "I am still pondering it." He came to a halt, compelling her to stop as well. "But it was the most wonderful night of my life. I am more grateful than I can ever express, knowing that I am special to you."

"That you are." Molly started off again. "I would like to hold your hand right now, but appearances count for so much in this small-minded world. Have you ever heard of the Brehon laws?"

"No."

"They were the most ancient laws of Ireland. Even the kings

were bound by them. The Irish were more enlightened fourteen-hundred years ago than all of Europe and America today. The lowest clansman stood on equal legal footing with the king. Women had the same rights of property and education as men. In marriage, a woman was an equal and not property. Women might serve in the armies and could even lead. But the reason I mention this most enlightened set of laws is that these ancient people recognized that life is a journey in which everyone changes. Marriage was absolutely sacred. If you committed adultery while married you were put to death. However, if the couple agreed that the relationship no longer benefited them, they could formally declare a parting of the ways. No crime. No sin. I wonder how we became so stupid in fourteen-hundred years."

Molly regarded the wares in another shop. "Oh, that material is exactly what I am looking for!" She turned to Allan. "I know you must continue your search. I will expect you at six for supper."

"If I am not there, it will be because of more good luck," he told her, while privately he thought it could just as easily be very bad fortune, the kind that killed a man.

Molly dipped her head in a formal manner. "Then good morning to you, Mr. Pinkerton."

"And to you, Mrs. Brannigan."

By the time Pinkerton straightened up, Molly had disappeared into the shop.

The remainder of the day Pinkerton spent walking the wharves. He reasoned that a sailor such as Hewitt would seek to escape via the means by which he could also earn a living. He found that both the *Pocahontas* and the *Fleetwind* had departed the city. He purchased a newspaper and read about every ship entering or leaving the harbor, so that he might differentiate them from the idle ones and those being built or rebuilt. Baltimore was the second most important harbor in the country, the home of the world-famous Baltimore clippers that could outrace anything else on the seas and which had been outfitted by privateers for the War of 1812 and had captured more than a quarter of all the ships lost by the British. Off toward Fells Point, half a dozen of their number were being built. Closer by, Allan had to deal with watching several dozen viable ships.

At least once each hour Allan moved his location, every time staking out the widest possible view from a new vantage point. As he stood or sat idle, he alternated between scanning his surroundings and consulting his notebook. He decided to sift the few grains of wheat from the piles of chaff he had gathered. Very little was certain and verifiable.

Poe had left Richmond around midnight on September 27th, onboard the *Pocahontas*. That he had arrived safely to Baltimore was proven by the fact that the next morning he had called on Dr. Nathan Covington Brooks, who was out of town. Whoever had met him at the end of the wharf had done him no immediate harm.

At the time he called on Dr. Brooks, he was sober. And then he disappeared for four days. For a man so well known, precious few souls had seen him in the city. He was found outside Gunner's Hall, carrying Dr. Carter's cane and wearing rags. He did not smell of alcohol. By the time he reached the hospital, if not much earlier, he had lost his billfold and any money he had carried. However, he hung on to the cane as if it were a lifeline. He acted as if he were drunk or damaged in some mental manner, but he was able to think and speak clearly enough to summon Dr. J. E. Snodgrass, who rushed to the place with Henry Herring, Poe's uncle. The men got nothing from him but a name that sounded like Reynolds. Likewise, in the hospital he repeated several times and on several occasions what sounded like the name Reynolds.

Poe died at five o'clock in the morning, on Sunday, October 3rd, after days of semi-coherent rantings but without ever regaining total consciousness. It was, Pinkerton decided, a mystery beyond even the wildest imaginings of the victim himself.

At five o'clock, Pinkerton made a desperate visit to the Tavern on the Wharf. No one had seen Duke Hewitt. Nor had he returned to claim his belongings. The offer of a ten-dollar reward for information produced no reaction. Allan exited through the back door. Holding his nose, he used the last of the strong October daylight to inspect every inch of ground for any clue he might have missed the night before. He found nothing. Unbuttoning his fly, he was happy to leave the contents of his bladder with the rest of the waste.

Molly and Allan dined with Siobhan lying in her cradle beside them. Molly had fashioned a feast of breaded veal topped with a fried egg, wedges of cheese, snap beans, carrots, and rye bread. The memory of Molly's post-midnight guest room visit hung over the table like an intoxicating perfume, subtly changing the content of the conversation and the tones of their voice. In the private confines of four closed walls, she was able to touch his hand and forearm with loving pressure. *For all the world,* Allan thought in amazement, *this is the image of a happy husband and wife at supper. How she can carry this off without apparent guilt is beyond me.*

"To my mind, there is only one explanation for why Mr. Poe would not be seen for four days," Molly declared. "He was rendered incapable of controlling his own actions and confined, most probably within the limits of the city."

"I concur," Allan said, again admiring Molly's reasoning skills. He concealed a belch and added, "I had a revelation while walking back here. I had been cursing the fact that nearly every other investigation I have conducted has been so much easier than this one. Certainly the murder in Richmond and the theft of your belongings were. And then I realized that all the other instances were crimes of the hand: the boosting of a wallet, a stab with a knife, the raising of a window. But this is a crime of the mind. It is not a mere robbery or a cooping."

"No," Molly agreed. "It is the business with the replaced clothing that proves that."

"Exactly. And this is why I absolutely must visit this character Rufus Griswold in Philadelphia. The reason is not just the name 'Ludwig' in capital letters on that note; it is the obvious enmity expressed in the obituary he wrote."

"He may not, in fact, be in Philadelphia," Molly interjected. "You may travel up there and learn from someone that he is now in Baltimore. And that would virtually condemn him." She set her napkin down on the table. "Yes, sad as I will be to have you leave again, you must go."

Allan had a sudden image of gathering her into his arms and sweeping her onto his lap, where he would cover her face in kisses. It was what he burned to do. But Molly had initiated their intimacy, and she had defined her motivations and limits. *I lack her courage*, he thought, *or, perhaps, her recklessness*.

Molly sighed and smiled at Allan. "Dear man," she said, rising from her seat and moving to the kitchen. "English or Irish tea?" she asked.

Allan realized that he had not once craved alcohol since setting foot inside the house with the green door. Molly Brannigan was a far more powerful intoxicant.

The bedroom hinges complained faintly, just as they had the night before. This time, however, Allan had been fully awake. He discerned that this time Molly had removed her nightdress before entering the room. She moved with sure motions to the bed and drew back the covers.

"Hello," she said, softly.

"Hello," he replied.

Immediately, Molly straddled Allan. She bent to kiss him, letting her breasts graze his chest hairs. Then she straightened up, reached behind her, and took him in her hand. He realized that she meant to couple with him from the top, what he had heard described as 'riding a St. George.'

"I can't," he told her, finally knowing his mind.

Molly's hand stopped moving. "Have you never had your wife from below?" she inquired.

"I have not," he confessed.

"Do you think this is too salacious?"

In reply, Allan reached up under Molly's armpits and swung her off him, to lie prone on the mattress. "Anything you might do could only be deliriously splendid. But I am not of the same mind as you on this. If we continue to make love, you will become addictive to me. I will find myself pleading for you to leave your husband. You will reject me, and I will become disconsolate. Or perhaps you will succumb to my relentless overtures, and you, I, Joan and Shamus will all be ruined. I cannot put the physical act in a little yellow chest and open and close it when I wish."

"Then you want me to leave," Molly said, after an awkward silence.

"No, I do not," Allan answered. "I want to hug and kiss you and to have you lie beside me all night, as the fondest childhood friend might do. But that is as much as I can endure."

Molly gave out a little, wistful sound. "So, now the rules are to be yours, are they?"

"I can walk no farther down the path you have set us on."

Molly wriggled under the covers and fitted herself to Allan's length. "Very well. I accept this innocent sinning." Her hand stole to his chest and began to curl the hairs into little knots. She planted a light kiss on his shoulder. "But if you change your mind, do not neglect to wake me."

# CHAPTER SIXTEEN

*Thursday, October 25, 1849*

Among his many talents, Allan Pinkerton could set his mind as others could set a twin-bell alarm clock. He himself had no idea how he did it, but if he needed to arise at six in the morning, he would invariably open his eyes between five fifty-five and five minutes after six, even if he had had only two hours' sleep. So it was on the morning he wished to go to Philadelphia.

When he rolled over, he remembered instantly that Molly had gotten up sometime around four to breast-feed her daughter. She had not returned. He wondered if she had realized how awkward these very moments would be and had elected to avoid them. He climbed out of the warm and comfortable bed and went to the washbasin to cleanse his body.

Try as he might, Allan could not dress or pack his valise without sound. In fact, as he lifted the valise to carry it downstairs, it banged noisily against the brass bedpost. He winced when he heard Molly's bedroom door open. A moment later, he heard a soft knock.

"What time does the train leave?" Molly whispered, after opening the door a crack.

"Nine o'clock," he replied.

"Good morning, Mr. Pinkerton."

"Good morning, Mrs. Brannigan."

Molly opened the door all the way. She stood in her nightdress, her rich tresses wild and, therefore, utterly enchanting and arousing to Allan. "Then you'll have time to take breakfast."

"I will."

Molly crooked her finger. "I want you to see something." She backed across the narrow hallway into the other bedroom.

Allan followed.

"Stop at the threshold!" Molly said, in a soft but urgent tone. "It was terrible having that thief invade the sanctity of this room. I must be able to tell my husband truthfully that no other man has ever set foot in his bedroom."

Once again, Molly was establishing a rule. This one especially bewildered and perplexed Allan. Molly Brannigan had allowed, had in fact invited the most private of intimacies with him, and yet he could not step quickly in and out of a space that would never tell of his presence and never be altered by him. But Allan understood the power of symbols, so he made no comment.

While he thought, Molly lit a whale-oil hurricane lamp and set it down on the dresser. She pointed proudly to a bookcase that was positioned close to the door but angled so that Allan could see the books in it.

"Our collection," Molly said, whispering so that Siobhan would not awaken. "The ones on the top shelf belong to Shamus. Mostly nautical, you see. The rest are mine."

Allan registered two cookbooks, a sewing primer, several histories, and a book of prayers. The rest, numbering around twenty, were novels and anthologies.

From the middle shelf, Molly drew a narrow publication, more a thick pamphlet than a book. She handed it to Allan.

"I did a bit more shopping than the fabric store," she said, referring to her post-jailhouse foray of the previous day. "It's a traveling present for you."

For a moment, Allan was transfixed by Molly's pleased expression. Then she gestured for him to read the cover.

"Franklin's Popular Tales," she read for him, shaking her

head with disapproval. "I love how the truly unscrupulous ones put a famous man's name as the editor, to borrow that authority as boldly as they steal the stories inside. I really shouldn't have provided whoever it is an income, but it was so perfect for you."

Allan opened the cover and read the contents. Inside, four of Edgar Allan Poe's stories had been reprinted. They were "The Pit and the Pendulum," "The Cask of Amontillado," "The System of Doctor Tarr and Professor Fether" and "The Gold-Bug."

"It just arrived on Tuesday," Molly shared. "That's American industry for you. A man isn't dead a month, and the living are growing fat on his remains. But it is so perfect a gift, don't you think?"

In that moment, looking into the glowing, happy face of Molly Brannigan, Allan had a revelation. *This is true love*, he realized. *The unselfish compulsion to give.*

Molly blinked, and her expression changed to one of surprise. "Your eyes are tearing," she said.

"Oh. It's hay fever," Allan prevaricated. "I get it in the morning this time of year."

"I see." Molly pulled her right hand back into the sleeve of her nightdress so that she could capture the hem and turn it into a makeshift handkerchief. She gently daubed at the corners of Allan's eyes.

"I get that sometimes, too," she offered.

The distance from West Pratt and Greene Streets to the terminal depot of the Philadelphia, Wilmington, and Baltimore Railroad was more than a comfortable walk. Moreover, due to the early departure of the train, Allan elected to take a cab. The weather was overcast and dank, and if he had to travel he figured this was as good a day to do it as any. He and Molly had parted fondly after breakfast, again as if they were a comfortable couple. He frankly did not know what to make of the woman or her liberal philosophies, but she was the flame to his moth. He knew he would return for as long as his money held out. Allan figured he had no more than five days before needing to get back onto a Baltimore and Ohio train. Either the trip to Philadelphia would yield something monumental, or else he would have to settle on his triumphs in the Linden Row Inn and on the Baltimore wharf as justification for the sizable outlay of Edward Rucker's cash.

The PW&B's ticket window sat not far from the tracks, and while Allan stood in the line he watched one of the awe-inspiring engines backing up to connect with the passenger cars. It had four leading "pilot truck" wheels and four driver wheels, a long boiler, and a towering smokestack with spark suppressor. The engineer leaned out from the controls, far above the track.

"Next!" the ticket clerk called out.

Allan turned from watching the behemoth machine and moved to the window. "One way to Philadelphia."

"Yes, sir."

"Do you know anything about the writer Edgar Allan Poe taking this train in late September?"

"I heard something about it," the man said. "But the stationmaster is the one you need to speak with." He jerked his head back. "His office is on the opposite side of this building."

Pinkerton hunted down the man, who was not in his office but after further search was found in the baggage storage area.

"Nobody in our entire company knows anything," the man said, looking exasperated. "But everyone outside apparently does! We've read that he got on without a ticket and rode all the way to Philadelphia drunk. Then we were supposed to have shipped him all the way back here. Another said he got off at the Havre du Grace stop. Another one said we have his trunk in storage. Listen, mister, as far as we know he got on no PW&B train."

Pinkerton thanked the man and returned to the track where the morning run to Philadelphia was being prepared. The indisputable facts were that Edgar A. Poe was in Baltimore on September 28th and in Baltimore on the morning of October 3rd. Allan was confident that at least one employee would officially have come forward if some bizarre occurrence on their line was connected with the death of a famous man.

Alternately, Pinkerton knew human nature well enough to understand that if ten persons actually witnessed a notorious event, within hours one hundred would claim to have been there. Like Dr. Moran from the hospital, a great percentage of the population would gladly lie if it meant they could borrow the limelight. A drunk in a black suit had probably gotten on a northbound run, and, upon learning of Poe's death days later, other passengers assumed in retrospect that he was the one.

Allan shifted his valise from one hand to the other. As he did, he thought he saw the top half of the figure of a man in dark clothing staring at him from around the corner of the depot's main building. When he turned fully, the figure was not there. He jogged to the place where he thought the man had stood and looked about. He saw several men wearing dark suits, either waiting or moving with purpose. Not one glanced at him or seemed interested in his presence. More importantly, he recognized none of them.

"All aboard!" the conductor cried out. The engineer reinforced the imminent departure by tooting his locomotive's steam whistle.

Allan climbed onto the train, praying that he would not spot any criminal games.

The train sped along on the relatively flat terrain of Maryland, offering splendid views of the turning autumn leaves. When the panoramas proved too repetitive, Allan would take out Molly's gift and read one of Poe's short stories. The slowest leg of the journey came when they reached the wide Susquehanna River and were forced to detrain and ferry across to another iron horse. He overheard someone saying that the railroad would soon transport an entire train across the river on a ferry. Allan had no doubt that even such a mighty river would be bridged within his lifetime. In spite of several stops, the longest at Wilmington, the train arrived in Philadelphia in the middle of the afternoon, giving Allan hope he could at least locate Dr. Rufus Griswold's place of residence, determine for certain if the man was in fact in Philadelphia, and make an appointment to interview him.

Pinkerton arrived on Printer's Row at four thirty. After a few abortive stops, he was finally directed to *Graham's Magazine*. Allan counseled himself the moment he set foot on the street that he needed to discard all his preconceived negative notions about the writer of Poe's national obituary. He hoped that at least one person from the staff remained who could direct him to Rufus Griswold. To his delight, he found the magazine's editor still at work. He was ushered into Griswold's office by an assistant editor and was greeted like a conquering hero.

"Mr. Pinkerton! You are the detective from Chicago investigating the death of Edgar Allan Poe!"

Allan was unprepared for the man who rose to greet him. He had expected a person of at least fifty years of age, ponderous, grey, and heavyset. Instead, Griswold looked fit and in his mid thirties, considerably healthier than Poe had looked at that age. He wore a fringe beard that was completely brown. His hair was wild, as if he had spent the day running his fingers through it. His smile was gentle and his eyes large. He had a high forehead, long nose and arched eyebrows. Pinkerton's immediate assessment was "pleasant of demeanor and appearance." He worked with his jacket on, and he sported a black bow tie at least as ostentatious as that Poe had worn. Allan wondered if such pieces of apparel were common affectations among the literary class.

"My reputation outstrips my accomplishments," Pinkerton said in a self-effacing manner.

Griswold made a florid sweep with his hand, indicating the chair beside his desk. "Not according to what has been written about you."

"I have not seen the article," Allan replied. "However, I refer to my lack of forward motion in this Poe business."

"And how do you think I may be of assistance in providing forward motion?" Griswold obliged.

Succinctly, Pinkerton focused on the finding of Poe in clothing he literally would not have been caught dead in and how this pointed to a guilty party with animus against him.

"Do you think I am a likely suspect?" Griswold asked with doubt.

"Have you satisfied anyone in law enforcement that you

were nowhere near Baltimore from September 28th to October 3rd?"

Griswold shook his head. "Well, that's certainly blunt enough. And you wonder why you have not moved forward?" He rose from his chair. "I will deign to answer your questions provided as restitution you take me to the finest dining establishment in this part of town and buy me dinner and a drink."

A drink did not sound bad. He had not touched alcohol since leaving Aaron Pelglade on the *Pocahontas*. Molly Brannigan's scintillating company and her intimate attentions had more than substituted for drink; but now that she was hours away, the thirst was on him again.

Allan stood as well. "I accept your offer with gratitude. I am sorry to have been so blunt, but at the same time I have too much respect for your intellect, sir, to have feigned other than my agenda."

"Well spoken!" Griswold fetched his hat and coat from the coat tree standing just behind his door. He took a step toward the door, remembered something, grabbed several pieces of paper from his desk, and reversed himself. "Peterson!"

"Yes, Mr. Griswold?"

"This is far enough along that you can finish it. Then you may go home." His tone was imperious.

Peterson accepted the sheets. "I shall."

"Charles Peterson of Philadelphia, Allan Pinkerton from Chicago. Where was I between September 28th and October 3rd, Peterson?" Griswold demanded of his assistant editor.

The thin, nervous-looking young man started slightly at the question. "September…Why, you were here, Mr. Griswold."

"In Philadelphia?" the magazine editor delved.

"Certainly in Philadelphia. But I meant here at the magazine. Morning to night. You have not missed a day since late August."

Griswold spun to face Pinkerton. "And how is that for impromptu honesty? *Andiamo*, Mr. Pinkerton!" he said with élan, striding toward the front door and leaving the detective and the assistant editor staring at each other.

In the City Tavern, Rufus Griswold ordered a double bourbon. Allan ordered ale brewed to a George Washington formula, hoping that he would be satisfied by just one glass.

"Most venerable of buildings! This is where the Founding Fathers retired to refresh themselves during the various Continental Congresses," the editor imparted, speaking over the clavichord music that wafted from the large room opposite the central hallway. "Don't leave the City of Brotherly Love without visiting Independence Hall or Ben Franklin's grave, sir."

"I will endeavor to play the tourist for at least a few hours," Allan said, as he consulted his notebook and began stroking his beard. "I first heard your name in association with a lecture delivered by Mr. Poe in Baltimore. January of 1844."

"My, you have gathered information," Griswold exclaimed. "Yes, he delivered that same lecture on the state of fiction writing in America in several cities. As I heard it, for all his imagined fame he was only able to command twenty-five cents a head." A slight sneer swept across the editor's face.

"He did not have good things to say about a work you had written," Allan said, poking the man with a verbal stick.

Griswold seemed unprovoked. "My critical anthology, *The Poets and Poetry of America*. It has been so well received that I am right now working on the second revised edition. Three printings in all. And that success is precisely what galled Eddie."

"Not some of the selections of poets and story writers you made?" Allan asked.

"That was his stated objection. But jealousy was behind his remarks. How well do you think you know Edgar Allan Poe, Mr. Pinkerton?"

"I did not know him at all when I began investigating two weeks ago," Allan admitted. "But I believe I am getting as good a sense of him as I can get."

"Then let me enlighten you as only someone who knew him intimately can. And pardon me if I cover aspects of this complicated man's life of which you're already aware. You must know he came from poor theatrical stock but lucked into a life of privilege."

"I would hardly call losing one's father and mother in quick succession luck," Allan rejoined.

Griswold was unfazed by the reply. "It should have been greater luck than he made of it, but he insisted on living life his own way, with no accommodations to those who lavished love, money, and education on him. The first thing that should be made crystal clear to you is that Edgar Poe was a lifelong ingrate."

"Why is that?" Pinkerton asked, taking first a long sip of his ale and then applying pencil to pad.

Griswold imitated Pinkerton's motion and swallowed an even bigger gulp of liquor. "Because he was absolutely convinced that he was a genius and that the world owes geniuses not only fame but fortune."

"Do you not think your friend was a genius?" Pinkerton challenged. Watching Griswold's Adam's apple work up and down, he hit upon a plan. If he could keep the writer talking long enough to get several more drinks into him, the alcohol would surely loosen his tongue and free up inhibitions. Truth did not only come from wine. He caught the eye of the waiter and gestured for refills.

"Absolutely, Eddie was one of a kind. That is the main reason I endured him. But having great literary gifts should not excuse bad behavior. He was shamefully spoiled by his foster mother...as only a woman who can't have her own children will do."

"Shouldn't John Allan's demanding nature have counterbalanced that?" Allan asked.

"No. It made his wife all the more sheltering and forbearing."

Griswold rested his elbow on the table, curled his three smallest fingers against the angle of his chin, and stretched his forefinger toward his temple. It was, as the conversation wore on, an obvious habit.

"What say you to the both of us eating here?" Griswold said with sudden emphasis. "You may have my company for as long as you like if you will buy me a good cut of beef."

Pinkerton willingly agreed to the editor's terms. He picked up a menu and then said, "Is there no wife, no children, wanting for you at home?"

"My first wife died very young," Griswold said. "My second wife and I are separated and, in fact, contemplating divorce." While his tone seemed matter-of-fact, rather than allow a moment for his interrogator to ask another domestic question, he added, "Another important thing for you to understand is that Eddie adored being considered a genius, but if anyone else got half the attention for similar merit, he was jealous beyond reason. That is the problem I faced, time and again."

"You are something of a genius then," Pinkerton said.

"Others, not I, have used the term. But I will say that I have gotten to where I stand not by having the benefits of travel and private education lavished upon me, as Poe had. I grew up on a farm in Rutland, Vermont. My parents recognized my talents and sacrificed that I might be as exposed to les belles-lettres as anyone else in rural America. I earned the 'Dr.' in front of my name by becoming a Baptist minister." Griswold finished his first drink.

The waiter arrived with the second round. "Keep them coming," Allan told the man, "and bring us two beef tenderloin dinners." The man nodded and moved out of the room.

"You see," Griswold said, shaking his finger to emphasize the point, "I really did like Eddie, and he really did like and respect me, down deep. Over the past seven and more years, we had many laughs together, shared many thoughts on the nature and trends of fiction writing. Even shared a great many intimacies. For example, to how many men do you think he would have confided that he never once slept with his wife?"

This shocked Pinkerton. "Not many, I am sure. But why was that the case?"

"Because she was his cousin and more like a child to him than a wife. He cared for her like a father. She was very delicate, both of body and mind. Something of a singer. I attended the party where she was singing and suddenly started hemorrhaging blood. It was the first indication of the consumption that killed her. I shall never forget it. Red stains all over her pretty white gown. So sad. She died in '45, you know."

"I read it in his obituary."

Griswold smiled. "Why, he and I were even friendly rivals over a woman in later years! I admired a large part of his oeuvre very much." He let a good deal of bourbon go down his throat. "But he was wildly uneven."

"'The Gold-Bug' versus 'The Man Who Was Used Up,'" Allan commented, thinking how he now had Griswold's and Aaron Pelglade's agreement on that issue.

"Precisely." He made a little noise in the back of his throat. "What first set him against me was that I took his place as editor of *Graham's Magazine* when he had to be let go."

"Why was that?"

"Because he went off on drinking or laudanum binges and missed deadlines left and right. Through lackadaisical behavior, he let other magazines snatch up the best writers. He thought he could simply fill *Graham's* with his own stories, poems and criticisms. And this was not the first time he was let go. He worked at *Burton's* here in Philadelphia as well, not only failing to get the periodical out on time, but Burton also caught him stealing the subscription list for his own intended effort. Something he quite sophomorically called The Penn. Pee Eee Double-enn. He actually had the nerve to be outraged when Burton sold the magazine and did not offer it to him."

Griswold finished his second drink in a rush, as if he intended to tax Pinkerton's wallet for the defense he was having to mount. Allan was happy to allow it. "He used to crow about how *Graham's Magazine* quadrupled its subscription rate while he was editor. From 5,000 to 20,000. Well, I've doubled it to 40,000, and that's again as much as when I started! An even greater feat, I'll allow."

Allan thought, *Crow, indeed! And now this one crows. Birds of a feather*. Aloud, he said, "So might I understand that you two had a love/hate relationship?"

"Well put. We both admired and disliked each other, and for the same reasons."

"So, what you wrote in the *New York Tribune* was to your mind even-handed," Pinkerton led.

"What did I write?"

"The obituary for your friend. Under the name LUDWIG."

"Who said that was me?" Griswold evaded.

"Come, Dr. Griswold," Pinkerton said gently, as he turned notebook pages back. "You may have signed yourself as LUDWIG at the end, but you more plainly signed yourself at the top by using several lines of text to promote your anthology: 'The family of Mr. Poe – we learn from Griswold's *Poets and Poetry of America*, from which a considerable portion of the facts of this article are derived – was one of the oldest and most respectable in Baltimore.'"

The editor did not seem overly offended by Pinkerton's accusation. "It was no more than he did to me many times in print, always using a pseudonym. And I will say that I put much thought into the text and believe it is most honest."

"But you submitted it to the *New York Tribune* and not to a Philadelphia newspaper."

"Because they asked me to write it. Since I am an authority on the man." Griswold glanced out the window, at the passing traffic on the brick pavement and the cobblestone street. "If you think poorly of me because I lowered myself to Eddie's level, I will tell you that I never stooped to pandering, as he did. First of all, he was never critical of me to my face, while I was bold enough to voice my thoughts on his poorer work to him. He was ever borrowing money from me, because he was constantly quitting jobs and refusing other work he deemed beneath him." He looked straight at the detective. "He stooped so low that he would spend his precious time with anyone who would buy him a few drinks."

Allan had all he could do not to burst out laughing at the irony of the remark, even as the third drink was placed in front of Griswold.

The editor's eyes narrowed. "There was this man living in Philadelphia for a time and who visited from out of town on a couple other occasions who used to take Eddie out drinking. At any other time, Eddie would refuse to suffer fools lightly. However, this fool was generous to him. Eddie said that he was always suggesting ideas for plots. Eddie said they were uniformly awful. However, then the man began accusing him of stealing the plots. He said that Eddie could have the fame; all he wanted was to be fairly paid."

This digression sounded extremely interesting to Pinkerton. "What was his name?"

Griswold struggled to remember. He took a sip of his drink. "I can't recall. That is, if he ever told me. He used to call him 'the homunculus.' Or else, Blackie. Yes, that was what he called him; Blackie!"

Allan thought of the nurse, Mrs. Lukauskis, speaking of Black Reynolds. In an offhand manner, he said, "I knew of a Blackie who was a career criminal. They called him that because of his black heart. But he worked exclusively in Ohio, Illinois and Indiana." Then, as if a minor afterthought, he added, "Might this Blackie's last name have been 'Reynolds'?"

"Well, it might have been. It might have been Washington or Jefferson for that matter. He never told me the man's surname!" Allan noted that Griswold's carefully- constructed avuncular persona was finally beginning to slip. "Eddie once said that he enjoyed keeping company with the fellow because it was like having a one-man retinue. Like he was a king, and 'the homunculus' was his court jester."

"Something like his short story 'Hop-Frog,'" Allan mused aloud, even as he thought how that court jester had exacted a terrible retribution upon his king.

Griswold's face suddenly lit up. "I remember more about him! About this Blackie fellow. He was a mortician's assistant. He actually hunted Eddie down the first time because he had personally experienced a corpse awakening. He wanted to explain the event and his feelings in detail, so that Eddie could incorporate these into his writing."

"It must have been a virtual love affair," Allan said.

"Indeed. The writer who was obsessed with dying and premature burial meets the passionate admirer who made his living working with the dead. And, of course, the man was in awe of Eddie and knew that he could bribe his attention with drink. Eddie told me he thought the man might be a necrophiliac. That subject even he would not touch in print. Such a sick obsession may have been the reason the man disappeared from Philadelphia; he might have been fired once or twice for desecrating bodies. He moved to New York, I know, and he and Eddie renewed their acquaintance."

Off in another room, a tray of dishes crashed to the floor. Allan's stomach felt as if a similar accident had taken place inside it.

"Can you describe the man?"

"No. I never saw him. Eddie told me about this in yet another begging letter. But hear me, Mr. Pinkerton: You must understand that I do not take especial umbrage for my mistreatment by Eddie's hands. He abused Charles Peterson, my assistant editor, mercilessly. Used him as a whipping boy. He abused his 'homunculus.' He abused many other writers. Even Charles Dickens. Can you imagine? We both met the great Englishman on his American tour. Back in March of '42. Eddie had a basketful of complaints about the man's style and characters. But he wasn't too proud to steal from him. Do you know Dickens' work, *Barnaby Rudge*?"

"No."

The beef tenderloin dinners arrived, dressed with mashed potatoes and carrots.

"Well," said Griswold, tucking his napkin under his chin, "Barnaby Rudge is a simple hero. He owns a raven whom he has named 'Grip.' It rides in a basket on his back. The bird constantly repeats the phrase, 'Never say die!' Does that sound familiar?"

"I had heard that the idea for 'The Raven' was given to him by the son of a friend in Saratoga Springs."

"Oh, that wife he was shagging. You know, you could never believe what Eddie said. It's like he wrote in his 'The System of Doctor Tarr and Professor Fether': 'You are young yet, my friend,' replied my host, 'but the time will arrive when you will learn to judge for yourself of what is going on in the world, without trusting to the gossip of others. Believe nothing you hear, and only one-half that you see.'"

"One second," Allan said, while Griswold dug into his meal. He reached down to his valise and pulled out Molly Brannigan's gift. He thumbed to the story of the insane asylum where a man visits and only slowly realizes that the inmates have taken over. He found the passage the editor had just quoted and read it to himself.

"Extraordinary!" he marveled. "You quoted that word for word!"

"I have a photographic memory," Griswold said, smiling so broadly with self-satisfaction that the food caught between his teeth showed.

"You are not the only friend who is able to quote with unerring accuracy," Allan said. "You must know Aaron Pelglade."

"Who?"

"Eddie's friend Aaron Pelglade. A whiskey drummer."

"Yes, Eddie would make sure to befriend a person in that business. And yet I can't place the name. How do you spell it?"

Allan obliged.

"Strange. Never heard that name."

"He said it's English…meaning 'through the glade.' He –"

Griswold had stopped chewing, his eyes fixed on the thin book Pinkerton held. "May I see that?"

Allan passed it over.

Griswold read the cover, then the inside information, then rapidly paged through the four stories. "Son of a bitch!" he exclaimed. "Where did you get this?"

Allan repeated what Molly had told him.

"No place of publication, of course," Griswold said, more growling than speaking. "You know that Eddie made me his literary executor?"

"I had heard of the letters passed between you and him," Allan acknowledged.

"This is precisely the sort of thing that I want to stop. Do you know that I went down to testify before a session of Congress in Washington precisely about the lack of enforcement of copyrights. Horrible!"

Having spent the past hour with Poe's embittered friend, Allan thought that the man's deep rancor would guarantee no effort on his part to keep Poe's works alive. Pirated publications such as Molly had purchased were sure to do more on Edgar Poe's behalf than anything Griswold would do.

"Who would benefit financially if his work was reissued through you?" Pinkerton asked.

"I suppose his mother-in-law." Rufus Wilmot Griswold's eyes narrowed as he looked at Allan. "And you are thinking that I, as editor, would end up the main beneficiary." He shoved some of the potato Pinkerton was paying for into his mouth and swallowed. "Well, let me tell you, sir: If that came to pass, it would only be justice. He must have approached me twenty times begging for loans. I am sure I gave him close to forty dollars over the years, and never once did he repay me. Dickens called him 'a disappointed man in great poverty,' and that is precisely what he was. He was so desperate that he continued to pester Graham to publish his work even after he and Graham had that monumental falling out." Griswold shoved a forkful of beef into his mouth, chewed and swallowed. "Talk about needing to swallow your pride! He brought that piece of claptrap 'The Raven' to us, and Mr. Graham rightly rejected it. But we all felt so sorry for him that I, the clerks, printers, devils, and even Charles Peterson passed around the hat and raised fifteen dollars. Pathetic. There is another man in town here who you must arrange to see. His name is John Sartain. He's a publisher and illustrator and a great supporter of Edgar Allan Poe. Nevertheless, he will tell you exactly how jealous, petty, spiteful, paranoid and, yes, even insane the man was."

Tired of hearing the same accusations over and over, Allan asked, "Why did you use the name Ludwig?"

"Because Beethoven was deaf at the end of his life. And so have I been to the cloying praises of the legion of braying jackasses who say that Poe is America's greatest writer to date. Rubbish."

Allan knew the time was right. He could read in the editor's glassy eyes that he was more than a little drunk. He reached into his jacket pocket and took out the piece of white paper that he had found behind the Tavern on the Wharf. He passed it to Griswold.

"What's this?" Griswold wondered aloud and then, blinking a few times to help focus his bourbon-clouded sight, he read. Griswold set down the paper.

"'My continued gratitude for helping bring Poe to me. If you wish to remain free and unconnected to his death, you must help me take care of another man. I will again pay you $20. I am staying in the same place. LUDWIG," Allan spoke, taking his own turn at reciting from memory. He related to the editor the circumstances surrounding Jack "Duke" Hewitt and finding the note.

"When did you find this?"

Pinkerton told him.

"I can produce my entire staff to verify that I have been

nowhere near Baltimore this entire week." Griswold folded his arms across his chest. "You also know from my assistant that I was in this city all the while Eddie was dying. This is a pathetic attempt to use my obituary as a means to deflect blame onto me. Do you think I harbored enough hatred against him that I would hire others to do him in?"

"In spite of the power he gave you over his works once he had died, I do not," Pinkerton said truthfully, even as he knew how happy the pitiful editor was to have his supposed friend dead, even as he realized just how blindly self-deluding and naive Edgar Poe must have been to have entrusted his immortality to this jealous, small soul who did not have the guts to physically kill his rival but who would gleefully work to kill Poe's legacy.

Griswold put his forefinger to his temple again. He offered Allan his most ingratiating smile. "It comes down to this: We had ambivalent feelings toward each other. Have you never loved a woman for her face and figure, Mr. Pinkerton, and hated her for her tongue?"

# CHAPTER SEVENTEEN
*Friday, October 26, 1849*

Allan intended to be out of Philadelphia as soon as possible. The return train to Baltimore departed at two-thirty. To speed his Friday, he had stood outside Independence Hall late the previous evening, craning his neck up to admire the stately central tower. He had visited Betsy Ross's narrow brick house with both the original flag of the united thirteen colonies and the present national flag flying from poles beneath its second-story windows.

The detective had lingered for many minutes, staring through the wrought-iron fence at the well-cared-for corner grave of Benjamin Franklin. All these he did in spite of his aversion to walking the streets of a strange city in the darkness. Ever since leaving Chicago, Allan had experienced a conversion from a man who felt no need to read to a convinced appreciator of the power of the written word. Nothing quite hammered that power home as stories he knew to be completely made up but which nonetheless pierced straight to his imagination and his heart.

Standing above the gravesite of a native son many in America considered the greatest genius it had yet birthed, the lesson was reinforced. Franklin's epitaph was not devoted to his many inventions, his philanthropies, his crucial involvement in the cause of independence nor in framing the Constitution, nor his service as foreign ambassador. Instead, it read:

The body of
B. Franklin, Printer
(Like the Cover of an Old Book
Its Contents torn Out
And Stript of its Lettering and Gilding)

Lies Here, Food for Worms.
But the Work shall not be Lost;
For it will (as he Believ'd) Appear once More
In a New and More Elegant Edition
Revised and Corrected
By the Author.

Allan had returned to the hotel room he had rented, still a little tipsy from his four ales and trying not to think too much about the infuriating Rufus Wilmot Griswold. Not because he was obliged but because he wanted to, he reread "The Gold-Bug" and "The Cask of Amontillado," both of which he judged were extremely well written and entertaining.

Directly after breakfast, Allan visited the nearest telegraph office and addressed identical messages to the chiefs of police of Manhattan and the City of Brooklyn. Then he moved with focused purpose to the address that Griswold had given him. He found there the offices of *Sartain's Union Magazine*. He also found the proprietor, editor, and engraver. Allan needed only one sentence from the man's mouth to discern that he was not only English but from London. He looked to be about Poe's age, but Allan would not have been surprised if he was a little younger, given to the fact that he had lost most of the hair on his crown and combed over the bald area. He had a full face, with a thick nose. Tufts of hair flowed over his ears, and his moustache and beard were not connected. He both moved and spoke with deliberation.

"I am most apologetic for interrupting you unannounced, sir," Pinkerton said, handing the man his calling card. "However, I am investigating the death of your friend Edgar Allan Poe, and I am on a strict schedule."

"I understand completely," Sartain allowed, "and I thank you for your interest in Mr. Poe. I cannot tell you how it grieves me that he is no longer with us. I knew him much of my time in America. One of my dearest friends in England is the painter Thomas Sully, and Edgar was the schoolmate friend of Thomas's nephew, Robert. We had common ground to explore from the very first, you see."

"How long has it been since you saw Mr. Poe?" Allan asked.

"The end of this past June he came to Philadelphia on business, to engage writers for his new venture, *The Stylus*. According to him, he took the ferry, the *John Potter*, from Manhattan across to…is it Perth or South Amboy?"

"I wouldn't know, sir."

Sartain laughed and rubbed his ear. His fingers were stained with black ink and left a mark. No, you wouldn't, would you? One of them is where the excellent Camden and Amboy Railroad terminates, running all the way down to our sister city across the Delaware."

Pinkerton nodded and decided now was the time to take out his notebook and pencil.

"At any rate, on the way something must have happened. You know how men take to chatting, gambling, and drinking on trips. I fear someone may have offered Eddie a bottle, either of alcohol or laudanum. He claimed to have overheard two men seated behind him plotting to murder him. Even though they whispered, he was sure he understood them."

"Did he describe the pair?"

"He said they were white, about his age, bearded. Nothing distinguishing. He said he jumped off at the last second at

Bordentown and gave them the slip. Then he got on the next train and ferried over to Philadelphia. I was the first one he came to. I will say that he was visibly shaken. Somehow, he had left his carpetbag behind, or it had been stolen. He also did not know what had happened to the fifty dollars he left with. His look was haggard and wild-eyed, which was exceedingly strange, since he said that his mother-in-law, Mrs. Clemm, had seen him off in New York. She surely would not have let him travel in that condition. And it is not that long a trip."

"But drink did terrible things to him and with precipitous reaction, if I am to understand correctly," Pinkerton said.

"Most true. Frighteningly true," John Sartain said. "When I say I was the first one he came to, this was on July 1st. Yet he left New York on June 29th! He had been wandering Philadelphia for the better part of two days."

An assistant excused himself to pluck a metal ruler from Sartain's desk.

"This sounds exceedingly like his last days in Baltimore," Allan observed.

Sartain drew a shade to shield the invasion of the morning light. "It does."

"Might he have been going insane?" Allan wondered aloud. "Are there not types of insanity where one is deranged for a period of time and then returns to perfect rationality?"

"I do not know. He had a great personal fear of losing his mind. He talked about it all the time. You may know it was a fixture of his writing."

Allan nodded as he recalled a line from "The System of Doctor Tarr and Professor Fether": "Why, as for that, a madman is not necessarily a fool." Allan was more than willing to believe that a genius might easily be a madman as well. Then he remembered how the tale's narrator wondered why the inmates of the asylum were well dressed but often not wearing the correct sizes. Poe discovered raving in rags the wrong size made his story seem either amazingly prescient or else wickedly ironic.

"He showed up at my house," Sartain went on, "with only the clothes on his back. I tried to hide my astonishment. 'Mr. Sartain,' said he, 'I have come to you for a refuge and protection. Will you let me stay with you? It is necessary for my safety that I lie concealed for a time.' His look was wild and haunted, but his voice was astonishingly calm and low in pitch."

"How disturbing," Pinkerton voiced before he realized it.

"Well, I thought it best to continue with the engraving I was working on, as if nothing untoward had happened. I listened to his story about the two men as if in an abstracted manner. I tried to reason with him and asked what motive they could have for wanting to kill him. He said, 'It was for revenge.' I asked for what. He said, 'Well, a woman trouble.' And then he abandoned that tack and began to talk about suicide."

The expressions on the editor/artist's face were so motile and serious that Pinkerton could almost envision the scenes as he described them.

Sartain continued, "No sooner did he talk of ending his life than a sly look appeared on his face and he said that the men had identified him by his moustache. He needed, he said, a razor to shave it off. Well, in that condition there was no way I would let him handle a razor. I said that I did not have one but that I used a scissors to trim my beard. He allowed me to cut off his moustache that way...which was quite difficult."

"Does Rufus Griswold know this story?" Allan asked.

Sartain picked up an engraving and held it in front of him without looking at it. "Griswold? No, indeed! I have shared it with only one other person: Edgar's close friend, Mr. George Lippard. Griswold would be the last I would confide in. But there is more." He set the engraving down. "Toward nightfall, he said that he wanted to go out. I asked him where, considering he had been so afraid of being spotted. He said he had to go to the Schuylkill River. He had on my slippers because his shoes were so worn down at the heel and had chaffed his feet. I decided not to make a scene about it. I said that it was a nice night and that I would be pleased if he would let me come along I thought he meant to drown himself.

"We walked to Ninth and Chestnut Streets and from there took an omnibus. He talked about wanting the portrait I had painted of him to go to his mother when he died, by which I understood he meant Mrs. Clemm. We alit and walked toward the bridge. Then we climbed the stairs that led almost to the top of the reservoir. There was a bench there. He sat and, in a strangely calm voice, said that he needed to confess to me where he had been."

"The previous few days?"

"Yes. He said he had been locked up in Moyamemsing prison because he had tried to pass a counterfeit fifty-dollar bill he had unwittingly brought with him from New York. While in his cell he had looked out his window and seen a young woman standing on the battlement tower, brightly radiant like silver dipped in light. Despite the distance, she addressed to him several questions. As with the two plotters on the train, she whispered and yet he could understand her perfectly. He said he was compelled to answer her truthfully, or else the consequences would have been terrible. Then he went on about an attendant taking him to a cauldron of fire and torturing him by making him watch Mrs. Clemm having her feet, then ankles, then knees, then thighs, then hips cut off."

Allan Pinkerton's mind reeled. He wondered how such a mind could have recovered sufficiently within a few weeks to have convinced the people of Richmond that he was perfectly sane. And then he wondered if the artist who held the engraving was the insane one. If Edgar Poe had not been found outside Gunner's Hall after vanishing for several days and then died ranting and incoherent, Allan would have believed nothing else.

"I had heard enough," Sartain went on, "so I gently lured him down the stairway and back to my house. I endeavoured to put him to bed, but he begged for laudanum. I gave him a small quantity, made up my sofa for him, and myself took up watch, lying across three chairs."

"You are indeed a wonderful friend, and I know how much he appreciated you," said Pinkerton.

"How is that?"

"Because he slyly embedded your name several times in his 'The Gold-Bug.' Whenever the black servant Jupiter wants to say 'certain,' he says 'sartain' instead."

The Englishman nodded and grinned. "You are the first person who has ever mentioned that to me. You are indeed a clever detective. Yes, Edgar was very fond of being secretly clever. He was always dabbling in word plays, anagrams, and riddles. But he was not especially adept at cryptography, you know. The cypher for finding the treasure in 'The Gold-Bug' was simply the one-for-one substitution variety."

"What happened the next morning?" Pinkerton asked, quite cognizant of the passing time and needing to re-track the editor.

"He got up sounding much more rational and went out for a walk while I worked. When he returned, he said that apparently his natural imagination had been working overtime and concocting new stories. He came to this revelation, he said, by lying in a field of grass and inhaling the smell of the plants and the earth. He thanked me for my solicitations and left. I later learned that he went to the home of the same George Lippard I mentioned earlier and stayed with him for several days. He lingered until George, I, and three other friends pooled together the sum of ten dollars, which was enough to get him as far as Baltimore. He left on Friday, the 13th of July. That is the last I or anyone else in Philadelphia saw of him."

"I wish I had time to go to that prison," Allan said.

Sartain looked quite crestfallen. "I went. They told me that Edgar had spent only one of the nights. In the morning he was brought with others before Mayor Gilpin, who recognized him. Without even asking what the charges were, Gilpin ordered him released. So part of Edgar's wild tale at least is true."

"He foresaw his imminent death," Pinkerton said, referring to the mention of bequeathing his portrait to his mother-in-law.

"He was convinced he was psychic and told everyone he knew," Sartain supplied. Then the editor sprang from his seat and began to pace back and forth. "But, confound it, the irony was that he was more upbeat when in his senses those last days than I had ever known him to be. He spoke with such enthusiasm about his new periodical. He said that the old love of his youth, who lives in Richmond, was a widow and that he was convinced she would accept his petition of marriage. He looked forward to moving to the South, because he said he had grown tired of the cold New York winters. Does that sound like a man who is suicidal?"

"Not to me," Allan answered.

"But I have even better proof," said the publisher of *Sartain's Union Magazine*. He walked to a pile of papers and dug out a large sheet of paper upon which a poem had been beautifully scribed in ink.

"This may very well be Edgar Poe's last poem," John Sartain said soberly. "You tell me the state of the author's mind."

Allan accepted the sheet and read.


I
Hear the sledges with the bells –
Silver bells!
What a world of merriment their melody foretells!
How they tinkle, tinkle, tinkle,
In the icy air of night!
While the stars that oversprinkle
All the heavens seem to twinkle
With a crystalline delight;
Keeping time, time, time,
In a sort of Runic rhyme,
To the tintinnabulation that so musically wells
From the bells, bells, bells, bells,
Bells, bells, bells –
From the jingling and the tinkling of the bells.


II
Hear the mellow wedding bells –
Golden bells!

What a world of happiness their harmony foretells!
Through the balmy air of night
How they ring out their delight!
From the molten-golden notes,
And all in tune,
What a liquid ditty floats
To the turtle-dove that listens, while she gloats
On the moon!
Oh, from out the sounding cells
What a gush of euphony voluminously wells!
How it swells!
How it dwells
On the Future! -how it tells
Of the rapture that impels
To the swinging and the ringing
Of the bells, bells, bells,
Of the bells, bells, bells, bells,
Bells, bells, bells –
To the rhyming and the chiming of the bells!

III
Hear the loud alarum bells –
Brazen bells!
What a tale of terror, now, their turbulency tells!
In the startled ear of night
How they scream out their affright!
Too much horrified to speak,
They can only shriek, shriek,
Out of tune,
In a clamorous appealing to the mercy of the fire,

In a mad expostulation with the deaf and frantic fire,
Leaping higher, higher, higher,
With a desperate desire,
And a resolute endeavor
Now -now to sit or never,
By the side of the pale-faced moon.
Oh, the bells, bells, bells!
What a tale their terror tells
Of despair!
How they clang, and clash, and roar!
What a horror they outpour
On the bosom of the palpitating air!
Yet the ear it fully knows,
By the twanging
And the clanging,
How the danger ebbs and flows;
Yet the ear distinctly tells,
In the jangling
And the wrangling,
How the danger sinks and swells,
By the sinking or the swelling in the anger of the bells –
Of the bells,
Of the bells, bells, bells, bells,
Bells, bells, bells –
In the clamor and the clangor of the bells!

IV
Hear the tolling of the bells –
Iron bells!
What a world of solemn thought their monody compels!

In the silence of the night,
How we shiver with affright
At the melancholy menace of their tone!
For every sound that floats
From the rust within their throats
Is a groan.
And the people – ah, the people –
They that dwell up in the steeple,
All alone,
And who tolling, tolling, tolling,
In that muffled monotone,
Feel a glory in so rolling
On the human heart a stone –
They are neither man nor woman –
They are neither brute nor human -
They are Ghouls:
And their king it is who tolls;
And he rolls, rolls, rolls,
Rolls
A paean from the bells!
And his merry bosom swells
With the paean of the bells!
And he dances, and he yells;
Keeping time, time, time,
In a sort of Runic rhyme,
To the paean of the bells,
Of the bells –
Keeping time, time, time,
In a sort of Runic rhyme,
To the throbbing of the bells,

Of the bells, bells, bells –
To the sobbing of the bells;
Keeping time, time, time,
As he knells, knells, knells,
In a happy Runic rhyme,
To the rolling of the bells,
Of the bells, bells, bells –
To the tolling of the bells,
Of the bells, bells, bells, bells,
Bells, bells, bells –
To the moaning and the groaning of the bells.

Allan handed back the sheet. "Well, it does grow somber and then sad in the last two verses, but the first two use words like 'delight' and 'merriment' and 'happiness.'"

Sartain had stopped pacing, waiting with expectation for his guest to finish reading. He set the poem down on his desk, within reaching distance of Pinkerton. "That is not because he is lapsing into sadness," he explained. "It describes two things: first the joy and elation that small bells instill and then the relatively greater solemnity and weight that bigger, lower-toned bells impart. He goes from smallest to largest, you see."

"Now I do."

"But he is also speaking of life. In the spring of life, when we are little children, we have no cares. Our parents take them on for us. Then in our middle size – as youths – we have independence, abundant health, and a world of possibilities ahead of us. All is still wonderful. But in the third quarter – our full size and autumn if you will – of our lives, things become more serious. The responsibilities grow. And then comes old age, ill health, and finally death. The verses grow longer, and the pace of the syllables slower. It is in early youth and old age that time seem most important. And so he repeats the words about time and the Runic rhyme. Bells are used to toll out time and occasions. The seasons, the passing of time is not sad; rather it is simply the nature and the toll, if you will pardon a pun, of life."

"How excellent," Allan admired. "And is there truly such a word as 'tintinnabulation'?"

"There is," Sartain confirmed. "It comes from the Latin word for 'little bell.' It belongs to a group of words called onomatopoetic, that is, the ones that use the sounds they stand for. Like buzz."

"I have a great deal to learn about writing," Allan admitted. "And what does 'homunculus' mean?"

"It refers to a dwarf or a small, manlike creature. That word is not in the poem. Why do you ask?"

"According to Rufus Griswold, Edgar had a sometime friend whom he called both Blackie and 'the homunculus.' Did he ever confide this to you?"

"No. Around me he was rarely negative. Almost never vicious, which that remark seems to be. Perhaps it was due to, or even provoked by, Griswold's company."

"I would not doubt it," said Pinkerton. "Another friend was Aaron Pelglade. Do you know him or know of him?"

"I do not."

"What about the name Reynolds?"

"Reynolds…" John Sartain tried to remember. "He was a drinking companion I believe."

"Did he live in Baltimore?"

"I don't think so. Either here or in New York City."

"Griswold said that this Blackie lived in Philadelphia and New York City," Pinkerton said, checking his notes. "Yes, here it is. Further, he thought that the man was a mortician or a mortician's assistant."

"That does not ring any of my bells," Sartain said, allowing himself to smile. He did not lose the smile when he added, "You may keep that copy of 'The Bells.' It is in Poe's own hand."

"Oh, that is too much," Allan said, even as he wanted to snatch the sheet from the generous editor's desk.

"I think not. He gave me two copies. Who is paying you to investigate his death?" He picked up the poem and handed it to Pinkerton.

"No one. I am doing it on my own," Allan said, admiring the calligraphy.

"And you come all the way from Chicago. Then you at least deserve a souvenir. Don't think it is so extremely valuable, Mr. Pinkerton. I know for a fact that there must be at least three more copies. You see, as friendly as Edgar Poe and I were, the leopard could not change his spots. He sold the poem to me for fifteen dollars. In about a month I will be the first to publish it; but I have recently learned by putting out reprint inquiries that he sold the same poem to at least three other publishers – exclusively – as well."

# CHAPTER EIGHTEEN

*Friday, October 26, 1849*

A key to the Brannigan house back door was hidden under one of the path bricks that led to the outhouse. Molly had entrusted the information to Allan before he had left for Philadelphia. When he arrived on the property at eleven in the evening, he quietly unlocked the door and placed his things inside. Then he stripped naked, went outside in the near-total darkness, and doused himself with water from one of the rain barrels. The water was intensely cold, and yet it felt good to rinse away the soot, dust, and sweat of travel and to cool the hot ache of his feet. Moreover, the shivering made his tense muscles relax. He ran inside, grabbed a kitchen towel to dry himself, and then dug into his valise for his nightshirt. Once he had stopped trembling, he dashed outside again, hid the key, cupped his hands to take a drink, and retreated once more into the kitchen.

After locking the door, Allan crept upstairs with as much stealth as he could manage. He found both bedroom doors open. The moment he entered the guest room he knew why; Molly lay in the bed. She rolled over as he entered.

"You're back! Did fortune smile on you?"

"I think so," Allan said, setting down his valise and the protective folio folder he had received from John Sartain.

Molly sat up. "Do you know who killed Poe?"

"I believe I do."

She scooted herself over to the far side of the bed. "Allan! Who was it?" He sat on the mattress with his back to her. "I don't want to say until I hear from the police in New York."

Molly threw her arms around Allan's back. "It's someone from New York! How amazing. And you won't even confide in me?"

Allan smiled into the darkness. "Most assuredly not in you."

313

"What? Do you think I am a fishwife, telling tales over the backyard fence?" Molly ended by lightly biting his shoulder.

"No. Because your good opinion matters a great deal to me."

"What a wonderful compliment!"

Molly yanked her nightdress over her head and pressed herself against Allan's back. Her nipples, hard from the cold and passion, traced twin paths parallel to his shoulder blades.

"Molly…" he said, with no conviction. Again, in preparation for his return to her, Allan had refrained from taking a drop of alcohol all day. He admitted to himself that, like Edgar Poe, he liked drink too much and found it difficult to stop once he had started. He determined to stay away from it at all costs. But habits were most easily broken if replaced with other stimulations, and he could think of nothing better than the sexual attentions of Molly Brannigan.

"I know. But this is the last night that it would be safe." Molly's fingers stole over his flanks and down into his pubic hairs. "All things must end. When pain ends, we are happy. When pleasure ends, we are sad. But if we make fond memories, the parting is easier to bear." Her mouth had come up to his ear. He felt the warmth of her breath and then the tips of her teeth teasing his lobe. "Since you will not tell me yet who was responsible for Mr. Poe's death, you will do this for me."

Allan swung around and gathered the very clever, very desirable woman into his arms.

# CHAPTER NINETEEN
*Saturday, October 27, 1849*

Molly served pancakes for breakfast. They were stuffed with bits of apple glazed with a sugary syrup and rolled in cinnamon. She called them apple fritters, and they were delicious. Allan thought of the last time he had been offered an apple. It was by Aaron Pelglade, in the cemetery beside Edgar Allan Poe's grave. He thought of the incident, and a chilling frisson rippled down his spine.

When they had finished eating and Allan had detailed almost all the incidents of his visit to Philadelphia, he said, "In short, it was a critical journey."

"I fear that Mr. Poe would have been confined to an insane asylum soon enough if he hadn't died when he did," Molly said. "What a peculiar story, I mean about the woman beckoning to him through the bars of the prison cell! Do not people who contract certain venereal diseases go slowly insane?"

"I believe that is true."

"And, from what you have said, he had his share of women. As well he would need to, never sleeping with his wife!" Molly declared.

"But he was finished off before he could kill himself," Allan reminded her. "So, having heard all the clues I have presented over the past week and more, tell me who the guilty party is."

"I will not," Molly said.

"Why is that?"

"Because I might be wrong, and your good opinion matters a great deal to me." Molly smirked as she echoed the words Allan had delivered to her the night before.

"I will give you a present if you tell me." Allan got up and reached under the shawl that lay on the rocking chair. When he had descended to the parlor, Molly had been engaged in preparing breakfast. It had given him the opportunity to hide the folio folder he had received from John Sartain. He held it up to the level of his head.

"Very well," Molly relented, her eyes bright at the anticipation of another gift. "I say it was Rufus Griswold."

"Your reasoning?"

Molly ticked off her points one by one on the fingers of her left hand. "First, because Poe had insulted him so many times and so publicly. Secondly, because he proved his anger in the obituary he was too cowardly to sign. Thirdly, because Poe had recently made him the executor of his literary estate, providing the man income. I say he had his rival killed by proxy, being very careful to be in Philadelphia when Poe was made sick and died. Oh, and this is my fourth proof: He was so happy to use his assistant editor to prove he himself had no opportunity."

"But you have ignored the fact that I said the guilty man is from New York," Allan pointed out.

Undeterred, Molly said, "He could have worked for some time in New York City, between his youth in Vermont and his hiring at that *Graham's Magazine*. You may be waiting to learn of a criminal record he has in New York. I certainly know that Griswold must have a good connection to that city, because the obituary he wrote for Poe was published in the *New York Tribune*."

Pinkerton realized that, in spite of her acute intelligence, Molly was like the majority of the population, trying to force the wrong piece into the machine because one end fit perfectly.

"What about 'the homunculus'?" the detective asked. "Why

do you not think it was the bizarre mortician's assistant Poe called 'Blackie'?"

"Because the bizarre are often the most harmless. They cannot help but exhibit their peculiarities, making everyone wary of them. Thus suspected, they are scrutinized most carefully and rejected as friends if appearing at all dangerous. Besides, why would he be in Baltimore, and what would he have gained?"

Without answering, Allan handed over the folio.

"Then I am right!" Molly exclaimed. "It is Rufus Griswold! And what is this?"

"Open it," Allan said gently.

Molly slipped the sheet of paper carefully from its protection. She gasped when she read the signature at the bottom. She glanced at Allan. Tears welled up, and she quickly wiped them away and held the paper at a distance to keep from running the ink. Her eyes moved back and forth, from line to line.

"It is his last poem," Allan shared. "I think it is very good."

Molly made no reply until she had finished reading. Then she stood, set the poem on her chair, moved to Allan, and hugged him. "Nothing could be more wonderful than this. I will have it framed under glass and display it forever."

Allan wondered how Molly would explain its appearance to her husband.

A knock on the front door disturbed the silent moment. Molly daubed at her eyes again and crossed the short distance to answer it.

"Good morning, ma'am," a male voice said. "I believe that Mr. Allan Pinkerton is lodging here."

"Yes." Molly stepped back. The man entered.

The members of the Baltimore Watch did not have uniforms such as were worn by the policemen under Sir Robert Peel in London. However, the men had taken to wearing a de facto uniform, so that they could recognize their brethren from a distance and so the people of the city could recognize them. It was a short, black version of a top hat, a dark coat that reached just below the waist, and a red or russet shirt beneath. This man's shirt was new and flame red.

"My name's Leudeke, sir," the watchman said. "I'm here on behalf of Chief Magistrate Foster." He handed over a folded piece of paper.

Allan read it. To Molly, he said, "They found Jack Hewitt"

"Wonderful!"

"Not so wonderful. They found him dead." Allan shoved the note in his pocket and looked at Molly. "Do you know if your handyman will be in Baltimore today and tomorrow?"

"I'm sure he will be. Why?"

"Ask Mr. Burton if he is willing for five dollars to play a part for me. It will take very little acting ability and not too much time. I believe I'll be back before supper."


"One good thing about salt water," Magistrate Foster remarked, "it cleans wounds."

Duke Hewitt's corpse lay on the boardwalk planking, just beyond the limits of the Tavern on the Wharf. It was quite bloated and dripped water. Pinkerton noted that he had two circles of rope tied to him, one around his right ankle, the other around his right wrist. Both had been cut from water-soaked lengths of rope that lay on the planking, tied to two large stones. The sailor's throat had been slashed.

"Amazing how buoyant a body becomes when it begins to release its gases," Foster observed dispassionately. "He floated up just high enough for someone to spot him. Are those the clothes he was wearing when he got off the *Pocahontas*?" he asked Pinkerton.

"They are. He had left his other clothing behind in the tavern before he went missing the first night. I believe it takes several days for a body to fill with gases in such cold water, so that fact more than the clothing would indicate he was killed soon after debarking the *Pocahontas*."

"I trust your logic."

Pinkerton noted that Foster wore the simplest of ties, which the man had just taken off. This the detective took as a symbol of a no-nonsense attitude, that the official was more interested in maintaining his position through honest work rather than fashion. Allan himself wore a tie only when occasion demanded it. He squatted and examined the fatal wound. "Cut left to right, from behind," he observed. "Not especially deep but severing both carotid arteries. Hewitt wasn't conscious for very long after that. Did he have any money on him?"

"No. His pockets were empty."

"I saw the captain of the *Pocahontas* pay him just before he left the boat. And I gave him three dollars."

"Do you think it was merely a robbery?" Foster asked.

Pinkerton stood, thinking for a moment about the note he had found on the walkway. "An extremely timely robbery, as far as my investigation of the Poe case is concerned. Perhaps it was a secondary motivation, to cover the primary one."

"Indeed," the chief magistrate agreed. He turned to an underling. "There's nothing more we can get out of this. Take him over to Washington University Hospital."

"To use as a practice cadaver?" Pinkerton asked.

Foster stepped back from the still-dripping corpse. "Since he has no identification to inform next of kin, I think he might serve his fellow man at least this once."

"Might I suggest you hold the body somewhere until Captain Massey returns with his boat? Massey said that he did not know the man before September, but I would think he might be able to make some inquiries in Richmond."

"Good idea," said Foster. "I would hate to have his family pestering me for the corpse in two weeks and need to gather all the pieces. No matter how diligently you do your job, things like that can blemish your reputation forever."

Pinkerton understood. "One other thing I know from the body;" he said. "Whoever weighted it down was not a sailor. Those are just a series of overhand knots on his ankle and wrist. A sailor would have used something quicker but just as secure, like two half hitches."

"Would you like to quit Chicago and work for the City of Baltimore, Mr. Pinkerton?" the chief magistrate asked, looking quite serious.

If Molly Brannigan had been single, Allan would have sent an immediate telegram, asking his partner Edward Rucker why the detective agency could not just as easily set up headquarters in Baltimore. But the reality was different.

"I'm sorry. I can't," Allan said.

"I'm sorry as well." The chief magistrate of law enforcement set his hand familiarly on Pinkerton's shoulder.

"Let us return to my office. I did as you promised and took special care of Mrs. Brannigan's travel chest and scrimshaw. We can release it to you this morning."

"Good," Allan said. "Speaking of traveling luggage, has Mr. Poe's carpetbag turned up?"

"Unfortunately, no."

The two men started walking in the direction of the center of the city. Allan said, "We may not need any clues from Mr. Hewitt's death. I believe I may already know the identity of the person responsible for leaving Mr. Poe in the rain outside Gunner's Hall."

Foster regarded his companion with a look of even greater admiration. "Truly? Who is it?"

"Your office should receive confirming telegrams from the police of Manhattan and the City of Brooklyn in the near future. I am hoping they arrive today, but it may be on Monday."

A carriage awaited the chief magistrate. He gestured for Allan to climb in first.

Allan added, "If I am correct, it still does not guarantee that we can tie him to Poe's death beyond a reasonable doubt. This is not a case where the murderer is found standing over a plugged victim with smoking pistol in hand."

"I understand. Back to my office, Honor!" William Foster commanded the driver. To Pinkerton, he said, "Then what, if anything, can be done to serve Lady Justice?"

"I am hoping the man can be tricked into incriminating himself before reliable witnesses. One of those witnesses would be you."

Foster seemed both pleased and intrigued by Pinkerton's

words. "Continue."

"Let me tell you detail by detail why I suspect the particular man," Allan said. "And when I have finished, I shall tell you my plan for trapping him."

Between the time when the respected out-of-town Chief Detective Allan J. Pinkerton alighted from Chief Magistrate Foster's carriage and when he exited the justice building carrying Molly Brannigan's travel chest, more than an hour had elapsed. William Foster had been sincerely impressed with Pinkerton's process of narrowing down suspects and focusing on one man regarding his Poe investigation. However, when it came to the detective's method of proving that man's guilt, the chief magistrate was not nearly as sanguine.

His somber facial expressions indicated several times that he was in a frame of mind to balk. Aware of the offense it might cause, Allan nevertheless was reduced to reminding Foster that he had solved seven Baltimore robberies without costing the city one cent. A grudging acceptance of his plan was then given, along with the promise of Watch Force assistance.

As Allan walked down the front steps of the building, he was brushed by a boy of perhaps thirteen years moving with haste. Allan caught sight of the telegram in his hand.

"Is that for Chief Magistrate Foster?" he asked.

"Yeah, but you ain't him," the youth called back.

"Is it from New York?"

The messenger slowed his rush, turned, and regarded Pinkerton with a degree of awe.

"Answer enough," Allan said. He gestured to the boy to complete his delivery, following behind. As he climbed through the labyrinth of halls to Foster's office, trying not to bang the corners of Molly's luggage, he thought of the identical telegrams he had sent to New York:

Chief Magistrate Baltimore Watch requests
description and first name NYC mortician
assistant Reynolds with arrest record STOP
Mid forties

Allan followed the messenger as far as William Foster's office door and waited. Foster registered his presence, accepted the telegram, read it, and held it out for Pinkerton.

"You were right."

Allan read the message. Tersely worded as it was, it told him the majority of what he needed to know.

Jerel Reynolds served eight months
for necrophilia Auburn prison 1846
STOP forty seven years five foot five
black hair spectacles harsh voice
STOP refer Judge Barnaby Bristol

"Necrophilia!" Foster proclaimed. "Having sex with a corpse! What an unspeakable monster. And now he's a whiskey drummer."

"I am fairly certain that he is only masquerading as a whiskey drummer," Pinkerton declared.

"Very bizarre. How long since you've seen him?"

"Since I returned from Richmond. That was this past

Tuesday."

"Three-and-a-half days," calculated the chief magistrate. "What makes you think he's anywhere near here?"

"Two reasons. The first is that he said he would personally reclaim the Poe story he loaned me. The second is that I believe he returned to Baltimore for the sole pleasure of watching me investigate and fail." Allan set down the chest. "I know that sounds egotistical, but he said as much the first time I met him, in the Westminster cemetery. If I recall his words correctly, he said, 'I came from New York for this purpose.' At the time, I thought he meant that he had rearranged his sales visits to pay respects to his old friend. Now I realize he was being cheeky to my face."

"How could he have known you would be here?" asked Foster.

"My partner released a story to a number of prominent newspapers even as I was en route. At least one among their number was a New York journal. I was made out to be the greatest solver of puzzles since King Solomon."

A precious orange, no doubt shipped to Baltimore from Florida or Cuba, sat on Foster's desk, giving off a wonderful aroma. It caused a pertinent association in Pinkerton's mind.

"Yes, he was mocking me and Edgar Poe that afternoon. He had brought an apple with him. What he did not eat he tossed beside the grave and spoke about how it was white at the moment but would quickly turn brown and then rot."

"Ghoulish bastard!" Foster exclaimed. "By all means, we need to bring this miscreant to justice."

"It is precisely his hubris that will undo him," Pinkerton added, glad that his words were making a more enthusiastic accomplice of the chief of Baltimore police.

"But what if he does not visit you today?" Foster wondered.

"He will," said Allan with assurance. "Either he or a flunky has been watching my comings and goings. He longs to hear from my lips what I learned and did not learn up in Philadelphia. And he will stay in your city until I skulk out with my tail between my legs. Knowing him as I do now, he cannot resist being present for such a triumph." Allan changed the subject from theoretical to practical. "My friend, Mrs. Brannigan, tells me that Baltimore is very keen on theater."

"Indeed," Foster verified. "Our Holliday Street Theater rivals that of Philadelphia's Walnut and those in Annapolis. I count myself as a devotee."

"Might you have influence with any producers or actors?" Allan asked.

Foster's chest elevated slightly. "As chief magistrate, I have influence throughout Baltimore. What is it that you require?"

The two men talked for several more minutes, with the detective specifying needs and timetables. Then Allan said, "If we would see that he keeps to our schedule, I must leave here and make myself available."

Foster rose from his desk and offered his hand. "Starting at nine-thirty, my men and I will be awaiting and available to you."

Even though the walk was long, Allan elected to hike over to the Lexington Market, saving what little of his money remained. There, he nosed about the many shops and stalls, hoping that Jerel Reynolds would appear, pretending to meet by chance. He bought a sachet for Molly and placed it inside the chest. After loitering half an hour, he crossed the street to the Maryland House hotel and approached the desk clerk.

"You have had a guest here, off and on," Allan said. "Aaron Pelglade. So high. Black, shiny hair. Gravelly–"

"Yes, sir. I know him," said the clerk. "He stopped by early this morning."

"Did he? Is he staying here?"

"No. Not tonight. He asked to leave a message. Might you be Allan Pinkerton?"

Pinkerton took out his billfold and presented his calling card.

"Very good, sir." The clerk went to the wall of pigeonhole cubicles behind him and pulled out a sealed, cream-colored envelope. Unlike the one Allan had found behind the Tavern on the Wharf, the note was on light blue paper. He grunted in appreciation that the man was careful enough to change both handwriting and stationery.

Allan allowed himself a smile broad enough that it caused the clerk's eyebrows to raise. He thanked the man and started for the foyer doors.

Walking out into the street, he pulled the stationery out of its envelope and re-read the words thereupon, as if to confirm his first perusal.

Saturday, 27 October

Dear Allan–

As the preponderance of my business is now between Philadelphia and Richmond, I have decided to relocate my residence to Baltimore. I have taken a lease on a house. Meet me tonight, O'Grady's at 8:00. Please bring my copy of 'The Murders in the Rue Morgue.'

Your obedient servant,
Aaron Pelglade

"I will be there, Aaron Jerel Pelglade Reynolds," Allan said softly to himself. "I will be there wearing bells, bells, bells, bells, bells, bells, bells."

"Why is there a need to stage a charade for a man who's already known to be a criminal?"

Molly Brannigan looked angry on behalf of every person who admired Edgar Allan Poe. She sat in her parlor, bouncing Siobhan up and down on her knee while Allan sat at the table disassembling and cleaning his revolver. She had already praised him once more for recovering her property and added thanks for the thoughtful sachet. With those concerns addressed, she focused fully on the matter of bringing Aaron Pelglade/Jerel Reynolds to justice.

"As far as I know, he has only been found guilty of misusing the dead, not killing anyone," Pinkerton pointed out.

"He had an excellent reason for killing that sailor." Molly watched Allan's eyes grow wide. "I mean, from his point of view. The way I see it, Reynolds came up from Richmond with Poe, getting him drunk on the way. Then, he made sure to be in Richmond when you were there and take the same packet back to Baltimore, to learn what you learned and to control your interpretation."

"I think he might only have arranged to be at the Baltimore wharf when Poe arrived," Allan countered. "Otherwise, there was too much danger of any one of the crew recognizing him from only a few weeks earlier and commenting in my presence. And Hewitt said no one came up with Poe."

Molly looked a bit less sure of herself. "You're the detective."

Allan looked at the woman and then around the room. With very little trouble, he could imagine her as his wife and the little girl in the cradle his daughter. The place was cozy and exceedingly pleasant. Then his eyes fell upon the painting of the sailing ship above the hearth and the scrimshaw on the mantel, and he came back to reality. "You do quite well, given your lack of experience," he praised.

"And you did say Reynolds carries a knife long enough to slit a throat.," Molly added.

"Certainly long enough to slit an apple. Reynolds had to have some acquaintance with Poe. That much is clear from his intimate knowledge and anecdotes. Then it is not difficult at all for him to greet 'Eddie' at the wharf as if by chance and invite him…"

"Where?" Molly asked.

Allan set the weapon down on a pile of rags and applied a bit of gun oil. "That is a good question. Reynolds would not want the two of them to be seen carousing together for several days. Again, it would associate him too clearly with Poe's end."

Molly laid the baby in her cradle and set it rocking with her foot. "Fine. Then the sailor chances to see Reynolds at the dock."

"And I ignorantly tell this to Reynolds on the packet. Hewitt holds his tongue before I ask him, either because he cares nothing about Edgar Allan Poe or else he doesn't want to become involved in an affair with no profit to him. However, once I offer him money he is all too willing to link my traveling companion with the man who met Poe on Spear's wharf weeks earlier." Pinkerton's eyes narrowed. "I believe I recall a sly smile on Hewitt's face as he looked beyond me. That look focused on Reynolds and also betrayed his amusement that I had no idea the man I sought stood directly behind me."

"But where did Reynolds lead Poe the night he landed?" Molly pursued.

"It would not be Maryland House, where Reynolds has been staying this time. That's the most frequented part of the city."

"Mr. Poe was missing for three or four days," Molly mused aloud, her blue eyes flashing. "If I were the Watch, I would arrest Reynolds at O'Grady's Tavern tonight, dump him down some black hole for three or four days without food or light. I would douse him with cold water every hour, to be sure he was extremely uncomfortable and could not sleep. Then I would drag him out and interrogate him. If he failed to answer, I would beat him with a hose until he did!"

This barbaric bent was a side of Molly Brannigan Allan had not seen. The fall air outside had grown unseasonably cold in the past few hours, and insects were seeking shelter. Allan picked up a ready fly swatter and whacked one of the pests that had settled on the dining table.

"Yes, like that," Molly said, speaking of Jerel Reynolds.

"I'm glad you are not queen of America," Allan said.

"I should think you would be happy to provide the beating," she replied. "He came down to Baltimore precisely to impede you and to gloat when you failed."

"He also saved me from a good beating at Ryan's 4th ward," Allan pointed out. "That alone merits some clemency."

Molly uttered an unconvinced sound. "He did it to ingratiate himself."

"I hope you have a pair of pliers in your house," Allan said.

Molly stood. "If we don't, Glenn Burton certainly does." She walked into the kitchen.

Allan had already emptied the revolver chambers of their bullets. He picked one up. "Is Mr. Burton hesitant about performing a part?"

From the next room, Molly said, "He wishes to know the specifics."

Briefly, Allan recited the details.

Molly responded, "For a quiet man, Glenn can show a dramatic flair at parties. I am sure he will be quite intrigued and willing."

"Make sure he understands that he will be safe. I am doing all I can to see that no possible danger can come to him. Do you think, given that this is the last weekend of October, that we will have privacy in the cemetery?"

"Oh, I think the superstitious believe that the souls will soon be rising. They will be sure to avoid the burial-grounds. The thing to do is to post a sign saying the cemetery is closed. No mere sign will dissuade Reynolds if you succeed in your part."

"It is a pity that we could not have staged this four days hence," Allan regretted. "While there is a deep ocean of knowledge I do not possess about Jerel Reynolds, I know for certain that he is as obsessed as Edgar Poe was with death and with the dead rising. He told me so himself, several times. Of all holy days most evocative to the imagination, All Hallows Even is beyond peer. Molly, I also need a candle and matches."

Molly rummaged noisily for a time. "Here are your pliers. What are all these items for?" Before Allan could reply, she said, "What I do not understand is why he would harm his friend."

"Surely some of it was for money. From what the people in Richmond said, Edgar Poe was carrying more than he had ever held in his life."

"How would Reynolds know that?"

"Because, like theater folk or law enforcement officers, the literary community are a tight pack who makes it their business to know what is happening…particularly if someone has money to buy stories. I am sure the word spread like wildfire that Poe was carrying a thick roll of cash to buy works for his new periodical. But I am convinced money was not enough to have caused Reynolds to travel to Baltimore and arrange such a grotesque end for his supposed friend."

"Do you think you can get the truth out of the man?" Molly called out.

"Yes, if I play him most delicately. Reynolds is not stupid. In fact, he prides himself on his intellect."

"And yet he is only a whiskey salesman!" Molly said with disdain, as she carried a pair of pliers, a candle, and matches to Allan. "That must be at least one step down from mortician's assistant. Brilliant careers!"

"I don't believe he actually is a whiskey drummer," he replied, as he had to Magistrate Foster. This time, however, he elaborated. "First of all, his display case looks new, which may mean he purchased it or had it made just for his charade. Secondly, he treats it badly. I watched him set it down in a puddle and bang it against several chairs and tables. It would not look new unless it in fact is. Thirdly, it occurred to me as I was returning here that when he opened it, he never had any order forms inside. It was extremely dunderheaded of me not to have noticed that a week ago."

Molly sat again. "So, he thinks he's gotten away with murder at a distance from where he lives and is safely back in New York City. Then he reads in the *New York Sun* that a live version of Poe's Detective Dupin is on his way to investigate. So he takes part of the money he's stolen from Poe and buys a case and whiskey and comes down here to watch you from arm's distance. 'Keep your friends close and your enemies closer,'" Molly quoted as she watched Allan work. "Who said that?"

"Sun-tzu, a Chinese military strategist who lived before the time of Jesus. Yes, that's precisely what Aaron Pelglade sought to do. Now the man will pay for his assumption that he controls me. Blackie Reynolds, as Poe called him. You recall I asked you the color of Mr. Poe's hair?"

"Yes. Because that chief physician at the hospital said Poe's hair was black."

"But we both agree that jet black hair is rare indeed, and the writer did not possess it. However, Jerel Reynolds' hair is truly black. My, how Poe loved to play with words. To play with words and to mock with private, esoteric jokes."

"Goodness!" Molly exclaimed. She jumped up and went again into the kitchen.

"What is it?"

"Keep working. I will show you."

Allan made good use of the pliers and then lit the candle. Molly came back into the parlor carrying a scrap of paper and a pencil. She had written letters in a rough circle:

\* \* \*

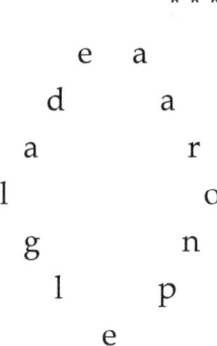

"Do you see the whiskey drummer's name in the circle?" Molly asked.

"Yes," Allan said.

"I will use each character once." As Molly wrote each letter in a line below the circle, she crossed the corresponding one off above. Within seconds, she had used them to spell:

'edgar allan poe.'

"Edgar Poe was not the only one who mocked with words. Reynolds does not respect you very much at all," Molly observed, "dangling this clue day after day in front of your nose."

Allan shook his head with deep misgiving. "And I did not earn his respect by seeing what was literally before my eyes."

"Why take Poe's name? "Molly queried. "Why not use an anagram of his own?"

Pinkerton nodded slowly. "I believe I know the answer to that, but I will find out for certain tonight."

"Don't be too hard on yourself," Molly said. "He spelled it for your ears, not your eyes."

Allan returned to his labors. "Even so. But now it is my turn to assail Mr. Aaron Pelglade's eyes and ears."

# CHAPTER TWENTY

*Saturday, October 27, 1849*

Pinkerton strolled into O'Grady's Saloon at twenty minutes past eight o'clock. He held in his hand the periodical that contained Poe's 'Murders in the Rue Morgue.' The place was packed to the rafters and vibrated from the rowdy energy of the patrons. Saturday night had arrived; revelry was required by the crowd. Three drunks were attempting to sing *Three Blind Mice*. Over the course of the next few minutes they never once finished the round and laughed with increasing hilarity each time they failed.

Jerel Reynolds sat exactly where he had sat the first time he and Pinkerton had rendezvoused in the gin palace. He glowered at one patron who looked to grab the empty seat, like a Pomeranian pretending to be a pit bull. He did not have his display case with him. He stood to greet the detective and held onto the back of his chair as he did.

"Allan! I thought you might not show up." He fixed his stare, just as he had done in the cemetery. His eyes blinked, if anything more frequently, behind the thick glass of his spectacles, and his voice was as scratchy as ever. He held out his hand. For an instant, Allan thought it was for a friendly shake. But instead, Reynolds reached for the periodical.

"Was it not one of the most splendid stories you have ever read?" Reynolds asked.

"Aaron, you are a connoisseur of the first order," Allan replied, making the man grin.

"We'll have a round here and then retire to my new house… where the drinks are markedly cheaper." Reynolds indicated two half-filled glasses already waiting at the table. He plopped himself down on his chair.

"Pike's Hill rye?" Allan asked of his pour.

"Not here, but at my…yes, the perfect word is 'digs.' Visiting their distillery was what pulled me away from Baltimore for two days."

Allan made a mental note to tie up loose ends by having William Foster inquire of the distillery what, if anything, they knew about the diminutive man.

"But my days were boring!" Reynolds insisted. "Tell me what you learned in Philadelphia."

In between small gulps of his drink, Allan repeated the stories of Rufus Griswold and John Sartain. He omitted every mention of 'Reynolds,' 'the homunculus,' and 'Blackie,' but made much of Griswold's negative statements and Sartain's detailing of Poe's hallucinatory episode.

"One or the other surely explains Eddie's end," Reynolds declared. "Will the Philadelphia police investigate Griswold's bank account to see if he made a large deposit soon after Eddie disappeared?"

"I passed along my suspicions to the chief magistrate of this city," said Allan. "And that is as far as I can go. I have run out of time."

Reynolds affixed a look of deep distress. "Oh, my. But you must take solace in the knowledge that you delved so much deeper than anyone else. And perhaps Griswold will be found guilty."

"Perhaps."

The two men engaged in talk of the rail route between Philadelphia and Baltimore and other astonishing advances in mechanization until they had both drained their drinks. Then Reynolds clapped his hands together.

"Come see the digs!" he exclaimed, "You will be my very first guest."

Not far down Pratt from the saloon, they hailed an unengaged hack and climbed in. Reynolds directed the driver to a number on Gay Street.

"Remember that sailor who told me he had seen a man greet Poe when he got off the *Pocahontas* from Richmond?" Allan asked, pretending to look past Reynolds at the passing cityscape.

"Right, right! I assume that came to nothing?" Reynolds disguised his thoughts well. Pinkerton expected nothing less.

Allan said, "He never showed. I believe he saw no one. His sole intention was to steal my three dollars."

Reynolds nodded with force. "That's why I neglected to ask you. I was sure it would be the case, but I didn't want to discourage you."

"Yes, he vanished. Left me standing on the wharf. But at least I was able to catch a pair of thieves." Keeping his eye on the route, Allan rattled off the tale of the house burglars.

"You must be the most accomplished and successful detective in America," Reynolds granted.

"Possibly the world," Allan said, keeping his face somber.

"Possibly," Reynolds echoed. "It is all the more wonder that this Poe business has confounded you. Because someone dressed the man in shoddy, worn-out clothing, and that was not a kind act."

"Indeed someone did, and indeed it was not."

The hack turned the corner off Pratt and stopped soon after.

"This is it," Reynolds announced. "Close to the wharves so that I can race to the packets at the last moment."

Allan looked toward the harbor and saw that they were

close. Soon, however, he would not be able to see more than harbor lights from the distance. A temperature inversion was creeping in, and the first wisps of fog descended. He resisted glancing at his watch. Although not as accurate as his internal sleep clock, his waking sense of time was good. He estimated that the hour was a little after nine. William Foster and one of his most fleet-footed men would be concealed in the cemetery in half an hour. The chief magistrate had not deemed more than their participation and that of Glenn Burton necessary. In case the set-up went awry, the circumspect city official wanted as few witnesses as possible.

"Come inside," Reynolds invited, after paying the cabman.

Allan looked up at the townhouse. The structure was two-storied, relatively old, rather rundown, and somewhat narrow.

Reynolds stopped directly after opening the door with an old key. He bent, picked up an oil lamp sitting just inside the door on the floor, found some matches, and brought the lamp to light. He moved into the house without looking back.

When Allan entered, he found himself looking at a townhouse laid out in the same pattern as Molly's. The stairs leading to the second floor lay just beyond the front door. Unlike the Brannigan home, the parlor contained only three items of furniture: a single bed with a wooden frame, a café table, and one chair. The whiskey display case and two wooden crates holding liquor were on the floor near the bed. The room had no other illumination except the oil lamp, so shadows dominated.

"It's not much yet, but it will be home once my belongings arrive from New York," said Reynolds, adjusting the lamp to its full but still feeble brightness. "So, you'll want that Pike's Hill rye. Please pick out a bottle for you, and bring me the opened one of bourbon."

While the little man seemed at ease and totally unaware of Allan's plans, nonetheless the detective knew him to be a dangerous adversary. Thus, he was pleased to see that not only was Reynolds willing to allow him to pick out his own bottle but that every flask was also sealed. He handed the two flasks to his host.

Reynolds went to the side window, which lay in darkness. He opened the flasks and poured out two fingers' worth into each of two glasses sitting on the sill. Then he came back into the light and offered the rye to Pinkerton.

"Bottoms up! To your very good health, Mr. Pinkerton!"

"To your long life, Mr. Pelglade!" Allan said, thinking, *And may it all be spent inside a prison.* Allan upended the glass as if drinking all its contents, but when he began to lower it he let half of what he held in his mouth trickle back.

Reynolds emptied his glass with an appreciative little growl. "As the guest of honor, please sit on my bed. Now that you have read a goodly number of Eddie's works, which do you like best?" He fetched the opened flasks, handed the rye to Allan, and kept the bourbon for himself. Then he plopped down on the solitary chair.

Allan had eaten several pieces of bread just before leaving the Brannigan house, so that they might absorb the alcohol he expected to consume and release it only slowly into his system. He suspected that his adversary drank every night, and in spite of Allan's greater weight and height, unless he consumed the bread he would have no advantage. Necessary to the plan was to get Reynolds drunk enough that his mercurial emotions and wild imagination would overpower his logic and reason. He was happy to enter into yet another of Reynolds' protracted dissertations on Poe if it meant keeping him drinking. He sat on the bed. The mattress and webbing were not particularly comfortable.

"As we have both agreed," Allan began, "'The Murders in the Rue Morgue' is not only clever but also very instructive as to the methods of good detection. The plot is outlandish, but it must be – to allow Dupin to solve the seemingly impossible."

"I was going to strike you," Reynolds said, albeit affably, "until you explained yourself there. What other stories?"

"I like 'The Gold-Bug' very much."

Reynolds nodded. "And?"

"And 'The Pit and the Pendulum.'"

Reynolds' eyes lit up. "Yes, yes! Superb! What about 'The Mask of the Red Death'?"

Pinkerton took another sip, mimicking in miniature the long draft taken by the pretend whiskey salesman.

"Not so much."

"What? It is outré in the extreme! Readers have had nightmares for months after reading that tale."

Alan shook his head. "You can see it coming from a mile off. There's no surprise."

"That's because Poe ruined it," Reynolds insisted. "He took a perfectly splendid plot and telegraphed the ending. It was his poor writing that made it less than perfect."

"So, he gets a bullseye for the plot and a near miss for the rest," Allan suggested.

"He gets nothing for the plot!" Reynolds snapped. Then his face took on a petulant expression, and he lapsed into an eerie silence. After another swallow of bourbon, he looked left and right, cocked his head, and stared at Allan through his thick glasses, blinking away.

"What?" Allan asked.

"Are you all right?"

Allan realized that he was not, in fact, all right. His vision had begun to unfocus. He looked down at his glass. He was sure he had seen Reynolds break the seal on the flask of rye. How could it be tampered with?

"What about 'William Wilson'?" Reynolds asked, as if abandoning his concern for his guest. "What a sea change from the works immediately preceding! He must have used fecal matter for the ink pigment when he wrote 'The Devil in the Belfry' and 'The Man Who Was Used Up!" Reynolds rose from his chair and drew his frail self to his full height. "I'll tell you what Edgar Allan Poe was, Mr. Pinkerton: he was a Stradivarius without a decent tune to play!"

Allan, too, attempted to rise. He found his equilibrium severely wanting and sat back as quickly as he had stood, flailing his arm behind him to keep from bouncing prostrate onto the mattress.

"He was a brain without legs," said Reynolds. "Just as you are." And then he laughed.

Allan summoned all of his determination and rose again. He lumbered in the direction of the door and put his hand on the knob. And then he was struck from behind. What little light had illuminated the room suddenly went out.

When Allan Pinkerton awoke, he found himself securely bound to a chair. It was a damp and low-ceilinged interior, with rough-hewn beams exposed above. The floor was hard-packed dirt. There was not one window. He figured he was in the cellar of the townhouse where he had lost consciousness. An oil lamp identical to the one he had seen in the front room upstairs emitted a feeble, yellow light from its place on the floor. Moreover, the space seemed the same dimensions as the old townhouse had been.

The cellar smelled musty and dank. Under the steps, beyond a pathetic bed, sat a closed trunk, topped by a carpetbag and a handyman's tool carrier.

The back of the detective's head, his shoulder blades, elbows and buttocks ached. He realized he had been dragged unconscious down those wooden steps. As he struggled vainly from side to side against his bonds, he realized that both peripheries of his vision consisted of wall. He looked up. Less than three feet above his head was a curving ceiling formed of hard-packed dirt and stone. He saw that he and the chair were inside a small alcove that had been dug out of the far end of the cellar. He registered the sand, the powdered limestone, and the trough for mixing cement directly in front of him. Beyond these lay several piles of bricks. Enough to wall him completely in the alcove. Just as Fortunato had been sealed up for eternity, in Poe's "The Cask of Amontillado."

A door opened above. Grunting with each step, Reynolds descended into the cellar. He carried in both hands a large wooden bucket.

"Awake sooner than I expected," Reynolds observed when he turned into the open space. "Now you know why I call it my digs!" He laughed uproariously at his own joke. "It turns out I lied; you are not my first guest. But welcome to my pit anyway," his scratchy voice added.

Pinkerton's host set down the bucket and then sat on the bed. It was far inferior to the poorly-made one upstairs. This one looked like an antique Reynolds had rescued from the city dump. It had a mattress but no sheets, pillow, or covers. On the mattress lay Pinkerton's revolver. "Do you like your view? It's different from the one Eddie had. I had only begun to excavate the space you're sitting in."

Allan chuckled.

His captor's face went slack with astonishment. "Why do you laugh?"

"Those ragged, filthy fingernails. You didn't get them from helping someone replace a wagon wheel; you got them from excavating down here."

"Correct! You indeed have a mind like a steel sieve. I was amazed at how much material came out of that little space you're in. Or should I call it 'crypt?'" Reynolds' voice, though annoyingly raspy, was calm. As if to amplify his pacific attitude, he crossed one leg over the opposite knee. He swung out his right hand in a casual manner. "Here is the result of my labors. I haven't tried to move any of it yet."

Allan noted the several piles of dirt and rocks and the pick and short shovel lying atop them. Beyond the piles of brick and limestone and the mixing trough was a coal scuttle.

Allan saw that Reynolds had changed to work clothes. His pants were rough, and his shirt was of a checkered pattern. He wore low-quarter boots. He stretched behind himself, to the workman's carrier, and produced a trowel.

"I've never used one of these before, but how difficult can it be?" Reynolds reached under the bed and carefully picked up a two-thirds-drained whiskey flask. He drank deeply and slowly from it, as if he had all the time in the world. He set the flask down under the bed as carefully as he had lifted it, stood, and came closer to Pinkerton. "Eddie imagined the bricking process rather well in 'The Cask of Amontillado,' don't you think? Considering he had no idea…no idea at all. One never saw his fingernails split and dirty."

"What time is it?" Allan asked.

"It's half past ten. I actually thought you'd be unconscious for much longer. You know the reason you woke up so soon? I was only able to put the thinnest line of knockout drops in your glass. Otherwise, you'd have seen the liquid glimmering, even in the darkness." He smiled. "But I'm glad you're awake. It's so much nicer having someone to talk with while one works, don't you think?"

"You're going to wall me up, just like in Poe's story."

"My story!" Reynolds shouted. "Don't you understand even yet?" He fetched the bucket with a pained grunt, went to the scuttle and poured half its contents of water into it, and then emptied the rest into the mixing trough. He talked as he methodically mixed the limestone, water, and sand into cement. "Is this so difficult to understand? If you're the most successful detective in the world, I must be the most successful criminal, because I've certainly bested you!"

Allan declined to disabuse his captor of his belief. He studied more closely the alcove that surrounded him. It was deep enough that he would be almost two feet from the wall Reynolds intended to re-create. He tried to kick out his feet. They were securely bound to the legs of the chair. He could feel that his arms and hands were secured by metal behind his back.

"I used your own handcuffs," Reynolds said in an off-hand manner, pulling Pinkerton's ring of keys from his pocket and dropping them on the earthen floor. "Thanks so for showing them to me. The scene will be that much more gruesome two months or two decades from now, when someone opens the wall and finds your skeleton shackled to that chair. Then, if they haven't been removed long before, the person will see that salvation lay just inches away, on the opposite side of the wall."

"And why do you feel you need to do this?"

Reynolds laughed. "Well, because I can. And because you are moderately clever. You might tomorrow stumble across some idiot who saw me and Eddie together."

"You learned via the literary grapevine that he was heading north through Baltimore, with money to purchase stories," Allan said.

"Correct."

"Then you came down from New York and waited for him to arrive by packet. You knew he would come that way, because the railroads are not connected between here and Richmond."

Reynolds grunted as the mixture became thicker and more resistant to stirring. "Isn't that exactly what I told you?"

"You pretended the wharf side encounter was by chance, of course."

"Of course."

"And did you have your display case of whiskey at that time, or did you purchase it just for my benefit?"

Jerel Reynolds scowled. "Think harder...or is your mind still fuzzy? I had both it and my story of a new profession made expressly for him. Because Eddie could not resist free alcohol. The poor are so easily seduced by free things." He drew in a deep breath and dragged the trough up to the edge of the alcove. "I also had this townhouse by then. Had to lease it for three months, but I only paid for two up front. I cursed the landlord back then, but when I read in the *Sun* that you were on your way, I was damned relieved to still have its use. Whenever he was in Baltimore and unable to gull a friend or relative into taking him in, the best Eddie could afford was Bradshaw's Hotel. It's a dive right beside the B&O Railroad terminal." He began shuttling bricks close to the scuttle, two at a time. "So I said to him, 'Eddie, old buddy, I've been mad at you for a long time, but who can stay mad at a genius forever?' And do you know what the fool – the one who never suffered other fools – replied? 'Certainly you can't, Blackie.'"

"He called you Blackie because of your hair," Allan said.

Reynolds pointed the trowel at the detective. "Dead on. One point for the corpse-to-be. And then I told him how I had moved from New York just three days before and invited him to stay with me overnight. Once again, that inveterate moocher could not resist. Freeloading was his forté."

Reynolds had evidently researched the task at hand. He brought the smaller bucket close to the wall, and dipped his eight bricks in the water. Then he buttered each brick and laid it on the existing foundation stones. "This was originally going to be Eddie's fate. I thought it so…what's the word…ah, yes… poetic!" Again he laughed. "But then I thought, 'He will suffer thus, but disappearing will make him a vanished genius to the world.' Ever elegant and sober in their minds. So much better to dress him in rags and leave him in a gutter, like the sneaky drunkard he was. Indeed! Ruining his reputation while stealing the money for his precious periodical was a far better idea."

"You're doing a very neat job," Allan observed.

"Thank you. I'm so glad you understand that no amount of pleading or reasoning can save you. You won't start to scream 'For the love of God!' when I reach the tenth course, will you?"

"Not I." Allan tested his bonds again while Reynolds busied himself fetching more bricks. He found that a rope had been tied around his waist and woven around the seat, the back, and the legs, so that he could not stand. He also saw that the knots were the same simple ones the man had used to tie Jack Hewitt's wrist and ankle to the stones.

Reynolds stacked his bricks and continued the process.

"You chose this house because it was not far from the wharves," Allan said.

"And because I could not afford anything better, since I did not yet have his money."

"Fifteen hundred dollars," Allan recited.

"Wrong! I told you that was a ridiculous figure on the boat. They either lied to you in Richmond or else stole the balance after he died."

"How much did you get?"

"Seven-hundred-and-fifty-three dollars and a few cents."

"Not a bad haul," judged Pinkerton. "What a skilled craftsperson makes in a year."

"Not quite, but more or less what I believe he owed me." Reynolds was working fast and puffing hard with each breath. He was already halfway done with the second course.

"Because you gave him all his best plots," said Pinkerton.

Reynolds made a little bow. "Yes! At last someone understands!"

"Tell me how that came to be," Allan invited in an affable

tone. "You met him, you said, in 1835."

Reynolds set down his trowel and regarded his captive as a monologist would a rapt audience. Allan knew this was a moment for which the man had been awaiting for so many years. "No. I lied a bit. It was 1838, in Philadelphia. He was working as an editor and earning a pitiful few pennies writing his execrable short stories. Then I offered the idea of the man who kills his spiritual self, his conscience…'William Wilson.' It was as if flint had struck steel. Heaven ordained that we meet each other and collaborate. At first he resisted. He told me the story was unworkable. But then he wrote it. And it made him money. And it gave him added stature." Reynolds studied the two courses of the wall and resumed his labor in a desultory fashion as he spoke.

"He was given fifteen dollars for that masterpiece. I told him afterward that he was degrading himself and letting the greedy publishers know how cheaply he was willing to sell a work of genius. But he was always behind in his earnings, always owing to someone. And so he took the money and continued on the sorry path of selling himself…and me…short."

"How much did he give you of it?"

"Five dollars." Reynolds laughed ruefully. "But it was five he owed me, so it was in essence nothing. Without my plot, he had nothing."

"Why didn't you write the story yourself?" Allan asked.

"That's just it. I told you already, days ago. I can come up with the most unique ideas, the most captivating notions. But I lacked his control of language, his ability to…to breathe life into an exquisite corpse." Reynolds leaned in close, across the first two courses of bricks. "We were perfect complements to each other. Like Rich and Gay."

"I don't know who you mean."

"No, of course you don't. But you do understand what I said about my part of his fame."

Pinkerton saw his opportunity. Pushing up on his toes, he threw his weight as forward as he could. The chair pitched, throwing him onto Poe's murderer. Reynolds let out a surprised yelp. He threw up his hands, but they were too late to prevent Pinkerton from falling on him. The two men went down, Reynolds on his back and Pinkerton face first into the man's chest. As he fell, he aimed his nose to catch one lens of Reynolds' spectacles. The impact whipped them from the man's ears and the bridge of his nose. The crunch of glass shattering on the little pile of bricks was unmistakable.

"You stupid bastard!" Reynolds yelled. "My glasses! Ah! My only pair!"

Allan hoped they were. "I'm sorry," he offered, as Reynolds rolled to the side and he was left to fall to the dirt, nose painfully twisted. "I hoped to knock you out, so that I could escape. I didn't mean to harm your spectacles."

Reynolds worked his way to his feet. He pressed the fingers of his left hand lightly against his left side, wincing as he had done in the Westminster cemetery and O'Grady's saloon. He dug into his trousers and pulled out his jackknife. He swung it open, moved to where Allan could see him with one eye, and brandished it. "But you did harm them. I ought to cut your tongue out. Why shouldn't I cut your tongue out?"

Allan kept his voice as calm as possible. "Then I won't be able to answer any of your questions."

"Then why not gouge your eyes out?"

"Then I won't be able to suffer the darkness that will close in on me when you slide in the last brick."

Reynolds' chest heaved up and down. His tongue protruded from his gasping mouth. Clearly, Allan's words made sense to him. He shook his head, closed his knife, and thrust his fingers into the opposite trouser pocket. He pulled out the tiny tin box that held his digitalis pills.

Reynolds popped one of the pills into his mouth and swallowed it dry. "'Abandon hope, ye who have entered here.' Do you think I lie to you about my critical contributions to Eddie's fame? Do you think I am some deluded maniac? No, indeed. I can tell you every work I provided the plot for. Also the month I shared the idea with him. The month he got each story published. Every idea of mine – unlike his own works – was published."

He picked up what remained of the spectacles and set them on one of the stair risers. Once he was breathing more naturally, he bent for the handyman's tool carrier and took out a hammer and two very long nails. As he worked, he mumbled, "October, 1838, 'William Wilson' is published," recited Reynolds. "Number Two: 'The Fall of the House of Usher,' 1839. Number Three: 'The Murders in the Rue Morgue,' 1841."

Reynolds left Pinkerton lying awkwardly on the floor, his stomach aching from the jumble of bricks under it. Allan heard him begin the process of hammering the two nails into the rocklike dirt above and behind him.

"I read the news about an escaped ourang-outang and told Eddie that such a wild but manlike creature would be perfect for committing a crime. He took the story from there. He developed all the subtle clues by first inventing them and working them in as actions. Fine. But he could not be the inventor of the detective in fiction without me."

The hammer rang out again and again. Reynolds' breathing again became ragged and labored. He let the hammer drop and went back to the tool chest for a length of rope. Then he wrestled Pinkerton and the chair upright, passed the rope twice around Pinkerton's midsection, and secured the rope to the nails.

"That will hold you until doomsday," he said portentously. He plodded over to the poor excuse for a bed and sat heavily on it, his small lungs heaving. "Number Four: 'The Mask of the Red Death,' May of 1842. Twelve dollars! He let that go for twelve dollars. To goddamned Graham, who so misused him as an editor. And how much did I receive? Nothing. Four classic tales that may still be read in five hundred years, and my share is nothing. Eddie was cheated of money, but at least he gets everlasting fame."

Reynolds shook his head, stood, and returned to his labors. "God, the cement is starting to set! Don't slow me down again, or I will slit your throat."

Reynolds bent to his work, wetting and buttering bricks, muttering how he had salvaged more than half of the ones from the original wall and how that effort had saved money and the need to haul so much new material down. Twice in the ensuing five minutes he went to the bed and reached under it for his fortification of bourbon.

"'The Gold-Bug' was his. He could have it. Just too precious and unbelievable. What brute of a pirate is going to draw up a substitution riddle map? 'Marie Roget' was his. God, the man was a true detective. Did you know he solved the plot to

*Barnaby Rudge* several issues before it came to its conclusion? He gave the solution to Dickens personally, and the Englishman was flabbergasted that Eddie had figured it out. He was a demon at two things: calculation and creating worlds and moods from pure words. That's why I chose him for my plots, you see? Number Five: "The Tell-Tale Heart.'"

"That was a corker," Allan allowed.

"Thank you. Number Six, another favorite of yours: 'The Pit and the Pendulum.' Also 1843. Another twelve dollars! God Almighty, the rich spend that much on an intimate party at a good restaurant! Down their fat gullets and out the next day as shit. But 'The Pit and the Pendulum' is immortal. And then what happened, Mr. Pinkerton?"

Reynolds paused with a brick in each hand, eyebrows raised and myopic eyes wide, inquiring as if Allan were leaning over a fence and shooting the breeze with him.

"I don't know."

"Then I'll tell you. In 1844 he produced 'A Tale of the Ragged Mountains' and 'The Spectacles.'" Reynolds glanced back in the direction of his ruined glasses, then shook his head at Pinkerton. "Do you know these tales?"

"No."

"Of course you don't. Even those who read them cannot recall them. Or they would rather forget them. Because they were drivel. Rubbish. Dross. And do you know why?"

"Because you didn't suggest their plots," Allan said, not expecting contradiction.

"Because he was back on his own at that point. I had finally reached the end of my tether. Eddie kept promising me that when the works were reprinted, I could have all the earnings.

But, of course, by the time I had met up with him again, some new dire emergency had occurred, and he had spent my part. One evening, in late 1843, in a tavern that looked very much like O'Grady's, I told him that he could kiss future fame farewell, because I would never share another plot with him as long as I lived. I stalked out of that saloon and fired one parting word at him. And do you know what that word was?"

With confidence, Pinkerton said, "Nevermore."

Reynolds' head jerked back with surprise. Then he quickly recovered. "Good guess. That's precisely what I said: 'Nevermore!' 'Nevermore!' Just like that." His voice, always raspy, sounded almost precisely like that of a large black bird.

Pinkerton stared at the brilliantined black hair, swept back on the diminutive man's head. He stared into the blinking, birdlike eyes. Then he laughed outright.

"You find that funny?" Reynolds asked with a look of injury.

Pinkerton thought of Professor Throckmorton lecturing him about William Shakespeare: the borrowed plots were secondary in importance. They were merely existing mortar bowls the greatest genius of the English language used to mix and grind his characters in, compelling them to struggle, to reveal their natures and mettle, to triumph or fail. "Surely not as funny as Eddie did," he replied.

This time Reynolds blinked in his surprise. "Yes, Eddie was immensely amused. He thought 'The Raven' was the funniest lampoon a man could ever devise, the greatest literary thumbing of poetic nose the world had ever read but not understood. I was the bird-brained creature with the shiny black covering who visited him uninvited and imparted nothing important. And yet he was able to use my presence to awaken his genius."

"And he never told anyone what the poem really meant," Allan said.

"Of course he never told anyone. He either said he was inspired by a child of some married woman he was copulating with or else that he had been inspired by Dickens' *Barnaby Rudge*. How could he tell his world about me without having to admit I was the other half of his own personal William Wilson? His better half. 'The Raven' was a hollow triumph, wouldn't you say?"

The clue of the homunculus called Blackie that Pinkerton had received in Philadelphia had been the key allowing so many other facts to unite. Suddenly, on the train ride back to Baltimore, the strange appearance of the cawing, black-haired little man in the cemetery made sense. His obsession with Poe made sense. But, most of all, his constant downplaying of Poe's talents before he and the poet had met and his insistence that the plots in Poe's earlier stories were the vital missing element pointed the finger directly at Reynolds as the person with the greatest animus against the writer. The ragged clothing, precisely Reynolds' size, provided physical proof of his plot. The telegram by the police from New York had merely corroborated what Allan knew of the little man's sick mind and provided a first name.

Pinkerton calculated the time elapsed since he had awakened from his drugging. He wanted Jerel Reynolds to arrive at the Westminster cemetery as close to midnight as possible. In spite of his discomfort, he decided to let Poe's murderer chatter on. The man was, after all, divulging fascinating information. And there was much yet to share that

Reynolds might not be inclined to reveal once he was in custody but would babble to a rival he was sure would soon be dead.

"'Nevermore,'" Allan said, blandly.

Reynolds laughed. "Yes. But I have answered his jest with the gravest of replies. Poe will write, breathe, laugh and love nevermore. And neither will you, my ambitious friend. I estimate that you will have perhaps half a dozen hours to regret coming to Baltimore before the lack of air circulation finally asphyxiates you. I will leave some holes in your tomb, not for water weeping, but so that you may have sufficient time to contemplate your end and do your own weeping. Then, when you are as cold as these walls, I will close up the holes so that your rotting corpse does not stink up the entire house."

"How considerate," said the detective.

"January of 1845 that insult 'The Raven' was published," Reynolds remembered bitterly as he resumed work at a considerably slower pace. "But, you know, much as I was abused by the man, insulted, and used, I loved him for his genius. I am not ashamed to admit it. And he could be charming. As Fortunato was charming. 'The devil hath powers to assume a pleasing shape.' So in 1846, I relented and gave him one last chance to repay me. I gave him the plot for 'The Cask of Amontillado.' And as I did, I said to myself, 'The table turns. This time, he will not apprehend your private joke on him. If he does not repay you, you will see that he suffers the supreme irony and dies behind a wall.' Because he was stealing from me. Plagiarizing and claiming as his own. If you did not understand it before this, Allan Pinkerton, then you will understand it before you die: Plagiarism in the literary world is the same as murder in the real world."

Reynolds sneezed.

"God bless you," Pinkerton said amiably.

Reynolds regarded him quizzically. The mask of unabashed triumph faded from his face.

"How many blocks is this house from Gunner's Hall?" Allan asked.

"Four. Why do you ask?"

"That's why you chose the place to dump him. Close and a drinker's paradise." Allan straightened up in his seat. "You tempted him here with liquor and free lodging. He insisted on visiting Dr. Brooks, but he hadn't made himself helpless yet. So, you let him do that. You must have been very pleased when Brooks wasn't home."

"Immensely relieved, I will admit. But I knew he would be back for the free drink and bed. When he returned, he got himself roaring drunk," Reynolds revealed.

"But," Pinkerton jumped in, "I believe, after another day at the most, he would have stopped drinking on his own. I am certain of this because he had a dream to fulfill, a dream far more powerful than the lure of alcohol. So that means that you introduced something else into his whiskey. I am guessing it was laudanum. And what else? What killed him, slowly but surely, Aaron?" he asked, being sure to use the name Reynolds had given himself

"Arsenic. It was arsenic," said the delicate man. "And I had to hold him here for several days, because a lethal dose had to be introduced gradually to produce a cumulative effect. Ever since 1836, there has been something called a Marsh test. It can detect the presence of arsenic in a corpse years after death. I have been told that arsenic destroys every system of the body. It first produces stomach pains and headaches, then tenderness everywhere, dryness and tightness of the throat, hoarseness and difficulty of speech, cramps and convulsions, delirium, and then death."

With only a few sentences, Reynolds had precisely described the death that the doctors and nurses of Washington University Hospital had witnessed.

"Because Eddie was both a binge drinker and a user of laudanum, I employed both liberally, with small pinches of arsenic. I knew that everyone in Baltimore would assume it was booze or opium and never guess deliberate poisoning. Finding a corpse in the street would necessitate an autopsy. Slow death after he was in their care, however, allowed them to think whatever they wanted. Alcohol poisoning, brain lesion, rabies. I never read so many theories about one man's death. And yet no autopsy. Brilliant, no?"

"Very clever," Pinkerton granted. "So you locked him down here in the darkness. And that is the cot you allowed him. Perhaps you thought the damp air would add pneumonia as well. And you gave him a tiny bit to eat and no water. But he received all the alcohol he wanted."

"Why are you so clever all of a sudden?" Reynolds wondered aloud, the bravado gone from his raspy voice.

"His constitution was already delicate. And when he was permanently incoherent and you were ready to drop him off, you exchanged his clothes. No, that's not right! You stole his clothes early on, while he slept. And you left those rags down here for him to choose to wear or freeze. Oh, the indignity and embarrassment! Further, they were your clothes. I'll bet they were clothes from one of your low periods, and you hung on to them for just this purpose."

"They were."

"Did you not give him the idea for 'Hop-Frog,' where the king degrades his jester and makes his nobles wear costume rags?"

"No. He stole that story from another source. But it gave me an idea."

"By exchanging clothing, you became the important partner and he the unimportant one."

"It is as if you were talking with him," Reynolds marveled in a breathy tone. "As if you were down here listening. How can you know so much?"

Reynolds' inviting question signaled the entrapped detective to become the trapper. Since receiving the man's note at the hotel, Pinkerton had planned to invite himself to Reynolds' new home. Within the privacy of its walls, he would have the latitude to spin a tale as bizarre and grotesque as any Poe had ever concocted. Unlike the simple goal of the Gothic author to bring shivers down his reader's spine and create a nightmare or two, Allan's purpose was to galvanize Jerel Reynolds to actions that would prove him to be Edgar Poe's murderer.

"But you allowed him to hang on to that cane," Allan plowed on. "The cane whose owner, Dr. Carter, supposed he had switched by mistake. The truth was that Eddie was frightened, carrying so much money. He had never owned a pistol, but he assumed he could defend himself with the sword hidden inside the cane leg." Pinkerton thought of Reynolds' favored left flank and braced himself for a leap of insight. "And he did use the sword. Didn't he, Aaron?"

Reynolds rushed to his flask of bourbon. He fought open the

top and chugged the last inch of the amber liquid. "Yes, he used the sword! I thought he was helpless down here, but he came at me, drunk and drugged as he was."

Reynolds yanked up his shirt, exposing a closed but red wound about an inch long.

"He stabbed me! I was lucky he wasn't more sober or he could have killed me – and after all I did for him!"

"You took the cane away, but you gave it back to him when you dumped him on that bench."

"That's right. I wanted him to believe it made him safe. I wanted him to lie there and not cry out or try to crawl away."

"Yes." Allan knew that he had set the hook deeply into Jerel Reynolds' psyche. "The black suit you wore when you arranged to meet me in the cemetery; that is Edgar's suit," he went on. "You had a tailor take up the sleeves and the trouser legs. Finally, you were the visible part of your William Wilson."

Reynolds' eyes narrowed. "You are mocking me, just as he did. How can you have such nerve, tied to that chair and awaiting entombment?"

Pinkerton laughed softly. "Because I have spoken with Eddie."

Allan had heard the expression 'the color drained from his face,' but he had never seen such a dramatic demonstration as occurred that minute to Jerel Reynolds.

"You are a clairvoyant?" he asked, in a tone almost reverent.

"No! I mean the living Edgar Allan Poe. The one you and the rest of the world thought died but who did not."

Reynolds collapsed on the bed, trembling. "Impossible! Every newspaper reported his death. There was a huge funeral. He was buried."

"I will not even ask you to untie my hands, because in a few moments you will do it of your own free will. You will understand that killing me can only result in your certain execution."

Pinkerton had carefully refrained from making any remark about the dead sailor, Jack Hewitt. "Right now, you can only be accused of attempted murder."

Allan's captor sat in silence, shoulders heaving, glaring at his prisoner.

"Listen to me before you make one more stupid mistake," Allan ordered in his commanding baritone. "You dropped Eddie off at Gunner's Hall, and he was found and brought to Washington University Hospital exactly as reported. He was nursed for four days and seemed to actually have died. Because he had no money, the doctors, staff, and even the medical students pooled their spare coins and bought him a poplar coffin. It was stained to make it look like a more expensive wood, but it was very cheap and poorly made. You know from personal experience that poorly made coffins allow enough air for a man barely breathing to live. Eddie shared with me only a few days ago that you were a mortician's assistant. You know first-hand about true premature burials."

"My God!" Reynolds exhaled.

"In that capacity, you once saw a person revive. Eddie said you told him that when you first met. You also know that Washington University Hospital is a teaching hospital and that it has in the past few years fallen on hard times. Consequently, the staff has been reduced to robbing graves in a few surrounding cemeteries for anatomy cadavers. Think about the recent disappearance of that young lady from her parlor. What was her name?"

"Margaret Jensen."

"Yes! You told me about the true story of the woman put alive into the mausoleum in Baltimore, the one who Eddie included at the beginning of his 'The Premature Burial.' You also know that Westminster is all the way on the other side of town. There was no grave robbing in Eddie's case. Instead, the doctors conspired to take an unclaimed body from their cellar, one that was too rotted and beyond usefulness for dissection, and substitute it into Poe's coffin. But only half an hour after the grand viewing that had taken place under the hospital's rotunda was ended, when they went to make the switch, Eddie gave out a groan. He had fallen into a catatonic state, but that period of total rest had allowed his body to recover.

"You read that there was no trace of alcohol on him when he was found outside Gunner's Hall. Likewise, the laudanum had worn off about that time. It was only the arsenic's work that rendered him so pathetic in the hospital. And because you had been so careful not to administer a lethal dose, he was able to weather it. Just as the Borgias did by taking increasingly large doses over time, to build up their immunity to poisoning. He was beside himself with joy that all his premonitions had come true and that he had actually survived premature burial."

Allan was careful to end his recitation with mention of premonitions. Aaron Pelglade had voiced his belief early on in their acquaintance. During Pinkerton's protracted speech, Reynolds made not one sound. He hardly seemed to be breathing. Finally, he rallied a bit.

"If he is still alive, why has he not come from hiding and accused me?"

"Oh, he intends to," Pinkerton assured. "But you know Eddie better than all of us; he waits for the absolute best moment to resurrect. For Jesus, it was a Sunday morning. For Eddie, it will be this Wednesday night. What day is Wednesday, Jerel?"

"You know my real name," Reynolds said.

"Of course I do. He told me. So you would have proof that he is still alive. Unlike me, he is a wizard at solving riddles. The name you have been using with me is an anagram of Edgar Allan Poe. He said you did it because you are convinced you are as much the famous author as he is."

These words struck the little man like a dagger through the heart. His hand pressed unconsciously against his chest.

"What day is Wednesday, Mr. Reynolds?" Pinkerton asked again, in a hypnotically smooth voice.

"October 31st."

"And what is October 31st?"

"All Hallows Evening."

"Exactly. Hallowe'en. When the dead rise from their graves. Now, not being from Baltimore, I had no way of knowing. But of course Eddie did: This city celebrates the occasion with more fervor than anywhere else. He says the reason is because New England is predominantly Protestant. However, Baltimore has many Italians and, since the potato famine, a flood of Irish. Both are Roman Catholic, and have strong traditions of joyously celebrating religious holy days. Tell me if Eddie is wrong: In Baltimore, there are many 'play parties,' where people bob for apples and tell ghost stories, trying to win a prize for telling the most frightening tale. Here, the Irish display their Jack O'Lanterns, to commemorate the legendary hero who treed the devil. People even wander the streets dressed as ghosts and ghouls and devils."

Reynolds did not try to contradict his captive.

"Nothing pleases your friend more than perpetrating a colossal hoax on the public. His balloon hoax will shrink to insignificance. Imagine when Edgar Allan Poe, the master of the macabre, literally rises from the dead on Hallowe'en! Imagine it, after every newspaper in the country has declared him dead. His new periodical is certain to gain an initial subscription rate of 50,000 or more! Think of the time he'll have attacking that traitorous obituary writer Rufus Griswold and rescinding his offer to have Griswold serve as executor! And the best part is that the public cannot become infuriated at him for this hoax. He was only the innocent victim. All of America – eventually, the world – will turn its hatred upon you, Jerel Reynolds. And to think you ran from his house after bringing him home drunk because you feared becoming…how did you say it…'the man who created the downfall of America's greatest fiction writer.'"

The chalk color of Reynolds' face gradually changed to pink and then red.

"You are much more clever than I could have supposed," he said to Pinkerton. "Somehow, you pieced all of this together from your interviews, from your study of Poe, even from what I told you. And you must have made guesses. Amazingly, all of them were correct. But he is dead. You think you can convince me to let you walk out of this house because of mere words?"

"I wouldn't if I were you," Pinkerton said. "No siree. Leave me tied up here and hurry your backside down to the Westminster burial ground. Dig up gravesite number 27. Prove the truth for yourself. You will find a poplar box, and you will find a corpse, brown and shriveled as an old apple. But you will not find Edgar Allan Poe. It's a damned good thing you decided to drug me and bring me down here," Allan extemporized, "because otherwise nobody was going to tell you about the Hallowe'en hoax. I was convinced to stay in town to hold you here…since you obviously came back from New York specifically to meet and match wits with me. Eddie is, even as we speak, contemplating the best way to manipulate you to precisely where the public will be able to tear you limb from limb. Oh, when you've seen the wrong corpse in the hole, please come back and release me."

Reynolds turned and snatched Pinkerton's revolver from the bed. Then he grabbed the short shovel that lay against one of the dirt piles. Having filled his hands, he spun to face the detective and glowered at him.

"You have bought yourself a few extra hours," he said, through short, clavicular breaths. "But when I dig up that grave and do find Eddie, I will return. And your death will be infinitely more painful. You, like Edgar A. Poe, will die regretting that you have ever made sport of Jerel Reynolds!"

Having had his say, Reynolds climbed the stairs. He did not bother to extinguish the lantern. Pinkerton listened to him turning the key in the cellar door. A few moments later, the same sound repeated from the house's front door.

Allan felt completely enervated. He exhaled and willed himself to breathe in deeply. Then he set to freeing himself. When it came to being forehanded, no one exceeded Allan Pinkerton. He stayed awake nights thinking of how he might plan for every eventuality. One that he had hit upon, several months earlier, was the remote possibility that someone might get the jump on him and ensnare him with his own handcuffs.

To prevent such an eventuality, Allan had had spare handcuff keys sewn into the inner left sleeve of his jackets. He reached up with his right hand fingers, found the key, and snapped it off of its binding threads. Within seconds, he had sprung both wristlocks. Once his hands we free, he had no trouble untying the amateur knots. He reclaimed the keys left on the ground and headed for the cellar steps only two minutes behind the ex-mortician. As he moved, he felt the missing weight of his revolver. He shook his head and continued up the stairs.

Several kicks to the cellar door were all that he needed to break the lock. The front door was another matter. Allan elected instead to throw the little table through one of the front windows, then use the chair to clean away the remaining glass shards. Within seconds he stood outside. He sprinted toward the harbor, where more public conveyances were likely to be roaming in search of fares. The problem was that the fog had rolled in thickly during his hours of unconsciousness and confinement. Even standing under a city lamp, he could not see more than seventy feet ahead.

The sounds of a horse's hooves rang against the cobblestones. Allan moved toward them. An empty hack appeared from the swirling mists. Allan ran to intercept it.

"Get me to Westminster Church within ten minutes, and you've earned yourself two dollars!" he cried to the hack man as he climbed up.

The driver shouted to his horse and cracked his whip. The carriage bolted off, throwing Allan against its lightly-padded back rest. He was glad that the man was at least fifty. Chances were better than even that experience would allow him to navigate Baltimore with his eyes closed.

Traffic was light as the midnight hour closed in. Every minute or so, another horse, carriage or wagon appeared out of the fog, its approach hidden by the mists and the loud clopping of the hack horse's hooves. Then reins were drawn tightly, voices shouted out in warning, horses whinnied, and wheel rims groaned from the hasty application of brakes. But generally, the cab continued its mad dash toward Westminster.

"Tell me when we are within a few hundred feet of the place," Allan called back. "I want to approach quietly."

"And why would that be?" the hack man asked.

"Because I want to catch a ghost," Allan replied.

No more questions were asked.

Only a few minutes later, the hack pulled over to the curb. "As you wish, and I have earned that two dollars."

"Here they are," Allan said. "Turn around quietly, if you please. I don't want the ghosts frightened."

"Good hunting," the driver wished.

Allan oriented himself by the bulk of the church and then walked with long but quiet strides along the sidewalk, past the forbidding sign and through the opened gate of the cemetery. He heard another person moving ahead of him. With the help of the hazy, fog-filtered moonlight, he could just make out the man's form. It was Jerel Reynolds. His stride was jerky, indicating the full flask of bourbon he had drunk and perhaps his fear of the place, the hour, and the possibility that Poe was alive. He held the shovel in his left hand and the revolver in his right. How he had convinced a cabbie to take him as a fare was beyond Allan's imagination. He thought that possibly the barrel of the gun had convinced someone, precisely by not speaking.

Allan stepped off the gravel path and chose instead the

muffling surface of the grasses around the headstones. He skulked as quickly as he could toward the back of the cemetery, knowing exactly where Reynolds was headed. Because Allan moved with more caution, Reynolds reached Poe's gravesite in advance. The wet air carried well the sound of the shovel thrusting into only half-hard dirt. It bit and flung, bit and flung.

Just as Allan came close enough to see the back of the burial ground, he caught sight of a figure emerging out of the fog on the far side of the cemetery fence. It was five foot eight or nine, a thin man wearing a black suit with a high neck wrap and an elegant bow tie. The hair on the top of the man's head was dark, full, and wavy, parted on the left. His left eyebrow, just barely visible through the gauzy fog, was lower than his right. He wore a moustache. And he carried a cane with a brass handle.

"I'm not down there, Blackie," the man said, in a deep but husky voice that sounded like a throat that had been damaged by arsenic.

Reynolds, who had been transfixed by the apparition, yelped.

"Why did you do it to me?"

Reynolds dropped the shovel. Even in the fog, Pinkerton could see that he was shaking like an aspen leaf in a whirlwind.

"Everything I ever wrote was mine alone," the unmoving figure provoked.

Allan was certain that without his spectacles, Reynolds could not possibly see through the disguise. He expected that the man would rush up to the fence or shrink back. He did neither.

"No!" Reynolds shouted with fierce anger. "No, no, no!" He reached between his jacket and trouser waist, brought out

Allan's revolver, pointed and fired five times. With the first report, the figure of Poe jumped. It retreated quickly at an angle with the second. It ducked behind a tree trunk for the third. Then, after the fourth and fifth reports cracked through the night air, the figure stepped back into view and slowly advanced.

Blackie stared at the weapon, trying to figure out how it had blasted a huge hole in the ceiling of Gunner's Hall and yet did nothing to the familiar figure closing on him. The revolver dropped from his hand. Then the homunculus clutched at his chest. Aaron Pelglade took a single step backward. Jerel Reynolds fell to the gravel walk, precisely where he had met Allan Pinkerton. He lay very still.

"Glenn, are you all right?" a female voice cried out from the far side of the fence.

Allan recognized the sound of Molly Brannigan.

"I'm fine. My God, was that supposed to happen?"

"No," Allan called out, as he moved to the man lying on the path. "But you played your part wonderfully." He reached out and felt Reynolds' neck for a pulse. He found none.

"Is he dead?" Chief Magistrate Foster asked in a tense tone, materializing out of the mist.

"Yes." Under his breath, Pinkerton expelled another, profane syllable.

"Blast! Exactly the sort of thing I feared."

The Watch assistant emerged from behind a large grave monument. He said nothing.

Allan closed the man's eyes. "He had a bad heart. He spent the night drinking and doing heavy labor. Go home, Mrs. Brannigan. Go home, Mr. Burton," he called out. "You must not become part of this."

Without a word, Molly caught the costumed Mr. Burton by the sleeve and guided him into the masking fog.

Allan could not resist raising the bottom of Reynolds' trouser leg and reassuring himself that it had been recently altered. He picked up the dropped revolver and placed it in his holster.

"How did he get your weapon?" Foster asked.

"He drugged me and tied me up. I thought I had everything planned, but his intention was to murder me tonight."

"Why in God's name would he do that?"

Allan shrugged. "Fear. Insanity. His reason to me was because he could."

"Well, it's a mercy he failed. Two men dead by his hand are enough." Foster turned a complete circle, peering into the rolling mists. "How did he miss your Edgar Poe from such close range?"

"A precaution. I removed the lead from the bullets and replaced it with little plugs of candle wax."

"How clever of you," said Foster.

"Not half clever enough," said Pinkerton.

The chief magistrate turned to his underling and issued several barely-audible commands. The young man saluted smartly and trotted toward the street. "Well, I think it is safe to say that this shall make you famous throughout the country," Foster said to the detective.

Allan sat on the stone bench, weary beyond his capacity to stand. "No, it won't."

"Why is that?"

"First, because he didn't make a confession. More importantly, if we contend that this man is the murderer of

Edgar Allan Poe people will demand to know the reason."

"And what was the reason?" Foster asked, chaffing his arms against the cold.

"Jerel Reynolds assured me that he provided several of Poe's most famous plots. He said that Poe promised, over and over, to share payment, but he never did." Allan then wearily pointed his hand at the lifeless Reynolds. "According to him, he was cheated of fame and fortune."

Foster snorted. "What poppycock! The man was a lunatic."

"Just because a man is insane doesn't mean he can't devise unique plots," Allan argued, glancing up at the soft orb of the moon. "In fact, when you consider how bizarre and grotesque Poe's tales were, many people would believe only a lunatic could have invented them."

"Then you believe he told the truth?"

Pinkerton looked at the body, which seemed so much smaller in death. He remembered back to sitting alone in the Richmond inn and reading Poe's early, less famous and surely more disturbing tales. He recalled thinking that someone's influence must have turned Poe to a better, more mainstream writer. Perhaps it was the unintended contributions of a number of friends, lovers, and other authors. Or perhaps the specific suggestions of only one. "I don't know. I don't think anyone ever will. But I do know that if he is declared Poe's murderer, then people will remember their relationship, and his reason will need to be revealed. And then, true or false, Edgar Allan Poe's memory will be diminished. That is as great a crime as murdering him."

Foster stared at the Chief Detective of Chicago for a while. He cleared his throat. "After all the distance you've come, all the money and time spent, all the dangers you faced, you are willing to walk away with no credit?"

Allan Pinkerton mustered the strength to rise from the stone bench. "Two weeks ago, I would not have contemplated such a decision. But since that time I have learned to appreciate the value of a great writer. For all his shortcomings, Edgar Poe was an American treasure. We have too few of those to tarnish." He faced the fresh grave and bowed his head in respect. "I have solved a few other crimes on this journey. I have gotten more than I had hoped for."

Foster glanced once again at the dead man and then at the recently dug grave. "One way or the other, the whole of Edgar Poe the writer lies here. You need to rest, Mr. Pinkerton. I'll watch over him until the wagon arrives. As far as the world will know, one of Poe's friends collapsed and died from grief while viewing the grave."

Through the gloomy atmosphere, a single, deep bell from a distant church slowly tolled midnight.

# CHAPTER TWENTY-ONE

*Sunday, October 28, 1849*

Under the cellar stairs of the house Jerel Reynolds had leased were a trunk and a carpetbag. The trunk belonged to Reynolds. Although several inches at the bottom were filled with Poe books, periodical contributions and newspaper articles, it contained only one personal item from the writer. A piece of notepaper held the words:

Thanks
Edgar A. Poe

Reynolds had spent more than two hundred and fifty dollars of Poe's subscription money in the space of a month. Allan suggested that the remainder be sent to the reporter Oscar Penn Fitzgerald, care of the *Richmond Enquirer*, so that the young man might see that the remainder was returned to Poe's supporters. The story would be that the money was found when Poe's carpetbag was belatedly discovered.

In Edgar Poe's bag, little of material value was found except correspondence from relatives, friends, and colleagues. Not one letter was found from Jerel Reynolds. If Poe had received any, he had not deemed them important enough to save. And yet he had called out Reynolds' name many times before his death, and the embittered Rufus Griswold had heard of 'the homunculus' and 'Blackie' from the author's own lips.

By the time Pinkerton returned to the house with the green door, Sunday morning was half finished. The city's church bells competed with each other to announce the Lord's day. The fog had blown out to sea. Warmer, sunshine-blessed weather had settled upon Baltimore.

Allan found Molly working in the kitchen. She had slept the

night with her bedroom door closed, and he had been too tired to give that a thought. He stood by Molly's side and dried dishes as he told her about his decision to leave the Poe case unsolved. She nodded often but rarely spoke. Likewise, when he detailed the contents of the trunk and the carpetbag, she made little comment. He wondered if witnessing Reynolds' death had shocked her or if possibly she was annoyed with him for what he had hired her handyman to risk. He did not ask her outright but was content to let his thoughts about the remainder of the day improve her mood.

"Today promises to be a grand one," he said.

"Yes. I saw when I hung out towels."

"There won't be many this nice for the rest of the year, I'll wager."

"Probably not."

Allan put his hands on either side of Molly's waist and gently turned her. "What I am saying is that you ought to get out. I have made this a trying week for you. I want to make it up to you by taking you out."

"Taking me out," Molly echoed. Her voice had no hint of pleasure in it.

"Yes. Perhaps a picnic."

"You will compensate me in full if you pay me the remainder of the bed and board you owe."

Allan laughed lamely, looking for the humor behind her words. "Of course I will. But I want to do more. Can't you get Mrs. Burton to watch Siobhan?"

"Mrs. Burton watched her all of last evening. Her and two rambunctious boys of her own."

"Then we could bring her along," Allan suggested, sensing

the coolness under Molly's perfectly calm tone. "And Mr. Burton as well.

"Where?"

"Anywhere."

"Allan, every bit of 'anywhere' is outside. Even a restaurant is a place beyond these walls. A concert is beyond these walls. I am a married woman. I cannot go out with a man other than my husband."

"Even with your friends as company?"

"Yes, even then."

"Perhaps just a carriage ride–" Allan began.

"Don't you understand? Appearance must be maintained. I must live in this city. You will go...tomorrow or the day after... and I will stay. As a Catholic and a woman of Irish descent, I know that I may only rise so much, but my sights are set as high as possible. I wish to have political power and influence, and I will not get it by picnicking with a detective from Chicago or riding with him in a carriage."

The very calmness of her voice was what infuriated Allan the most. He let down his hands and took a couple steps backward. "So, let me understand. There is a commandment in the *Bible* against adultery, but you are fine with ignoring that. However, 'Thou Shalt Not Flaunt Appearance,' which is nowhere in the *Bible*, you must obey as if you are the Pope himself."

"I have explained myself with crystalline clarity," Molly said.

Allan's heart had never hurt as much. He sighed heavily and then said, "In the past week or so, I have heard of several divorces. Divorce is not the impossibility it was even twenty years ago."

"Are you saying you want me to divorce my husband for you?"

"Would you contemplate it?"

"And you would leave Joan and your children?"

"I would see that they are taken care of."

Molly took Allan by the hand and led him into the parlor. She pushed him gently onto one of the chairs.

"You do not know me, Allan."

"I think I do," he countered.

"No. You cannot, because I have not let you see all of me. I have made myself better than I usually am for your sake. And I strongly suspect that you have done the same for me. I know that you do not smoke, because you could never eradicate all the smell from your clothing. But you may well drink. You may well gamble."

"I don't–"

Molly set her fingers across Allan's mouth.

"Don't you see? I want to be perfect for you, and I want you to be perfect for me forever. The only way that can be is if it ends now. You will go, and you will never change in my mind's eye. Time will not diminish you. I will not need to promise 'through sickness or health,' 'richer or poorer,' or even not to betray, as I did my husband. Let us take the gift we made together for each other and honor it by letting it be."

Allan was forced to recall her words, which were not said as a warning but in anticipation of this moment: "I do believe that the day after you marry you may turn a corner and meet the man of your fondest passions. In that case, the answer is to satisfy your passions, then return to your marriage and never look back." He realized with deep astonishment that, while he would never be a fiction writer, he had co-created a convincing romantic fantasy that nevertheless had no basis in reality.

"You are more than I suspected," he told her.

"I like who I am and where I live. I will have power and a modicum of wealth," Molly asserted, looking down at him. "And I do not want to be 'the other woman' who destroys your marriage."

She took Allan's head and slowly drew it to her chest. "A poem. We made a poem together – one far lovelier than even the great Edgar Allan Poe could have written."

Of that, Allan Pinkerton was not sure. But he had come to realize already, through Poe's melancholy poems to lost loves, that the dead and those left behind were indeed much easier to adore. He allowed his face and hair to be fondled for a few more seconds. Then he stood.

"I'll be gathering my belongings," he said. "My money was swiftly running out, and you know how tightly we Scotsmen like to hold onto it."

Molly managed a smile.

Allan looked for the last time at the painting of the clipper over the mantelpiece. He turned back to Molly and said, "I'm sure there will be a train leaving soon from the B & O terminal."

"You will have great success with your national detective agency," Molly predicted, as Allan moved toward the stairs. "I will read your name in the newspapers as I grow older, and I will think of us."

*And so will I*, Allan thought, as he ascended the stairs. *I will think of you, 'Many and many a year ago/In a kingdom by the sea.'*

# ABOUT THE AUTHOR

Brent Monahan has spent his life fascinated with and passionate about questioning the world – and arriving at unique, thoughtful, insightful and, quite often, spear-tip pointedly amusing answers that find their expression in his many novels. Whether he is offering a rational explanation to an historical haunting, as in *The Bell Witch: An American Haunting*, or delving into the psyches and machinations of such icons of financial and political power as J.P. Morgan in *The Jekyl Island Club*, Mr. Monahan does so with an unparalleled depth of research and smart, witty writing that has engaged decades of readers and garnered him considerable critical recognition from both reviewers and his peers.

Mr. Monahan has authored thirteen novels, two of which have been made into movies – including *An American Haunting*, starring Donald Sutherland and Sissy Spacek. He has taught writing at Rutgers University and Westminster Choir College of Rider University, even though his terminal degree was in musical arts from Indiana University, Bloomington. He lives in Yardley, Pennsylvania.

www.ingramcontent.com/pod-product-compliance
Lightning Source LLC
Chambersburg PA
CBHW051442260626

47162CB00001B/203